That Certain Spark

That
Certain
Spark

CATHY MARIE HAKE

BETHANYHOUSE
MINNEAPOLIS, MINNESOTA

Published by Bethany House Publishers
11400 Hampshire Avenue South
Bloomington, Minnesota 55438

Bethany House Publishers is a division of
Baker Publishing Group, Grand Rapids, Michigan.

Printed in the United States of America

Library of Congress Cataloging-in-Publication Data

Hake, Cathy Marie.
   That certain spark / Cathy Marie Hake.
      p.   cm.
   ISBN 978-0-7642-0320-6 (pbk.)
   1. Texas—Fiction. I. Title.
   PS3608.A5454T54   2009
   813'.6—dc22

                                                    2009007610

There are many forms of courage—

Blazing a new trail,
Taking an unpopular stand,
Stepping out in that moment of faith,
Laughter instead of tears for someone else's sake,
Enduring physical, spiritual, and emotional anguish,
Holding on to God with trust instead of desperation,
Forgiving as we were forgiven.
Loving one another.
Asking for help to bear a burden.

This book is dedicated to Jesus Christ, who showed the ultimate courage by going to the cross. His love cleanses me, humbles me, and woos me. With that certain spark only He can give and foster, I'm able to step out in faith. Jesus is my example, my Lord and Savior. I want to walk in His footsteps, sit at His feet and be brave enough to love as He taught. He is my everything, and I praise His name.

Books by
Cathy Marie Hake
FROM BETHANY HOUSE PUBLISHERS

Letter Perfect

Bittersweet

Fancy Pants

Forevermore

Whirlwind

That Certain Spark

That Certain Spark

One

November 1892
Gooding, Texas

Miracles are going to start happening, Karl Van der Vort. I can feel it in my bones." The labyrinth of wrinkles on Mrs. Whitsley's face added to the almost mystical quality of her comment. Blue eyes lively as could be, she winked. "Miracles."

Thump. Karl shut the door on her now-full coal bin. Humoring the sweet old woman, he asked, "Like what?"

"You're going to get your heart right with Jesus." Nodding sagely, she leaned on her cane and extended a glass to him. Silently agreeing it would be nothing short of a miracle, Karl reached for the drink; but to his surprise, the widow continued on. "Then you're going to find yourself a wife."

"A wife!" The idea rattled him so much, he was glad she'd held on to the lemonade a breath longer before letting go, lest it tumble from his grip.

Her smile widened, arranging her wrinkles into rays of delight. "Yes, a wife, Karl. The Good Book says, 'Seek ye first the kingdom of God, and his righteousness; and all these things shall be added unto you.' A blacksmith owning his forge and livery couldn't have a steadier job, and you have a home and dog. The only things that're missing are God's peace and a wife. Sure as we're standing here, you're going to find both. You've started coming back to church, and that'll set your feet on the right path."

Unwilling to respond, Karl chugged down the lemonade. He'd emptied half the glass before the sheer bitterness made him come to a shuddering stop.

"What's wrong?" Mrs. Whitsley swiped the glass from him and took a sip. "I forgot the sugar! I do apologize, Karl. This is terrible. Just terrible. I don't know what came over me."

Karl stooped and placed his hands on his knees, then tilted his head and tenderly kissed the old woman's cheek. "There." He straightened up. "That was sugar enough for me." He grabbed the handles of the oversized wheelbarrow he used to make coal deliveries and walked off.

Within a few strides, Karl muffled a groan as he realized he'd probably been too bold and shocked the poor old lady. *What was I thinking?* He stank at trying to figure out women, and the proof of that very fact was that at the age of twenty-eight, he'd not yet married. After a box social or a few after-church strolls, he'd inevitably scared off the few eligible young women he'd met—and if he couldn't handle a woman near his own age, how was he supposed to figure out how to treat a woman double, maybe even triple that?

He steered the wheelbarrow around a large jagged rock and toward the mountain of coal next to the railroad tracks. Lyrics from Sunday's hymn stole into his thoughts. *"When peace like a river attendeth my way . . ." I would like this. In my heart, though, there is yet a drought.*

Old Mrs. Whitsley said I'd have to make peace with God before I'd find a wife. My soul has been in turmoil now for fifteen years. Why should I even bother thinking of a wife at this point?

Karl shook the thoughts from his mind, and the remainder of the morning flew past while he delivered coal to his neighbors and filled the huge bins at the smithy. As he brought back the last load, his brother called out loudly, "Come! We have cookies!"

Karl didn't need any explanation. The slight edge to Piet's voice warned that Linette Richardson had delivered the cookies and was making a nuisance of herself. He and Piet regularly rescued each other from Linette's husband-hunting schemes.

"Cookies!" Karl set down the handles of the wheelbarrow and went into the smithy.

"They're shortbread and torn pants." Linette grabbed hold of Karl's arm. "Your favorites." Coming from Mrs. Orion, the woman who ran the boardinghouse and bakery, *torn pants* was merely a whimsical name for cookies. Recently she'd hired Linette, however, and Linette saying *torn pants* was enough to make both brothers determined to send her off immediately. Even Skyler, their faithful collie, slunk into the corner instead of wildly wagging his tail in hopes of earning a treat for himself. Smart dog.

Karl frowned down at his arms and Linette's hand upon him. "I'm covered in coal dust, Miss Richardson. I'd better wash it off. You'll want to wash right away back at the boardinghouse before you start helping Mrs. Orion again."

"You're a hardworking man. Both of you are." Linette's green hair ribbon started slipping as she looked around the shop. Due to a fever her hair had been chopped short, so she wore a ribbon to try to keep from looking mannish. She turned loose of him and slid the ribbon back into place. "This place is bursting with proof of your industry."

"*Ja*, and it's shouting at us to get back to work." Piet turned back to the anvil. A second later, the clang of his hammer filled the air.

Karl timed his words to fall between the hammer strikes. "Much obliged for the cookies. Know you have to get back to work, too." He turned to the side and plunged his hands into the water barrel—a not-so-subtle dismissal, but it wasn't right to give the girl false hope. Sluicing icy water over his arms and face felt bracing. Even in the dead of winter, the forge put out so much heat that Karl relished the cool relief of the water. Even greater, though, was his relief that she'd left by the time he shook off the last splash of water.

Just off to the side stood a plate of cookies. The twisted and fried "torn pants" were crispy, just the right mix of butter and sweet. But best of all—shortbread. His long, thick fingers dwarfed the flaky chunk. How did Linette know it was his favorite? The poor girl. He pitied her. The eldest in her family, she didn't have a beau, yet the next two sisters in line were both planning their weddings. If Linette had her way, it would be a triple wedding. Piet and Karl vowed neither of them would fall into that trap. No matter if she occasionally came by with a delicious treat, no bribe was sweet enough to convince either of them to pop the question.

Though known for flattery, Linette had spoken the truth. Their business thrived. Blacksmithing required brute strength; by working together, they were able to fabricate impossibly heavy and unwieldy items. They never lacked for work. In fact, when another blacksmith opened a forge in town, they'd tried to send business his way—but

Baumgartner did shoddy work. Once his laziness became apparent, Karl and Piet no longer referred clients to him. Soon Baumgartner packed up and moved on, leaving Piet and Karl with as heavy a workload as ever.

Piet paused momentarily. "It took you forever. Mrs. Orion must have fed you. Next time, I deliver the coal."

Karl cocked a brow. "Only if the hammer says so." Their father taught them their trade and how to settle arguments. A hammer tossed straight up would fall, and the direction of the handle would dictate the result.

Leaving a sooty smear across his forehead as he wiped away sweat, Karl's brother scowled. "Then I toss the hammer. My hammer."

"Fair enough."

A few big bites of shortbread, then Karl covered the plate with the napkin. Later, he'd eat his other piece. Piet was right: He'd filled his belly earlier with Mrs. Orion's tasty breakfast after delivering her coal.

Karl pulled his work apron from the nail, and the thick latigo leather, supple from years of use, filled his hands. Scarred and stained, the piece bore mute testimony of untold times when it had protected him from the sparks and shards that abounded in his profession. The strap ruffled past his hair and rested at the base of his neck. Instead of a bulky tie at the middle, a belt buckled behind Karl's waist—loose enough to let a little air circulate. That modification was Karl's idea. Matteo over at the saddlery had been happy to affix the belt and buckle when the wraparound ties snapped. Ready for business, Karl picked up his hammer.

"What," *bang*, "are," *clang*, "you," *bang*, "working," *clang*, "on?" Piet spaced his words between each blow, but because he wanted to elongate the iron bar as well as flatten it, he swiveled his hammer and struck the bar with the side of the hammer every other blow.

"Hooks for Widow O'Toole to hang her velocipede."

Piet snorted. "A woman who wears bloomers and rides a bicycle."

"She's a lonely old woman."

"Not really that old. She wouldn't be so lonely if she stopped scolding grown men for enjoying a drink now and then." Piet hefted his hammer. "But since you've been going to church, you're getting holier-than-thou. Judging everybody. Saints—" he pointed one direction with his hammer, then the other way—"and sinners."

"I've judged no one!"

"You're arguing with me and standing up for her right now. That says it all." Piet's hammer crashed down in an attempt to cease the conversation.

Karl didn't allow that ploy to work. "You're a grown man. You make decisions for yourself. I am a man, and I make the decisions for *my*self. I decided to go to church, Piet. It does not make me a saint. I sit there and know how far from God I have wandered."

Ever since he'd started attending church without his brother, Karl had been paying an unexpected price. Piet was growing as sour as Old Mrs. Whitsley's lemonade. Like all brothers, they'd had a day here or there in the past when they were put out with one another—but it had been weeks now, and Piet showed no signs of letting up. Compared to Piet, Widow O'Toole might be a pleasant change.

At that preposterous thought, Karl picked up his own hammer, pulled a long iron rod from the furnace, and started to work on the orange, glowing end. Again, the hymn in his mind kept the heartbeat-like cadence of strike and rebound strike of his hammer.

"Whe-en. Pea-eace. Like. A. Riv-er." The iron didn't feel right. Shoving it back into the fire, he shouted, "Did Clicky telegraph an order for more iron?"

"Ja." Steam rose as bubbling and hissing filled the suddenly quiet shop when Piet plunged the bracket he'd made into the water bath. "Tomorrow it will come."

Thinking of the previous winter when they'd had some appreciable snowfall, Karl twisted the rod in the fire. "Weather's turning. Next time we'd better double our order."

"Tripled it." Piet lifted the bracket from the water but looked past it, directly at Karl. "Though I didn't need to. You stand around jawing and go warm a pew while I'm the one working."

Anger flashed through him. "The forge has never operated on Sunday. For me to go to church makes no difference in how much work gets done. When I get home from church, you're just rolling out of bed."

"Home from church?" Piet scoffed. "Home with a full belly."

So that's what this is all about! "The same people who invite me to Sunday supper would gladly have you over, too."

"But I'm not good enough because I'm not there."

"That's not why." Karl let go of the rod, turned, and looked at his brother with disgust. "Saturdays you drink so much, you're sick most Sundays, thus I've had to thank them for their kind offer and turn them down. Even then, you cannot complain—the women have still sent plates of food for you."

Piet bristled. "I'm a man. I don't complain."

"You just complained that I don't do my share of the work because I worship on Sundays when our forge is closed." Piet's face grew thunderous, but Karl stared right back. "Have I ever once complained about how you like to drink beer? About you getting so drunk I had to clean your mess and work alone the next day? No. Not once have I complained." He refused to let his brother minimize the truth of the problem. "It used to happen very seldom—but it is once a week now. Sometimes twice."

"That's none of your business."

"Your drinking is my business." Now that he'd finally broached the topic, Karl refused to back down. "I clean up after you and work without you, so our shop earns less."

"Get back to work. This is exactly what I meant. You stand around jawing. That's why there's less money."

"Always in the past, we've held our funds in common, but you're drinking away the profits and the savings. It's time for us to split the money so this is a partnership. That way, you can drink away your half if you wish, and I can save mine."

Only the crackle of the forge sounded in the entire place.

"Hullo! Hullo in the smithy! Could I please have a bit of help?"

Karl started toward the barnlike doors. Suddenly, he crashed to the ground. *My own brother kicked my legs out from beneath me. My own brother.* Piet sauntered on out. "Mrs. Creighton, how may I be of service to you?"

That was it. He'd taken all he'd take from his brother. Grabbing his hammer with his right hand, Karl reached for the iron rod with his left. Until Piet came back in, he'd pound out his anger. Two solid, satisfying strikes, then he gave the rod a quarter twist. But with the next blow, a portion of the rod splintered off and shot backward.

Karl dropped his hammer, shoved the rod into the water bath, and picked up the bucket of sand to tend to the sparks and embers. Pouring water on the embers only resulted in steam, but sand smothered out the air. Convinced he'd averted any fire danger, Karl finally focused on the searing pain in his thigh.

It took a moment for him to realize he had to remove his huge leather gloves. That done, he leaned into a workbench, curled forward, and wrapped his hands around a metal shard. The part sticking out of his leather apron was long as a ten-penny nail and every bit as thick. Rough-edged, it tore at his hands as he tightened his grip. Gritting his teeth, he yanked.

"Decided to pull your weight, did you?" Piet said as he came back in.

The shard had barely moved—but it sent his thigh into horrific spasms. Karl clamped his jaw and broke out in a cold sweat. Sensing his need, Skyler came over beside him and let out a soft whimper.

Piet started toward the forge. "You—Karl!" He rushed over and manacled his brother's hands. "Tongs. It will take tongs to pull that out. Standing, you make the muscles tight. Sit down. Here. Ja. Ja. *Goed.*"

Bracing his thigh in both hands, Karl gritted out as his brother dithered, "Just get the tongs."

"No. First must I cut off the apron from you. If not I do this, it could on the way out break off or cut you more." For the ugly fight they'd had minutes before, his brother's love was still evident. The most telling thing was how Piet mixed up his word order. On rare occasions when he grew extremely upset, he'd speak in English but revert back to Dutch word order.

It took a couple of well-placed swipes before Piet hacked off the bottom quarter of the leather apron. He rose and picked up the tongs. "Now has come the time."

"Do it." *And, God, if you're listening, please help me.* Gritting his teeth, Karl braced himself as his brother clenched the shard with the tongs. Just the contact hurt, yet when Piet began to pull, the tongs lost traction and slipped off.

Piet groaned.

Karl gritted, "Rubber band."

With the aid of a rubber band's traction, the tongs stayed in place on the second try. Piet dropped back down to his knees. "I cannot tell if out all of it came."

"I can bandage it. Just grab a clean bandanna. I'll be fine."

"*Nee.* I'll go get Velma."

Karl gripped his brother's forearm to keep him from dashing off. "Don't bother. New doctor's coming tomorrow. If I need help, he'll be the one."

"This is no bother. It's important."

Karl used his brother's help to get back up on his feet. Cold sweat broke out on his forehead as fire exploded in his leg.

"It is no bother for me to get Velma," Piet repeated. "She is skilled enough to help you."

"Don't get her, Piet. I refuse to drop my pants for a woman healer."

◇·◇·◇

Huffing like a great asthmatic beast, the train pulled out of the last major stop before Gooding. Veterinarian Enoch Bestman cast a glance at the door to the bedroom of their Pullman car. Exhausted from a complicated emergency case, his twin—a physician—now slept with the same intensity their father and grandfather had after long nights working on patients.

Back in Chicago, Enoch had been champing at the bit. Nothing in particular triggered his restlessness, and in spite of a booming practice where he'd been content for four years, a feeling that he wasn't where he was meant to be besieged him.

All of that was behind him. " 'Remember ye not the former things, neither consider the things of old. Behold, I will do a new thing,' " Enoch quoted from the forty-third chapter of Isaiah. That verse had come to him right after he'd seen the advertisement from Gooding, Texas, for both a physician and a veterinarian. It couldn't be more clear, and he hadn't once doubted that this was God's will for him and his twin.

A few strides carried him to the window. Land stretched out before him in a seemingly endless expanse, free and open instead of cramped and crowded. Every mile of progress the train made now carried him closer to a new life.

Lord, thank you for working out all of the details so Taylor would come. I praise your name for the opportunities awaiting us in the days and years ahead.

Taylor eventually emerged and stopped at the table for something to eat. "Why didn't you wake me up?"

"You needed the sleep."

"If this town is as rural as we suspect, I'll end up sleeping away the next four years."

Enoch hitched his shoulder. "Then again, rural places without decent medical care could easily have a few very pressing cases waiting for the arriving physician."

"And a rural town devoid of veterinary support must have citizens poised to pounce upon the vet as soon as he disembarks from the train, too." Giving him a sly smile, Taylor added, "In a farming and ranching community, animals must outnumber people by a landslide. That being the case, your need for sleep will be far greater than mine."

Enoch pinched half of the gingersnap from his twin and tossed it into his mouth.

"That was the last one!"

"They'll undoubtedly have food for us in Gooding. Besides—" he flashed a grin—"I'm bigger and older."

"Taller by a single inch and older only because you were pushy."

"Hey!" He gave his twin an outraged look. "I was doing you a favor. Everyone knows they always spank the first twin the hardest."

Taylor laughed. "Doctors don't spank babies."

"No?!"

"Enoch," Taylor said, drawing out his name with greatly taxed patience, "human babies aren't like the animals you treat—"

"My wee ones are much more talented. Seconds old, and they're already standing. Minutes, and they're taking their first steps." Nodding, he professed, "Animals are much better off."

"As I was saying, human babies are different. Babies' little necks are weak. Even if they didn't go flying—and that's a frighteningly real possibility—"

"Frightening? Entertaining. All you'd have to do is have someone in the right place to catch them."

His twin chuckled. "For a moment, you had me convinced you knew nothing about this."

Enoch shrugged. "I don't. I did think you doctors gave the kids a whack on the backside. I'm just as glad that you don't. It's always seemed that such a blow could cause irreparable damage to a newborn. You'd be wise to find a local woman to help you with the births. I wasn't kidding about not knowing anything about the babies."

Taylor's green eyes glinted dangerously. "You're tardy with that revelation. You pledged to assist me as needed since your medical knowledge far surpasses anything these people will have."

The train began to slow. "I will assist you . . . with everything else." Diverting attention, he gestured toward the window. "Look. There have to be at least thirty people here to meet us. I'm sure you'll find a woman or two right there to help you out. And they hung a banner. 'Welcome, Drs. Bestman.'"

"I'm going to appreciate the fact that they didn't give in to the temptation of writing 'Bestmen.' Judging from those thunderheads, we'll praise God that He sent all these neighbors to help us get things unloaded and moved before the weather turns."

"Exactly." The train stopped and they disembarked.

A portly man swaggered up with a woman in tow. "Welcome, welcome to Gooding! I'm Gustav Cutter, the mayor."

Extending his hand, Enoch said, "Enoch—"

"The vet!" The mayor bellowed, "This here's the one for all the critters, folks. And looks like he's already got himself hitched to a right pretty filly."

Surprise and temper glittered in Taylor's eyes as she cast a hasty glance at Enoch. He'd negotiated the contracts and made the arrangements for their move to Texas.

Enoch murmured, "They know, Sis. Dr. Glendale's letter of recommendation is clear about you being a woman."

A look of relief smoothed her features before Taylor laughed. "My brother? Married? Oh, Mr. Cutter, after our long trip, that joke has to be the best welcome possible."

"A fine welcome indeed!" Enoch took the cue. "Mr. Mayor, permit me to introduce my—"

"Tell us she's your sister!" one of the men shouted.

"And that she ain't hitched!" another added. Activity rippled through the other men standing behind the mayor. One twisted his moustache while two tried to tame wild-looking hair and another elbowed his way forward. Several stood taller. *I'm going to have my hands full keeping men away from Sis.*

"Awww. She's got powerful cute dimples," one hapless man declared, thereby insuring Taylor would never extend anything more than civility toward him.

The mayor's wife turned around and took a few steps back. "If you cannot summon together a few clear thoughts, at least scrape together a modicum of manners. You've interrupted Dr. Enoch Bestman when he was going to introduce this young lady. Of course she's his sister. With that sable hair and the same smile, the family resemblance is quite clear. Miss Bestman wouldn't have come with her brothers if she were married."

"Yeeee-haw!" One of the cowboys grabbed Mrs. Cutter and swung her around.

The mayor went to rescue her.

Smiling at Enoch through gritted teeth, Taylor hissed, "What have you gotten us into? She said *brothers*. Plural."

He'd picked up on that, too. They'd have to brazen their way through this. Apologizing to her or acting worried would make it worse. Instead, he resorted to teasing. "Don't suppose you have a tonic that'd make you instantly sprout a beard, do you?"

Taylor's eyes widened and her lips twitched with suppressed laughter. "All the times I threatened to swipe a pair of your trousers but you told me to take pride in being a woman, and now you're trying to pass me off as a man in a skirt?"

Spirit. Gumption. Humor. He'd never been more proud of

her. "Forget it. You're stronger than any man I know. Whatever lies ahead, we'll face it together."

"From the looks of things, it's a good thing God's with us."

Mopping his face with a monogrammed handkerchief, Gustav Cutter returned with his wife in tow. "I beg your pardon. Dr. Bestman, you were going to introduce us to your sister and to your . . . twin." The mayor craned his neck to look past Taylor toward the train as he spoke the last word. "Where is he?"

Enoch cupped Taylor's elbow. "Mr. Cutter, permit me to introduce my twin, Miss Taylor MacLay Bestman."

Two

T win." The mayor's eyes bulged, then his complexion took on a decidedly ruddy cast.

"The doctor is a woman!" a young woman blurted out gleefully.

Taylor nodded at her. "Indeed, I am."

A knot of men formed off to one side. They kept casting hostile glances at her. It took no imagination to figure out what they were discussing.

"You're Dr. Taylor Bestman." Mayor Cutter looked in dire need of a dyspepsia remedy.

Taylor gave the mayor a cool businesslike smile and pretended he'd actually welcomed her. "It's a pleasure to be invited to Gooding. Unless there are any pressing medical or veterinary cases waiting, my brother and I would be delighted to meet our new neighbors before unloading our supplies and taking them to the clinic. You're all busy, hardworking people, and we're honored you came to greet us. Aren't we, Enoch?"

"Yes." Enoch nodded politely toward Mrs. Cutter. "Though I'm not married, Mr. Cutter, let me congratulate you on finding such a lovely filly of your own."

During a few more introductions and a proper word or two, the crowd thinned tremendously. At least a dozen men cast dark looks at Taylor and stomped off.

Enoch rested his hand on her shoulder and said to no one in particular, "We've freighted a considerable amount of goods with us on the train."

"I'll be happy to help cart your things to the clinic." A man stepped forward. "Daniel Clark. I own the mercantile."

"And I'm Millicent—Millie, his wife." A woman with wind-swept curls shifted a bright-eyed toddler to her other hip. "While the men see to that, I'll take the doctor over so she can see the place."

The tension in Taylor's shoulder eased slightly. *Even with an awkward start, we'll make this work.* "How very kind of you."

Taylor followed Millie and two other ladies who joined her, but they let the doctor enter the building first. Wide open double doors off to the left showcased a surgery that left Taylor breathless. She hastened in and made a rapid assessment of the instruments and layout. "This is magnificent!"

"You have Velma to thank." Millie nodded toward the older, squatty woman. "She ordered, organized, and cleaned everything. Until now, we've depended on her for all of our medical care."

Velma seized the opportunity and took control. "Millie, take Doc on upstairs and show her around. Doc, to my reckoning, you've got four minutes before the men plow in here with all your stuff."

"Less than that, Velma," said the pregnant woman by the wall, tugging the toddler away from Millie. "I told Tim no one was eating until all of the Bestmans' possessions are delivered."

"That was clever of you, Mrs. . . . ?"

"Creighton. But do call me Sydney."

"Syd, if you're going to hold Millie's little Arthur, you sit on down," the bossy older woman fussed.

Taking the opening, Taylor smiled. "When are we going to welcome your little baby?"

Velma bristled and interposed herself between Sydney and Taylor. "I'm right glad to have you here, Doc. I've done my best by folks, but times I knew my best wasn't good enough, I bundled 'em up and put 'em on the train to go to a genuine doctor. But the midwiving—no need for you to horn in on that."

Managing a polite smile with her firmest tone, Taylor said, "The mother-to-be deserves to select who gives her care. Millie, I'm ready to look at the upstairs of this splendid place."

Taylor climbed to the second level. In the first chamber she ran her hand along the floral-carved cherry footboard. "What a spectacular bed!"

"It is pretty, isn't it?"

While Millie Clark watched, Taylor closed the navy blue curtains. "I couldn't hope for more. If I'm out on an all-night call or have an emergency midnight surgery, being able to block out the sunlight and sleep in the daytime is a blessing."

"Of course! That makes sense." Millie whirled around. "Over here's your brother's room."

"Enoch's an early riser. He'll appreciate the east window."

27

The woman started toward the hall. "We thought you could use this last one as a patient room if need be."

"How charming!" Taylor looked into the third bedroom, a huge room with several cots ready for patients. "You ladies outdid yourselves in readying things for our arrival. I'm most appreciative."

A loud thud sounded downstairs. "The thing that will make the men most appreciative is dragging everything in here as quickly as possible. We've a lovely spread laid out over at Old Mrs. Whitsley's. Everyone's supposed to go eat as soon as the crates are all in."

"Then I'd best go help make room." Sydney had mentioned the food, too. After having had nothing more than half a cookie in a long while, Taylor needed no encouragement to hasten things along. Quickly descending the stairs, she found Daniel Clark dumping a second crate into the surgery.

"Dr. Bestman, your brother said these boxes were the most important." He accepted a crowbar from his wife and proceeded to pry off the tops.

"Thank you, gentlemen. Could you please take that to the first bedchamber on the right?" As the men carried up a heavy steamer trunk, Taylor murmured to Velma, "Do we normally keep a crowbar here?"

"Haven't the faintest. I only ordered the instruments and supplies. Once that quack we just sent packing got here, the good Lord only knows what's gone on." As she spoke, Velma reached into the first crate and pulled out test tubes and microscope slides. "Put these off to the far corner. That's where the other stuff like this is."

Taylor didn't take kindly to being ordered around in her own surgery—even if that was exactly where she would have placed the items. *But she's the one I have to thank for this place being outfitted so spectacularly.* "Actually, it's ludicrous for me to unpack my supplies whilst there's so much else demanding my attention. Thanks to you, the surgery is in outstanding form."

Face alight, Velma nodded. "It's good to know you understand what all went behind setting this up. The doctor we had here before you didn't appreciate half of what he had and didn't know what the other half was. That nitwit like to destroyed it all."

Sydney cast an unreadable glance about the room. "For the first time in her life, Velma's not being blunt. This place was a medical pigsty. Dr. Wicky shoved all sorts of boxes and bottles and bandages and instruments into the armoires and dumped them in heaps over in the corners."

"After I'd taken such pains to set up such a fine clinic for him! Hmpf! And the junk he'd brought in! Dr. Meldon's magnetic girdle."

"For the treatment of social ills and baldness." Sydney giggled. "I couldn't believe it when Orville drove up and took all that worthless garbage."

"I believed it. Mark my words. That misfit'll be using the quack's machines on folks any day now. I shoulda had Big Tim bash and burn 'em all. Anyway, I came in and tried to reorganize things again while the others cleaned." Velma stepped to the side. Reverently pulling open a drawer, she revealed white cotton cloth covering several long slender bundles of instruments. "Most of all, I sterilized everything so it's all ready for you in case of an emergency. Boiled and double wrapped."

"Exactly as I would have prepared them." Taylor smiled. "I know it took a lot of time, and I thank you again—"

"Pshaw," Velma interrupted as she shut the drawer. "Anytime you need help on a hard case, you just call for me."

"I'll definitely keep you in mind." Taylor smoothly turned

the tables. "Likewise, I'm available should any case of yours be difficult."

"Things're gonna work out just fine between us, Doc. Clicky! Don't go dumping that down there. Haul it on upstairs."

Taylor pulled her black wool skirts close and squeezed between the crates. Looking at the tall, gangly man, she raised her brows. "Clicky, is it?"

"Yes'm. Or Miss. I mean Doctor. I'm really Clive Keys, but since I run the telegraph, folks gave me the handle of Clicky."

"Well, Mr. Keys, I'd very much appreciate your taking that big load of things up to either of the bedchambers. I'll sort through it all later."

"Your brother said you would. And he asked me to tell you he's hauling a mess of his stuff over to the livery. Hey!" He turned to the side and barked at a pair of older schoolboys. "Ozzie and Lloyd, set that box down before you drop it!"

Trunks, crates, and barrels flooded into the place over the next half hour. When Enoch showed up, Taylor smoothed her hair and turned toward Sydney, who was merrily arranging the family china in a solid-looking buffet. "I believe we should gather up all of these hardworking men and go on over for that dinner now."

The words scarcely left her mouth before her neighbors stampeded out the door. Their haste was all for naught, however. Upon their arrival to Old Mrs. Whitsley's home, Velma scolded, "You all go to the pump and wash up. Everybody knows the guest of honor eats first anyhow. Parson Bradle's gonna ask a blessing."

A suitably short prayer ensued, given the men's hunger and a warning clap of thunder. The words were clearly heartfelt enough not to require senseless embellishment, and the pastor said amen.

Millie handed her a plate and urged, "Get started! Everyone's waiting to go after you."

"It all looks delicious." *And I'm ravenous. This is going to be the last decent meal I'll eat until we get a housekeeper.* "I don't know how I'll ever decide what to take. I'm sure you ladies are talented cooks."

"Take some of everything and be quick about it." Velma gave her a stern look. "You're not in the city, where women eat like birds."

Mrs. Whitsley patted her arm. "The ladies will be insulted if you don't taste what they brought."

Enoch immediately charmed the dear Old Mrs. Whitsley right out of her shoes, insisting upon carrying a plate for her and teasing her about the tiny servings she took. "Now, where would you and your bitty bites and dibby dabs like to go?"

Mrs. Whitsley brushed aside his sweet talk. "I'm going to sit right there in the parlor by the window. Doctor, you come sit by me. Your brother can wander off, but I aim to have a word with you."

Taylor sat beside the old woman, put her own plate aside, and took the shawl from the arm of the settee. Wanting fresh air shouldn't mean chilling old bones into arthritic pain. Wrapping the length of soft wool about the old woman's frail shoulders, Taylor praised, "You have a lovely home."

After a few moments of polite chatter, the hostess tapped Taylor's wrist. "Velma's been treating all of us for so long, she was wary about you coming. I don't know what's transpired, but you've certainly won her over."

"On occasion it will be helpful to have a pair of capable hands." Determining just how capable Velma was when it came to actual medical practice was a whole different matter. Nevertheless, a willing person could be taught . . . unless they thought they already knew everything. Then those so-called practitioners became the bane of every physician's existence.

Others joined them in the parlor. Like a child who couldn't wait until after his meal for dessert, Clicky took a huge bite of pecan pie. "It's going to be confusing for us to have two Dr. Bestmans."

"Initials—" Taylor started.

"—would be stuffy," Enoch cut in, settling the argument they'd had on the train. His eyes glinted. *I win.* "My sister is Dr. Bestman. I'm Doc Enoch."

Two can play at that game. "Just as we'll refer to his veterinary barn as the clinic and the place for humans as the surgery." Since she'd run a clinic and also had a surgery in Chicago, Enoch wanted her to have nothing less here. He'd simply wanted his veterinary place referred to as a barn.

"We'll raise the clinic this Saturday," the mayor said.

"The almanac calls for rain on Saturday," a farmer said. "How 'bout Monday? It should be clear by then. Parson Bradle could remind folks about it at the Sunday meeting, too," a farmer suggested.

"Monday it is, then," the mayor agreed.

"Stop right there, you varmints!" Velma's booming voice caught everyone's attention.

"Hooo-eeey! Set this aside and give me my cane!" Old Mrs. Whitsley shoved her plate at Taylor and twisted around with the agility of a woman one-third her age.

A knot of men halted on the porch steps. As the parlor jutted out perpendicular to the house, the porch wasn't but a couple of feet away from them. Swiftly placing her plate on the adjacent table and turning, as well, Taylor looked out the window.

"This dinner's to welcome the doctors," Velma said from the

doorway, flapping her arms at the men as if they were nothing more than pesky children underfoot.

"This ain't your place, you bossy old woman, and we're not going away."

"You've got a whale of a lot of nerve, turning your back on the doctors, not helpin' move their things, then showin' up just to eat all the vittles."

"Stuff all got moved anyhow," one of the men mumbled.

"And the food will all get eaten somehow, too." Velma folded her arms across her chest and nodded as if to say, "You can't argue with that."

"It's rainin' out here, Velma."

Mrs. Whitsley stuck her cane out the open window and poked the first man on the arm. "You're not so sweet you'll melt, Orville. And if you had the sense God gave a gnat, you'd know better than to show up here."

Just then, Big Tim Creighton and Daniel Clark bracketed the man and escorted him out to the property line.

Mrs. Whitsley patted Taylor's hand. "No matter where you go, there are good sorts and bad 'uns. Orville there tried to cheat me and a couple of other widows outta money. If ever he sets foot in your office, make sure you got your brother or one of the men you see in here now with you."

"In my profession, discretion is essential, and I'm careful to exercise it at all times. Nonetheless, I appreciate wise counsel such as yours."

Gnarled fingers played with the cane. "The wisdom is from the Lord. Any foolishness is all mine." The old woman got up, then paused. "If you find a cure for old age, you let me know."

"I'll do that as soon as you're old enough to need one."

The men out on the porch had formed a huddle. "Y'all got rid of Orville. Now how 'bout lettin' us in? We promise we'll help build the barn for the vet."

"Better late than never," Mrs. Whitsley called out. "Let 'em in."

No sooner had she vacated her seat than the mayor's wife came and sat beside Taylor. Her eyes sparkled as she scooted a little closer—a tiny move that rarely presaged anything good. Taking the offensive, Taylor grabbed her plate and lifted a bite of pecan pie. "The food is all so tasty. Had my brother known it would be so delicious, he would have rushed me to arrive before Thanksgiving."

"This is pecan pie—my great-memaw's recipe." Mrs. Cutter crammed a bite from her own slice into Taylor's mouth.

"Mmm. Magnificent."

Mrs. Cutter bobbed her head. "No boast or brag; it's a fact."

"I hope your memaw passed this recipe down to all of her granddaughters and has opened a bakery or a diner here in town."

"Wasn't that so sweet of you? Mercy Orion, who owns the boardinghouse, sells her baked goods through the mercantile. Could use a little more cinnamon, bless her heart, but a widow with a little girl has to cut corners where she can. As for the diner . . . it closed a year ago."

"Oh no," Taylor moaned. Upon seeing Mrs. Cutter's gape, she couched the truth in such a way as to keep from utterly humiliating herself. "Since my brother and I often keep odd hours, we've appreciated the convenience of a diner." It took every shred of her willpower not to cast a look over at the buffet and concoct a means by which to take supper home for that night. *One last decent meal before we're doomed.*

"Yes, well, you did come from Chicago. Big cities have all of those conveniences and exciting possibilities. Gooding's always been a plain-old ordinary God-fearing town full of salt-of-the-earth citizens—with Orville being the notable exception." Mouth twisting in a less-than-sincere smile, Mrs. Cutter added, "Until today. Now you, Doctor Bestman, are the most notorious thing that's ever happened to Gooding."

Three

"E dna Mae!" someone nearby gasped.

Clicky set aside his pie. "Orville's the worst liar and cheat any of us knows. You have no call, comparing Dr. Bestman to him."

"There's no denying the truth." Mrs. Cutter's jaw and voice hardened. "Ever since the train arrived, my Gustav's about had his ears scorched off. He's not here now because there were still three men in his office, bellowing at him. Once the news spreads that a woman doctor bamboozled us, he says we'll have a revolt on our hands from the locals and Gooding's going to be the laughingstock."

"Madam, I regret your husband is not here." Enoch scanned the suddenly quiet room. "I personally sent the letters of recommendation and verification of our degrees. I assure you, no secret was made of my sister's gender. If there's any question—"

"There can't be." Parson Bradle's wife shook her head. "Edna

Mae, you and Gustav were down with the grippe, and I brought over soup. I read the mail aloud to both of you. Among the papers in the packet Dr. . . . . Enoch sent were two letters from physicians who plainly said Dr. Taylor Bestman is a woman. I might add that they gave her glowing accolades. 'Diagnostic acumen and extremely deft in the operating theater' and 'nonpareil in obstetrics' are among the remarks that stand out in my mind." She gave her husband a faltering smile. "I didn't feel it proper to reveal that interesting tidbit since I learned it reading their mail to them during a sick call."

Parson Bradle patted her hand. "You did the right thing, Mama. But now the air's been cleared. No trickery was intended nor deception perpetrated."

Taylor rose. "That explains it, and we'll reserve notoriety for shady politicians and prisoners. I've vowed to serve the Lord and practice my profession honorably. Holding steadfast to those vows is—"

"An assured fact. My sister is undoubtedly one of the most stubborn people I've ever known."

Laughter eased much of the tension in the house.

Taylor smiled and went to stand next to Enoch. "Indeed, I'm one of the most stubborn my brother knows. Second, of course, to the image he views in the mirror each morning."

Enoch slapped a hand over his heart. "I'm wounded by that truth!"

Mrs. Whitsley banged the floor with her cane. "Then it's a good thing she's a doctor."

A minute later, Edna Mae Cutter came over and clutched Taylor's hand. "I was wrong about you and hope you'll forgive me."

"Of course."

Instead of looking happy, Edna Mae's expression showed greater distress. Her voice dropped to a mere whisper. "Please try to forgive my husband, too, because Gustav won't ever admit something slipped by him. He's planning to stir up trouble, and nothing will stop him."

◇~◇~◇

Karl mopped his forehead and leaned more heavily on the workbench. With the rain's moisture and the forge's heat, the smithy turned into a muggy swamp all its own. Waves of heat warped the air, making everything in its path turn blurry. Even after wiping his eyes, the board with all of the local brands burned into it seemed to shimmer and undulate.

Even if I had not hurt my leg, I still would be seeing these same things. It's nothing more than the weather and the location. Nevertheless, Karl swiped the back of his neck and jammed the handkerchief into his pocket before his brother appeared. No use in giving Piet any cause to fret. His older brother fussed more than a biddy hen on her first egg.

"Here." Piet held open a coat for him. "Get this on. The train— it has gone already. I'll hitch up the buggy."

"What for?"

Hovering like an impatient mother, Piet tried to stuff him into the coat. "Though you have tried, you are not hiding the fever from me."

"It's nothing." Karl jerked away.

Piet let out a frustrated growl. "It is a doctor you are needing. And soon."

"I'm fine. I changed the bandage."

CATHY MARIE HAKE

Piet glowered at him. "The storm will worsen. In the dark of night, I cannot risk our horses because you were too foolish to leave now."

"Skyler could drag me through the mud over to the doctor if the need was so great."

Piet nodded. "Ja. This is true. If you were in so great a need, it would not trouble you at all that the new doctor is a woman."

"Your mind is as warped as Widow O'Toole's gate." Karl practically snarled the accusation.

"You think about this I would tell jokes? No. Never once about this. They came on the train and I have seen them with my own eyes. The doctor and the other one."

"They're both doctors."

"But one is a people doctor and the other is for creatures. The one who for the creatures gives care, he is a man."

It took too much energy to argue with his brother over this. To state "he is a man" was redundant and normally would have struck Karl as ridiculous. In his current state, making a sarcastic comment seemed quite reasonable.

Piet already thinks I judge him. It's best I not say anything. Karl turned from his brother.

"Are you listening to me? The doctor who for the people cares, that one is not a man, but a woman. With my own eyes, I saw her."

"Then get spectacles. Once you have a pair on, you can change your mind."

"Don't be a fool, Karl."

Pretending his leg didn't burn, Karl walked toward the forge, picked up his hammer and prepared to toss it. "I win; you leave me alone."

"Two must agree before the hammer is thrown. I've not agreed."

Fingers flexing around the smooth wood of his hammer, Karl glowered at his brother. "So what is it you name so that you would agree? I want to work; all you do is squawk like a wet hen."

"I win, and you see a doctor—I let you choose which one: the woman new here or I will help you to another town. I lose, and I will say nothing more—"

"Goed!" Karl's hand started on the upswing.

"Unless I feel you are sicker still—"

Karl halted his action, but it wasn't easily done. Feeling hot and impatient, he didn't have the tolerance it took to deal with his brother's overprotective nonsense.

Pretending he had every right to dictate the smallest detail of their lives, Piet bobbed his head as if he'd negotiated the Magna Carta. "Ja. Then will I throw the hammer."

Thoroughly irritated, Karl sent his hammer aloft. It wheeled end over end in the air, then spun toward the soft dirt floor of their shop.

Thud. A small cloud of dust swirled, and Piet let out a smug sound. "It points to me."

"It does not. It most certainly tilts toward me."

Karl and his brother leaned forward, and Piet stared at the hammer, then back at him. "It's mine. I win."

"And I still say it veers slightly toward me. It might possibly be dead square in the middle. That's the most you'll get from me. I'll throw it over again."

Piet gave him a look of disgust and snatched the hammer from the dirt. "Same arrangements." A flick of his wrist, and the hammer flew clear up to the rafters, where it banged. Usually when they tossed the hammer, they just flicked their wrist so the tool spun end over end and landed in a gentle, controlled action. This wild display made Piet's frustration abundantly clear.

Thump. Again, the dirt swirled but higher and more than usual. Karl grunted, "See? I won." Wordlessly, Piet turned and stomped away.

Starting to squat sent stabbing pain through Karl's thigh. With Piet out of the shop, Karl straightened. "Skyler, fetch."

The collie didn't hesitate to come, even though the area was normally forbidden. Because of the ever-present shower of sparks, Skylar knew his place lay on the other side of the chain, where distance and a divider provided safety. Karl indicated the hammer, and Skyler picked it up and gave it to him. He scratched the spot between the dog's ears that the pet liked so much. "Goed hond, Skyler."

The dog went back, and Karl continued making the pieces he'd pledged for the vet's barn. The rain outside couldn't have come at a better time. Karl positioned himself so he stood directly in a draft. Cold air ran straight by him, stealing away some of his fever's heat. When he stepped even a foot away from that stream of air, the forge felt like the inside of a volcano.

He always rolled up his sleeves and left the top two buttons of his shirt unfastened when he worked. Plenty of blacksmiths didn't wear shirts at all—a very tempting thought. Instead, Karl reached in and unfastened every last button on his shirt.

"You're hot." Piet's accusation came out in a flat you-can't-argue-with-me tone.

"Ja." Why lie? "I have a little fever, but the forge and the rain together—they make it muggy and sticky in here." He operated the bellows, feeding the fire more oxygen so it burned hotter. "Did you stir the beans?"

"Ach!" Piet headed to the other side of the forge. Pitiful cooks, they'd learned a trick from another blacksmith. A pot of beans set by the forge all day would be ready for supper—all they had to do was remember to stir it occasionally. Many was the time they'd forgotten and endured burned beans. From the way Piet moaned, tonight would be yet another.

Karl reviewed the list of items and determined he needed to make some bars. They'd be just wide enough to hold a folded towel, but the brief length held a specific reason: Bolted securely, the bars could be used to hitch an animal. He'd put some in at the livery and found them handy. Surely a vet would find uses for them.

Waves of heat continued to shimmer, and all of the hammering echoed his pounding headache. *Odd, my hammer is heavier than usual.*

The water barrel hissed and sizzled as he plunged the sixth bar in to temper and cool. *I'd rather dive into the water, myself.* The bar barely cooled, he then used a punch to drive the holes into the ends. The task completed, Karl rewarded himself with a trip to the water barrel. Merely letting his arms drop in clear up to his elbows felt delicious. Cupping his hands, he realized just how filthy they'd gotten. Karl didn't care. He lowered his head and splashed water onto his face and neck.

Skyler gave his short, light friendly bark.

"Piet. Karl." Creighton entered the smithy.

"Tim," Piet said.

Karl nodded, then wished he hadn't. It made him dizzy. *I'm shivering, too.* Though he'd been roasting ten minutes earlier, now he breathed a sigh of relief that he'd rooted around and found a pair of his father's old balbriggans to wear because he'd been so unaccountably cold this morning.

"With it raining, I left Sydney and Velma over at Mrs. Whitsley's. They insisted on me bringing over some food so you'd have a decent supper." He handed a covered tray to Piet. "I saw you briefly at the welcome. Because Van der Vort Livery signed the contract to provide the Doctors Bestman with horses and a buggy as necessary, I know you'll stand by your word. Some folks are liable to kick up a ruckus about a woman doctor, and I admit it took me by surprise, but she's got enough schooling to cast five men into her shadow."

"We're men of our word." Piet sounded funereal. "We'll honor the contract."

"You were to stay and meet the doctors," Tim pressed.

Karl resented his brother being questioned. "We've spent the day making the pieces we promised for the barn."

Tim viewed the array of pieces and gave a low whistle of approval.

After he left, Piet whipped the cover off the food. "He thinks everything is fine."

"Neither of us said so. Sometimes it is better for a man to hold his opinion to himself."

"The only thing I want to hold is a fork!"

A heaping tray of excellent food, but Karl scarcely dredged up enough of an appetite to eat half a plateful. Every time he moved his left leg, pain shot through him. *I'm tired is all.* Pushing away from the table, he grunted. "I'm going to bed."

"You should eat more first. 'Feed a fever, starve a cold.' "

"No. It's 'Starve a fever, feed a cold.' " Karl tried to keep his voice strong and steady as he stood. If he let on how it pained him, Piet would start kicking up a ruckus all over again.

"That lady doctor would know." Piet's eyes narrowed. "She would know, too, how better to make your leg feel. I should have taken you to a doctor earlier."

"I'm still on my feet. That proves I didn't need a doctor." Knowing he'd pushed himself as far as he dared, Karl headed for bed. Stripping off his suspenders and shirt was easy enough. He couldn't get out of his jeans unless he pulled off his boots—but the movements necessary for unlacing them were nothing short of agonizing. *What does it matter?* Karl rolled onto his back on the bed and left his feet hanging over the end.

He grew hotter, then freezing, then hotter still. Disjointed, impossible dreams jumbled together. Piet shook his shoulder and said something to him. Sure it was a dream, Karl closed his eyes.

"Uit bed met u!" Piet shouted, tugging on his arm as if to help with his command to get out of bed.

Falling back onto his pillow, Karl shook his head.

Piet robbed him of his boots. *"Kom met me."* The room whirled, then righted, but only for a few moments. The loud clomps of Piet's boots on the stairs made the only sound in the cabin. *Come with me?* How could his brother ask him to come along and leave him behind? A second later, cold air and cold metal hit him all at once as Piet dumped him into something. Karl let out a roar.

·◇··◇··◇·

"Mmmm." Enoch smiled. "This pie is good." They'd come back and steadily unpacked for the past four hours.

Taylor searched for a place to put a pair of silver candlesticks.

"I still can't believe you suddenly grew so sentimental over everything."

"There's no reason why you shouldn't keep the wedding gown—just in case God surprises you."

"Surprise? It would be a shock, and a dreadful one." She gave up and set the candlesticks on the table. "I don't know of any woman who's successfully juggled being a wife and physician. When I took the Hippocratic Oath, it was tantamount to wedding vows. I'm married to my profession. I only agreed to bring the gown because it would be lovely if your bride wanted to wear it."

"If you don't mind, I'd like that. But you need to have the china and candlesticks."

Taylor let out an exasperated laugh. "It's hardly fair to scrape my burnt offerings onto the same china upon which our great-great-great-grandmother—"

He chimed in, "—served the queen." Waggling his forefinger at her, he said, "That's why the dishes had to come. Someday we'll be eating a meal, and you'll tell your nieces and nephews about that story."

"What do you want to bet they ask how the queen tasted?" Taylor quirked a brow. "Any child of yours will undoubtedly have a sassy mouth."

"I distinctly recall we asked the question in unison."

Hitching her shoulder, Taylor dismissed the accusation. "Mr. Burke drilled the evils of that type of sentence construction into us only hours before. It was inevitable."

"For as long as I live, I'll never forget how Mother laughed as Father tried to calm down Grandmother. Leaving behind the china would have been abandoning all of that."

"And these candlesticks?" Holding up her hand, Taylor gave him an exasperated look. "Let me guess. They're to remind me of the years of early morning piano practices."

"Not at all. They're practical devices that can perform any number of tasks. Hold up slippery windows. Cosh robbers on the head . . ."

Her dimples deepened as laughter spilled out of her. "Enoch, if you ever tire of doctoring animals, you ought to think about writing. Your imagination works overtime."

He shook his head. "Never. I've heard about starving artists." He set aside the empty plate. Having nested several boxes and crates inside of one another, Enoch put them out the back door.

Finally Taylor allowed herself the freedom to go on into her surgery. Ascertaining that much of what she'd brought duplicated the stock of this amazingly well-stocked surgery, Taylor had already sent some boxes and crates up to the attic that afternoon. Velma had unpacked the patient gowns, surgical drapes, and other clothware, as well as the laboratory equipment. Now—*now* Taylor could familiarize herself with where everything else was, change things around to suit herself, and indulge in hours of perfecting details.

Enoch returned with yet something more to eat. Leaning against the doorframe of her surgery, he moaned. "Superb."

Taylor slid the jar of tincture of iodine onto the shelf and turned around. "Save me a bite."

"Absolutely not." Enoch scooped up another huge forkful.

"Oh well. If that's how you feel, I'll bow out gracefully." Taylor lined up a few other jars, lifted her skirt, and made a quarter turn toward the pharmaceutical shelves. She could see Enoch's reflection in the just-cleaned glass panes. "Never let it be said I stood in the way of your holding up your end of the bargain."

Snatching up the last bite with his fingers, he gave her a baffled look. "Huh?"

"Oh, don't give me that astonished look, Enoch. You know it's your responsibility to hire our housekeeper this time."

Looking as if he'd been given a terminal diagnosis, he groaned. "The men mentioned a girl—Linda?"

"Linette already works at the boardinghouse. But with the dearth of marriageable women, I think you'd better think about a matronly woman of later years."

Taylor unpacked a physician's treatment ledger and continued. "Too bad Velma's already taken. She can cook and clean, handle rowdy men, and deliver babies. Add to that, she's nimble enough even at her size and age to climb onto her mare and ride out of town."

"You should have put a bow around her neck."

Taylor shot her brother a wry look. "Velma's, or the mare's?"

"Velma's. She sounds like God's gift to Gooding. I don't suppose she has any sisters?"

Enoch's face fell when she shook her head. A rapping on the door brought him to his feet.

My first patient here. Spying the plate with cake crumbs, Taylor grabbed a small towel and used it as a drape.

"Don't want anyone to think you're Marie Antoinette, eating your cake?" he teased as he strode through the surgery for the front door.

She stepped into the entryway behind him. "You ate it. If anyone gets beheaded, it ought to be you."

"You'd sew my head back on."

"Of course I would." She smiled. "Backwards." Having gotten in the last word of their banter, Taylor nodded to her brother to open the door to her patient.

"Yes?" Enoch sounded slightly puzzled as he opened the door.

"We saw your light on, so we came on over." Millicent and Daniel Clark entered, each holding a covered dish.

"We won't bother you by lingering," Daniel added, "but if you need help moving anything, I'm happy to stay and help."

Millie smiled back up at her husband. "Goodness knows how long you'll all stay up—Daniel worked the night away when we first arrived here. I thought you could use a little something to nibble on."

"That was very thoughtful of you." Enoch shut the door and practically grabbed the food from them. "The boxes and trunks were placed in the correct rooms this afternoon—an enormous help, to be sure."

"The ladies worked with astonishing speed, as well. All of our dishes, my clothing, and some of my medical goods were unpacked before we went to eat."

"Daniel, she had every box labeled with what was inside." Millie smiled up at her husband, but her smile turned into a poorly concealed yawn. Color suffused her face.

Daniel slid his arm around Millicent's tiny waist. "Dear, we need to go."

As Enoch opened the door, he scanned the street. "Those gas lamps do an excellent job of lighting the street."

"The mayor's house has gas piped into it, too. Since the town doesn't pay all that much, it was something extra they threw in. I feel obligated to confess that our mercantile had a grand-opening drawing and the prize was a velocipede. The widow next door to you won it and is . . ." His voice died out, leaving no doubt as to the reason for his warning.

"Widow O'Toole's dangerous riding swept me into Daniel's arms for the first time, so I don't complain," Millicent said, leaning into her husband.

With that slight move, Taylor saw something. She stepped out onto the porch in time to see someone in a wheelbarrow being pushed by a frantic-looking man. Yanking up her skirts and running down the steps, she called back, "Enoch, I'm going to need your help here."

"My brother, his leg—the iron went into it." The man stopped pushing his burden at the edge of the boardwalk, directly in front of her surgery.

"Where?" Taylor had already taken in the patient's rapid, shallow breaths and sizzling flesh and concluded the accident must have happened a day or two ago.

"Linker."

Linker. It was close to German's *linken*. She immediately looked at the left leg. Confined by jeans, the swelling was still noticeable. Taylor's heart plummeted. Had the wound been near the knee or below, she could have amputated. This high up on the leg, so close to the lymphatic system and arteries, the outlook was grave.

It took Enoch, Daniel, and the patient's brother to carry the slack man into her surgery. Millicent squeezed Taylor's hand. "We'll be praying for Karl and for you. I put water on to boil. I didn't know what else to do."

"You did the right thing. Thank you." Taylor slipped a heavy white apron over her head and tied it about herself, knowing while she did so Enoch would slice off the patient's jeans. Though her hands looked clean, she washed them anyway.

A strangled groan sounded.

"Off cut it!" The brother grew emotional and loud. "The leg—off cut it! Karl is the only brother I have. This is what you must do to save him."

Piet's anguished shouts pulled Karl from the heated darkness. Pain enveloped him, yet he still heard Piet's plea, "The leg—off cut it!"

"We'll do what must be done," a deep voice pledged.

Regardless of his fever, Karl's blood ran cold. Opa's leg had been amputated. He'd suffered horrendous pain, never found a false leg that worked right, and cursed the day he'd agreed to the operation. To be like that was not to live.

"I have the instruments set out." The woman's voice sounded calm and kind. "Mr. Clark, please—"

"Come on, Piet."

Waves of pain and scorching heat engulfed Karl. The strange man said something about getting leather straps and a saw. Karl refused to give in to the fever's pull. Eyes open the merest slit, he didn't recognize where he was. Cool, sure hands tested his forehead, then fingers pressed against the pulse in his wrist. Seizing at this one chance, Karl grabbed the woman's sleeve.

For a heartbeat, she stilled, then she said in a steady voice, "You're in the surgery. Your leg is wounded."

"No amputation." Despite his lack of strength, his voice came out in a harsh imperative. "Don't let him." Something wavered in her eyes. Sympathy? Help?

"Your life is more important than your limb."

"No!" The denial tore from him. He had to bolt or they'd cut. Karl rolled and shoved himself at the same time, forcing himself off the table and onto his feet—or foot. The moment his injured leg moved, pain froze the air in his lungs. Still, he refused to show any outward sign of difficulty. He had to convince this woman to help him.

Bracing his shoulders, she ordered, "Ease back to sit on the table and tell me why you're so opposed to surgery."

"*Opa.* Lost. Leg." Every word was an effort. He wouldn't sit back. The doctor would return any minute. If only he could concoct a way to get out of there! *A horse. I can't walk, but if she brought me a horse . . .* Satisfied with that plan, Karl tried to wipe the sweat from his brow and almost fell over.

"Here." The woman saw to it. "Let me help you."

She was an angel. Compassion and mercy radiated from her. "Promise you'll help?"

"I promise." Her green eyes only reached his chin, but the directness of her gaze showed plenty of spunk.

Deciding he'd trust her, Karl squinted over the woman's shoulder. The way the room rippled reminded him to hurry. "Have a plan."

"Whatever it is, you'll have to lie down under that sheet first."

"No. Get m'horse."

Her head dropped back until she stared up at the ceiling. "Balbriggans aren't decent. You need—"

"Awww." He nudged and tugged to turn her away, so why did he feel off balance? After embarrassing her half out of her skin, he wished he could oblige and crawl back under the cover for a few minutes until they concocted a way to get him some jeans—only he didn't have time. "Sorry, angel."

Lips pulled back in a grimace, Karl inhaled slowly, then curled his lower lip between his teeth and let out an ear-splitting whistle.

$\mathcal{F}$our

At the piercing sound, the double doors to Taylor's surgery flew open and her patient's brother ran in. "Why have you done this?"

"I didn't do anything yet." She struggled to keep the injured man from crumpling to the floor. "Help me, please."

Daniel wedged past Piet. "I'll take care of Karl. You'd better take care of matters before they get out of hand."

Taylor guided Karl's shoulders while Daniel hefted the rest of him onto the surgical table. Enoch showed up in the doorway and shoved something into Piet's hands. "I found the leather straps, but I still need another saw blade."

Her patient grimaced—and understandably so—until Taylor noticed his lower lip curled inward over his teeth. *Oh no.* "Don't wh—" Clapping her hand over his mouth, she stopped the sound before it built to full volume. Unadulterated fury flashed in her patient's ice-blue eyes. He'd already demonstrated far more fight than imaginable, but he couldn't afford to waste a scrap of energy. If she could keep him calm until anesthesia put him out . . . "Shh." She withdrew her hand and leaned close.

He glowered. "M'plan."

"Our plan. Remember? I promised to help."

The merest nod and a small grunt, and he lost consciousness. Piet blanched and dragged in a harsh breath. "He didn't— He isn't—"

"Unconscious."

Enoch gave her an apologetic look for riling her patient and his family and went back to find a saw. A moment later a loud noise on the porch had him calling out, "I've got it!"

Regardless of whatever case had just presented at their door, Taylor couldn't divide her attention. Enoch would have to see to it. This surgery couldn't wait. If she had to administer the anesthesia herself, she'd need to use a sponge instead of having Enoch drip chloroform onto the cone she'd set out. Until she determined that for certain, a judicious splash on a piece of gauze . . .

But the commotion outside intruded, finally forcing Taylor to look up. Disbelief washed over her. "Enoch, get that horse out of here!"

"I'd . . . love . . . to." Both heels dug into the floor and hands full of mane, Enoch couldn't keep the beast from ducking her head beneath the lintel and plowing from the entryway into the surgery. "Sis," Enoch said in his excessively low, keep-calm tone, "get out of the way."

Piet and Daniel struggled in vain to keep back the biggest horse she'd ever seen. Without a halter or lead, they had nothing to hold.

"My brother—he whistled." Piet planted himself directly in

front of the horse. Iron horseshoes gained little traction on the wooden floor, but the beast's sheer weight gave her an unmistakable advantage.

"Sis, out. She's twitchy."

Careful to match her brother's tone to keep the horse from panicking, she ordered, "Stop worrying about me." Taylor eased around the perimeter and whisked off the cloth napkin she'd draped over the cake plate just minutes before. "Sugar. Sugar, girl!" She imitated the sound Enoch made when he was enticing a horse to take a treat.

The behemoth paused, looked over her shoulder, and executed a turn worthy of a ballerina.

Enoch nodded at her. "Now back out into the entryway, Sis."

"I'm not leaving my patient. Daniel?"

Daniel took the plate and lured the horse out. Once the tail cleared the doorway, Taylor sprang into action. Shutting the doors, she surveyed the damage. She'd never given much consideration to precisely how much dirt and dust a horse's coat held . . . until now. The evidence covered the floor, the trays of now-contaminated instruments, even her patient and herself.

After all her hard work, Velma would have apoplexy.

It took several of Taylor's spare sterile sheets to drape everything—the floor included. A new surgical apron, scrubbed hands, fresh instruments, and she was ready. Enoch reappeared. "Piet's taking the Trakenhner back to the livery."

"Did you call her a train? She was big as one."

Enoch chuckled as he started to scrub his hands. "I knew you'd find humor in the situation. Good thinking about the sugar— Daniel and Piet are impressed."

She shook her head. "These people are crazy as foxes, and I

think *we're* the ones who've gotten hoodwinked. We're stuck here for four years!"

"Take heart. We'll either grow accustomed to it or starve long before then."

⋄⋄⋄

For all of the surgeries Taylor had ever performed, Mr. Van der Vort's rated as the most challenging. Even with Enoch's help, she still could have used two more pairs of experienced hands. Imbedded deep in his thick thigh muscles were not one or two fragments of iron, but three. Two were dangerously close to nerves that could partially paralyze the use of his limb, and the third was nestled beside an artery. All three sites had grown infected. In truth, the blacksmith had come very close to being buried in the cold ground.

After the surgery, Mr. Van der Vort's fever raged all night, and he was in danger of hemorrhaging. Remaining by his bedside, she'd kept watch and prayed. Only as the sun started to rise did he slide from the last vestiges of the chloroform haze and drift into a restless sleep.

Casting a look over her shoulder as she exited her patient's room, Taylor frowned as she recognized the melody of "Massa's in de Cold Ground."

"Enoch! Stop that whistling!"

Chortles overtook the tune. "Bad choice, huh? What about this?" The first few notes of "Old Folks at Home" quavered in the air.

Heading down the stairs, she ordered, "None at all."

"Don't worry, Sis. Horses won't be interested in Stephen Foster's tunes."

"That wasn't funny in the least."

"My comment or Van der Vort's stunt?"

"Neither. It's a marvel I'm not deaf from his whistle."

"I wonder if he'll have any hearing left after you serve him a piece of your mind. Though," he mused, "I think you're complicit since you did promise to help him."

She raised her chin. "I didn't specify what type of help."

Taking an apple from the basket he'd hauled inside, Enoch buffed it on his sleeve. "I overheard you when I came back with the leather straps." Eyes twinkling impishly, her twin kept the debate alive. "You laid equal claim to the plan."

"I agreed to help him. Febrile irrationality is the only explanation for his summoning his horse—that or simplemindedness."

"Horses are highly intelligent creatures. I'd like a good look at that Trakenhner. She's a beauty."

Folding her arms across her chest, Taylor gave her brother an incredulous look. "There's nothing beautiful about a horse in my surgery."

"It was stupid and dangerous for you to stay when I warned you to get out."

"In the future, if you don't let a horse in, I won't be put in such a position." Though tired, she couldn't help smiling at her brother. They constantly matched wits. "It's a simple matter of cause and effect."

Enoch examined the red apple. He was peculiar about them— they had to be perfectly shiny before he'd take a bite, but Taylor wasn't fooled in the least. The action served to smother his smile. "Piet mentioned Karl has a different whistle for each of their horses. You're lucky. He could have summoned a seventeen-hand black Shire."

"No doubt he can call hogs, too. That doesn't mean they belong in my surgery."

"Aha! I knew it! You're jealous."

"Only of your apple." She held out her hands for him to toss it to her.

"It's just an apple." Enoch lounged against the banister and continued to shine the fruit. "You have to wait for your patients to come to you—"

"And all you need to do is pucker up?"

"I've never had to do that for my patients, but I've been known to enjoy it with an owner or two."

"I'm disappointed in you." Taylor paused for the sake of timing. "A gentleman doesn't kiss and tell."

"I didn't tell who. I just said I enjoyed it. You might want to try it sometime." He winked, tossed her the apple, and started whistling another song as he walked off.

Weariness dragged at her. Concerned about blood poisoning, infection, and possible hemorrhage, Taylor needed to return to her patient's bedside. She finished the apple, gulped a mouthful of last night's leftover cold coffee and shuddered, then went back into the sickroom.

Once at the bedside, she picked up her stethoscope to listen to the blacksmith's heart and lungs. Especially after he'd received chloroform for the prolonged surgery, making sure his breathing remained stable was essential. The conical wooden stethoscope her grandfather and father had used didn't transmit sound as well as this modern binaural model. Originally miffed that she'd not wanted his piece, Father had soon changed his mind when she had him borrow hers to discover its superior sound transference and the added bonus of freeing the physician from having to be within mere inches of a patient's chest.

Overall, her examination yielded good results. Mr. Van der Vort's heart and lungs sounded excellent. The surgical dressing on his leg showed no bleeding. If only he didn't have a fever . . .

Skimming a vinegar-water cloth over his furrowed brow, heavily muscled arms, and wrists allowed for significant evaporative cooling. It wasn't until he opened his eyes that she realized she was humming the tune Enoch had been whistling as he'd left. Mortified, she shot a frantic prayer heavenward. *Please, God, let this man be too sleepy to remember what I just hummed.*

Karl floated on the haze of mostly asleep and felt an odd pressure on his chest as the strains of a song teased the edges of his mind. Something cold and wet kept bothering him, too. His nose tingled from the odd smell of . . . vinegar? Nothing was making sense.

"Beautiful Dreamer." His eyes shot open. A dark-haired, green-eyed temptress was leaning over him, humming the song in a sultry key. He didn't recognize her or the location, but only one kind of woman wore scarlet. A strong blink didn't make the color of her shirtwaist fade one iota. So much for giving her the benefit of the doubt—but then, there really hadn't been much room for uncertainty. No decent woman would hover over a strange man's bed, humming a love song and caressing him.

She cleared her throat. "Your fever is coming down. I'll get you something to drink."

"Nee. No. I'll go home and have water." What he'd mistaken for vinegar must have been the mingled odors of beers and whiskey.

A gigantic hammer and anvil pounded in his head already. The last thing he wanted to drink was alcohol.

"I have water right here." Dropping the cloth she'd mangled into a bowl, she rose.

Karl wasn't about to wait for her return. Jackknifing—or attempting to jackknife—put him flat on his back, teeth gritted against a wave of pain.

"Mr. Van der Vort, foolish actions could very well start bleeding or rip your sutures." Face puckered like a sour schoolmarm, the chippie came back over. "Prop yourself up on one elbow."

"Bossy," he muttered. Raging thirst made him comply as he strained to recall when he'd last had anything.

"Sip it. If you do well, you may have broth next."

"Broth?" Another reason he knew he had to leave. This woman planned to starve him.

"Yes. Now please attend to what I say. You sustained significant damage to your quadriceps femoris. The most powerful muscles in the human body are in the lower limbs, and of them all, the quadriceps are the strongest. With the . . ."

She said a few more words that made absolutely no sense to him. Then suddenly, it all made perfect sense. Karl choked on the last gulp of water and bellowed, "You're that woman doctor!"

$\mathcal{F}$ive

S is?" It took all of five seconds for a man to appear in the doorway. His voice sounded casual and even lazy, but his intense stare told Karl the doctor's brother considered himself to be her champion and defender.

"Mr. Van der Vort is surprised to meet me, Enoch."

"Furious." No use mincing words. Karl directed his instructions to the man. "Give me my jeans. I'm leaving."

Enoch didn't move, other than to face his sister and shrug. "At least he didn't ask for his horse this time."

"Don't give him any ideas." Focusing back on Karl, the doctor gave him a no-nonsense look. "Your pants have fewer stitches in them than your leg and—"

"That's why a woman should content herself with sewing quilts." Bound and determined to leave, Karl pushed himself into a position where he half sat on the edge of the bed, battling the sheets and a blanket. Just before he tossed them all aside, he realized the folly of that action and dropped them in a wadded mess around himself.

"Trousers will not fit over your dressing."

"Lady, there's enough wrapped around me to fill the Grand Canyon halfway."

"There's a hole in your leg to rival the canyon, sir." The minute his fingers closed around the knot on that bandage, her voice turned just as hard as the iron he worked each day. "Any less pressure or padding, and the benefit accomplished by the surgery would be for naught. That must stay in place, just as you must severely curtail your activity until the immediate postoperative period has passed."

His thigh started throbbing like anything. Fancy as all her words sounded, it didn't mean she knew beans about how to doctor folks. She must have done something wrong to his leg—probably wrapped it too tight. Once he broke free from here, he'd loosen it up, get a gander at it, and decide just what was necessary under the circumstances. Mind made up, Karl moved again—all of a pathetic inch that left him breaking out in a cold sweat and gritting his teeth.

"I won't keep you here if you insist upon leaving. Just know this: Your wound is liable to open up and bleed all over my nice clean floor. If you're well enough to make that kind of mess, you're obligated to clean up after yourself." Her green eyes held challenge.

Frustrated by his weakness and vexed by the way she was goading him, Karl muttered, "A woman's place is to sew clothes and mop floors, not to sew men and order them around."

"I understand." The doctor nodded slowly. "Women to the cradle and coffeepot; men to all great endeavors."

Karl gaped at the so-called doctor. He couldn't have heard her correctly. "All women feel the cradle is their greatest endeavor."

Her brother didn't manage to cover his laugh with a cough. "You would have stood a better chance of gaining her agreement if you'd said everyone aspired to making a good pot of coffee."

"That would be a lie. Piet and I, we gave up. Ours is always burnt. I'll wait to leave until I've eaten breakfast and had coffee." He grunted as he slid back to the center of the bed. "Doc, he wasn't always so good at fixing sick people, but anyone who came here for help knew they were welcome to the coffee on his stove. He always brewed the best in town."

"Even if he wasn't a woman? Imagine that!"

Karl shot the woman doctor an impatient glower. He should have anticipated her reaction. "You've got plenty of perk, but there have to be grounds to brew the right cup. Same with doctors. Women don't have the necessary . . . grounds it takes to serve as physicians."

"If it would instill confidence in you, I'm willing to show you my medical degree."

Staring at her, Karl took in the fire in her eyes and all the strands of hair that had worked free and coiled into touch-me curls at her temples and nape. "There's not a piece of paper in the world that could make me look past your dimples or forget your humming."

Taylor blushed. Enoch scarcely believed it. With society's prejudice against female physicians and doctors themselves being the most stalwart subscribers to that ignorance, Taylor had endured untold ridicule during her years at medical school.

She'd been the butt of jokes, she'd been the victim of sabotage in the laboratory, and she'd endured every possible type of accusation. But after the first week of medical school, Taylor had ceased blushing.

"Speaking of coffee, I put some on the stove." Enoch purposefully omitted the fact that he was merely reheating last night's. He gave his sister a questioning look. "Only you know what's okay for Van der Vort to eat."

"My appetite is good. Strong. Lusty." As soon as he used the final adjective, the blacksmith went ruddy.

"Then I'll find us some breakfast." Taylor left.

Launching in as soon as she was out of earshot, Van der Vort said, "You're a veterinarian. You have medical skills. Surely you can render care to me."

"No."

"Why not?"

"My sister doesn't treat animals, and I don't treat humans. It's that simple." He allowed a rueful grin that kicked up the side of his mouth. "Well, almost that simple. I've been around when Taylor's had to treat some men who acted like jackasses, but she still treated them."

"You love your sister."

"I do."

Looking at him intently, the blacksmith ordered, "Then send her back to your parents. She'll be unhappy here."

"We've both signed four-year contracts. We're honoring our pledge."

"Then she'll stay, but she'll have to stop this nonsense of doctoring." Van der Vort yanked the blanket up and clamped it in place beneath his arms.

Is he trying to shield Taylor, or is he embarrassed that she's worked on him?

"The wrongs permitted in big cities aren't acceptable in our small town."

Now Van der Vort had crossed the line. Enoch expected men to ask him to treat them, but he always refused. People might give their opinion about women as physicians. Though it wasn't necessarily enlightened or kind, Enoch tolerated such blather. But the blacksmith had just judged and condemned his sister. "There is nothing wrong with someone—man or woman—using the gift God gave them. You, of all people, should be grateful."

Taylor's patient glowered at him. "I'm not going to be a testimonial for her."

"She didn't ask you to."

"Good thing." Van der Vort closed his eyes. "Anyone can sew."

"Know many who can take three metal shards out of a man?" Slamming a handkerchief onto the bed next to the patient's hand, he ordered, "Open that." Anticipating Taylor would have to prove herself, Enoch had saved the pieces she'd removed during the surgery last night. Jagged and sharp as could be on many points, all three measured about an inch long.

Van der Vort let out a long-suffering sigh, complied, then flipped the edge of the handkerchief back over the mean-looking pieces. "The part my brother took out was bigger and longer."

"Is that all that matters to you—what you can see on the outside?"

A single crack of a laugh blurted from the patient. "Very clever. A man who loves and protects his family—I can respect that. But your sister . . ."

"You will treat her with the utmost respect." Enoch stared at the blacksmith as he gave the command. "My sister is a godly woman and a lady."

"Who does a man's job."

"More than a man. We fought last night. Your brother and I told her to amputate. She didn't just save your life; she saved your leg."

For a moment, Van der Vort went silent. "I won't treat her disrespectfully. That much I give you, but don't expect more. I still believe what she does is wrong."

"No one asked your opinion."

"I get an opinion. I'm in a bed, and she's in and out of this room."

Staring a hole through him, Enoch bit out, "Now that you're conscious, she'll never be here alone with you."

Dishes rattled on the stairs. Taylor was coming. *Lord, please open this man's eyes or close his mouth.* When Taylor reached the landing, the floorboards creaked.

"Talcum powder."

Taylor entered the sickroom. "You need talcum powder, Mr. Van der Vort?"

"No, you do." He grinned at her.

"That's enough." Enoch thrust himself between his sister and the man.

"Dump talc on the floor and rub it into the cracks. It'll sift down to the joists and stop the creaks."

Setting the tray on a three-drawer bureau, Taylor smiled. "For that, you may have coffee and a little something to eat."

The blacksmith fell upon the baked goods like a starving man. A pang shot through Enoch. Keeping this man here would mean feeding him whatever food they'd been given. Other than that, the kitchen didn't have anything in it. With her patient in a better mood, Taylor removed the dishes. "My brother will assist me in examining your wound."

"He'll look at it and tell you how it is."

"The relay has begun, and you chose your partner. You cannot change that now."

Van der Vort's fair eyebrows slammed together and his blue eyes turned to ice. "I did not choose you to be my partner."

"Ah, but you did. Furthermore, I carried out my part of the agreement. I helped you, and I didn't amputate your leg." Taylor gave him a stern look. "On the other hand, your only contribution to the partnership was whistling me deaf and getting a horse in my surgery."

"See?" He turned to Enoch. "Fanciful imaginations are just another reason women aren't intended to be—"

"Your grandfather's leg was amputated. Or at least I assume it was your grandfather. You called him *Opa* when you asked for my help. Yes, you grabbed my wrist, rolled off the table, and begged me to help you escape before they could amputate. Please don't feel I'm making fun of you, because I'm not. I take ethics quite seriously, and all of this goes to the heart of that matter. You did indeed ask for my help, and you specified no amputation. I honored your wishes on both accounts."

"Honor them now. I want you to stop treating me."

Taylor shook her head. "It would be unethical. No one else is close enough to oversee your care. As I tried to tell you earlier, you are in great peril of hemorrhaging, contracting blood poisoning, or having any of several other complications. In three days, if you still

69

wish, I will sign off on your case and send you to another physician. By then it should be safe for you to travel."

"Three days!"

Proud of how she'd taken charge of the whole situation, Enoch inserted, "You heard the doctor. Three days."

Now that she'd managed to distract her patient, she motioned Enoch to pull back the covers. "I have deep scratches in my entryway floor downstairs and in the surgery from horseshoes, and though I wouldn't have known what to call that huge brown mare, my brother tells me she was a Tran-Tranek—"

"My Trakenhner? You expect me to believe a sixteen-hand Trakenhner came inside?"

"And into my surgery because you whistled for her. I hope you have a different mare to hitch to my buggy, because that one and I aren't on good terms."

"You cannot have it both ways, Doctor. You, yourself, aim for good results, and your brother says respect from your patients is enough. So why does it matter if you're on good terms with the mare, as long as she gets you to the right destination?"

Enoch drew off the cover and cut the knot holding the bandage in place. The whole while, he fought the urge to let out a booming laugh. Most men were so cowed by Taylor's intellect, accomplishments, and profession, they avoided trading anything more than the briefest essential salutations. Occasionally there was one who found basking in her reflected limelight and benefiting from her wealth much to his liking—but those were invariably arranged dates for charity suppers Taylor attended for the one evening and wisely sensed those men were not for her.

But this man?

He'd ascertained that Taylor was loved and wanted her to be

sent back where he thought she'd be happy. Now he lay there offering his opinion, telling her what to do with her new home, and calling her out for what he perceived as hypocrisy. Enoch looked from his sister to her patient and back again, a smile tugging at the corners of his mouth. This man wasn't like any she'd met before.

"You don't have to look at that. I will." Van der Vort exerted himself to get into a sitting position.

"I'll show you precisely what I did." Taylor started unrolling the bandage.

They're going to have a tug-o'-war here in a minute. Enoch thought he probably ought to be ashamed of himself for finding the whole situation entertaining, but the guilt didn't stop him from watching.

"That is unnecessary. I'll be able to see."

"Tell me, Mr. Van der Vort: Are all Texans as stubborn as you are?"

"Tell me, Miss Bestman: Are all women doctors as bossy as you are?"

Always one to appreciate a rousing conversation or debate, Taylor burst out laughing. "I propose a deal. I examine your incision and you hitch that feisty mare to the buggy when I pay visits to my patients."

"Done."

Pronouncing the operative site excellent, Taylor started to bandage it up. Someone knocked downstairs, so Enoch nudged her. "I'll finish this."

With her gone, Van der Vort said in a low tone, "Dimples actually has a sweet temperament."

"She does, but don't ever call her that again."

"I was talking about the mare."

⟨∘⟩⟨∘⟩⟨∘⟩

"I tend to be rather practical. I usually make stew on the day after I do laundry and thought I'd bring some over as a welcome."

"I'm very thankful," Taylor said at the exact moment a mouth-watering aroma hit Enoch.

"With the storm coming, I had to run and pull everything off my clothesline instead of coming to meet you yesterday," the woman said. "Hearing that some people marred your reception with a narrow-minded viewpoint distresses me. The Bible says there's no slave or free, no male or female, and as far as I'm concerned, I actually like you being female. There are times that . . . well, having a woman for a doctor would make me feel more comfortable."

Enoch knew he couldn't walk out right then and embarrass the petite woman standing with his sister, so he eased back up the stairs for a minute. He and Karl had shared a sound laugh over the Dimples matter, and Karl was still letting out an occasional chortle. That would give the women the impression they were still alone.

Taylor led the woman to the parlor, and Enoch strained to hear her cute Texas drawl. His stomach growled and a wry smile twisted his lips. Instead of searching for a housekeeper, maybe she'd just found him. The women continued to talk for a few more moments. At the point he figured they'd probably gotten beyond whatever "woman talk" they needed, he cleared his throat to warn them of his presence and went down the rest of the stairs.

"Here's my brother. Let me introduce you. Mercy Orion, this is my twin brother, Enoch. Enoch, this is Mercy Orion."

"I'm pleased to meet you, Miss, Mrs. . . ."

"Mrs. Mercy Orion," his sister clarified.

Mrs. Orion nodded her head, and he did the same. "Mrs. Orion." Hmm. When he'd entered the parlor, he'd thought her dress to be pinkish. Up closer, he determined she was wearing mauve. Women had rules for how long they wore black for mourning before they added gray and mauve, but he'd never paid attention to them. She was a beautiful woman, and he couldn't help wishing it was her husband she mourned. What a terrible thing to do—selfish, too—yet Enoch couldn't keep from hoping to turn such a sad misfortune into the ultimate happiness for both of them.

"Mrs. Orion, you're wearing mauve," Taylor probed. "I hope you don't mind my asking . . . ?"

"It's for my dear husband. I lost him at Fort Bend's Jaybird-Woodpecker War."

Enoch struggled between feeling compassion for her loss and delight that her grief wasn't fresh. "My condolences. That was four years ago, wasn't it?"

She looked astonished. "Yes, four years in September."

"Being a veterinarian, my brother immediately spied the headlines."

"Such an odd and frivolous name for something so tragic. It must have been hard for you." Enoch watched her features carefully.

"The first years were a blur, I was so heartbroken. But time has helped. I'm blessed to have many happy memories and a very sweet daughter to remember Hamilton by."

"A daughter!" The fact that she had a child surprised yet delighted him. "I hope she has your beautiful brown eyes." And stunning eyes Mrs. Orion did have—wonderful large eyes with a thick, dark fringe of lashes. A man could get lost in those eyes.

Taylor shouldered up beside him, putting some distance between him and the widow. "Yes, I noticed your remarkable eyes right away, as well. Our mother always referred to them as doe eyes. Enoch, Mrs. Orion made us a delicious stew, and I'm getting hungrier by the minute just smelling it."

"So am I." He patted his stomach. "The aroma could bring a man to his knees."

Mrs. Orion laughed. "I don't know about that, but since it was believed that you were both bachelors and men tend to have a sweet tooth, I figured many of the women probably made you some of their tastiest desserts. With the weather turning cold, I thought something wholesome and hot might be appealing. You probably haven't had time to finish unpacking or get things squared away, especially with you already having had to do surgery. . . ." She turned her attention from Taylor to him. "And I understand that the doctor . . . well, you, Doctor . . ." Her hands moved in a little flustered gesture.

"Let me make it easy for you." Enoch took the stew from Taylor, set it on a nearby table, and motioned for Mrs. Orion to have a seat.

"Thank you, but no. I already told your sister I have something in the oven."

"Far be it from me to make someone else burn anything. I already do enough of that for at least ten people all by myself!"

She laughed—a soft, husky laugh.

"My sister is to be called Dr. Bestman. I've already invited everyone to call me Doc Enoch. It makes it easier for all involved so there's no question as to who is Dr. Bestman. Now that you know it, you won't run into that awkward doctor/doctor confusion again."

Mrs. Orion's carefully folded hands now formed a nervous knot. "I don't know. . . . It carries with it an altogether different type of awkwardness because it's too familiar by far."

He smiled. "I don't consider it familiar in the least, but as simple common sense. I wouldn't take offense, and I don't expect anyone to invite me to address them by their Christian name—especially not the women. As a lady who's practicality is proven by the delivery of a hot meal on a late November day, Mrs. Orion, surely you understand the straightforward reason behind it."

Taylor didn't disappoint him. She latched on to the word. "Practical." She smiled at Mrs. Orion. "That does settle the matter, doesn't it?"

"I suppose it shall. I'm sure you need to tend to your patient, and I didn't mean to keep you."

"Taylor and I haven't had a chance to do any marketing and our larder is empty. As you pointed out, my sister's busy here, but I won't have the slightest idea what to buy. Would you have some time to help me select a few essentials at the grocer's?" His sister looked at him like he'd gone out of his mind, but Enoch didn't care. He'd have Mrs. Orion help him buy thread, needles, and fabric for new slip cushions if that's what it took to spend more time with her.

Taylor's foot nudged his. "I thought you wanted some soup."

His sister just didn't understand. Often they were so close they could almost read each others' thoughts; yet now of all times, his twin was oblivious. Enoch glowered at her. She gritted her teeth and stared back at him.

Mrs. Orion cleared her throat. "If you don't mind making do with the stew today, tomorrow would be more convenient for me. Linette Richardson and I are baking quite a bit today, and we've already mixed up most of the dough. I'd be happy to help you, though. Could I meet you over at Mr. Clark's mercantile tomorrow at nine o'clock? Maybe then you could both come."

"Excellent." He'd find a way to leave his sister at home tomorrow. Enoch walked over and opened the door for Mrs. Orion. As she passed by, he inhaled deeply. She smelled of cinnamon. Cinnamon and vanilla. Other women tried to smell of roses and lilac and honeysuckle and all of those sweet, sticky, smelly sorts of things, but Mercy Orion smelled of home and welcoming and warmth. He was in love. It was love at first sight, and he knew it. He'd met the woman he wanted to marry.

Enoch turned around, and his sister looked at him with nothing short of frustration. Holding the stew pot again, she shook her head. "It's an utter waste to buy groceries until we get a cook."

"We need all the staples. And oatmeal. I can buy that type of food. Those things don't go bad, and we can make oatmeal." *I don't want Sis to ever think I wanted Mercy just so we'd have a cook. Nothing's further from the truth.* "We don't do too badly with eggs and soup. We could probably get by for awhile."

"I don't want to, and not just for the sake of my stomach." Taylor glanced at the ceiling. "At least when I have patients, having someone else around would be wise—maybe a morning woman and an afternoon one. Even if there are some troublesome men around, Gooding has a lot of nice ladies."

"Yes, it does." Leaning against the doorframe, he tilted his head toward the woman walking down the street. "And I'm going to make that one my wife."

Six

O h, good heavens!" Taylor dropped the pot of stew, and it splattered everywhere. "Look what you made me do! We've sacrificed almost half of a good pot of stew because you've lost your mind. I can't believe it! I'm starving and so are you, and the only thing you can do is be ridiculous over a woman you've only seen for three minutes. Not even three minutes. Enoch, you have gone round the bend!"

She waggled her finger for emphasis. "Stop and think. In the past, you had all sorts of fun running around with whichever woman suited your fancy. The two of you tired of one another, and you waltzed on to someone else. This is a small town, and you can bet all the men know Mercy Orion's every move. I guarantee you she has men panting after her, and if this tastes half as good as it smells, men clutching diamond rings line up at her doorstep."

She started pacing around the mess. "Help me clean this up, and you're going to just . . . you just . . . you don't get a bowl of this at all because you wasted your share by shocking me so deeply that . . . Oh, you made me a blithering idiot!" Taylor glowered at him some more.

"Take the pot on into the kitchen, Taylor. I'll clean this up."

Taylor picked up the pot. "I'll help you clean it up," she said with a definite lack of grace in her tone. "But part of this has to go to my patient. I'll share anything that's left with you."

"No, I'll just have a taste of it, then you can have the rest. I'm planning on having hundreds more pots of that in my future."

She shook her head and muttered, "Crazy man. Thoroughly crazy man. He's gone round the bend. Whoever thought my own brother would be the one I'd have to treat for insanity? What am I going to do? I'm in a town that doesn't want me, and my brother's going insane. If Mother were here, she'd be telling me to watch out because trouble always comes in threes."

Enoch didn't mind that his sister was muttering to herself. Courting Mrs. Orion was going to be fun.

After a quick cleanup, the siblings returned to the kitchen, where the remaining stew went into bowls for Van der Vort and Taylor. She took a bite and smiled appreciatively, then asked, "So where were you this morning, that you came back with that big basket of apples?"

"Out . . ." He shrugged. "Looked around a little bit."

"You usually tell me about your cases."

"Nothing much to tell." Was this deception? He couldn't very well tell her exactly where he'd been. The case had turned out to be a ruse, where two men had urged him to make his sister cease practicing medicine in Gooding. "It wasn't really a case. People are rather anxious to see how I am around their animals. Since we're from the city, I get the impression some worry I don't know much about livestock. Think they figure I'm a dog-and-cat man who could also take care of Aunt Bertha's prized canary in a pinch. One man—a farmer named Smith—flat-out said he'd voted against bringing me."

Taylor handed over the bowl with the rest of her stew. "It's so hearty I'm already full. For him to be in town when he'd normally be doing his chores . . ."

Enoch took a huge bite. "He had good cause: a wagonload of what seemed like two hundred kids he drove to school. His opinion was that the town ought to have waited till a Texan applied. Gooding's been without a vet entirely, so another month or year without shouldn't have made that big a difference."

"Until it's his cow or pigs or plow horse that's in trouble." Affronted on Enoch's behalf, she started pacing around the table. "Times like this, I'm so tempted to give in to my vengeful spirit. If that Smith doesn't trust you or have faith in your professional ability, he oughtn't call you out to help care for them."

"He had a pair of decent-looking horses hitched to the wagon. Maybe he has a natural talent with animals and won't need help. There are plenty of other animals in the area. I'll be busy enough."

"So you strolled around and gave hitching-post consultations?"

He seesawed his tongue at the corners of his lips to get the last speck of flavor. "Suppose you could say that. It started out with my going over to visit the barn site. Men would pause and visit for a minute or so, just to get a feel for my medical opinion on anything from ticks to torsion."

"And whether you'd treat them because they refused to have a woman as their physician?"

Enoch met her gaze. "A few asked. You know my answer. Give them time, Sis. They're backward. You can't take it personally."

A brave smile flitted across her face. "Enough about that. Tell me all about the barn."

Her attitude about some of the men's ignorant stance was far better than he could have hoped—but it was all he should have expected. Taylor wasn't one to moan and fuss, so he went along with the change in topic. "They did a really nice job, Sis. Since you didn't have a chance to see it yesterday, maybe later today we can go out and take a look at it together. It's all exactly to my specifications."

Taylor smiled at him. "I'm so glad for you, Enoch." She'd given up the maternity/pediatric practice she'd slaved to achieve in order to come here for his dream, and what was she getting? Not much. In fact, she was getting a whole lot of difficulty. Yet her voice rang with sincere pleasure for him. "So what kind of consultation earned you a basket of apples?"

"None at all. Clicky dropped them off. Maybe I'm not the only man in town experiencing love at first sight."

"Then he'll need to go to Austin to get his eyes and head examined. I—"

A loud crash upstairs cut short whatever else she planned to say.

Seven

Enoch charged upstairs with Taylor on his heels. With every single step, she rued women's fashions. He stopped in the doorway of the sickroom, and she slammed into his back.

"Move," she ordered, trying to shove him aside. Any number of terrible images flooded her mind. The blacksmith lying on the floor with a concussion . . . or a broken leg . . . or worse still, lying there hemorrhaging . . .

Enoch moved out of the way, but laughter shook his frame.

Work-scuffed boots were sticking out from under the bed— each attached to a leg! One she could only see the calf, and the other she saw just past the knee. Disbelief shot through Taylor. "Mr. Van der Vort, get in that bed this instant."

"Just a minute" came the muffled reply from beneath the bed.

"A minute is more than I'm willing to give you." She marched over and stared down at the feet. How had he gotten those boots on? For that matter, how had he gotten to them—or the jeans—at all? "I took pains to explain the risk of your hemorrhaging."

"And I just thought you were the pain." A head and broad shoulders rose from behind the far side of the bed. It was Mr. Van der Vort, giving her a jaundiced look.

Taylor's focus darted to the floor, confirming that those big booted feet remained in place. *It's physically impossible for those legs to be his. Then who's under the bed?* "Enoch, please assist Mr. Van der Vort back into bed."

"I'll be okay." A foot attached to that voice thumped the floor as proof of the claim. "Well, blast. Maybe not. These are my favorite suspenders."

Her patient shot Enoch a look. "Piet—my brother—is stuck. Help him. I can take care of myself."

Curiosity burned within her. She wanted to ask why his brother got stuck. But Enoch started snaking under the bed, so he'd be able to tell her later exactly how the man was stuck.

"Mr. Van der Vort, you must remain in bed. It's vital for you to rest." Stepping over the booted feet, Taylor headed toward the far side of the bed.

"Just what are you doing?" Mr. Van der Vort barked from his seat on the floor.

It wasn't his tone that stopped her; it was the realization that instead of the roomy calf-length cotton nightshirt he ought to have on, he was sporting a blue flannel shirt. She jerked her chin upward. "Sir, I expect you to be in that bed, covered up, when I return to this room in exactly one minute."

"And if I'm not?"

"I want to watch this," Piet declared. The whole bed shuddered from his attempt to wiggle free.

Wild threats whirled around in her mind. "If you're not—" Taylor's focus drifted down from the ceiling and locked with her patient's eyes—"I'll be back in here, and you'll still be down there." A smug little smile tilted her lips. "Now, I don't think either of us wants to give even one more second's thought to that."

"You might not . . ."

"Enoch!"

Roars of masculine laughter filled the room.

He betrayed me. Just for the sake of a few laughs. She'd dealt with male jeers, derision, and heckling in medical school. Automatically drawing on the skills that had gotten her through then, she pasted on a half smile. Jaw tight and head held high, she turned and marched from the room. *I'm going to return just as I said I would.* Those men were acting like naughty children, testing her limits. Fine. They'd soon discover Taylor MacLay Bestman stood her ground.

But it was Enoch's jesting that made her heart ache. Already he'd declared he'd fallen in love and found his future wife, and now he'd chosen coarse male camaraderie over what had once been an unshakable allegiance to her. Taylor walked into her own bedchamber and collapsed onto an empty trunk near the door.

"With or without you, I'm going to Texas." Remembering his words to her now triggered a panic. Had Enoch truly wanted to come by himself? Had she stifled him when he wanted to break free?

The same crash that had brought her running upstairs sounded again next door. "Piet, are you trying to crack all your ribs?" Enoch asked, sounding mildly irritated. "I told you to wait."

He coerced me into coming here. "Come with me, Sis," he had pleaded. *"I sold my practice. You and I have always been a team. Look to the future with me. Come."*

Well, I came. He got what he said he wanted. Now we'll have to make the best of it . . . If Saint Paul could learn to be content in prison, I can do well here. A wry smile twisted her lips. Until that moment, it had never occurred to her that Paul had written he'd learned to be content. Heartened by the knowledge that he'd had his share of struggles or he wouldn't have had to learn, she decided not to feel quite so guilty about being upset.

One minute—she'd given the men more time than that. Squaring her shoulders, she smoothed her hair. Regardless of how she felt, she had a job to do, and she was going to get it done.

Karl heard her coming—not because of the creaking floorboards but because of the I-mean-business drumbeat of her heels. Until now she'd always walked silently, so he knew she fully intended to make this racket. It had been downright funny watching the doc go all prissy and proper, jumping to the wrong conclusions. She'd probably do the same thing again as soon as she spied him. Sitting on a chair in the middle of the floor, halfway between a small bookcase and the bed, he was supposed to hand Enoch books to prop up the legs of the bed.

With a Sears' nightshirt on, Karl felt ridiculous. A couple months back, Piet had been so delighted to have found something with a seventeen-and-a-half-inch collar and long enough to hit their shins that he'd sent away for a pair of the dumb-looking things. Rarely did ready-made clothing come of a size to accommodate the muscles that years of blacksmithing developed. Since his jeans wouldn't fit over the bandage, he was stuck in this getup for a day or so. Definitely no longer.

As soon as Doc cleared the doorway, her eyes locked onto his.

Only the momentary, very slightest widening of her eyes gave away her surprise. "Mr. Van der Vort, you're not where you belong."

"Doc," Piet whined from beneath the bed, "do you think I wanna be stuck under here?"

"Then you should let me cut off your suspenders," Enoch said, accepting the last few books from Karl.

"Nee!" Piet paused a moment. "Mama—these she gave to me."

"Of course we won't slice them off." The doctor's thumb went to trace the small silver chatelaine at her waist as she turned to him. "Mr. Karl Van der Vort, remain in that chair with your limb raised while my brother and I see to extricating your brother."

Her resolute expression invited no discussion and her order rubbed him the wrong way, but for an instant he'd seen her features soften and heard the compassion in her tone when she reassured his brother. That alone bought his cooperation. Nodding his head was a waste of time. She'd already turned away and started dragging over a sturdy little table.

"I'll get that." Enoch yanked it into place. "We're going to need more books. I'm going to stack them up, lift the bed onto the piles, crawl under, and untangle him."

Once her twin left, the doctor just stood and studied Piet's boots. Feeling slightly guilty for having embarrassed her, but not enough to apologize, Karl decided to lighten things. "At least this time I didn't summon a horse to free me."

The doctor glanced at his brother's feet and back at Karl. "If it weren't for the boots, I wouldn't be able to tell the difference."

Was that a— No, she couldn't have smiled. Had she? "Matteo made those boots. Runs the saddlery down the street."

She got down on her knees by his brother. "So Matteo dresses man and beast."

"Ja."

"I'll have to go see him."

Karl jumped at the opportunity. "You are not a man. Matteo makes things only for men and horses. Nothing else at all. Nothing for women."

"I see. Then I'm going to advertise for a woman cobbler to come to Gooding."

"You cannot do that!"

She arched a brow. "Are you one of those tedious men who believes all women should be barefoot and breeding?"

"Nee. But this is not your town. You cannot advertise for someone just because of a whim."

"Of course not. I'm doing so out of need. No matter how attractive a shoe might be, a bad fit makes one miserable. Both women and men are entitled to something so basic and essential."

The woman had spunk. No getting around it—she was smart and had a surprising wild streak in her. Maybe not wild. Spirited. But that also translated into her being headstrong about carrying on a man's profession. He could admire the quality without approving of how she applied it. What a pity, though. She was like that shoe—attractive, but the wrong fit for her own gender.

Unaware of his thoughts, the doctor delicately cleared her throat. "Mr. Piet Van der Vort, this is awkward."

"Nee. I am okay. Not comfortable, but not bad. It would be better were I flat."

"The right rear shoulder of his suspenders is stuck, so he's . . ." Karl stuck out his hand and twisted it.

She closed her eyes. Her shoulders rose and dropped with a

slow, deep breath. "I was referring to my questions and solution to the problem. Your braces—suspenders, that is—are they two-sided in the back?"

"Nee. Just the middle is where they button to my pants."

"Good. Good. I'm going to reach in sideways and see if I can unfasten the back." A minute later, her voice a touch strained, she said, "Are you able to undo the front now that the tension is lessened?"

Bumping and rustling ensued. "The right side, that could I do. Linken—I lie too heavy on that side. My hand is too big." A moment of silence stretched. "Doctor, I . . . you are . . ."

"Very well. If you'll pardon me, I only mean to extract you." Still on her knees, the lady doc had to reach in and strain. Finally she sat back on her heels. Letting out a deep breath, she carefully made sure her black skirt was covering her properly.

Freed, Piet started a clumsy exit.

"Hold it!" Enoch dropped a huge armload of books. "You're going to tow that bed and mow it over my sister!"

"Come on out, Piet Van der Vort," the doctor said as she rose. "You're big and strong enough to tow just about anything, but I'm not one to be mowed over."

Enoch gave the books a dark look, then began to gather them up. "Piet, how'd you get there, anyway?"

"I wanted to see my brother. You were busy, so I did not inter-rupt. I just came up the stairs."

"And crawled under the bed?" The doctor and her brother exchanged an incredulous look.

"The chamber pot—it was not by the edge." Piet emerged and stretched. "I thought perhaps it was deep in the middle, in the shadow."

"You were kind to want to assist your brother. We have a wash-room next door, and I'll provide your brother with crutches." While she spoke, the doctor tugged Piet over to a chair. He sat down, but from the adoring look on his face, he'd do anything for her. "Does anything hurt? How is your breathing?" She proceeded to examine him. "You're fine. With that bed crashing on you, you might well have fractured some ribs or given yourself a concussion."

"But you would make me well." Piet's head bobbed with absolute certainty. Enoch handed him the suspenders, and everything was fine. "I think just as you are two Bestmans and it was confusing at first, we are two Van der Vorts. It was confusing today." Piet chuckled. "But now we are all friends. You will call me Piet and my brother Karl."

Oh brother. He got stuck under the bed, but Piet might as well have fallen at the doctor's feet. In less than a day, she'd won his allegiance and adoration. Exasperation pounded through Karl's veins. He'd counted on Piet springing him loose. That woman had just charmed his brother into becoming her ally, and Piet would merrily strand Karl here for a month if it provided an excuse for him to come over. Which just proved Karl's point: A pretty young woman and medicine didn't mix.

Eight

T hat's where I draw the line. A man has to have some pride."
Karl gritted his teeth and pushed away from the new table they'd put in the smithy for him. He'd champed at the bit to come back to work today, but not for this. "I'm not repairing it."

Piet looked at the ugly contraption through the wide-open shop door. "I don't know. It has some charm, don't you think?"

Karl snorted. "Charm?"

"Beauty is in the eye of the beholder." Piet sounded far less certain now that he'd come over and had a chance to see the swan-shaped silver wall sconce up close. The fact that he hadn't picked it up spoke volumes.

"The beholder is Mrs. Cutter."

"Ja, now it all makes sense." Piet shrugged. "She's willing to pay for you to repair it."

Prodding it with the dull end of a pencil, Karl muttered, "I'd pay her to take it away."

"You made a bargain with the doctor that though you could not yet do all work, silversmithing was reasonable."

"Reasonable? That woman doesn't know the meaning of the word."

"If the deal you struck is not to your liking, you can stop and go lie down."

"Of course it's not to my liking." Karl scowled. "But I'd do anything to get out of that surgery!"

Smirking, Piet looked at the sconce. "Anything?"

"You made your point." Karl grumbled, "It was a deal I didn't want to make."

"You are a man of your word and you said—"

"Don't remind me. All of this broken garbage is reminder enough." Karl looked at the array of pieces everyone in town came up with the very moment word went out that he'd be doing this kind of repair work. Silver, that he could do. The gold? Ideally, it would go to a goldsmith, but there wasn't one. Tapping out dents, straightening kinks, repairing chains, and tidying engraving—that was all doable as long as he kept in mind gold was much softer than silver.

But this wall sconce? The beak had fallen off the swan in protest of being attached to something so ugly. Karl shoved aside the project. "I'm not going to do it. I refuse."

"Your word has always been your bond, so there is no doubt that you'll meet your obligation."

"Condemned by faint praise." Karl grabbed it back again. He went over each step mentally as he got started. He filed the edges until they came together smoothly again and cleaned them with the "pickling" solution, carefully joined them with the flux, and then added the solder. Using the torch from inside the swan's narrow neck demanded his complete concentration. He finished the job, cleaned it up a little bit, then polished the silver so that it would look good—well, as good as anything that awful could look, anyway.

The next piece was a dandy little item. It deserved his attention, and he wanted to get it done right away. Doc Enoch had slipped it to him. It was a chatelaine that the doctor wore clipped to the waistband of her skirt all of the time. Whether anything was hanging from it or not didn't matter; she always had it clipped there. Most chatelaines had a simple bend of metal that tucked into the waistband, but hers bore some kind of interesting latch to secure it.

Karl now studied the mechanism. When flipped down, it locked, securing the chatelaine to the waistband more closely, or it would—but at present it was broken. He'd have to figure out how to fix the piece. If he added a semicircular tension spring, maybe that would take care of the problem, but he'd have to manufacture one . . . but exceptionally small, and of very strong wire, too. The challenge energized him. Anything to make the time pass quickly. He'd told the doctor he wouldn't do any blacksmithing for the next three days if she let him out of that place. Having Doc Enoch and Piet flanking her as she extracted those words turned a purposefully vague comment into a solemn promise.

The smithy's soot didn't allow for proper jewelry soldering, so some of the men had taken canvas and configured a three-sided structure for him just inside the smithy, but outside the forge area. After two more days of doing this soldering, he would make up for lost time, wielding his hammer on the anvil from first light until the kerosene in the lanterns gave out at night.

Grudgingly, he had to admit silversmithing was a good use of his time until he gained more strength. His leg was healing nicely, and each day he could feel it growing stronger. Truthfully, he was thankful to the doctor for having done all of the work she had. Grateful—but not convinced that a woman ought to be a physician. For all the orders she gave, she would have done well to enter the military and aim to become a general.

But the one good thing that developed from this whole affair was that his brother hadn't a drop to drink ever since Karl got hurt. Indeed, Piet suddenly turned a corner. He seemed . . . well, different. Karl hadn't mentioned it—wasn't sure he wanted to— but he was praying and waiting. Piet wasn't a man to be pushed or pestered. Contrary as he'd been, saying something might very well send Piet straight back to the saloon.

Winding the wire for the tension spring, Karl considered the inevitable mental and physical descent that overtook drunks. *If wounding my leg helped spare my brother that fate, it was worth it.* Karl leaned forward and glanced at his brother. *Even if Piet had been right and the doctor had to cut off my leg, I would have agreed to it if I knew the result would be him turning his life around.*

Snap! The end of the spring he'd been forming suddenly broke off. Deep in thought, he'd formed five coils when the application called for three or four. Setting down the delicate pliers, he reached for more wire.

"I'm taking these over." Piet loaded cross braces, hinges, hitching posts, and a variety of hardware for the vet's barn raising into the wheelbarrow.

Squinting out the smithy doors at the almost barren trees, Karl nodded. "The weather will be good."

Piet slugged him on the shoulder. "I sent word that the doctor would call on some folks this week. As pledged, you will drive her."

"We pledged a buggy, not a driver."

Piet scowled. "We don't know if she can drive a rig, and she doesn't know where she's going. Even if that were not the case, there are bad feelings about a woman doctor."

"I'm not getting in the middle of that."

Jaw dropping, Piet stared at him. "Your life—she saved it." He shook his head. "The least you can do is protect her in return for what she has done for you."

What kind of idiot am I? Though I paid for my surgery, I didn't consider that some debts cannot be canceled with mere money. It is true. I owe her.

While Karl thought, his brother sustained his tirade. "If the doctor was a man, after he saved your life, you would ride with him. Even if you do not approve of a woman doctor, it is not like you to be ungrateful and unfair."

Karl held up his hand. "You made your point. Many points. And all of them are right. I'll drive her. I neither approve or disapprove of her."

"You should be ashamed." Piet turned and walked off.

Karl turned back to the doctor's chatelaine. *There's nothing wrong with being neutral on an issue. Not everything has to be a fight; instead of the extremes, some things can be in the middle. So it is with how I feel about the doctor. I have no call to be ashamed. I'm grateful for what she did—but she lacks modesty to do her job. If she limited herself to treating women, perhaps that would be a good thing.*

He returned to his work and by the time he was done, the clasp would secure just about anything. Certainly it could hold whatever little frippery the doctor might want to put on it. The old latch must have given way out of sheer exhaustion. Some of these pieces got

95

handed down for generations. Judging from the heavy patina of the silver, this was one such treasure.

The convex oval shape was common enough, but instead of the usual floral pattern, Dr. Bestman's bore an intricate Celtic knotwork engraving around the edge. A faint engraving in the center of the metal piece demanded a closer look. At the foot of the cross lay a sideways heart.

Lay my heart at the foot of the cross? Karl found himself wishing such an act were as easy as it was to retrace the engraving, refreshing the design.

Gritty paste oozed through the cloth as he prepared to polish the silver. No piece left the smithy unless it was perfect. The inside came first. A shepherd's crook–like hook that hid inward from the bottom of the chatelaine allowed women to attach all sorts of things from it. Tender memories of his mother and cousin assailed him. Women in Texas didn't seem to wear chatelaines much, but *Moeder* had put hers on each and every day.

The hook gleamed to his satisfaction. They never needed to bear much weight. On marketing day a tiny coin purse would dangle from it. Other days, a quartet of fine chains held a set of sewing and needlework necessities: a silver thimble, a little triangular holder for delicate swan thread scissors, a fan-shaped pincushion the size of his thumbnail, and a slender needle holder. The pieces would lie silent in the folds of a woman's skirt when she walked, but as she turned, they'd tinkle. For church or to go visiting, the chatelaine would hold a clip for a frilly handkerchief or gloves. Moeder and Annika always had something else hanging from theirs—the tiny book and pencil. Thinking that would be a useful addition for the doctor, he'd created a second hook and painstakingly balanced the piece. He hoped she'd be pleased. After all, she'd saved his leg.

I'm returning it to her brother. He sneaked it to me, and he can give it back to her. I don't want her to think I have feelings for her—especially after I caught her singing to me. Appreciation and affection are two very different kettles of fish.

"Ouch!" Karl jerked back his hand. The smaller hook jabbed beneath his fingernail. Though no polish remained on the back of the chatelaine, plenty of the paste had seeped into the tiny hole beneath his nail and made it feel like a wasp sting. *I could get stung by that doctor who hummed to me just as easily if I don't keep my guard up.*

"What did you do now?" Piet shouted at him.

"Something stupid. My hands are too big for all these small things. Silversmithing for me is like when we went to the circus and saw that clown riding the baby's rocking horse."

The whoosh of the bellows amplified the roar of Piet's laughter. After he finished with the bellows, he trundled over to the edge of the canvas, right at the opening that led toward the work area in the smithy. Chin high, he inspected the array of items on the table. "Complain all you want, but this is a need of the people here we never knew of. I'm thinking it would be a *goed idee* for us to do this sometimes."

"You must have hit your head with the hammer."

Folding his arms across his chest, Piet's brows slammed together with disapproval. "Opa was known for his silverwork. Just because you're chafing to do something different, you complain like a thwarted child. You shame yourself acting thus and insulting Opa's profession."

Astonished by his brother's reaction, Karl rose and hobbled toward him. The pain in his thigh didn't matter. "I didn't mean to insult his profession. I was speaking of my own incompetence.

As far as us stopping business and taking up silversmithing every once in a while—" he reached over and smacked his hand on an inch-thick stack of orders—"I see no practical way to do so. The other night, when we argued, there was contention over who was getting enough done. Right now, everything is falling on your shoulders, and—"

"It is my place as the older brother to care for you." Piet's arms opened all of a sudden and yanked Karl to him in a desperate embrace. "You are my *broeder*. You are all I have. Nothing else matters. If I had lost you that night, I would have died along with you. Once was bad enough. Never again."

Karl's arms flexed just as securely. "There is nothing like the love I bear for you." Years ago their little brother's brutal death had shook them both to the core. The bands of grief were starting to fall away for him. If only Piet could have a scrap of that comfort. "No one loves you more—" he paused just a heartbeat and added— "except Father God."

Piet stiffened and his arms fell away.

Quickly curling his hands around Piet's shoulders, Karl stepped back and shook his brother. "You should know I'm too ornery to die."

Piet batted one hand away. "Enough talk. We both have a lot of work to do." As Karl turned to walk away, his brother tacked on, "Opa always waited until noontime to polish everything he'd done in the morning."

"Then I will, too." Hating to admit just how much he needed it, Karl eased back onto the stool. The doctor told him his leg would be weak, but it still alarmed him.

The one compensation for having the makeshift silversmith tent was that Skyler's favorite place to flop down happened to be near the far edge of the table. He'd sit right at Karl's side, but when Karl needed to use chemicals, his collie would trot back to his bed. Odd how that extra bit of contact and companionship enriched Karl's morning.

It wasn't much later that Skyler sprang to his feet and gave his someone's-coming yip. In swept none other than the doctor. Karl rose at once. "Dr. Bestman, what are you doing here?"

"I should ask the same of you, Mr. Van der Vort," she said, "only I know we struck a deal."

"Not a good one, but I'll live with it."

"I agree it was not a good deal. I would rather you were not working yet at all. Since we live next door, I thought I'd stop by to see how you were doing and see if you needed anything from me. I thought perhaps we could go upstairs so I could examine you—"

"My leg is good. You no longer need to care for me."

She gave him a quizzical look, then understanding crossed her features. "I see. I'm glad you're feeling much improved."

"Ja. I stand very good now."

"I'm not sure how you manage that feat." Humor enriched her tone and sparkled in her eyes as Skyler circled her again, brushing heavily against her leg.

"Skyler! Nee!"

"He can't help it. He's bred to herd. I understand." She came over of her own accord, but Skyler seemed quite proud of his accomplishment, and she praised his dog. "If you would please sit down on that stool there, I can show you some exercises that would help strengthen your damaged muscles."

"Fine." He sat down.

All of a sudden she burst out laughing. It wasn't one of the little titters that most women did but a full-throated, wonderful laugh.

He couldn't help but smile, almost join in as a matter of fact. *So when I thought maybe she'd smiled about comparing Piet to a horse when he was stuck under the bed, I was right. The woman actually has a sense of humor. But what's so funny?* She strove to regain her self-control as she touched the swan piece. "I wouldn't have laughed if there were any possibility you'd made this, but anything this atrocious must have taken days to dream up."

"It's a nightmare, and I wasted my time repairing it."

Tilting her head to the side, she winced. "Perhaps it's the day in the fairy tale when the ugly duckling becomes a swan."

"The duck would have made a good meal."

"I can't tell where you fixed it." She studied it very carefully.

"Here, by the beak."

Running her finger over the area, she closed her eyes. "I don't feel anything."

"Hmpf." That was a good trick. He'd remember it. With his eyes closed, he'd be able to concentrate on the slightest dip or roughness.

The doctor put her hands on his knee and thigh; Karl scowled. Just like that, she went from being a pleasant neighbor lady to a woman doctor. It was just plain wrong. Manacling her wrists with his hands, he rasped, "Your brother—he should be here and do this."

"My brother is helping Mrs. Orion at the boardinghouse. It seems she needed a few repairs."

"Groceries—Mrs. Orion helped Doc Enoch buy them." Karl nodded curtly. "An exchange. Trading is done and we all try to give the widow the better end of the deal. I can wait until your brother is done there."

The doctor gave him a stern look. "My brother treats animals.

He assists when a true need exists. It may seem uncomfortable, but I'm a physician; therefore, it is not improper, Karl. You must allow me to do this in order for me to treat you. Again, that muscle has been badly wounded, and what we both want is for you to recover fully."

"Fine." He nodded curtly.

"Concentrate here and here, where my hands are. What I want you to do is tighten these muscles, and as you tighten them very slowly, notice how it straightens your leg and how your foot comes up. Do you see this?"

"Ja."

"Now I want you to do that again, only this time, instead of having your boot flop, I want your toe pointing toward the roof. Karl, this isn't a race. Do it slowly."

"I want my leg to get better fast."

"That's dangerous. If you overstress the muscle by doing several exercises quickly, it can tear clear through. The quadriceps here are the strongest muscles in the entire body, and you're a powerful man. I repaired the damage with great care, but the fragile silk sutures are no match for heavy exertion. As the tissue knits back together and heals, I believe your muscles will repair adequately, but the actual range of your knee and hip's movement will rely upon faithfully doing these exercises." Her eyes locked with his. "Slowly."

He nodded his understanding. As she motioned for him to lift his foot, he did so.

"Don't stop when your foot comes to there." She held her hand higher. "I want you to reach this point."

"My leg—I cannot get it all the way straight."

"No, you can't. It's just a little bit shy of being perfect, and I want you to have a full recovery." Suddenly an impish gleam hit her eye. She drew her hands away. Crossing them behind her back, she leaned forward and murmured, "Think, each time as you do the exercise, that you are kicking the ugly swan sconce."

"I'll recover very quickly now."

"That's what I hoped for."

"Are there any other exercises I should do?"

She showed him a few more, then suddenly she froze. "What are you doing with my chatelaine?"

"Your brother sneaked it to me. Perhaps he didn't want you to get your hopes up if it couldn't be repaired." Pride filled him as he picked up the piece. "But I fixed it. It's good as new now."

Reverently accepting it, she rubbed her thumb along the knot-work edge as if to refamiliarize herself with a long-parted friend. She tried the lever and inspected it from the side. A soft look of wonder went over her face. "You did something different with it. As I work the lever, I sense it has more strength than it used to."

"Whatever originally held it and provided the tension was gone, yet something was clearly needed in that place to make it hold. So I made what I thought might have been there. I hope you will find it satisfactory."

"This is outstanding. My chatelaine's never really had the strength I required. I've considered having the flat piece on the back elongated. . . ." She turned to stare at something off to the side that suddenly seemed of great interest. "But it's not possible."

Karl knew why she'd suddenly avoided eye contact. This topic edged toward indecent. While the pretty part hung outside over the side of her waistband, women tucked the inch-and-a-half to two-inch flat metal back inside their skirt to anchor the piece in place and bear whatever slight weight they'd attach to it. If the inside metal piece were any longer, it would poke the lady in the hip each time she moved.

"If you want it stronger, I could widen it through here." He took a pencil and drew on his table. "See here? Instead of it just being straight, what I can do is add by making it shaped thus." He showed her how he could widen it.

"Like the petal of a flower."

"Ja, ja, so."

She looked at him. "Not like the beak of a swan."

"No, no, not the beak of that stupid swan."

"I'd appreciate it if you could do it." Her fingers didn't quite want to let go of the piece, and he saw her hesitation.

"I'll do it right now."

Dr. Bestman looked at all the other pieces he had in line waiting. "That wouldn't be fair. You have other people waiting on your work, as well."

"Ah, but you see, yours was still being worked upon. No work is done until I polish it. I had not yet polished your piece, so that means it was still unfinished."

Her jaw dropped. "You polish silver?"

"I polish each thing that I do. Piet!" he called. "Piet, tell her, do we not always polish each thing that we do before we put it out?"

"Of course. It would not be right to send it out raw. We are not just workers, we are craftsmen."

"A master craftsman, indeed." She handed the chatelaine back to Karl. "I thank you very much for doing that for me. I'll be back later today to fetch it."

"You need not do that, Doctor." Warmth radiated from the metal, reminding him of how closely she'd held it. "I will bring it back over to the surgery."

Just then the mayor rushed in. "I came in to ask a favor of you, Karl."

"What is that?"

The mayor caught sight of the doctor and muttered something about physicians and confidentiality. He grimaced, furtively looked about, and leaned toward Karl. "I want to ask you not to, ah . . ." His voice died out as his hand came up to momentarily cover his eyes, then slid back as if to wipe a horrid thought from his mind. Again he looked at Karl. "You didn't, did you?" he asked, hope quavering pathetically in his tone. "Not yet?"

"What didn't I do?"

"Fix it—my wife brought in tha-tha-that—"

"Are you talking about the swan?" The doctor shouldered right beside Karl.

The mayor groaned and nodded.

Karl clipped, "Ja. It's fixed."

"I may as well take it home to her." Staring down at the piece, then closing his eyes, the mayor said, "A lesser man could have been blinded by having to work on it."

"Please excuse me for the interruption, but you've missed the point, gentlemen. A lesser man did work on it. That is precisely why the piece exists."

Though flattered by her praise, Karl didn't dwell on it. He simply named his price for the labor, and the mayor paid him.

"I hope the two of you won't ever mention what happens next. I am a very clumsy man, you know." The mayor took two steps, dropped the wall sconce, and trampled on it. When he picked it up, every last segment was bent. Actually mangled—all except for the swan's beak, which remained perfectly intact. Mayor Cutter lifted it and looked very satisfied. "My only problem tonight is going to be trying to paste on a sorrowful look, you know."

Eyes narrowed, the doctor stared at the mayor. "If you didn't like it, why did you have it in your home?"

"Edna Mae likes them."

"There is more than one," the doctor stated in a calm tone.

Karl marveled at her self-control. He'd almost blurted out the same words, but in a roaring question of disbelief.

Glad to have a sympathetic audience, the mayor nodded. "My wife brought a pair of them into the marriage and is sentimental about some cockamamie story about what they represent." He held up the mangled piece. "With one ruined, she'll have to take the other down."

Karl and the doctor remained silent. They'd shared the same opinion of the sconce, but a man deceiving his wife rankled.

"My wife likes symmetry, you know, and with just one wall sconce, the house won't look right. Karl, show me something masculine, something you could make now that you're doing this kind of work for the next few days."

"No. I'm only doing this till the end of the week, and I have far too much to do already."

"I'm sure you can find something simple . . . anything!" The mayor went to a sample book at once and flipped through it. Every other page, he'd nod his head and say, "Um-hm. Oh this, yeah, oh, very nice. Very nice."

The doctor slanted Karl a look. "You must not overdo, else the incision will open and you'll begin to bleed. The work you have before you is the limit."

Karl wasn't about to have a woman order him around. Caught between a bossy woman doctor and a conniving husband, he scowled at them both. "Nothing's gotten done since the two of you got here."

"Come, Mayor Cutter. Like all the men in Gooding, he's a gentleman and won't sit in a lady's presence; so he won't ease back onto that stool until I leave." Dr. Bestman closed the book on the mayor's hand and pressed the sconce into his arms. Her voice dropped. "With the pain he's enduring, it's a wonder he's not roaring like a wounded bear."

His leg hurt, but he didn't want her announcing it. *I'll take that up with her later. Doctors supposedly take a vow to hold things in confidence.*

"Pain?" Mayor Cutter cast a disapproving look his direction. "You're given to exaggeration, young woman. He's fine. That just goes to show how little you know about medicine."

"Mr. Mayor, are you questioning the veracity of my degrees or the value of my experience?"

"Diplomas can be falsified, as can be letters of reference. So few citizens here are willing to have you treat them, it's impossible for you to have gained any level of experience whatsoever."

The doctor grabbed a slip of paper from the worktable, looking as if she would merrily toss the mayor down the closest well. She snatched up Karl's pencil and with quick, sure strokes, listed the names of no fewer than eight different references. She handed the page to Cutter. "As you've questioned my integrity, professional ability, and experience before a witness, I hereby demand you confer with any of these individuals. Until you have all the facts, Mr. Cutter, mind your words. I'll look past them this once, but if this is repeated, you'll knowingly be committing slander. As a politician, you know well the importance of the words you employ and their ability to build consensus or the potential damage they can cause. It is my hope we'll work together for the good of this community."

Karl had to give her credit. She'd kept her tone crisp and businesslike, even gave the mayor leeway that he didn't rightfully deserve after implying she was a liar. Any man would have called him out; she provided facts and roped him in before he rode roughshod over her.

"You could conjure up any number of names." The mayor dropped the paper.

"Among them, the dean of the medical college in Chicago?" Doc arched a brow. "And the chief surgeons of two different hospitals? Or—"

"Quit chippin' your teeth. Nag a man half to death—that's what women do. It's one more reason why they oughtn't be doctors!"

While Skyler growled, Karl again swept the doctor behind himself. "Don't raise your voice at the lady."

The mayor sneered. "I didn't raise my voice at a lady."

Every muscle tensed with the need to fight for this woman's honor. From behind him, he felt the slightest brush of a hand and the softest whisper, "I forgive him."

"You forgive him, but I do not." He continued to stare at Cutter. "Get out."

"I don't need your forgiveness." Clutching the crushed sconce to himself, Cutter marched out the door.

Unable to wheel around without his leg tearing apart, Karl yanked her into view. Before he could open his mouth, she stabbed her forefinger into his chest. "I forgive that blustering windbag, Karl Van der Vort, but I don't forgive you!"

Nine

Forgive me? You should thank me!"

"I don't need rescuing." Punctuating each word with a poke to his chest, Taylor added, "Do you understand me?"

Karl snorted. "You need to be rescued from yourself, if this is what you believe."

His observation brought her up short. Taylor sucked in a sharp breath, then started laughing. "You're not going to rescue me from myself any more than you're going to get me to thank you."

Sagely nodding, he finally sat on his stool. "I knew you to be a stubborn woman when first I looked at you. My mother—she had the same line to her jaw."

From the way he'd spoken of her in the past, the hulking man loved his mama. Because of that, Taylor overlooked the insult of being called stubborn. "Women must use their wits because we don't possess brute strength."

"You didn't use your wits just now. Not with Cutter."

"Of course I did, and you're going to want to know how, aren't you?"

He started to rummage through some scraps of silver. "No."

Astounded, she leaned closer. "Why not?"

"Forgiveness is not of the mind; it is of the soul." He seemed to have some method to his actions, and Taylor found pleasure watching the way he strove to manipulate his large fingers around a plethora of minute tools lying atop a faded square of maroon felt on the workbench. For all the deft-handed, long-fingered surgeons who'd practiced with laudable skill, she'd never seen a sight she admired more than when his fingers dusted a spot and gently set her chatelaine in the center, where the lighting glowed best. "I'll have this to you by the end of the day."

"Thank you. I'm sure my brother told you how important it is to me."

"Earlier, Piet and I discussed respecting the legacy given us. So it is with you."

◦◦◦◦

"You're a smart feller, Doc Enoch."

Enoch looked up from the coon dog. "Smart enough to know you've helped your dogs whelp plenty of times, Mr. White. Why don't you stop wasting your time and mine and say what you want to?"

A sheepish grin crossed the man's face as he glanced over at his wife. "Said you was smart. Feller like you's gotta see reason. It's better for you to do the doctorin'." The second Enoch started to react, the man hastily half shouted, "You can do the critters, too. Goodness knows we've all been needin' help when our horses or cattle take sick."

If it weren't for his Christian scruples and his promise to his sister that he wouldn't damage his knuckles defending her, Enoch gladly would have punched the smile off the dolt's face. In a deceptively bored tone he said, "If you try telling me how to run my life or my practice again, you could only hope to have a physician as talented as my sister to attend you after I finish reining in my temper."

"Are you threatenin' me? You can't do that!"

"It wasn't a threat; it was a promise. On the other hand, you implied a threat when you said it was better for me to assume both practices. As I know my sister's skill is unequaled, that could only mean that you must believe some other threat exists—and the only logical assumption is that harm would befall either my sister or me."

"You're mistaken." Mrs. White gave Enoch a stingy thin-lipped smile that didn't reflect in her eyes. "I'm sure my husband merely felt compassion for the bachelors of Gooding. You can treat man and beast, and we can send away for another physician; but finding an attractive, marriageable young woman who's willing to come live here is exceedingly difficult."

"Yeah. That's what I said. It'd be better if she stopped doin' a man's job and set about seein' to a man's pleasure. There's a heap of men who'd be tickled to have a gal wearin' their ring, cookin' Sunday suppers, and singin' lullabyes to a passel of their young'uns."

"I just came from the Richardsons'." *Or more accurately, barely escaped from there.* "You can pass the word to all of those bachelors that Richardson has a daughter who's unspoken for. His wife informed me that double wedding they have planned could be a triple easily enough."

"Men round here are desperate, but they ain't fools."

Mrs. White added, "Linette means well, bless her heart—"

"She'd probably say the same thing about you. She seemed to be a sincere young woman." Enoch rose. "It'll be ten cents for my visit."

"Ten cents! Nuthin' was a-wrong!"

Hooking his thumbs in his pockets, Enoch looked at White. "There was plenty wrong—just not with your dog. You want me to betray my sister by asking her to give up the thing God's called her to do, and you expect me to assume responsibilities for which I'm not trained. But I am a veterinarian, and even though it was under false pretenses, you summoned me out here on a professional call for your animal."

"Ten cents is robbery. 'Specially since you done nuthin' I couldn'ta done myself."

"Prized coon dog like this needs mindful tending when she's due to whelp, but if you needed professional help, it should have been with that bird dog."

"Netta?"

The retriever came at the sound of her name. Enoch commented, "Something's wrong on her left hindquarter. She's limping." He examined Netta and found a splinter in the fold of her leg. After removing it, he rubbed her belly. "Oh, so Queenie's not the only one having babies here."

"Huh? What?!" White perked up and groped her belly. He shook his head. "Nope. Shouldn'ta got my hopes up like that."

"Let me show you. Hey, girl." Enoch stroked her side before moving to her belly. "Between twenty and thirty days, there are firm, discrete lumps from the pups' placentas. In a few more days, the lumps will be spread out through the womb and easy to mistake for her intestines. Here." He ran the edge of his thumb over one spot, then another. "And here. Feel those."

White did so. "Well, I'll be. We were all laid up with a miserable complaint, then harvest was upon us and we all had to get out to the fields. I just didn't notice Netta—"

"She and Dash throw off fine pups," Mrs. White interrupted. "How many will she have?"

"Can't say for certain. I'd estimate six. Maybe a runty seventh. She'll probably whelp mid-January."

"Farming families don't keep much cash, Doc Enoch." Mrs. White wrapped her arms around her ribs. "Would you wait and take a puppy or maybe take one of Queenie's?"

"A fine coonhound is worth far more than a dime, Mrs. White. So's a retriever."

"How 'bout chicken? You'll take home chicken, won't you?"

Crisp, golden-fried chicken? "You bet!" Enoch figured he'd made an excellent deal until Mrs. White handed him a squawking gunnysack. *Bartering instead of being paid is part of country living. I expected that. Maybe not this soon, and certainly not with live chickens.*

"These will make for a couple of nice suppers."

"Indeed, they will." *I just don't know for whom.*

"By the way, Doc, we got a son—Ozzie. Him and Lloyd Smith are fast friends and hardworking boys. They've dreamt up that you'll hire them."

"I suppose I could scare up odd jobs for the boys to do. Mucking, too." Enoch couldn't be sure who squawked more over that news—the chickens or Mrs. White. He mounted up and started for home, then looked down at the sack in his grip. What was he going to do with chickens?

⟶⟵

"Sis!"

"Merciful heavens." Taylor set aside the treatise on asthma she'd been reading and rose from her desk. She tried to recall the last time Enoch had yelled for her. *There must be an emergency.* Grabbing her bag, she dashed through the kitchen and out the back door. Her momentum almost carried her right down the steps, but she caught the rail just in time when she noticed her brother standing alone. "What's wrong?"

"Nothing."

"Why did you shout for me? I was reading a fascinating piece on asthma and—" Her eyes widened. Enoch pulled a gunnysack from behind his back. It wiggled. *He brought me a puppy! He knows how long I've wanted one. Only I'm not going to say anything. I'll let him tell me.*

"I was over at the Whites'. They have a coonhound, Queenie. Even-tempered as could be. Anyway . . ."

Once he mentioned the coonhound, Taylor couldn't take it any longer. She dropped her medical bag and skipped down the steps. Just feet away, she suddenly froze. "Enoch, that gunnysack did not cluck."

"Not exactly. At least not the sack." He started to open the top.

"No." She shook her head as if her denial would change the facts. "There aren't chickens in there."

"Sure are. They'll make a couple of fine suppers."

Gaping, she stared at him for a full minute. "For whom? Neither of us knows how to cook."

"Maybe this new stove won't burn stuff."

"It's not the stove; it's us. When it comes to food, we're

114

pyromaniacs." Another thought occurred to her. Backing up a big step, she added, "I categorically refuse to kill or pluck them."

"You don't have to act so dramatic, Taylor. Bartering instead of being paid is part of country living."

"Certainly not with live chickens! Go do some more country living and barter them off to someone else." *And bring back a puppy this time.*

"There's not much I could get for a pair of chickens. Maybe what we ought to do is keep them in that coop. We'll undoubtedly wind up with more, and it has to be easier to parlay several chickens for something decent than to quibble with a pair. It's probably why the coop's here to begin with."

"Brilliant deduction," she said in a wry tone.

"You're going to have to help me. Mrs. White used twine to tie their legs together." They freed the fowl from the bonds and put them in the wire coop.

"So what about their coonhound . . . Queenie, was it?"

"Yes. She'll be whelping soon, and their retriever is having a litter in mid-January."

Taylor clutched his sleeve. "And I'll get a puppy?"

"They offered, but I didn't accept." Giving her an impatient look for the outraged sound she made, he said, "They're hard up for money and can sell a pup for a good sum. Besides, what business do you have, owning a puppy? Coming and going at all hours of the day and night—you don't have time for a helpless little creature."

"I put up with you."

"I'm insulted. I'm not a pup. I'm a wolf."

"Yes, you are." She reached up past his collar and checked. "Still wet behind the ears, though. That makes you a wolf pup." Not wanting him to sense her disappointment over not getting a dog, Taylor tousled his hair. "Helpless, too—at the stove and at the coop."

"And at the bedside of a man caught by his suspenders."

Taylor finally managed a true smile. "How is it you concocted such a complex solution to the problem when such a simple one existed?"

"I told you: I wanted to be in a position to watch your expression when you came back into the room."

"When did you— Oh!" Taylor couldn't believe it. She'd thought the worst of her own twin, that he'd betrayed her just for the sake of coarse male camaraderie, when he'd simply wanted to be in a position to watch.

"You swept into that room with the fire of an avenging angel. With Piet mistakenly thinking you were talking to him instead of Karl, all your aggression disappeared into nothing more than a mere wisp of smoke. The only thing that was more hilarious was watching beefy old Karl pull down the hem of his nightshirt and yank up his socks."

Disbelief and giggles shivered through her. "Like prissy old Great-Aunt Agatha?"

"No. Piet started yammering instructions from under the bed, worried lest his brother scandalize and offend you." A huge grin split his face. "Karl looked like a man passing out forks to cannibals before he had to crawl into a pot."

"He doesn't deserve that distinction; I do. Ever since I arrived, I've been boiling in oil and folks keep stoking the fire."

"Then scoot over. I'm hopping into the pot." Enoch's words couldn't be sweeter. His unswerving loyalty humbled her. "Where two or three are gathered, Jesus is with them, so He's with us. We're never going to burn."

"Like Shadrach, Meshach, and To-bed-we-go?" she teased, remembering the time he'd messed up that name in the Bible story.

"Yep." The chickens both fluttered and squawked.

"You hush." Taylor eyed their feathers. "Both of you ought to be the ones in the boiling oil, and you just might end up going to bed, too, as a nice fat pillow."

❧

Clip, clip, clip, clip. The distinctive sound of the doctor's purposeful footsteps approaching the smithy Saturday morning made Karl mutter to his dog, "If there was flint on the bottom of her heels, she'd strike sparks with every step." Skyler wagged his tail.

Hat at a jaunty angle, hair tamed and her pelisse folded over one arm while she held her medical bag in the opposite hand, the doctor appeared and announced from the double doors, "I'd like a buggy prepared, please."

"Where are we going?"

"I'm going to the Ochoa residence."

He didn't challenge her on the *we* versus *I*. Instead, he eyed her critically. "Go change while I hitch up."

"I'm ready to leave just as I am."

"You cannot go thus." His focus darted away. "Red—it is not a good color."

She laughed! "I always wear red. Except for Fridays, my pharmacy and laboratory day, when I wear a shirtwaist that's faded to pink. What difference does the outside make? 'Man looketh on the outward appearance, but the Lord looketh on the heart.' "

Karl couldn't find the words to tell her what kind of women wore red. Shaking his head, he went to get the buggy. Years had passed since he'd been to church, and now that he'd started attending again, he hadn't yet gone long enough to refresh his memory on all the stories. Though he'd hoped to remember names of the women of ill repute so he could cite them as examples as to the type who would be wearing red if they lived in Gooding, he couldn't come up with a single name. Frustrated, he led the rig to the front. "Let's go!"

Dr. Bestman had taken but a few steps before Skyler came running, scrambled up his familiar route, and perched atop the buggy. The doctor halted and gawked. "Call him down before he falls through!"

"He won't. I reinforced the roof."

"Nevertheless, we must be off."

"Ja." *This is going to be entertaining.* Karl folded his arms across his chest. "So get over here."

Eyes huge, she stalked toward him. "You cannot mean to allow that animal to ride atop the buggy. It's unsafe, for one thing. Furthermore, it's undignified."

"Skyler's been riding up there since he was a pup, and he's never been too worried about his dignity. I'm happy to have him ride along."

"It doesn't lend a professional appearance to my arrival," she gritted.

"Are you not the one who just said the outside makes no difference? That man looks on the outside appearance, but God looks at the heart?"

Her eyes narrowed. "I'm going to have to watch every word I say around you."

"Impossible. You talk far too much to succeed at that."

"I'm not going to worry about you any longer, Karl Van der

Vort. You're feeling well enough to be ornery. It just serves to prove what a fine physician I am—even if I wear red shirtwaists."

"How," Karl asked as the buggy pulled out of town, "did your father ever permit you to become a doctor?"

"My mother did; being a physician himself, Father couldn't very well disparage the profession."

Shaking his head as if to dislodge what he'd clearly thought to be the unbelievable first part of her comment, Taylor couldn't be certain he'd heard the second.

"That is even worse. Your mother—it is her place as a woman to keep the gentleness in your life. How could she permit this?"

Falling back on her stock answer, Taylor flashed him a disingenuous smile. "I'm pigheaded. It's more a matter of her being wise enough to know she couldn't stop me once I'd made up my mind."

"When you confided your wishes to her, why did she not go to your father and plead with him to dissuade you?"

Taylor turned toward the blacksmith. Others had probed this same issue—quite rudely—but he seemed genuinely distressed.

Furrows lined his brow and sadness lowered and slowed his tone. "It was wrong of me to ask. How can you explain or apologize for how your parents behaved?"

"Apologize? There's nothing at all wrong with the decision I made. As it happened, I didn't tell my mother at first. I announced my decision at the breakfast table to both of my parents at the same time. Mother applauded."

"You said your father was a physician."

So he did hear me say that. Taylor nodded and made a mental note of how Karl managed to hear and recall things, even when emotional. That was a good quality—one a doctor looked for in those who might be sought to assist in the event of an emergency. "Yes, Father and Grandfather were both doctors."

He gave her a meaningful look. "But not your mother or grandmother."

Laughter bubbled out of Taylor. "Perish the thought! You would have adored my grandmother. The poor woman fought an ever-losing battle against the rest of the family when it came to respectability. As for Mother . . . Father appreciated having her accompany him to work twice a month to care for 'shady ladies.' They dedicated themselves to doing so in the name of Christ Jesus, who showed tender mercy to such women."

"This all sounds respectable."

"You'd think so, but plenty of people expressed opinions about it. My mother loved God with all her heart, but she managed to see omens and portents in just about everything around her. Father said as a man of science that even he knew there was sometimes a kernel of truth in a fairy tale. He humored Mother, and she returned the favor by indulging his whim to educate me alongside Enoch."

"But your brother doctors animals."

"Until college, we were tutored at home. In addition to all of the academic subjects, we were taught fencing, shooting, and riding." Her features twisted. "They did, however, refuse to allow me to learn pugilism. I abhor violence, and the thought that Enoch was learning how to beat someone else appalled me. The notion that anyone might strike him incensed me such that I insisted Father or Grandfather go in order to render care if necessary."

"Thus you were indulged, as well—not just with them tending your concern, but with them permitting you to pursue the peculiar notion of doctoring."

She smiled. What a perfect opportunity God had given her! An intelligent man like Karl Van der Vort would come to accept her choice—even if he didn't support it. "There's a long family history of doctors—dating clear back to the MacLay healers of the Scottish Highlands—who were women. Becoming a healer is a family birthright. If you're unaware, my middle name is Mac—"

"Your name is not your destiny. This is not Bible times; this is modern times."

All hopes she had of him being reasonable fled. "Exactly. And in modern times, women can become doctors."

" 'All things are lawful for me, but all things are not expedient . . . all things edify not.' That is what Parson Bradle preached from the Bible last Sunday. Just because you could do this thing—this becoming a doctor—that does not mean it was the only choice or the best one."

Insufferable man! Sitting beside him in the buggy was trying every last bit of her patience. "How can you compare a desire to serve the needs of man with taking license and freedom to test the limits of God?"

Blond hair ruffled in the wind and he nodded curtly. "You have said this yourself—and thus, with your own words, you explain it all." When she continued to boldly meet his eyes without backing down, he eased his bulky frame over the slightest bit while resting his hand on his thigh. "To serve the needs of man is not something a woman should do."

It had been a while since she'd had this conversation. Each time it took a different path, and the challenge invariably invigorated her. From the start, Taylor had recalled the tutor's first lesson on debate: Adhere at all times to fact and eschew emotion. Facts are incontrovertible; emotions are anything but. His words of wisdom rang true. Being defensive merely caused others to become more firmly entrenched in their stance, so she'd been careful not to engage in this conversation more than necessary. To lose this debate in the presence of others would cause a man to lose face. Without anyone else around, however, the debate was on.

"Could you please repeat yourself, Karl Van der Vort? I'm sure I must have misheard you."

He stared at the horse's tail. "To serve the needs of a man is not something a woman should do." Color suddenly washed his neck and ears.

Laughter bubbled out of her. "I didn't realize you had such a delightful sense of humor!"

Looking entirely taken aback, he gritted, "That was no joke."

"But it had to be! Women spend their entire lives serving the needs of men."

Karl shook his head. "It is the man's place to work. He labors to meet the needs of those he loves."

She was silent a minute. "I agree with you." He gave her a startled look, but before he said anything, she continued on. "Yet I feel you've failed to credit women with the same loving dedication. Who cooks, cleans, does the laundry, gardens, and preserves food? I can see in your eyes you never thought of that as serving a man's needs, but it is. As a man who spends his days by a blazing forge, I'd think you have a better appreciation than most of what it takes for a woman to have to cook meals, preserve foods, and stand over a boiling washpot for hours on end."

"But that is for her man."

"So a woman shouldn't help a widower with these chores, just as a man would help a widow?"

Ice-blue eyes, the same shade as the inner flame of the Bunsen burner in the laboratory, glimmered with anger. "That's different, and well you know it. You do no good playing such games with me. There are matters of decency."

"And on matters of decency and propriety, I'm well versed. Since you've broached the topic, we'll address it immediately."

Ten

W hat?!" Karl jerked on the reins so reflexively, the horse and buggy halted at once. His greater weight and widespread boots kept him anchored. Taylor, however, had no such advantages, so she grabbed the side of the buggy.

A bar of iron slammed across her body like a sash. As quickly as Karl's arm shot over to keep her in place, he pulled it away. "I am sorry. Are you harmed?"

"I'm fine." Suddenly she leaned forward and tried to get out of the buggy while scanning about them. "Skyler!" Taylor felt a flood of relief as a happy bark sounded from above.

Karl took hold of her elbow and gently pulled her back down onto the seat. "My dog—he is fine. He is used to riding atop the buggy."

"I suppose he must be accustomed to your halting it that rapidly, as well, or he'd no longer be here."

Karl went right back to looking livid. "You think I mistreat my horses?"

Apparently there was no winning with this man. She'd tried to be agreeable about how he'd endangered one animal only to have him get angry about the other. "Clearly, your horse is well trained. He responded immediately to your signal to halt even though you gave no verbal command."

"Other men—they look upon your beauty and are easily misled by the truths you use to avoid answering questions. Trying that with me will get you nowhere."

A short laugh erupted from her. For the first time in her life, someone other than a tutor or male relative had challenged her to a mental duel. The novelty of Karl's tactics amused her because at the same time he was both complimenting her appearance and discounting it. Obstinacy personified, he sat there looking ready to throttle her for laughing.

"Surely you cannot mean to be so serious, Karl." She waved her hand at their unchanging surroundings. "We've been sitting here as if neither of us has a thing in the world to do. I couldn't help finding the humor in your assertion that my opinion wouldn't get me anywhere. Do you always remark on the obvious?"

Nary a twitch of his lips hinted at a smile, and his eyes continued to bore into hers.

Never one to back down from a challenge, Taylor stared right back. Under normal circumstances, such bold behavior in a woman would make it clear she was not a lady. But these weren't normal circumstances. Just because he owned the livery didn't mean he could control her every visit to a patient. The welfare of all her future patients relied upon her defining where she stood. "Very well, then, I'll take the reins—"

"You will not." The quiet of his tone didn't deceive her in the least. The deep bass that rumbled like a clap of thunder and the flash of lightning in his eyes told her she'd not been given a dare; she'd crossed a line and been put on notice.

Folding her hands in her lap, Taylor nodded. "I recognize that tone and look. I've used them myself when another physician has tried to horn in on one of my cases." Her eyes widened, and she didn't quite manage to choke back a moan.

He ignored the horse's snort and head toss. "What's wrong?"

"Nothing."

"I did hurt you." His words came out half accusation, half panic. Oblivious to the reins slithering away, he twisted toward her, jamming his elbow into her shoulder in the close confines of the small buggy. This time, he moaned.

"Don't twist like that. It's hard on your leg."

"My leg is fine, and ladies don't say *leg*." His fingers rubbed across her shoulder—an odd sensation, that. Few men ever bothered to come close at all, and those who did invariably commented on her height. Karl didn't give it passing consideration.

Only in that single second, she gave it plenty. "This is nonsense. I'm perfectly fine."

"I'll be the judge." Instead of listening to her, he kept his fingers braced on her shoulder and tested her clavicle with his thumb. Worry clouded his eyes. "The collarbone—it does not feel cracked. You must tell me what hurts. I'll take you to Velma."

"Nothing hurts, save my pride. Before leaving Chicago, I promised myself I'd not absorb Western colloquialisms."

Karl turned back into place, managing to bump her shoulder, elbow, and ankle in the process. "Velma will know how to treat this."

"This one is Velma's fault," Taylor muttered. "Let me explain. Colloquialisms are regional sayings, like 'horn in on.' In less than a week, I've used one!"

"Ja, you have." Karl bent to retrieve the reins. As he straightened, laugh lines radiated from the corners of his eyes. "It was just the first."

"You don't have to sound so pleased about it."

The buggy shuddered with his deep chuckles. "Even in defeat, you still smile."

"I haven't been defeated." She straightened her hat. "I changed my mind and decided to embrace my new land. So what do you think about that?"

A smile still tugged at the corners of his mouth as he drawled, "It was inevitable."

"Because I'm a woman?"

"Ja, but also because everything in Texas is better. For those two reasons, you'd change your mind."

"You, Karl Van der Vort, just implied that I'm both reasonable and logical. Perhaps I'm not the only person in Gooding who's changing. After all, change is inevitable."

"Not always." Just as suddenly as they'd shown up, his laugh lines and grin disappeared. His eyes went serious once again. "You can change yourself, but you cannot force another to change. Make no mistake about that."

Was he warning her, or did she detect an additional note behind his statement? Wisdom forced her to refrain from asking.

"The only change I'm looking for at the moment is a change of scenery, but before we go, I'll say what needs to be said: Men have no issue with sending their wives and daughters to male physicians. It is entirely hypocritical for men to suddenly cry foul about a female physician treating male patients. That being said, I am blessed to have my brother's able assistance so men and I are spared much of the awkwardness that might otherwise occur. Should specialized care be required, I'd refer a man out."

Karl seemed to find his horse's ears and mane infinitely interesting.

"That is what I intended to tell you when you halted the buggy and nearly sent Skyler and me flying."

"Never were either of you in any danger of flying."

"Granted, you prevented any mishap, but years of wielding a hammer forged such phenomenal strength in your right arm. That only accounts for me, though. Cannot you admit the obvious?"

"What is apparent to one person may not be the truth to another. You feared for my dog, not knowing the facts. You've seen how I reinforced the roof of the buggy for Skyler. What you did not see was the folding shield I pull up on his platform. Should he take a mind to, he can lie down. The instant he feels the buggy begin to slow for any reason, he's smart enough to sit. This keeps him safe."

Relief flooded her. "That's very reassuring. My brother is a highly skilled veterinarian, but Skyler's a fine dog, and I'd rather he not become one of my brother's cases."

"My horses respond to any command, no matter what form, because they are beasts of trust. Never have I whipped or mistreated them. Each of the animals in the livery knows the hand of their master is kind, so their obedience is full and immediate."

"What a wonderful analogy that is for Christ Jesus and us! When you next teach in the church or—"

"Nee." He cut her off abruptly.

"Forgive me," she said quickly. "It was impolite of me to speak of religion, just as it would have been for me to give my opinion on the recent election." She made an impatient gesture. "I need to get to my patient."

"Contradiction in a skirt," he muttered as he set the buggy in motion once again.

"Precisely what is contradictory about me?"

"You trouble yourself over the smallest of things, yet the big issues—you turn a blind eye to them."

"Faithfully seeing to my patients' welfare is no small matter."

"With this I agree, else I would not drive you there."

"You, Karl Van der Vort, are a contradiction in pants."

Utter amazement crossed his features. It soon gave way to a somber expression and a grave tone. "It is no mistake that I drive you."

"Yes, well, I do appreciate that. This appears to be quite a sprawling town. After today, though, I'll be able to get wherever I need to go. I have a fair sense of direction." *Compared to a dirt clod.*

"Nee."

Hackles up, Taylor glared at him. "It may be your livery, Mr. Van der Vort, but that scarcely gives you any call to—"

"It gives me every right to protect my investments. Weather's changing. Landmarks you might use one day suddenly don't exist the next. In the event of a rainfall, you'd likely run the rig off the road and splinter it into pieces."

"Just minutes ago, you boasted about your capable horses. Aren't they surefooted?"

"Even the most surefooted, well-trained animal is vulnerable when in the care of someone with questionable judgment. Until I am convinced that you can return from each trip safely, you're not going out alone."

"You're insufferably overbearing."

"Insufferable?" He cocked a brow. "A good doctor is supposed to know how to lessen pain."

"The stratagem is to find the root of the pain and get rid of it, thereby not just lessening, but alleviating the suffering." She paused and gave him a meaningful look. "I'm quite adept at reading maps, you know."

"Even if someone drew you a map—and that is highly questionable—it is still my decision as to whether you are permitted to drive alone or not. There is nothing more to be said."

"Yes there is." She heaved a very unladylike sigh. "You have the right to make this determination, even if I don't appreciate it. But at times like this, I almost wish I could relax my standards. If I did, I might console myself with the possibility of using a dull, rusty needle on you someday."

⌾⌾⌾

"The claims Mayor Cutter made regarding your fine preaching were well-founded," Enoch said, shaking Parson Bradle's hand as he exited the sanctuary.

"Thank you. We missed seeing your sister this morning."

"Taylor's out on a call. She asked me to express her regrets."

Mrs. Bradle's face clouded over. "Nothing serious, I hope. Daisy Smith wasn't here today. Neither was Fuller—"

The pastor smiled down at his short wife with an abundance of affection. "Mama, Doc Enoch couldn't say a thing about where Dr. Bestman went any more than you'd breathe a word about anyone upon whom I pay pastoral visits."

"My husband and I would like to ask you over to Sunday supper."

I should have anticipated this. "It's very kind of you to extend the invitation, but Taylor and I were already asked elsewhere." *And I can hardly wait to get there. I didn't get to sit beside Mercy during the service, and she slipped out right after the benediction so I couldn't even escort her.* Just over Mrs. Bradle's shoulder, he saw Mercy disappear inside her boardinghouse.

"Elsewhere?" The pastor's wife looked like a little girl who'd been told the last puppy of a litter had been given away.

"Yes. Perhaps another time?"

"Next Sunday." Mrs. Bradle claimed the day as if it were going to run off or be stolen.

"Next Sunday."

The alacrity of his agreement set both of the Bradles into smiles. The parson chuckled. "So you can't cook any better than I can?"

"Worse." Every man within earshot gave a gruff nod and the women laughed. Enoch didn't mind folks knowing he couldn't cook. For the next few weeks, if they took pity and dropped off food, he and Taylor would eat nicely.

After he married, there would be no need for Mercy to run a boardinghouse or bakery. She could finally stop working herself silly and relax. Do a little needlework. Bake and cook only as she'd like. Come to think of it, Linette would be out of a job, so he'd hire her to do the housekeeping and cooking—perhaps split her time between their place and Taylor's. After all, Taylor would come over for most of her meals anyway.

Big Tim slapped Enoch on the back. "If you've got an invite for lunch someplace, you'd best mosey on to it."

"Far as I'm concerned," Velma chimed in, "being late for Sunday supper ought to be a hanging offense." Sidling closer, she latched on to Enoch's arm. "Walk us to the buggy. Nothin' but trouble will brew if Mama Richardson sees you goin' to Mercy's for lunch. She's so set on getting Linette married off, she'll send her over to help out at the boardinghouse with Sunday supper."

How did she know where he was going?

Velma winked. "I'm old, but I'm no fool."

Sydney leaned heavily on Big Tim as she waddled along. "There aren't many secrets in a small town."

The slight delay worked perfectly. The Richardsons drove off. Enoch thought about going to Mercy's front door and knocking. She'd be in the kitchen, though. The last thing she needed was for him to pull her away from her work. Instead, he went around toward the back porch. *I should have thought to gather flowers. There's no time now. Not that there's much around this time of year, anyway.*

" 'Choose your partner, skip to my lou, skip to my lou, my darling.' " High and sweet as could be, the little girl's voice lilted from beside the back kitchen door. With eyes the same deep brown as Mercy's and hair the same hue—only worn in long plaits trimmed in pink ribbons—Heidi was the most adorable little girl he'd ever seen. A white kitten was tolerating her with remarkable aplomb, even though she'd dressed it in a bonnet and cape of some variety and was holding it upright so just the back paws barely touched the porch planks.

"Hello there, Miss Heidi. Who do you have there?"

She looked up, then quickly blurted, "Mama!"

The back door opened at once. "Hello. Heidi, I've asked Doc Enoch to come over today."

"No, Mama. No!" Heidi promptly burst into tears.

$\mathcal{E}$leven

What's wrong, sweetie?"

"Nothing's awrong. Tell him to go away!" Heidi gripped the cat so tightly around its middle, the poor thing started yowling. But when Enoch reached for it, she wheeled around and buried her face in her mother's skirts. The cat got lost in the yards of fabric. "No, Mama. Please . . ."

Sick to the depths of his soul, Enoch watched as the child rejected him. Her reaction was immediate and complete. He'd seen animals do the same thing, and when they did, they never warmed up to the handler or owner. It was instinctual—as if they sensed whether theirs would be a good match or not. Overwhelmingly warm as his feelings were toward Heidi, he'd expected it to be a mutual thing; clearly, it wasn't. The woman he longed for stood two feet from him, but she might as well be a continent away. He refused to come between a mother and her child.

Gravy drippings streaked down a dishcloth Mercy held. She tossed it aside and knelt down. "Heidi, what's the matter?"

"Him."

If I had any doubt at all, that put it to rest.

"Doc Enoch?"

Clutching the poor cat until the thing was in imminent risk of internal injury, Heidi wailed, "I don't want Tasha to be sick. Sick means dead. I don't want Tasha to be dead and gone!"

Relief flooded him. Plopping down on the porch, Enoch let out a sigh just for show. "Tasha can't possibly be sick. Nothing making that much sound can be sick!"

"Really?"

"Really." He patted his legs. "Come sit here and show me what Tasha is wearing."

Eager to show off her cat, Heidi scrambled over. In the process, Tasha's bonnet fell over one ear and the cape swooped forward to hang like a bib.

"So her name is Tasha. Hmm. And a fine specimen she is. Healthy. Fat and sassy." Slowly, carefully, he eased the poor kitten free. "Let's take a look—why, Tasha has a little gray on her ears and paws."

"Nuh-unh. The stuff on her paws is cuz she walked in the coal today."

Mercy cast a look back at the kitchen, and Enoch winked at her. "Go on in. We'll stay out here and talk about animals. I think Heidi likes them almost as much as I do, don't you?"

"Yep!" Heidi grinned. "Someday I wanna have a pony. That's a big animal, and Mama says I shouldn't pester God for something I don't need, but I think a horse is a good idea, don't you?"

"Horses are fine animals."

Murderous. The look sweet little Mercy shot him was nothing short of murderous.

"But horses are work animals; they're not pets. A cat like Tasha here, now here's a perfect pet. She can play with you, and you can hold her." He compared his hand size to Heidi's and said he couldn't hold a horse in two hands—how could she when her hands were so much smaller?

Their silly conversation wended through lunch. The boarders enjoyed chiming in at the huge table where everyone ate together. Mercy's boardinghouse held a cheerful, comfortable feel, and the boarders felt like a big family. Mercy treated them with respect, but her warm spirit made it seem as if they were her uncles and brothers. They treated her with deference and Heidi with humored affection. *But for all their joviality, these men are assessing me and acting like self-appointed watchdogs.*

Someone pounded on the door. "Doc! Doc Enoch!"

Jumping to his feet, Enoch excused himself and opened the door. Mr. Toomel stood there, still in his Sunday best, but muddy and bloody. "Todd Valmer's stallion spooked. He's shredded himself on barbed wire."

A small hand curled around his fingers and squeezed. "Can I come?"

"No!" Mercy gasped from directly behind him.

But that was a victory. *Heidi wants to be with me.* Enoch bent down. "Not this time, but another. I promise." He straightened up. "I hate to go so quickly. This was the finest Sunday supper I've had in ages. Thank you."

"You'll have to come back soon."

"I'd like that."

Heidi clung to his pant leg. "Promise with all your heart and sugar and spice on top?"

He tugged Heidi's beribboned plaits. "Sugar . . . and spice." Looking at Mercy, he wanted to add, *With all my heart.* Yet such a declaration shouldn't be made in front of a child or when he'd have to run out the door. Instead, he added, "Your mama's very good with sugar and spice. I'd be a smart man to come to this very place to make my promises so I could top them off here!"

◦◦◦◦◦◦

Viewing the men and wagons, the women who wended through the crowds with pots of coffee, and the huge piles of lumber awaiting the start of construction, Enoch felt a surge of excitement. Monday had finally arrived. The lumber was milled and sawn, and most of the mortises and joints had been cut according to the specifications on the blueprint he'd sent in advance—meaning the barn ought to go up fast.

"Karl! Doc Enoch!" Jakob Stauffer helped his wife down and swept his daughter from the wagon, as well, while his hired hand, Phineas, dallied over helping Annie from the wagon. Hope grabbed a big basket and called over it, "Phineas, you're not the kind of man to kiss without a tell, so bein' as I'm Annie's sister-in-law, I'm tellin' y'all to give her a kiss. If'n you don't, you won't get a thing done all day."

Enoch murmured, " 'Kiss without a tell'?"

Slapping him on the back, Karl chuckled. "That's Hope. She turns around sayings, yet they make sense in their own funny way. Jakob—he loves it about her." The blacksmith hitched a shoulder. "She won our fondness quickly, and no one ever corrects her."

Enoch understood the message. "No one ever should. I found her version of the saying charming. Now, as I—"

"Coffee." Just about to press coffee into his hands, Mercy tore her eyes from him and off to the side. "Heidi—"

At the mere breathless gasp of her daughter's name, Enoch spun to the side. Something raw and primitive made him surge in that direction.

"Skyler's with her." Karl's hand on his shoulder acted like a battering ram. The impact jolted them both.

Enoch didn't care what Karl said. *She's my little girl. I have to see for myself.*

"Ja, Skyler's walking with her." Pride rang in Karl's voice. "Little Heidi's coming to get Emmy-Lou from Hope so they can play together."

"I don't know who needs this more." Enoch wrapped his hands around Mercy's and lifted the gray graniteware mug—first to her mouth, then to his own. Mercy's already wide eyes blinked in surprise when he left the empty mug in her keeping.

"I'll get you more."

"Thanks." His raspy voice wasn't because of the burn of the coffee. He'd immediately adored Heidi, but he hadn't become conscious of the fierce love he felt already. *I hope she'll call me Daddy.*

Parson Bradle gathered the community together and asked God's blessing on the day's endeavor, safety for all, and that the barn would be a place of healing for all of the Lord's creatures.

"Thank you, Pastor. And thanks to all of you for coming out to help." Enoch clasped Taylor's hand in his. These people needed to know where his allegiance rested. A few had already felt him out about it, and he wanted to make the matter clear in case it made a difference before the work began. "It's been less than a week since we arrived, and my sister and I have seen the earnest and honest citizens of Gooding stand by their word and kneel before their Lord. We count it a joy to serve the almighty Father and to be your neighbors."

"Plenty'll be happy to use you, Doc Enoch!"

"And plenty of us'll be glad of having Dr. Bestman." Old Mrs. Whitsley poked the man with her cane. "I'm rickety and haven't a critter to my home, but I sure can beat some manners into a pup like you and tally up another patient for her if you think she won't have enough business."

Beloved as she was, the old woman earned plenty of laughter. Taylor managed to smile, as well, but she let go of Enoch's hand as soon as the man shouted out the pointed comment.

"We haven't discussed what types of physical activity are permissible—" ignoring Karl's glower, Taylor forged ahead—"given your stage of invalidism."

"I'm well." Karl strode away and decided to prove his point. He extended his hand. "Give me that."

The buck engaged to one of the Richardson gals didn't want to relinquish the beetle—a forty-pound wooden mallet. Young men liked swinging it to impress their ladies. Well accustomed to the weight of an ax and the fact that it cut into the surface it struck, those men weren't equipped to slam something so much heavier and have it meet complete resistance. More than once, a braggart had swung wild and damaged a beam.

"Let him have it," Mr. Richardson ordered. "He'll get us off to a quick start."

Begrudging at best, the man complied. Karl went to the center of the bent—a skeleton of wood made of side-by-side ladderlike braces. This barn would be wide—a three-bracer. Each of the lateral supports on the frame had to be knocked together with the beetle. Some of the men quickly assembled it, and Karl assumed the stance he'd always used. His stitches pulled—enough for him to know that if he could feel the skin tugging, all of the places the doctor had repaired on the inside wouldn't do well with the work. Unwilling to back down, he adjusted his position and gripped the beetle in both hands. Swing . . . and wham!

Even bracing for the impact didn't lessen the effect. It felt as though he'd somehow swung and hit his own thigh with the hefty mallet, but Karl absorbed the pain with a grunt. In no way would he let on how much it hurt. Neither did he count how many joints existed on this bent; he walked to the next. Counting would be admitting he wasn't sure he could last.

"Done with that one," Daniel Clark said shortly thereafter, carrying a large coil of rope over each shoulder toward the foundation.

Wiping his brow with his sleeve, Karl surveyed the completed bent. "Ja." His leg burned. More than he'd anticipated.

Dr. Bestman came over with a water bucket. She served the last few men working on the bent. The rest had moved to assemble the next. Last, she approached him. Dipping the ladle, she murmured, "Stop before you permanently damage your leg."

He grabbed the dipper. The cool water slid down his throat and refreshed him. Renewed him. "I need no one to tell me what I can do."

"Give me that hammering instrument before I wrest it away and knock some sense into you."

Karl grinned. The thought of her doing either thing was ludi-crous. "You can't. My head's too thick."

"Even Achilles had one weak spot." She stuck out her hand.

"You're a doctor. You should know there is a difference between a heel and a head."

"What I know is that I'm going to have to heal your head after I knock some sense into you." She waggled her fingers impatiently.

Karl chuckled. Matching wits with her made for a lot of fun.

"I've made light of this, but it's serious. You'll do yourself harm if you don't cease this exertion."

"Hey, Karl!" someone shouted from the second bent.

He raised the beetle over his head. "Don't worry, Doc. I'm healthy as an ox."

"Stubborn as one," she shot back as he walked off.

Karl approached the second setup. A cowboy who worked at Checkered Past waggled his brows. "Spirited filly, huh?"

"Sassy-mouthed woman." Jase Adderly, the new manager of the lumber and feed, spat off to the side. "Got no use for 'em."

Taking exception to the way both men characterized her, Karl growled, "Stop gossiping like a couple of old biddies. We've got work to do." Anger at them fueled his first blow. Anger at himself got him through several more. The men were right—Dr. Bestman was both spirited and sassy-mouthed, but that didn't give them call to speak about her disrespectfully. A woman deserved a man's regard and basic courtesy. The problem was, he didn't want to support the notion of a woman doctor. Even if she'd done a good job on his leg.

Well, maybe not so good. It burned like anything. Each swing and mighty blow made him grit his teeth against the agony. But he'd boasted that he was fine. Strong as an ox. To change his tune now would be a show of weakness. Karl refused to do that.

"Hey! Look!"

Karl turned to the sound of a commotion as a big team of men raised the first bent into place with pikes. The whole assembly shuddered as the main girder slid into place and the ends slapped against the stays that kept the whole piece from falling over in the other direction. A cheer went up when the piece was vertical.

"Phenomenal." Awe filled Dr. Bestman's voice.

Karl twisted about and saw the fascination lighting her features. *Phenomenal,* he thought as he saw the flush in her cheeks and fire in her eyes.

"Yep." Hope Stauffer walked alongside her. "All's well that's in well."

Karl looked up and tried to catch the doctor's eye. *Dr. Bestman doesn't know Hope can't read, so she mangles old clichés.* The realization shot through his mind, and Karl opened his mouth to say something—anything—so Hope's feelings wouldn't be hurt.

"Undeniably, it's in well," the doctor said in a breezy tone. "Perfectly, I'd say."

"It's gonna be the most grandest barn ever. Hey, y'all! We brung some more nice cool water. Reckon since Piet's team got two more bents knocked together, you got plenty of time to have a sip before goin' on to the next."

The coal in his forge didn't burn as hot as Karl's thigh. With the doctor standing there, he wasn't going to admit it, though. By moving in increments, he was able to look casual, and easing his weight over onto the other leg helped significantly. One more bent. Twenty more joints to strike into place.

"We'd best leave the men alone, Hope. I'm interested in hearing more about how you've given the men pickles at harvest. It's an excellent way to replenish the salt they lose, and it helps them hold water better. Can you tell me how much salt you use in the brine?"

The two women walked off—a pair of complete opposites. The doctor was tall, stately, and beautiful. Well educated and from a privileged upbringing, she'd never known want. A hat rested on her sleek dark hair, and she was dressed in expensive clothes. By contrast, Hope was average in height and appearance—though her joy for life always gave her a special brightness. An illiterate, itinerant cook, Hope had breezed into Gooding with nothing more than two cans of food. Even now, like all of the other farm wives, she wore dresses made of feed sacks. Everyone loved and accepted Hope—but she didn't upset their lives. The doctor had barged into town, taken over a man's job, and expected people to adjust to the change she forced on them. She and Hope got along. Then again, Hope got along with everyone. . . .

"The doctor—there is a fineness about her." Phineas spoke from across the bent to no one in particular. "Easily it came to her, to make Hope look smart. A woman like her with so much education and money could act uppity, but she opened her heart to Jakob's wife and didn't consider herself any better."

"Hope—she is a good woman and deserving of such regard." Karl voiced as much praise as a man should give another man's wife. "I wonder how many of us watched, worrying that she would hurt Hope's feelings. She didn't judge Hope at all, but we judged her and found her wanting—all without reason."

"It's something to think on," Adderly said, scratching his side. "Seems more sweet than sassy."

THUMP. The post tenons slid into the sill pockets, and the men started hammering a temporary brace into place. The fleeting respite was over. Two more bents for the barn. One apiece for Piet and him. Karl swallowed a last gulp of water. He'd rested as long as he could.

"Broeder!" Piet called as he swaggered over. "I thought to finish knocking these last two bents together all by ourselves, but some of the young wolves want to bark and howl."

"We'll be here all day if I'm supposed to have a go at it," Enoch called out.

Everyone shouted with laughter.

"As the elder brother, I claim this next one, Karl. You can organize the ones doing the last bent."

"You and I will each do half of this one."

Piet said under his breath in Dutch, "Your leg cannot take more."

Pretending he didn't hear him, Karl continued, "As the elder brother, you're used to being bossy—you organize them."

"As the elder brother, I will do two of the three braces on the bent, and I will eat twice as much dessert."

Karl gave his brother a shove. "When did you start losing your appetite?"

Until the second bent was up and secured to the first with a girt spanning laterally between them on each side, the original bent was unstable. Only three men stayed to help assemble the fifth. A particular piece was too long, so they had to borrow the identical one from the sixth set and assign someone to saw down the incorrectly sized one.

"Karl! Get that beetle over here." The second piece now slid into place with a resounding thump. Having slammed girts in place and relinquished the mallet, Karl figured he could ease off.

Skyler trotted over, yipped, ran away about ten yards, then turned to look back. It was his way of saying, "Follow me."

"Okay, boy." Karl saw his collie go around a clump of shrubs.

"Ow! Stop it!" The sounds of shouting from up ahead caused him to speed up. Rounding the greenery, Karl halted.

A half-dozen boys crowded around the doctor. She was kneeling on the ground, one hand loosely curled around one of the younger Smith boys' wrists. "I'm not doing anything at all. Here. Turn your hand this way so everyone can see what a splinter you've gotten." She rotated it slightly so the light angled off the heel of the boy's hand.

"Let go of him or I'm going to tell my dad!"

"The men won't take kindly to being disturbed while they raise that barn. You'll have to go get your mama and have her fetch her sewing basket so she can find a needle in order to get this ugly old thing out of here. Mmm-hmm. That's what she'll most certainly do."

Karl bent his arms akimbo and watched. She'd chosen her words shrewdly. Few things could be worse for a boy than to have to go to his mama in front of everyone as if he were a helpless baby—and know full well that when she did take a needle to him, he'd probably act like a baby, too.

"I ain't going to my ma. You take it out."

Skyler chose that moment to bark.

All the boys scrambled backward. One of the older Smith boys said, "Pa don't cotton to no woman doctor."

Slowly and carefully, the doctor set the little boy's hand down in his lap.

Leaning over, Karl made a dismissive sound. "It's just a stupid old picker. Go on ahead and yank it out, Doc."

"That's not possible. Now that I know the father wouldn't approve of my rendering care, I cannot do so. It would be against my canon of ethics."

"You got a cannon?!"

"The book kind, not the gun kind," Lloyd Smith said, tousling his kid brother's hair.

"Shouldn'ta told 'em." Ozzie White elbowed him. "We coulda joked on that for days!"

Doc rose and tilted her head to the side. "Mr. Van der Vort, may I speak to you for a moment, please?"

He gave a curt nod. Why did she have to stand on some dumb rule? It was just a splinter. They made it off to the side, and she dipped her head. When she started opening the five-inch-square leather purse hanging from the silver chatelaine he'd repaired, Karl's irritation evaporated. It pleased him that she wore the chatelaine clipped to the waist of her skirt every day. The extra effort he'd put into repairing her family heirloom had been well spent. There was something wholly feminine about how she'd go about the town with this pretty leather purse and often gloves, a hanky, or her slender three-inch sterling pencil dangling from the chain alongside the silver etched square notepad barely larger than a postage stamp.

And now the poor woman was probably fishing out a handkerchief because she didn't want the boys to see her getting teary-eyed and upset. Especially after Ozzie had just confessed to a plan to be a tease.

Opening the mouth of the purse to an unexpectedly yawning expanse, she skimmed her fingers along one side, delved down, and produced a pair of tweezers. "These will serve nicely. You'll have to do the task."

Karl pushed aside the tweezers and stared down at the neatly arranged medical supplies filling the purse. "What do you think you're doing, carrying those around? Do you think I repaired your chatelaine so you could use it to—"

"The tweezers." Her voice sounded as hard as the iron he would work tomorrow.

Wide-eyed, the children looked from him to the doctor and back. Realizing his gaffe, Karl chuckled as he accepted the tweezers. "I should have known better than to wonder what a woman had in her purse. My moeder—she kept everything in hers, from a ribbon and feathers for hat repairs to a pocketknife!" He motioned the Smith kid over.

All of the kids formed a circle off to the side around him, clearly avoiding the doctor. Since he couldn't hunker down, Karl pulled the boy's hand upward and quickly yanked out the splinter. "There. Easy as pie."

Dr. Bestman looked at Lloyd. "He ought to wash his hands."

Cramming his hands into his pockets, Lloyd shrugged. "Dad said dirt don't hurt nothin'. Farmers oughta be proud to have it on their hands."

Ozzie started snickering. Karl shot him a stern look. "If you boys aren't clean, you're not eating dinner." Once they left, Karl found he couldn't lambaste her about her medical bag. Instead, he held his temper. "Why? Why do you carry this with you?"

Wiping the tweezers, then tucking them back into a precise location, she simply said, "I took an oath."

"No one takes an oath to carry a bag."

"Why do the men of Gooding wear guns when it's a peaceful, God-fearing town?"

"It's not the—"

"Yes, it is the same—to save lives in cases of emergencies." She opened the purse as wide as it would go, which was only about two inches. Even so, she'd managed to put in a small array of things. "A pocketknife, tweezers, scissors, a tourniquet, four surgical clamps, three containers in which I have needles already threaded with suturing silk, gauze, pain medication, iodine mixture, soap, a handkerchief, a finger rosary, and a package of gum."

"Are you Catholic?"

"No, but some of my patients are, and I deeply respect their beliefs and needs. As for the gum—I make it a practice to give children a sweet after treating them." Clicking the purse shut, she looked at him. "It's enough to handle most emergencies. I can always use clothing for bandaging and slings."

"Men have pocketknives and the other women have needles and thread," he told her. "Soap and whiskey—"

"Are you suggesting that I eschew all moral and ethical responsibilities, hoping supplies might be on hand in an urgent situation? I'd certainly hope not. Diligence and preparedness often avert disasters, and life is sacred."

"Life is sacred." He reached down and batted at her purse. "This isn't."

"Quoting from my oath: 'I will follow that system of regimen which, according to my ability and judgment, I consider for the benefit of my patients.' I am able to carry these supplies about, and it is my judgment that it is best to have them on hand. Therefore, I'm honoring the professional oath I took when I became a physician. Normally, I wouldn't justify such a thing to anyone, but since you were so kind as to repair my chatelaine, I felt it only right to give you credit for assisting me."

Karl put his hands on his hips and assessed the doctor. He couldn't help but notice the way her cheeks had pinked during her speech. "If you'd stop chattering, we could go get lunch."

"You're the one who started the conversation by asking why I wear my purse."

"How was I to know you'd give me a full inventory of what you carry? Other women keep that a secret."

"I'm not like other women."

There's an understatement. "I have noticed."

⚬⚬⚬

"Stupid, childish stunt." Taylor threw yet another utterly filthy "sterile" wrap into the boiling washpot. Coming home before lunch to pick up some clean tweezers, she'd discovered muddy footprints all over her surgery. Worst of all, whoever had been there dumped some wet, loamy soil laden with worms, germs, and mold into the drawer containing the sterilized, carefully wrapped and ready-to-use surgical instruments. All that work for naught. She sterilized and rewrapped the instruments and finally gave the floor a final sweep. Now in case she needed to give care, she'd be able to.

She turned away from her instruments and shook her head at the incessant clucking from the chickens in the yard. Taylor found the combination of stink and noise had her wishing for the chickens' demise. Unless . . . A grim smile tilted her lips. She scooped up the bucket containing the dirt with the worms in it and headed to the coop. She had chickens to fatten up—the sooner, the better.

Wrists pecked unmercifully, Taylor finished feeding the hens. But as she turned to go, the hair on her nape tingled. It had nothing to do with her plans for fried chicken. Someone was watching her.

Twelve

Feigning that all was well in the midst of a crisis? Doctors honed that skill, so Taylor drew upon it now. She went back to the washpot, pulled out some cloths, and rinsed them. Clear and straightforward as could be, some men had let it be known they didn't want her in Gooding. With time, she would change their minds. In the meantime, no one was going to scare her into budging from her home.

"Hey, Doctor." Hope tromped over, and Taylor let the breath she'd been holding slowly escape. "Remembered me this place had a coop. Jakob and me—we don't wanna be owin' to nobody, so I though maybe you'd let me clean out the coop for credit."

Just before she agreed, an idea shot through Taylor's mind. "Actually, I'd rather barter something different."

" 'Kay. We can talk on it, but we'd better get back. The men're gonna start workin' again any minute, so I need to mind Emmy-Lou. I got me a funny feeling something's a-brewing. Just you remember righteous, almighty God ain't respecting persons who don't follow His Golden Rule."

"Romans 2:11." Taylor gave Hope's hand a squeeze. "I needed to be reminded that there is no respect of men with God."

"You and me'll think on that, but plenty of these knotheads are gonna try to tell you it don't say nothing 'bout women. Don't let it bother you none. They just wisht they was as smart as you. Now, what is it I can do to build me up some credit?"

You already have. Taylor kept that to herself. "When it comes to those chickens . . ." Hope accepted the plan with alacrity, and once they got back to the barn raising, they sealed the deal with a slice of pie.

A few minutes later Gustav Cutter stood before everyone and rubbed his hands together. "The barn's going up right quick, and we're mighty proud to have us a veterinarian. Toomel, White, Sawyer, and a few others have already used Doc Enoch and vouch for him being topnotch. As he said, he and his kid sis want to thank you for showing up and helping out.

"There were problems with the last doctor, and we all want to be careful this next time." Cutter smiled like a shark. "It's understandable. We need someone competent. Capable. There's no use having a town physician if folks won't use her."

Some pockets of folks went completely silent; others nodded and called out agreement. Piet shouted, "My broeder—among us he walks! There should be no questions. In Dr. Bestman, we have a fine doctor."

"I second that." Velma bustled over to Cutter. "You counted on me to know what we needed to set up that surgery, and you're going to count on my judgment about the doctor."

"You are just one person." Cutter curled his hands around his lapels. "I have made a decision. A very fair decision. There are one hundred twenty-three people in Gooding. According to Edna Mae, in the next three months, it'll jump to one twenty-five. On the first Monday of March, Doctor Taylor MacLay Bestman will provide me with a list of at least one hundred locals who commit to using her as their physician. Fathers can sign for their children. It stands to reason that if a substantial percent of Gooding's citizens hold confidence in the doctor, the burden of competence is, in part, demonstrated. Surely Dr. Bestman will agree this is a most reasonable arrangement."

Everyone turned to stare at her.

"Of course she won't!" Enoch's voice shook with rage. "She signed a four-year contract in good faith. So did I. Stand behind your word."

"You waited until the barn was half built before saying anything?" Toomel shook his head. "Was this to force Doc Enoch to stay?"

Taylor refused to allow everything to spiral out of control. "Mr. Mayor." She addressed him with chilling politeness. "I cannot agree with the arrangement—" People started talking, so she held up a hand to silence them. "My professional oath guarantees confidentiality between me and my patients. By providing you with their names, I deny them that right and break the sacred bond I pledged."

"Not only that," Mercy added, "someone could use the doctor and not sign the list. It wouldn't be honest or fair."

Like Karl Van der Vort? That thought shot through Taylor's mind, leaving a trail of pain. She shook her head. "I won't dictate another's actions. They are accountable to the Lord. I am, however, accountable for my own. I will not compromise my standards."

"Perhaps I could offer to stand in the breach." Parson Bradle stepped forward. "I'd be willing to maintain the list and merely report the number to the mayor, if we can all agree to that."

"Yes!" Cutter beamed. "That way, if anyone wants to remove their name, they can have you strike it off, too."

"You better have brought plenty of paper, Cutter." Enoch scanned the crowd. "Because my sis is the best doctor you'll ever meet. And if that's not enough for you, then you're missing out. But I won't. Blood's thicker than water. She and I'll go—"

"Nope," Cutter broke in. "You'll still be bound by contract."

Taylor thought of Enoch and his dream practice. His made-to-order barn. Mercy and her little daughter and Enoch's love for them and his happy future . . . Everything was imperiled. Taylor spoke loudly. "Parson Bradle, I appreciate and accept your offer to keep the list."

It had taken almost two years of medical school before approximately half of her classmates tolerated her; the others never accepted her. In four years she'd built up a highly successful practice in Chicago, but most of it consisted of women and children. Now she had three months to win over a preponderance of men and a pain-in-the-neck mayor. "I always did like a challenge."

Long after everyone else had left, Enoch remained at the barn. Entirely lining the longest two walls—with the exception of doors—were stalls, awaiting patients. Bins filled with oats and barley had been placed up front. From the roof, the pulley and rope hung ready to pull the bales of hay beside him up to the sizable loft. Concrete flooring jutted from the back wall for a distance of ten feet. The last stall's partition was a full-length wall, turning it into a room for him when he needed to spend nights at the clinic. He'd already unfolded a cot and tossed a few thick wool blankets on it. Off in the opposite stall were a boot brush and a pair of knee-high mucking boots, a leather apron, and rope tied into halters, leashes, and other uses hanging from ten-penny nails. Men could store tack there when they brought their animals in.

But Enoch's pride and joy rested against the back wall in the center. He'd shipped his instruments and medications in one-foot deep custom-made maple cabinets that hinged together face-to-face. Lipped shelves on both sides of one of the cases kept the larger instruments in place. Dozens of different sized, varying colored bottles and jars of an appreciable apothecary lined the shelves of the top half of the second case. Below them, drawers held everything from the smallest surgical instruments to blinders for horses. The final side of the second case would have looked like a jumbled mess had Taylor not arranged it: A narrow cupboard awaited his surgery apron or jacket, depending on the need of the moment; five reference books; lye and castile soap boxes; a set of nested aluminum washbowls; and four dozen folded towels.

First thing tomorrow morning, he would open the cases and Gooding would sport the best veterinary infirmary money could buy. And until Gustav Cutter had opened his big mouth after lunch, everything had been perfect. Now the barn represented not just a future full of dreams, but also one fraught with a heart-rending separation should most of these men stay narrow-minded. A toothpick measured wider than many of their minds.

Taylor can do it. She can prove herself. All she needs is the opportunity. Piet was right—seeing Karl walk ought to be all the testimonial necessary. Only it wasn't. It wasn't even close. So far, seventeen names limped down the list. He'd considered announcing a Bestman Plan, whereby he'd give a thirty percent discount to anyone on Taylor's list whose animals needed care. And he still would—if that's what it took to prevent her from being run out of town. But not now. Not until she'd had the opportunity to dazzle them with her skills. She deserved the dignity of proving herself.

Time. We have time. Three months. Enoch inhaled deeply. The sweet smell of hay mingled with the aroma of sawdust. Enoch let out a rueful laugh.

"What's so funny?" Orville Clark asked as he sauntered in.

"I was appreciating the smell—likely for the last time."

Smoothing back his sparse hair, Orville forced a laugh. "Suppose you got a point, but grand as we made the place, you can keep it aired out. I can help with that."

"It doesn't take much to shove open a few doors."

"Once you open those doors, you're not going to have time to close them. Mark my words: You're going to be so busy, you'll be running from head to tail." Orville jammed his thumbs under his suspenders and rocked back and forth with a big grin on his face. "Yes, sir. Folks'll come from far away, and you're going to need help. Someone to feed your patients. To walk them and to curry the horses."

"If I hire someone, their first and foremost chore would be to muck the stalls and pens."

Orville's lips thinned to a narrow white line. "You're the boss. The boss has the say."

"When I have all those patients you're predicting, I'll give the matter due consideration."

"You don't give yourself much credit, do you?"

"Animals can be treated in the field or in the owner's barn. The very sick or those requiring surgery will be brought here, as will those requiring temporary boarding."

Crossing his arms as if to hold in heat and scuffing the ball of his right boot on the concrete foundation, he muttered, "Winter's nigh unto here. Gonna be cold."

"True. Which is the reason the town council gave for building the barn—it saves me making extra house calls, and farmers can rest easy, knowing their sick beast is under constant watch. That, and the bad freeze that happened southwest and southeast of here in March this year. I heard animals drifted and froze. This way we'll have somewhere to shelter them."

Orville cast a glance toward the back corner as the wind let out a howl. "Barn's big as any around here. Might be, you could convince me to live here. Mind the creatures at night, keep an eye on things."

And I'd spend all my time keeping an eye on you. "I'm a vet, but I don't count my chickens. Should the day arrive when I'm as busy as you predict, I'll post the job."

Orville's eyes narrowed to slits. "Post it."

"At your cousin's mercantile." Enoch clapped his hands and rubbed them to stir up some circulation in them. "You're right about one thing—cold season's coming on. Nice as it is, a barn's always drafty. Let's get on out of here."

Orville dogged his every step until he'd locked the barn. Enoch headed toward the boardinghouse; Orville went toward the saloon.

The parlor light shone brightly through the swagged back curtains that framed Mercy as she sat crocheting.

Her head lifted at the sound of his footsteps on the

boardinghouse steps. Her smile would have warmed his entire barn through the worst blizzard.

He motioned her to stay seated and let himself in. By the time he'd stepped foot inside, she'd popped up and scurried toward the kitchen. Lounging against the doorframe, Enoch said in a low tone, "Now, how did I know I'd find you in here?"

Mercy turned toward him with a cup of coffee and a plate. "Pumpkin pie."

"You didn't need to do this." *Sweet pea.* He caught himself before he said it.

"I didn't do anything at all."

Enoch eased the cup from her hands and drank a big mouthful of the scalding brew. "Mmmm. Hits the spot."

"Mr. Michaelson says it's just above freezing again." She set down the pie. "Let me top that off for— Oh my!" she said, looking down upon the empty cup.

"You do make a fine cup of coffee, ma'am. Perhaps you ought to join me and have one."

He drank another cup while she went to the cupboard for a tray. She looked over her shoulder and laughed. "I suppose the tray is unnecessary now."

"Guess again." He grinned. "Good thing you have a boarding-house-sized pot. There are going to be times when you wonder if you shouldn't just pour directly from the pot to my mouth."

"You'd have to sit on one of Heidi's little chairs for that to work—I'd never reach otherwise. You're far too tall."

Enoch had never had a woman call him tall; he wasn't. And he couldn't help being disappointed in Mercy's statement. Honesty had to bind them together; any such falsehood would make another easier . . . until the cracks would make their love crumble.

Pretending someone was something they weren't invariably led to discontent.

"Let's be candid, Mercy. I'm not tall at all. I'm only five eight."

"That is tall! I'm only five feet. I barely come to your shoulder."

"Other men . . ."

She put down the tray. "I don't appreciate being compared to other women. I presume men don't like being compared to other men. If this is your way of asking about Hamilton, he was touchy about his height, so I never knew precisely what it was. My eyes lined up with his nose."

Enoch nodded and carried the tray into the parlor. Mercy set a single cup by one chair for herself, then the pie and two cups for him by the adjacent seat. "These teacups are ridiculous for you. I ought to get one of those large coffee mugs men seem to prefer." As soon as the words left her mouth, she turned five shades of scarlet.

Enoch pretended not to notice her embarrassment. "I'd like you to do that. Those teacups look pretty in your dainty little hands, but I'm sure I'm going to drop it."

"Despite its delicate appearance, china is surprisingly strong."

"Much like you," he murmured. Enoch knew she'd heard him. He wanted to praise everything about her. She was the most remarkable woman he'd ever encountered. He decided to see if the feelings ran even a fraction as deeply the other direction. "On the other hand, I've heard those big mugs don't last long."

"Anything lasts if handled with care. The sturdy shape of them would lend admirable stability. The larger size would extend a friendly welcome, don't you think?"

He took the cup and brought it up to his mouth. Holding it a fraction of an inch below his lips, he looked into her fathomless brown eyes. "Knowing one was waiting sure would warm my heart."

Thirteen

A few days later, Taylor heard noises within the house when she returned from visiting Millie over at the mercantile. She went through the door and peeked around the corner. Unable to see her office from the entryway, she thought about calling for help but decided it wouldn't come. She could clear her throat, but then she'd give someone a clue as to who was there already.

This was getting to be a problem, and Taylor determined she'd have to face it head on. Each time her brother went out courting Mercy, it seemed someone invited themselves into the surgery. Now, while that sneak didn't realize Taylor had come home, she could march in there and find out who it was.

Slowing her progress to muffle the sound of her sensible boots, Taylor reached the doorway of the surgery. "Mrs. O'Toole. Can I help you?"

The widow let out a yelp. "My goodness, I didn't hear you come. Are you trying to scare the liver out of a poor woman?" With her skirt clear up to her thighs and her black stockings pulled down to her ankles, she couldn't do much to hide her knees, which were skinned up much like a seven-year-old girl's. A bottle of witch hazel and a cloud of cotton bolls were spread across a small treatment tray.

"I didn't mean to frighten you. If you need care, I'm happy to assist you, but I don't expect anyone to be in my surgery when I'm not here." Taylor hoped her message got through. Perhaps this was a simple, straightforward explanation for the disturbances. "Did you have an accident on your velocipede, ma'am?"

"Well, it did slip a little. The ground was just the tiniest bit icy. It froze during the night, you know. The ground did, not my velocipede."

No evidence of a morning frost existed, but Taylor didn't mention that fact. "I assumed you were referring to the ground. It's quite a lovely velocipede."

"Would you like to ride it?"

Taylor thought for a moment. If she was going to be honest, she'd say yes. But she'd be a fool to try it. It would cost her every last name on her patient list and doom her forever. "I do believe that's probably an exercise I'd best leave alone. Since you've observed a morning frost, prudence would dictate that you store the velocipede away for the winter. Come springtime, you'll be able to enjoy it again." She picked up a cotton boll. "Let's go ahead and take care of you."

"I was just about done."

Taylor went ahead and dabbed on a bit more witch hazel. "It looks as if you cleansed it quite nicely." She wrapped some gauze around it, tied it in place. "I'm afraid your stockings are badly shredded."

Widow O'Toole sighed. "This was my last pair." After she admitted it, she looked like she regretted saying so.

"What you tell me never goes any further."

"I'd be mortified if anybody knew. You see, everyone already thinks I'm quite an oddity, going around on my bicycle." The woman's countenance went winsome. "It gives me such a sense of freedom, you see. They expect me to sedately stroll about in crow black all the time and do nothing more than my gardening. But that's not enough."

"No, I don't suppose it is." Up close, the lack of any silver or gray in the woman's hair and her still-youthful hands caused Taylor to drastically revise her estimate of the widow's age. Instead of edging somewhere around fifty, she was surprisingly a good decade younger!

"Seeing as they expect nothing more from me than that I garden or harangue them on the evils of their alcohol, it is only fair I should be permitted to enjoy my velocipede, don't you think?"

Taylor thought of all of the times she'd been told what she should and shouldn't do and how grateful she was her parents had supported her in the one thing she loved the most—that she'd been able to become a doctor. Yet acquaintances, so-called friends, and every single professor and student in the entire medical school told her what she'd chosen to do was wrong. She looked at the widow. "What you do should be between you and God."

Widow O'Toole beamed. "I knew you had common sense. Indeed you do." Limping slightly, she slipped out the back door. Just a moment later, the back door banged open.

Taylor didn't bother to turn around. "Yes, Mrs. O'Toole?"

"I almost forgot to tell you. Orville Clark is up to something again."

"And what would that be?" Taylor could have kicked herself for asking. She really shouldn't have invited any kind of gossip.

"That rapscallion's selling mail-order patent medicines."

Taylor muffled a moan.

"Yes, of all the boneheaded things, it's true. This isn't mere speculation, mind you. I saw him going door to door with a box filled with a plethora of bottles. Knowing how I feel about demon rum and its devilish relatives, he wouldn't dare come to my door."

Many folks had mentioned a recent cold snap, and there'd been a storm, too. Such weather inevitably tested the lungs of both the young and the old, so Taylor had seen some patients for problems ranging from simple colds and catarrh to more serious lung problems and dispensed different kinds of medications for them depending on her diagnosis. Even then, tinctures of time and rest were most effective. Well, those and several pots of honey-and-lemon-laced tea.

"People want a quick, cheap cure." *And more to the point, they don't want me as their physician. It's another tactic to keep prospective patients away from me. They're doing everything they can to see me fail.*

"Patent medicines are evil," the widow said. "Wicked, I tell you."

"They can be dangerous." Some of them could actually be quite harmful when paired with the medication she dispensed. Now she would have to make a point of asking each of her patients if they were taking any kind of a curative from anybody else. That would be awkward, at best. "Thank you for letting me know, Mrs. O'Toole."

"Well, I thought you should know. And since we live next door and you've seen my knees, I believe you should call me Eunice."

"I did need to know, Eunice. I appreciate that."

Eunice beamed. "I was just doing my duty." She waggled her forefinger in the air. "I won't call you anything other than Doctor, so don't ask me to. I'm so proud to know a woman physician, I'm going to relish calling you that every chance I get." Eunice O'Toole turned around and limped out.

I should have asked her if she needed help getting her velocipede home. A smile flitted across Taylor's features. She could just imagine what tongues would wag if anyone saw her walking down the street with the widow O'Toole's velocipede.

On the heels of that thought, she looked around her office. Had it been her imagination that someone was making clandestine visits for devious reasons? If so, then she didn't need to lock up. That would mean it was fine to leave the office open just in case of emergencies. People could come in and grab what was necessary, but did they know what was necessary? Most of these people seemed good-hearted and well-intentioned. But other than Velma, all of them confessed complete ignorance regarding medical issues. *Well, if I'm out of town, Enoch's in town and we both have keys. I'll start locking the building when I'm gone. It's just the smart thing to do.* Taylor looked out the window and let out a rueful laugh. She'd gladly loan her key to Eunice O'Toole if she could secretly ride on that velocipede.

◦~◦~◦

"Sure, I'll board her. She's a beaut." Enoch ran his hands along the mare's bulging side. "I noticed she's waxing up. Shouldn't be long."

Todd Valmer nodded curtly. "I can't watch after her. Not with me alone."

"Mares rarely drop a foal with an audience. They wait hours till you leave them for a few minutes."

"Yep. But wolves are bold this year. We've all set traps. The bad cold early this year killed off the weak elsewhere—the wolves are on the hunt here now."

"I have Ozzie White and Lloyd Smith here before school each morning to muck the barn, and though they've proven to be reliable, I still stay put. It would only take a schoolboy being careless once to let something in or out."

"Thanks. That puts my mind at rest."

"The first foal is in good position." Enoch made a mental note to point that out to the boys. Ozzie had a natural affinity for animals, and Lloyd hinted he wanted to pursue medicine. He had the aptitude, too. Enoch finished his examination and gave the mare an approving smack—just enough for her to feel appreciated but not enough to set her off. "That bodes well with twins."

"You'd know about twins."

Enoch laughed. "They'll watch out for each other when those wolves come around."

Studying his boots, Valmer said, "Watch out for yours. Wolves hunt in packs, and there's a pack after her."

A friendly warning? A threat? Enoch remained silent.

Valmer looked up. "I don't take to the notion of a woman doctor. But I won't set a trap or bear false witness. You can't blame us for kicking against her going against the natural order of things. But, Doc Enoch, you're good." He nodded toward his mare. "And if she's half as good as you, the town did okay in getting you both. Given time, she'll prove herself."

"Thanks for telling me. I am good; but she's ten times better. She's gifted." *If only enough men would recognize it in time.*

<O~O~O>

"Let me see you raise your arm now." Taylor stood in Mr. Toomel's kitchen and watched as he raised his arm. "Yes, now can you rotate your arm around? Let me see how far you can do that. Don't push it, just as far as you're comfortable." He was gritting his teeth. "Stop. Tomorrow you can do it a little bit more, but for now, I don't want you to strain."

The farmer stared out his window at the barren landscape. "I have too much to do around here. It's not going to get done if I don't do it."

"I sat in church and heard all of those people volunteer to come do your chores for you. Do you think I didn't know you had help?"

He got red under his light tan that hadn't faded from the summer. "I still go out and check."

"What man wouldn't? This is your land, your livelihood. I'd expect you to." Her comment helped him relax. She could see his other shoulder and the lines on his face ease. A strapping build helped him do all of the heavy labor on a farm. Nonetheless, it wasn't safe for a man to try to do that much work alone. No wonder he'd had an accident.

Toomel flexed his fingers. "My grip's no good."

Taylor clasped her medical bag shut. "Have you been applying the compresses from the cold well water as I directed?"

"I don't have time for that nonsense."

"That nonsense, Mr. Toomel, will take down the swelling. Just as it would treat a wrenched ankle, it removes the pressure surrounding the nerves responsible for your hand and arm. No doubt about it, the separated bones have stayed in place, but the ligaments aren't stable enough. Within a week you're going to be almost back to normal. But I still don't want you lifting any weight."

"What do you mean, lifting no weight? I have to—"

"Absolutely no lifting. The heaviest thing you're allowed to pick up at this point in time is five pounds."

"Nothing weighs five pounds around here. Nothing."

"Then I guess you'll lift nothing."

His brows slammed together. "I can lift something with my other hand."

"Yes, you can."

"And I can help with—"

"No, you can't." She looked at him. "You got injured when you were in top form. The likelihood of sustaining severe, permanent damage to your shoulder and arm cannot be dismissed. Think very carefully, Mr. Toomel, about whether the cost of your pride now is worth being a pained cripple for the remainder of your life. Like it or not, that's the cost."

Grim resignation creased his features. "When can I start lifting weight again?"

"By the end of next week you'll be doing nearly everything you once did. Beginning Thursday I want you to start lifting some weight each day. I'll give you gradations. Let me write it down on this sheet of paper for you." She wrote down progressive amounts of weight. "Now, I take it you don't have any weights here on the farm."

"Well . . ." He thought for a minute. "Not exactly. A bale of hay weighs a hundred pounds."

"Excellent." She wrote *bale of hay* next to the hundred pounds.

"A gallon of milk weighs about eight pounds." And so on, they went down the list and put something down for each of them. As they did, she'd add the day of the week beside it and how many times she wanted him to lift it with his healing limb.

"If you go ahead and progress lifting in this order and don't skip anything, you'll ease your shoulder so that by the time you're able to lift the bale of hay, you'll be able to continue to do all of your weight and not have a problem. It will also ease the muscle into the work so you won't be sore. The only things you'll not be doing after two weeks are the exceptionally heavy jobs—but you can push a bale of hay instead of lifting it."

He nodded curtly. "There you are, then. I'll help you back to your buggy."

"There's no need." She walked out of his home. Karl was waiting out there for her; she couldn't shake him. The man was like a bad cold. He still wouldn't let her take the buggy and go on any of her calls, though Taylor didn't know why. She knew her way around town and around most of the outlying country, as well. Blindfolded, she could probably direct the buggy to most of the houses close in, but he stubbornly insisted on driving and would sit out in the frigid wind or even the rain while she paid a visit.

Karl helped her back into the buggy, and his dog hopped up onboard. Not only had she come to accept the fact that Skyler would ride on top, but she actually enjoyed it. Ever since the barn raising when Skyler kept all of the children busy and safe, he'd truly proved his value. Not only that, but now that she wanted Karl to do more walking, Skyler trotted alongside him. Those walks were helping strengthen Karl's leg.

With the way Karl's leg and Mr. Toomel's shoulder each were mending, people in the community could see she was competent.

Women came to her quite frequently. Many of the men in town, however, were slow to come around. She knew they still went to Enoch to ask for medical advice, and he turned them away. He never said a word about it, though. He'd protect her feelings, but he was loyal to the bone.

The list of names now hovered at thirty. Almost a third of what she needed, but those were the easy patients. The rest were individuals who would be very hard won.

As the buggy started to roll, Karl grated, "I don't like you going into the houses where there are men like that."

"It's a professional call."

He looked at her. "They're still men and you're still a woman."

"I'm a woman with several sharp instruments at hand. I could carve a man up and lay him out like a frog on a dissection table."

"You wouldn't have the opportunity. Men are far stronger than women."

"I know men are stronger, Karl, but that isn't the issue. Men respect women. I've noticed that here."

He looked at her. "Not all men are respectful of what you do. You must know this."

It was easy for her to talk about it with her own brother, but with Karl, for some reason, she'd never said anything. "I'm aware of it," she finally admitted.

He looked away, then stared at the harness as they went on. "The men, they feel it is right for a man to be the physician. It is a man's job, not a woman's."

"And you, Karl, what do you think?"

"For me, I do not know."

His answer struck her, surprised her . . . but it also hurt. After all, she'd saved his life. Wasn't that enough? She, too, sat and stared forward.

"There was a time when I agreed with those men. You've changed my mind enough now that I am uncertain. For me to have changed my thinking at all reflects the favor I've shown you. But it is wrong for a woman to be with a man who is not her husband when he is unclothed. That is my objection. For you to be out like this in dangerous situations, that is not right, either. Then, too, for you to have a job; women do not work."

She tamped down a moan. "I've heard all of this before, Karl. Surely you realize that. Let me tell you what I think."

"Is there anything about which you do not tell everybody what you think?"

"Why is it that a man can tell everybody what he thinks, and we're supposed to hold his opinion to be right, good, and of great importance; but a woman is expected to strictly listen and agree and have no opinion at all?"

"Women are supposed to be directed by their fathers and their husbands."

"Don't you want to have a wife or a daughter who is smart enough that she can make good decisions?"

"Ja, but—"

"Then wouldn't she be smart enough to have a good opinion on things?"

"Yes, I would suppose so, but—"

"And if she were intelligent, wouldn't she read so she would be interesting to converse with? And if she was well-read, then wouldn't she also have enough in her mind, enough knowledge to increase the ability to form reasonable opinions and make wise decisions?"

"This could be the case."

"I'm not trying to be unkind, Karl, but you have to understand: We're not living in the Dark Ages—we're in a modern world. Girls read now. They have the same education boys do. As a matter of fact, many of the girls around here have had far more schooling than the boys have because the boys have been held out during harvest time while the girls have continued on at school. And then the boys have quit school after sixth grade or earlier than the girls because they're needed to do the heavy farm work while the girls have completed a high school education."

He thought for a moment. "True."

"So if anything, many of the women here are better educated and well-read. It's the case for the Whites, the Richardsons, the Bunces, and the Smiths—and those are families I can rattle off just because they're right along the road here." She sighed. "The only reason Lloyd Smith is in school instead of minding the fields is because Enoch pays him enough to satisfy his greedy father."

"Nevertheless, for me to agree does not give credence to your point. The things about which decisions need to be made—they have to do with the farm. For those decisions, the man's experience and knowledge count most, and so it is he who should be making those decisions."

"I grant that might well be the case."

He nodded proudly. "So I am right."

"Partially. But not all decisions are about the farm. Just the other day, Daniel and Millie were planning the window displays for the mercantile. He wanted to wait until summer to put a display of the yardage goods in the window, but Millie knew the sun would bleach the fabrics then so now is the best time. Daniel had to agree. So sometimes it's the woman who has the knowledge that makes a decision right." There. Point made. Her logic was undeniable, and she flashed him a smile. Surely he'd concede she'd won this debate.

"That's a minor thing, not an important matter."

Taylor let out a long-suffering sigh. "I'm sure you're not trying to goad me, Karl. In a way, I wish you were. I enjoy a debate just for the fun of it, but in this situation I can see you honestly hold the misguided notion that men are always in the superior position to make every decision. Sometimes they are, sometimes they aren't, and sometimes, decisions need to be made by consensus."

"Talk." The word rumbled out of him like it was something vile. "Too much time is wasted with all that talk. It is the way of the world that someone must lead. History proves it is the man."

"Might does not make right. Knowledge and skill count, too. Often, they're more important."

He shot her a sideways glance. "Men have skills and knowledge—like farming. You're talking in circles. If you can't come up with something concrete, then it's a theory—"

"We're talking about getting a church organ. You know how expensive organs are, and who's going to play that organ? A woman. So who should choose the organ?"

"The pastor, of course. Parson Bradle should pick the organ because he is the leader of our flock."

"You would have Parson Bradle choose the organ, though he's never played one; yet here we have Mrs. Smith, who has experience and has offered to play for the congregation, and you dismiss her as the wise and logical choice?"

"That does seem illogical. I suppose I see your point." The buggy crossed a rut and jostled significantly, yet before she could relish her victory, he added, "But that is not a decision within a marriage."

"Karl, I think I want to wring your neck right now."

He laughed. "You're a doctor. You don't wound people; you heal them."

"I just might make an exception in your case."

After a silent interlude, his hand swept up and down to encompass her. "You've done much thinking about family. Why have you not married, a fine woman like you?"

"Honestly, Karl—"

"Honestly, of course. Why are you not married? You are comely and healthy. Your mind is sound, even if you're of stubborn temperament. And if ever a woman was unafraid of hard work, surely it is you. Ja, you should be married."

Leaning away, Taylor stared at him. From his sooty boots that stuck out from beneath the lap robe to his windblown hair, she took stock. "Why haven't *you* married? You're handsome and remarkably strong. Intelligence, obstinacy, and diligence to duty are among your most prominent traits. Yes, you, Karl Van der Vort, should be married." His smile grew with every compliment she paid him. "But if you speak to other women the way you just spoke to me, it's a marvel I'm not constantly treating you for bruised shins."

"Ladies like compliments."

"Thus being treated like a broodmare is hardly flattering."

"Broodmare!"

"You decided I was healthy and intelligent, and you assessed my temperament and willingness to work." Taylor laughed at his flummoxed expression. "The only thing you left out was the condition of my teeth."

"They are nice and straight and very white." A sheepish smile crossed his face. "And what do you expect of a liveryman? And a blacksmith who acts as a ferrier?"

Laughter spilled out of her. "You're hopeless."

"Nee. You do not understand. People—they are like horses. Piet is like the Trakenhner—solid and huge and reliable. Enoch and Mercy are like second years that have been let out to the field by themselves for the first time. They have all the freedom and do not know what to enjoy first."

"That's true."

His voice changed, slowed. "You are like a Thoroughbred—intelligent and responsive. You come from important lineage. Thoroughbreds' manes are luxurious and their coats carry the finest gloss." He seemed to lift his hand toward her head, but then it turned out to be a mere gesture.

Disappointment speared through her, and she realized she'd wanted him to stroke her hair.

"Your hair—it carries such sheen and it's so thick. Your bearing challenges a fool to break your spirit."

And a wise man? She didn't ask. Instead, she shifted the focus away from herself. "So, as long as you're comparing me to a horse, what kind of horse would you be, then?"

He chuckled. "Shire. Ja. Definitely a shire."

Thinking of the huge gray Belgian draft horse he had at the livery made her smile. "You're not Belgian; you're Dutch."

He shrugged. "But I am big and plodding."

"They're gentle giants and there's much to be said for that kind of stamina and endurance. I appreciate how you drop everything to take me on calls." Every time she went out on calls like this, she'd see sparks in the smithy at sunset. In fact, after sunset, as well. "When other people finish for the day and close their shops, you're still working because you've helped me out."

"I don't mind. As long as you don't kick my shins for telling you about your mane."

"Shall we shake on it?"

"No. Keep tucked in. It's far too cold. Snow's on the way again. Oklahoma shares it too frequently with us."

When they neared town, Taylor hastily reached up to secure any loose tendrils. Around Karl, she didn't feel the need to be concerned about her image the way she was with other men. Grandmother called it "maintaining presence," and many was the time when attention to the details of spotless gloves, a well-tamed coif, a queenly posture, and a serene expression had carried her though situations men intentionally created to embarrass her. Karl might not endorse her being a physician, but she had to give him credit for the fact that he'd never once done anything to ridicule or humiliate her. As her chaperon of sorts, he was in an ideal position to do such things, but he hadn't. She'd come to trust him.

"Here you are."

"You didn't have to drive me here. I could have walked."

"It is no trouble." He jumped down and curled his hands about her waist. Instead of lifting her straight down, he took a few steps and set her on the boardwalk. "There's no use in you getting muddy. Let me get your bag."

"Thank you." She fumbled with her key.

"Let me get that." He took the keys, unlocked her front door, and pushed it wide. Once she'd entered, he stepped inside.

"I—" She turned around and almost ran smack into him. "Thank you."

"Think nothing of it."

Easier said than done . . . far, far easier said than done. At a time when her twin was busy meeting new clients, setting up his own practice, and besotted with Mercy, she'd essentially lost his companionship. Instead of being alone, though, she'd turned to find Karl Van der Vort at her side. Over the past days he'd become a friend. A good friend. In a way, it made sense. She'd always felt more comfortable with her brother and his pals than the giddy I-think-he's-looking-at-me! girls. Gooding was such a small town, Karl always knew why they were paying the house call as well as who the patient was. Taylor implicitly trusted he wouldn't break the confidence of any of her patients. In many ways, he shared the burdens, concerns, and joys of her practice far more than Enoch ever had in Chicago. The realization stunned her.

"I'll set your bag down. There. Now go have some tea and warm up."

She smiled. "You'll be warm by your forge in a few minutes. Good-bye."

Walking down the steps to the buggy, he called back, "See you soon."

I'm counting on it.

◦◦◦◦

"A month. That's all it's going to take. Mercy's going to be standing beside me at the altar a month after I met her—which means I have two weeks and two long days to go."

"Impossible." Taylor stabbed a clothespin onto the sheet while Enoch held the other end out of the dust.

The wait does seem impossible, but I'm not going to agree with her. This wasn't a time for banter. Upon meeting Mercy, he'd declared she'd be his wife and gone about courting his lady. Surely his twin comprehended his serious intent once she'd seen him in action. Only now, from her succinct answer, he realized she hadn't gotten over her initial skeptical reaction.

"Nothing is impossible with God. God gave me this love for her. I have faith He'll give her the same love for me."

"Even if—and that's a big *if*—Mercy shares your feelings of affection," Taylor said, cramming on a few more clothespins, "a month is hardly a proper courtship."

Enoch hooted. "Since when was propriety important to us?"

"It's not just you, Enoch. Mercy's a mother. She has to consider her child."

"Of course we'll consider Heidi. I already decided we'd have her carry a basket of something—I'll have flowers railed in." He felt inordinately proud of himself for having thought of that way of including her in the ceremony.

Pushing several damp strands of hair off her cheeks, Taylor gave him an impatient look. "I wasn't referring to the ceremony. Remember the Melverts?"

"Aw, Taylor, that's not even a logical comparison. Mercy, Heidi, and I will be happy together. That old man married Casey and Jan's mother and put them through purgatory."

"Or so they thought. That household was in an uproar for years. I'm still not convinced it was his fault."

"You never liked darling little Jan and her frilly parasols."

"Avoiding her became a pact among the girls. Spoiled little Jan stabbed us all with the tip of her parasol whenever no one was looking. I wouldn't be surprised in the least if she bedeviled that poor man. Her mother shamelessly indulged her."

Grabbing a fistful of wet dishcloths, he thrust them to the side. "Mercy does not indulge Heidi."

"She dotes on her, and rightfully so—" Taylor held up a hand. "But if you do get married, Mercy will suddenly have to divide her time and attention. Heidi isn't accustomed to having to share her."

"When we get married," he said, locking eyes with his twin, "Heidi will be gaining a daddy's affection."

"Don't rush things." Taylor shoved the dishcloths back one at a time. "I never thought I'd say this, but Grandmother was right. 'The achievement isn't worthwhile if it requires no endeavor.' "

"Bunk. God's grace is free."

She shook her head. "No. It was bought at the dearest of costs. Christ achieved it—we received it."

"True. It was His gift. The only thing more wretched than our taking that gift is refusing it, because we need it so desperately. The love God's given me for Mercy is the same type of gift. I'm not about to turn my back and walk away. I'm running full tilt toward it."

"The only thing you need to run toward is the telegraph office to send off that advertisement for a housekeeper."

"I've been thinking . . ."

She pointed a clothespin at him. "That's what landed us here."

He grinned. "It sure is."

"Lean over here."

"Why?"

"I want to check to see how bad the damage is." Before he could ask, she started prodding and poking at his head with her fingertips. "A horse had to have kicked you somewhere here. I'm sure of it. That's the only possible explanation."

181

"Sis?" He waited until her brows raised in silent query. "Which one of your patients kicked *you*?"

"None of them. It's contagious. I've grown quite mad, living with you."

"Then you ought to be relieved that I'll be moving out once I marry Mercy."

"You're counting chickens."

"I'm a vet. We're experts at these things. I just saw one in the kitchen, as a matter of fact."

"It would be better if you were an expert at hiring a house-keeper so we'd have one here to fry that chicken. I'm already trying to get the men in town to think of me as a physician, and they're seeing me doing laundry and other domestic chores. In their eyes, it undermines my professional credibility. I'm going to nag you unmercifully."

"Nothing you do can take Mercy away from me."

Taylor gave him a jaded look. "It's impossible to steal what never belonged to you. Don't get me wrong—I like Mercy. Someday she'll make a wonderful sister-in-law—but I'm talking about two seasons or two years from now. Not two weeks!"

Enoch planted his feet and crossed his arms. "I'm resolved."

"You're ridiculous."

"I'm fetching her in fifteen minutes. I said we'd pick up Heidi from school and take a stroll. It's astonishing how much I can learn about Mercy from her."

"You're using a daughter to spy on her mother?!"

"No. It's not like that."

"It's conniving and invasive, and it takes advantage of a little girl."

Jaw tight, Enoch stared at his sister. On one hand, he ought to be pleased she felt protective of Mercy and Heidi; on the other, her low opinion of him felled Enoch. *The only way she's going to understand is to see us together.*

So fifteen minutes later he returned with them, and Heidi skipped into the house ahead of them. Mercy gave him an apologetic smile. "She's curious."

"She's also charming, like her mother." He motioned her in. And at that moment, Heidi let out a shriek.

Fourteen

Enoch and Mercy raced inside. The second he saw his sister hastening to Heidi, he held Mercy back.

"I see you've found my skeleton. I named him Wilhelm. I'm Dr. Bestman. You must be Heidi."

"Yes, ma'am. Is he dead?"

"A long time ago. Probably . . ."

"Twelve years?"

Laughter tinted his sister's voice. "Maybe even twenty or thirty. But I use him to help me explain to people when they get hurt how I can fix them up. You see, the Bible says we are fearfully and wonderfully made."

"Mr. Wilhelm is fearful made, all right! He made me scared."

"You may hold my hand if you'd like. He's nothing but a pile of bones my brother and I wired together."

"Really? Like 'Dem Bones'?" Heidi launched into a creative rendition of the song.

"That girl's going to give us a run for our money." He looked down and watched as comprehension widened Mercy's eyes.

"Hello, Mercy." Taylor smiled at them. "Why don't we have Heidi keep me company while you go for a stroll? I could use some help."

Thanks, Sis.

A stroll along Gooding's boardwalk would invite folks to stop and chat, but Enoch wanted time alone with Mercy. Going to the wooded area across from the train station would only set tongues afire. So instead, he tucked her hand in the bend of his elbow and led her through the kitchen, toward the back door.

Her steps stuttering, Mercy made sounds of awe as they went past the worktable. Spread out with scientific precision, as if it were being dissected, lay a plump fryer. The legs, thighs, and wings had already been cut off, then placed back close together as if to approximate the bird waiting for a frying pan. "How did she carve it up like that? So perfectly?"

"Probably used a scalpel." He smiled at her amazement. Mercy then remained utterly silent the whole time he walked her out to the barn.

The weak evening sun slanted in on them, capturing her and illuminating the golden strands in her light brown hair. Enoch stopped and held both of her hands. "Mercy Orion, it's been two weeks since we met, but in my heart I feel like it's been a homecoming."

"What a lovely thing to say."

"It wasn't supposed to be lovely. It was supposed to be loving."

Her breath hitched and color suffused her cheeks. "If I could get away with it, I'd wed you today."

She pulled her hands away. "I find I've lied to you." Uncertainty flickered in her deep brown eyes.

The meals at her place . . . the late night coffee and desserts . . . I couldn't have misread all of that. "In what way?"

She bit her lip and seemed to search for words. "I said I didn't think men would appreciate being compared, so I wouldn't do so."

"And memories of Hamilton . . . ?"

She smiled. "You recall his name. Yes, well, Hamilton was a childhood friend. I knew him all my life. As you've pointed out, our acquaintance is quite recent."

She paused, and Enoch felt the pounding of his heart accelerate.

"Yet in that time, though I cannot explain how, I've come to feel I know you every bit as well as I'd known him after we'd grown up together and begun to court. Due to my own grief, then out of concern for Heidi, I've not considered a future with a man. At the risk of sounding horribly cliché, this has all taken me by surprise."

"Surely you sensed my interest."

"Of course I did. I refer to the emotions that have taken root and the speed with which they've flourished."

Her admission made him want to whoop with joy. Enoch fought the urge to grab her and give her a kiss. Instead, he took her right hand, lifted it, and looked over it. Their eyes met. Sparkling as hers were, he knew she'd not just mouthed words. They'd come directly from her heart. "Sweet pea, I'd be honored . . ." he said and then kissed the back of her hand, "if you'd be so kind—" he kissed it again—"as to allow me to pay you court."

She made some response, but breathless and stammering, she made no sense whatsoever.

"Shall I take that as a yes?"

"Please!"

He again kissed the back of her hand, and as she lowered it, Enoch wouldn't let go. "You may as well know something about me right away. About my family. Convention and propriety were constraints rarely observed anywhere at home except the front door and the dining table."

"Since your sister is a physician, I gathered that your family is . . . avant-garde."

"Was. It's just the two of us now." He stepped closer, leaving a scant two inches between them and lowered his voice. "But I'd like to change that. Soon."

A soft little sigh was all the answer he got.

"If I were proper, I'd settle for those gentlemanly kisses from a second ago." Slowly, he curled one hand around her nape. The slight pressure of her hand over his heart stopped him.

"You are a gentle man, Enoch Bestman. A strong and gentle man."

He accepted her praise and continued to dip his head, intent on claiming that kiss.

But her hand exerted a little more pressure and her head turned ever so slightly away. "You're honorable, too."

"I'm impatient," he half growled.

Nervous laughter twittered out of her. "So I noticed, but if this were Heidi and a young man she'd known only a short time . . ."

"I'd tear him limb from limb." Still, he didn't let go. Smiling, he whispered, "And afterward, I'd gather up our daughter just like this," he cradled her to himself and swayed to and fro. "And I'd press a kiss here on her temple . . . and another one here on her cheek . . . and tell her . . ." He whispered something in Mercy's ear.

"You wouldn't! You couldn't!"

Keeping her head cupped to his shoulder, Enoch calmly asserted, "I could and I would. It's the easiest and most effective way to gain control over a bull."

"But—"

"If that man didn't want a ring though his nose, he shouldn't have acted like an animal in the first place." He held her tight. "You're going to make me be content with holding you, aren't you?"

"Aren't you content?"

He waited a moment. "Yes. But I'd be delirious with a kiss."

"Paul said he had learned whatsoever state he was in, therewith to be content."

"Sweet pea, I only spoke half of the truth when I said Heidi was going to give us a run for our money. You're going to be even more of a challenge. It's going to take me a lifetime to figure you out."

<hr>

As tolerant as a saint, Tasha endured Heidi dressing her that evening in bonnets, bibs, and a cape. Finally, though, she started twitching her tail and getting an impatient tone to her meow. Enoch tapped Heidi on the shoulder. "That's definitely a 'Put me outside' sound, because kitties can't use chamber pots."

Heidi giggled as she let out the cat, then left the kitchen with her mother to put on her nightgown.

Mr. Michaelson sat back and nursed a cup of coffee. He'd been boarding at the house the longest and seemed to have appointed himself as Mercy's chaperon. "That cat doesn't put up with any nonsense or fuss. Along comes Heidi, and Tasha purrs and lets that little girl do whatever her heart pleases."

"I'm glad for Heidi."

Michaelson looked him straight in the eye. The man behaved in an avuncular manner toward Mercy. Probably because of his advice or meddling, Orville Clark hadn't been able to swindle Mercy, as he had most of the town's other widows. "Mrs. Orion—" Michaelson cleared his throat—"she's a lot like Tasha. Graceful and pretty as can be, but standoffish. Good woman's gotta be that way."

"Sadly enough, that's true. A stupid man is after what gratifies himself; a godly man is after what pleases the Lord and gladdens his woman's heart. With those priorities in order, other things fall in line just fine."

Michaelson set down his mug. "Sure am glad we sent for a vet."

"So am I!"

Heidi came skidding in. "Did you 'member the book?"

"I sure did. It's the Bible storybook my sister and I shared when we were children." They went to the parlor and Heidi snuggled beside him, looking at the book and sounding out some of the words. It wasn't long before the story was over and she'd fallen fast asleep. He set aside the book and played with the tip of her braid.

Mercy touched his elbow. "I'll take her upstairs, Enoch."

"No, not yet."

"Is she warm enough?"

I should have thought of that. "I'll keep her warm." Enoch lifted Heidi onto his lap and made sure her toes stayed beneath the hem of her heavy yellow-and-white-striped flannel nightgown. He wanted to cuddle her, enjoy carrying her upstairs with Mercy by his side, and tuck Heidi in together. He'd never put a child to bed. Concerned by his lack of essential fathering skills, he was determined to seize every opportunity to learn how to be the best daddy possible.

Mercy settled into the chair next to the sofa.

"Taylor was far happier playing with a microscope than a jump rope," he told her. "What are Heidi's favorite things to do?"

"Wiggle and make noise." Mercy smiled. "Heidi's always been lively." She regaled him with a few cute stories, then rose. "She gets heavy. I'll carry her upstairs."

"No you won't." Skimming an arm behind Heidi's knees and tightening the one about her ribs, he rose. Mercy lit a lamp and preceded him upstairs.

Grabbing fistfuls of his shirt, Heidi sleepily demanded, "Night-night kiss."

He couldn't answer her—at least not with words. Enoch drew her impossibly close and kissed her cheek. After slipping her onto the mattress, he stepped back and watched intently as Mercy whispered a prayer and kissed her, as well.

Enoch took Mercy by the hand, led her out of the chamber, and shut the door. "Did you see what happened tonight?"

"What?"

"She wanted me to tuck her in. Heidi wanted me to kiss her night-night. Me, Mercy." He smacked himself on the chest.

"It was darling."

"It was more than darling. She trusts me and accepts me. Until I met you, I scoffed at the notion of love at first sight. Even after recognizing I'd been wrong about that, I had to face three other hurdles. The first was whether it was God's will for me—and He led me straight to the Song of Solomon. Next I needed to know if you could have feelings for me, and even then, Heidi's acceptance was vital to family harmony." He traced the curve of her cheek. "I love you, Mercy. With all my heart, I love you."

Tears glossed her eyes and shaky fingers pressed against her lips.

I haven't misread this. "Mercy, marry me. Be my wife, my lover, and the mother of a handful of children whom I'll love as much as I do Heidi."

"I . . . love you, too, Enoch. This is all so dizzying."

He moved closer, trapping her against her wall and curling his hands about her slender waist. "Does this help?"

She shook her head. "Leaves me more breathless."

"Hmm." He dipped his head and kissed her. "All better now?"

She let out a small laugh. "Oh, Enoch, what am I going to do with you?"

"You're going to accept my proposal."

"Yes, I will marry you."

"Excellent." He started pulling her toward the stairs, then stopped. "Parson Bradle's already gone to bed. We'll have to wait until tomorrow."

$\mathcal{F}$ifteen

"Mama got enraged last night," Heidi blurted the moment Taylor opened the door to Edna Mae.

Taylor strove to keep from laughing as Edna Mae Cutter patted Heidi on the head. "You mean engaged, dearie." She then barged past Taylor and threw her arms around Enoch. "You darling boy! It's about time someone made that girl happy."

Stunned, Enoch tried to disentangle himself. "How did you know?"

"It's not a wedding without music, you know. Well, Daisy Smith lives too far out of town for anyone to go get her, especially since you're just having a small wedding at the parsonage, so when the parson went to get the county declaration forms for weddings, my husband suggested I play the piano. We're so happy to help you celebrate the pinnacle of your lives!" She beamed.

"Oh! And don't forget to invite Old Mrs. Whitsley," Mrs.

Cutter called out as she left. "It's a tradition for her to ask a blessing over the bride since she's Gooding's eldest woman."

"That's a sweet tradition," Taylor said. *But a very small parsonage.* Currently the guests included the Van der Vorts and the Clark family, since Heidi had asked if she could invite Fiona and Audrey, the Clarks' adopted daughters. *But unless we hang guests from coat pegs, we won't be able to take even a couple more surprises.*

"Yoo-hoo!" Hope Stauffer called as she came in through the Bestmans' back door. "Lord have mercy! Is everything all right?"

Taylor smiled. "Enoch and Mercy are getting married today."

"Ain't that the most wonderfulest thing you heard in a long time? Phineas is a-workin' on my sister-in-law, Annie. She's still a-scairt. Her husband—he beat the stuffin' outta her. Sins of that man still reach out of his grave and haunt the poor girl, but we're doin' our best to show her how good men can be tender and strong all at the same time. If'n all ya'll don't mind us a-comin', we'd be honored; but if there ain't room, could you mayhap squeeze in Annie and Phineas just so's we can help Phineas make her catch the marryin' fever?"

"Of course we'd love to have you all," Enoch said. Once Hope left, Enoch mentioned he'd gone to the barn and invited Lloyd and Ozzie since they were employees. He shrugged. "Having Hope's family won't matter since we'll need to move the wedding to the boardinghouse."

Taylor gaped at him. "How can you be so blithe? Mercy is going to be in a dither. It's her wedding day. She doesn't have time to fix up the place or see to details. I can just imagine what Mercy will say when she hears about this. Heidi's words were prophetic. Her mother's gotten enraged!"

He picked up an apple and started shining it on his sleeve. "Things'll work out. Love always finds a way."

"In this case, it won't. You can't see her before the wedding to talk to her about it."

"You'll do it for me, Sis. I know you will."

Not bothering to hide the irritation she felt, Taylor snapped, "What makes you so certain?"

"It's your job."

"My job is to either certify you as insane or to beat sense into you. I'm not sure which would be the kinder thing to do for Mercy."

"Go be my emissary. I trust you. You're my best man." He winked. "Your name recommends you, and the primary requirement is that the individual in question is to be the groom's best friend. No one else will do."

Her nose tingled and tears burned as she flung her arms around him. "I'm honored, and I love you. And yes, I'll even go do your dirty work."

He held her tight and kissed her cheek. "I love you, too. Thanks . . . for everything." As they parted, he handed her the apple. "Give this to Mercy and tell her she's the apple of my eye."

"I'll take it, but I'll give her permission to pelt you with it if she's so inclined."

She turned to Heidi. "Come on, dear. Let's go talk to your mama."

⟡⟡⟡

Thirty minutes later, Taylor returned home. Shutting the door, she called out, "Enoch, the wedding's been moved."

He came out of the kitchen with a cup of coffee. "I told you Mercy would be okay with it."

"Mercy can't have it at her place."

Coffee splashed in an arc as he swung the cup over to thump it onto the nearest surface. "It's not getting moved to a different day!"

"No. Now settle down. It's just that her boarders all invited themselves, and Clicky did, too. Then she asked me to be her maid of honor."

"She can't have you. You're already my best man."

"I told her that. So she decided on Sydney since Sydney was the one who pried her out of her black widow's weeds and made her stop living in the past. But you need to go get her while I speak with the pastor. We'll still get you married today."

⋰⋱⋰⋱⋰

"I lied. You're not getting married today," Taylor told her brother without looking up from the exam table as he came into the surgery. Metal found metal. "There." She slid the long-handled tweezers in next to the probe and removed the bullet.

"With my help, we'll get this done in no time." Enoch sounded determined. "What happened?"

"Equal parts stupidity and spirits."

"Heard a bunch of knotheads traded lead at the Nugget," Velma said as she entered the house. "Reckon we're gonna have to patch you boys up outta the goodness of our hearts because you're just too plain stupid to stay out of trouble."

The man waiting for the doctor looked a bit embarrassed.

"It's a crying shame, too. Doc Enoch here's getting hitched and invited the whole town to the shindig. Only he's not having a bunch of soused cowboys ruinin' his weddin' day." Velma *ts*ked. "Think of all the good food and dancing you boys cut yourselves out of."

Widow O'Toole descended the stairs. "The ones who have to stay are already in bed. Velma can bandage that one up, and I'll stay and clean up the mess. You two go on to the wedding!"

Enoch and Taylor ran to the church. Karl was pacing away from them, then turned and rushed toward her. "I'll seat you. Everyone is waiting."

"No. That won't be necessary," Taylor said as she clasped hands with Enoch.

Looking grim, Karl said nothing. He stepped out of the way, and Mrs. Cutter started plinking on the piano. Taylor looked at her brother. "Here goes nothing."

"No. Here goes something."

They got to the front of the church, and Taylor stood beside her brother as any best man would. A minute later, Karl was standing beside her. He gave her an odd look and jerked his head toward the pews. She ignored him.

With flowers being scarce and having had no time in advance to ship any in, Heidi came down the aisle sprinkling leaves along the way. Sydney Creighton waddled in, looking as radiant as any expectant mother could. Big Tim escorted her, then sat on the front pew once they reached the altar. As Mrs. Cutter started banging "Wedding March" with more gusto than skill, Mr. Michaelson escorted Mercy down the aisle. Enoch sucked in a deep breath. Taylor wondered if he even recognized his bride was wearing their mother's gown.

"Go sit down," Karl murmured. "You don't belong here."

Irksome man. What was he doing, butting in to her family's business? Taylor figured she'd tell him and get rid of him. "I'm a best man."

"Yes, you are a Bestman, but today, Mercy becomes a Bestman, too, and she is the woman who belongs by Enoch's side."

Tim tromped up and stood by Sydney. In a loud whisper he said, "If Enoch gets two people to stand up with him, then Mercy gets a pair, too."

Taylor caught the look her brother and his bride exchanged. As long as they were amused, that was all that mattered. She reached out and took hold of Heidi's hand, then lifted her up a step so she could see better.

The wedding proceeded according to the *Book of Common Prayer* and the couple exchanged vows. Hope and Annie sang a duet Taylor hadn't ever heard. As Parson Bradle said the closing prayer, Heidi started getting antsy, then exclaimed in a loud whisper, "I'm bleeding!"

Taylor bent down. "You've lost a tooth!" Reaching for her chatelaine, Taylor realized she didn't have it on.

Enoch took the handkerchief from his pocket, squatted down, and rolled it up. "Here. Bite on this." He kissed Heidi's forehead and rose.

Her eyes widened. "Daddy's married to me! He kissed me!"

"I'm proud to be your daddy," Enoch said as he stroked her cheek.

The pastor cleared his throat. "You may now kiss your bride."

Enoch did so with great exuberance. At that moment, Taylor knew she'd never regret coming to Texas.

◇◦◇◦◇

"You'll have plenty to eat, ja?"

"Ja!" Piet nodded appreciatively. "Go now. Do not delay."

Karl didn't need his brother to urge him. He'd been champing at the bit to get over to the surgery for the past half hour. With folks still dropping things off and milling around, it hadn't been necessary. But now that everyone was gone—well, it was different.

Walking up to the front door felt odd, but it was only right. He did so and knocked. Dr. Bestman opened it almost immediately. "Karl! What's wrong?"

"What's wrong is that you open the door, and you don't know who is there."

"Doctors often treat strangers. What do you need?"

He pushed his way in, took off his coat, and hung it on the hall tree. "I need to talk sense into you. You have men here still?"

"I have patients."

"Men. The patients are men—ones who got drunk and violent today. Safety and decency dictate that you not be alone with men." He looked around. "Where are they?"

"In the patient room, upstairs."

"Woman—they could kill you in your sleep."

"Impossible." She smiled. "I never did put talcum powder in the cracks of the floor, so it still creaks, and my door locks. Furthermore, Karl, they're not in the pink of health."

"You know nothing about men. I'll pump some water and carry it upstairs. You will stay down here."

As he topped off their water glasses, Karl noticed all of the patients were fast asleep; but what difference did that make? They could awaken at any time. Every last one of them was a troublemaker. That did it. No matter what she said, he was staying until these three were long gone.

He found Taylor in her surgery, intently looking at something. Karl peered over her shoulder. "That is not right."

She let out a breathless shriek and whirled around. "What are you doing there?"

"Looking at that mess, same as you were."

Smashing into the drawer backward so it would slam shut, she pretended to give a careless shrug. "One of the men who had too much to drink probably got into things while we were treating one of his buddies."

"Now. They are all leaving now."

"I haven't discharged them."

"Yet." Harsh as could be, the word curled in the back of his throat. He set her off to the side and yanked open the drawer. "You have surgical instruments in here, ja? Many sharp ones, for to cut. Three men, they are dangerous, and you have weapons on hand for them to take and use. And then you think you would be safe all alone at night? Nee."

"It could be a child's prank, too."

Karl snorted. "A childish prank, perhaps. More likely a dangerous one. Men who like to scare women—they are men who go on to find scaring them is not sufficient. Cruelty is that way. Darkness always grows darker."

She shook her head—an adamant move. "You're not going to scare me, Karl. It was probably just what I hypothesized: the work of a drunken fool. If not, it was a stupid stunt, nothing more. I refuse to let my mind be taken captive by your wild imaginings."

He stepped back. Had he overreacted? The jumble of instruments and soiled cloths in the drawer was at complete odds to the pristine order she maintained. But a drunken fool might well have fumbled and done something idiotic like that. *The woman's living all by herself—undoubtedly for the very first time in her life, and here I am, scaring her.*

"Get rid of the men." He almost purred the words. "Because then we can eat the food from the wedding. Until they're gone, you don't want to get out the food—they'll eat it all!"

"I ate enough to last me for a month of Sundays. Since they're all asleep, you don't have to worry about their discovering I have food on the premises. Go ahead and help yourself . . . but then you need to leave."

"I'm not leaving. By those very stairs. That's where I'm staying tonight."

"So you're staying upstairs and you'll mind them tonight?"

He gave her an irritated look. "I have no skills with sick people. You will sleep in the parlor. I brought down a blanket for you. For the night, I will sit in a chair to ensure that all will be well. It is not right for you to be alone in the house with men." *She ought to appreciate that. None of the chairs in this place look very comfortable.*

"Your logic is faulty. You're a man."

Standing with arms akimbo, he glowered at her. "Everyone knows my character. They know I would not act in an untoward manner." *Even if the doctor is a woman. A young woman. A pretty young woman.* He ran a hand through his hair. *I can keep an eye on things. If those men so much as let a shadow fall outside the door of that room . . .*

"This situation has to be accepted," she said. "It's not going to change."

Intentionally misunderstanding her, he bobbed his head. "I agree. You must accept that this cannot be permitted. It puts you in danger."

"I sat at your bedside all through the night after your surgery. Tremendously high fevers and high-risk wounds require vigilant care."

He didn't want to know she'd been by his bedside all night. The feelings that stirred up were ones he didn't want to untangle and examine.

Being beholden to anyone didn't settle well. And to a woman? Especially for the kind of gentle care he now knew she gave? "Troublesome woman!"

She had the nerve to let out a small laugh. "Maybe I'm not entirely different from other women after all. I understand men universally believe the women around them are troublesome, if not entirely impossible."

Exasperating. Her clever mind came up with fine humor, but at a time when he couldn't possibly enjoy it. "I won't be distracted from the topic by your humor. While your brother lived here it was marginally acceptable for you to have some kinds of male patients. Now it is out of the question."

"Karl, I don't tell you how to run your smithy. Don't tell me how to run my practice."

"You can't run it if you're dead."

"I can't run it if my patients are dead, either. You forget, Karl, that I must make the most of every opportunity to prove my doctoring skill. Time is . . . well, three months isn't long."

"Here we go." Widow O'Toole bustled in through the kitchen door as though she'd been invited. "I thought we might need a few extra quilts tonight."

"That was most thoughtful of you, Eunice." Taylor gave Karl a victorious smile.

"Ja, it was. Here. I will claim this one. You ladies will downstairs remain while I go upstairs. If there is need, I'll get the doctor." Karl flashed a smirk at her and headed upstairs.

Her voice trailed after him. "It's too bad, since all the great food is down here."

His step barely hesitated. "I'll make a tray for you, Karl," the widow pledged, and he let loose a low chuckle of victory.

◦~◦~◦

Early the next morning Karl stretched the kinks out of his back and yanked on his boots. Delicious aromas lured him downstairs. It wouldn't be long before he was waking up to decent breakfasts. *Well, maybe not soon, but perhaps not all that long. What am I thinking?* He shook his head. The doctor was interesting and intelligent and . . . very challenging to be around. Pretty. Definitely pretty. What did it matter that she was a doctor if she could still be a fine wife and a good cook and a loving mother? All of those things would make for a happy home. He needed to think more about it. Yes, he did need to think more about it.

And goodness, she made sure his coffee cup stayed full of the best-tasting coffee he could remember drinking in ages. That should have made him deliriously happy—but she did the same for the three shamefaced, now-sober men at the breakfast table. Widow O'Toole was gone, but instead of serving leftover wedding dessert for breakfast, which didn't sound like a bad idea to him because he knew the bachelors would have been satisfied with it, Dr. Bestman had gotten up early, made flapjacks, and put them in the warmer. All three of those idiots started making cow eyes at her. Karl herded them out before their plates were clean.

He walked back in. "For being smart, that was about as boneheaded as you could have been. All these men want a woman who can cook. You should have scorched the coffee and burned the food!"

"I'll remember that the next time."

"There's not going to be a next time!" Karl stomped out and slammed the door.

⋄⋄⋄

The day kept building from that morning's set-to. At school lunchtime, the teacher cut an apple and sliced her palm. Karl had been installing another coatrack at the school and told her the doc wouldn't mind her bringing all the kids over to sit and watch her get stitched and bandaged up. As Taylor motioned for the kids to enter the surgery, Lloyd Smith remained in the doorway with some other students, hanging on to his siblings, his face pale. He whispered, "I'm sorry. Dad doesn't . . ."

The teacher smiled warmly at Taylor. "Don't worry about me, Lloyd. The doctor is a woman, and so am I. Besides, I need someone to stitch this. I can't do it myself."

He transferred his worried gaze toward Taylor. "Are you good at sewing?"

"I'm better at sewing people than clothes."

"Wow!" one of the kids shouted. "A pirate bone man!"

That did it. The younger ones broke free and ran inside to see the skeleton. Lloyd came in, but he was also the first one back out. Taylor finished with the teacher, and as the group left, Karl rode up in the buggy. "You need to tend to a couple of cowhands on Checkered Past. Don't know exactly what the problem is."

Depending on who told the story, the fight had started over a deck of cards, some cigarettes, or a woman. As soon as she got there, Taylor knew she had a handful of fighters who'd been egged on by others. Karl bristled and tried to stand between her and the men. Tapping him on the back, she said, "If you'll stand to the side, I'll do what I must."

"By standing here, I'm doing what I must."

"Nonsense. Watch." She opened her medical bag and took out a pewter flask. "I'll treat the wounded here. If anyone dares raise his voice, I'll apply this to his scalp."

"What is it?" someone shouted.

"Come read the label for yourself."

The cowboy got there and lifted the flask. "It's a big word," he mumbled.

"It's two small words put together." Taylor took a few more things from her bag.

"Rrrring. Ring. WWorrr-ummm. Ring worm. Ringworm." He looked proud of himself as he announced it, then his features twisted in outrage. "Ringworm!"

No one made a sound the entire time that she was treating the injured cowboys.

As they left, she shot Karl a look. "I ought to pour this on your scalp."

"You would give me ringworm?"

"That's doubtful. This smells so atrocious, ringworm would run away. I put a ring of worms around it as I filled it with the most obnoxious fluid I could concoct, so the name is honest. Brawn is a fine thing, Karl, but since I lack it, I use my brains. You need to have faith that I can handle these situations."

"In this case, I admit things turned out well. It does not mean it would always be so. Why did you say you should pour this on my head?"

Taylor slanted Karl an exasperated look. "I told you last night not to run my practice. Last night and at breakfast, you took it upon yourself to try to get rid of my patients. Then you invited the whole school to come in!"

"Ja. This was fun!"

"No, Karl. You know there are families where I see the mother, yet the father disapproves of women physicians. Children shouldn't be put in the middle."

Karl scraped some mud off his boots. "Each day when I see my scar, I realize the same injury only three months earlier would have killed me. Doc Wicky would have cauterized my leg and left the metal inside. The children—if they see you doing the job with their own eyes, when they grow older, they will remember you are able. I wasn't thinking of now. I was thinking of the future."

She inhaled slowly. Deeply. "Karl, that was the kindest, most hopeful thing I've heard since I arrived in Gooding."

"Never mistake my misgivings about your profession—they aren't regarding your abilities. The proof of your skill is undeniable. You should know I have put my name on your list."

Her heart did a little jig, but she knew he didn't want her to make a fuss. "Thank you, Karl. I know that's been a difficult decision for you."

"Ja, it has been. I fear because of the dangerous situations in which you put yourself. Just as I said your skill is undeniable, a man's nature when he's around a beautiful woman is also undeniable." He paused and looked directly into her eyes, his gaze holding hers. "You are the most beautiful woman I've ever seen."

Immediately she turned away. *Oh no. He didn't. He can't feel that way.* "We'd better get going. We have to stop by the Richardson farm, and you don't want to be stuck there at suppertime."

Almost two hours later, Dr. Bestman ordered, "Karl, stop the buggy."

"Why?" He gave her a piercing look as he tugged back on the reins. The last thing he wanted to do was turn around and go back to the Richardson farm. Mama Richardson had a to-do checklist for Marcella's and Katherine's wedding. Every bachelor around knew "Lasso groom for Linette" and "Change from double to triple wedding" topped that list. She'd just changed the date to Valentine's Day, and everyone knew the reason was to allow more time to achieve that goal. He'd barely managed to haul Doc out of there before Mama Richardson had arranged an afternoon of charades and an evening of recitations.

Lifting the earthenware lid to a crock in her lap, Dr. Bestman said, "I can't wait any longer. I didn't get any lunch. Did you?"

"Does that ever matter?" Karl reached under the seat to get the forks and spoons they'd started carrying. "Skyler, down." The collie hopped down and raced around.

Taylor said grace. They'd started taking turns praying when they paused for one of these quick buggy picnics. Asking God to bless the food was straightforward enough—and that was all he did when it was his turn. On the other hand, the doctor took a few extra sentences to praise God, to thank Him, and to seek His guidance and wisdom. It wasn't ever more than just a few lines—heartfelt words that indicated a connection with the Lord that Karl knew he himself lacked.

There were times those few words left him feeling convicted, and he'd eat in silence. The doctor never bothered to make conversation in those instances. Likely, she had plenty on her mind. On other occasions, her prayers lifted his spirits and he'd think to tease her or talk about goings on in the town. This afternoon was one such time. "This casserole—it's good. We'll eat it all and hide the crock."

"Piet might have something to say about that when he sees those noodles sticking to your shirt."

Karl chortled. He knew full well Doc wouldn't allow him to eat all of the food. She was like that—always making sure to save part of whatever she was given to share with him when he drove her somewhere. Times when she went out alone someplace close by, she'd still come back to the livery and not have so much as sampled the food. Piet and he kept silverware and plates clean all of the time now—something they'd never bothered with before. "You'd better have more. The minute Piet sees you with this, it'll be a miracle if he helps you out of the buggy before he swipes it from you."

"I believe in miracles."

Karl squinted into the distance. "You're a doctor. You should believe in science."

"God created the laws of science that regulate the physical world in which we live." Her voice grew pensive. "But I don't ever want to limit the Lord to finite rules. He's the God of infinite possibilities, so even as a physician I believe in miracles."

"You didn't have to explain all of that."

"I didn't?"

He wished he hadn't backed himself into this conversation. It was sinking into depths he didn't want to plumb. Karl grasped for the easiest excuse. "You have to believe in miracles if you think I'll have left any of this food in the dish by the time we get back to town."

Taylor laughed. She was like that—she'd look at him for a split second, and in that half-blink of time, she'd detect some of the uncertainty he felt, the nagging doubts. She gave him that breath of time to decide how he wanted to handle things—if he'd like to talk about the matter, or sleep, or ignore it altogether and skip to a different subject. Most women weren't like that—at least none of the other women he'd ever known.

But Taylor MacLay Bestman was a woman unto herself.

She laughed and let him off the hook, diffusing what could have been an awkward, Bible-thumping moment. "You and Piet are fortunate Enoch's gotten married. Now you won't have to fight him for the food."

"It puzzled me that you didn't go eat with him and Mercy while they were courting. He's your family. Surely you'll do so now."

"Sometimes. My brother is so head-over-heels in love with Mercy and Heidi that he doesn't even notice having the big 'family' of boarders around the table every morning and night. Suddenly, if it were just Mercy, Heidi, and my brother, Heidi might feel like she's missing something. I enjoy going over now and then, but I'm just as glad it's not for every meal."

One more look at the crock, and Karl gripped his fork. "I'm glad, too!"

Back in town, Taylor handed the food to Piet with great pomp. Piet fell upon it ravenously, and Karl yanked it away. "It is not just for you. The doctor—she earned it."

Lacing her fingers and pushing them together to force the fingers of her gloves to fit the wedges of her slender fingers more closely, she laughed. "I couldn't possibly eat another bite. You men enjoy the rest. Thank you for driving me, Karl. Good evening."

Karl watched her walk to her home. *That little sneak planned this escape, and that's why she had me stop so she could eat on the way home.*

In an odd way, the fact that she had taken the first opportunity to run heartened him. If she felt nothing, she'd not be bothered by his interest. Clearly, he stirred up something deep within her. He hoped to continue to do so until the tiny spark turned to embers and finally flames.

⋄⋅⋄⋅⋄

BANG! CLANG! BANG! CLANG! Karl spent much of the next day working on the forge. Taylor came in early that afternoon, insisting she needed to go check on Toomel. Karl argued with her, but she stubbornly insisted on going—alone. Finally he gave her strict orders. "Go, but only to Toomel. Check on him, and come right back. Stop nowhere else. There's a storm on the way."

She promised and indeed, she was gone only long enough to make that trip. It wasn't long thereafter when she came back to the livery again. He looked out at the darkening sky. Even if it wasn't green, this was tornado weather if ever he'd seen it. "Where are you going?"

"The Smith children are having some trouble."

"As many of them as there are, someone can load them in a wagon and haul them to your office."

"Not in this weather. Not with lung complaints. I oughtn't have said even that much, Karl, but . . . please make haste."

He went ahead and hitched everything up. "With this storm on the way, you stay there if Smith advises you to."

"Don't worry about me."

He didn't bother to respond to that ridiculous comment as he guided the buggy out of the livery. "How did you know about the Smith kids?"

"They sent Mr. Richardson in. He rode by and told me Grandma said it was urgent."

210

"Ja, then. Off you go." He sent her off, then kicked himself. He probably should have gone with her. Smith had voted against having Doc Enoch come; he'd been volatile about getting rid of Dr. Bestman. But a father's love could make a man do anything for his children—even send for a woman doctor.

A half hour later she wasn't back. But she'd probably just arrived, so of course she wouldn't be back. Besides, she'd need time to work with the children. He'd give her forty-five minutes more.

Forty-five minutes later, Karl told himself he'd give her a half hour more. He was starting to get antsy. If the children were in such a bad way, perhaps she'd need something. He'd seen her gather supplies for her pediatric calls often enough, so he was familiar with the sort of things that she sometimes used with the children. Karl picked up the key to her surgery that she tucked under a stack of his invoices whenever she left on a call. But when he got there, the back door was unlocked. Either she left in such a hurry, she didn't take time to lock it, or Enoch was here. He pushed the door open. An immediate flurry of footsteps sounded.

Sixteen

Karl heard the front door open and raced toward the sound. But by the time he got to the porch, passing wagons blocked his vision of whoever had just darted across the street and obscured any footprints that might have been left.

As he walked back through the office, Karl looked through her surgery. Doc always kept it so tidy. Everything looked right, but appearances could be deceiving. Somebody had been in the office—but why? The only thing that made him feel slightly better was that Taylor hadn't been home. Maybe that was it: They were trying to rob her.

He took the stairs two and three at a time and didn't bother looking at the room he'd used as a hospital room. Nothing of value was in there. Enoch's old room remained neat and undisturbed. But the window in Taylor's room yawned wide open. Karl strode over to shut and fasten it. Books by the bedside, a Bible by the oak rocking chair, and a neatly made bed were tidy enough. The top drawer of the bureau was closed . . . almost. A sheer bit of cloud-weight cloth edged in spiderweb-fine lace hung out about three inches. His blood boiled. Someone had plowed through her unmentionables. She wouldn't have left anything like that out. Knowing someone had done this would spook her, make her feel . . . Karl didn't want to think how a woman would feel about such a thing.

It wasn't right for him to see the contents of such a drawer, so he turned sideways and tugged it open. His palms went sweaty, and Karl rubbed them on his pants, though a second glance proved they were far from clean. He looked around, then figured he'd nudge that lacy whatever back into where it belonged with that thin volume of . . . poetry. Sliding the book under something that didn't weigh anything, while not looking, proved to be impossible. Keeping his back to the dresser, Karl peered beneath his arm. The crimson cover of the book reminded him of Doc's shirtwaists. As he worked it beneath the unmentionable, Karl broke into a sweat. *Eucalyptus. Camphor. Mustard. What else does Doc take when she sees kids? Candy. Ja. Candy. And camphor.* Doc's pretty, lacy whatever disappeared, and Karl slammed the drawer with such anger, the whole bureau jumped a good three inches.

Dr. Bestman needed his help gathering medical supplies for this house call, but Taylor Bestman—the green-eyed, surprisingly feminine-beneath-the-surface woman—needed his help even more. No one was going to scare her or bother her again. He'd see to it.

What else had been going on? Had the dirty mess he'd found her staring at in her surgical instrument drawer the night Enoch got married been part of a cruel plot? He was going to find out. Karl would wrangle every last detail from her. No more secrets.

Back downstairs he gathered a few things he'd seen her use

before with the children. He wasn't quite sure how much should be taken, so he took some of the white jars with the pretty blue labeling on them and carefully put them in a crate. A length of the white flannel, another of the red. He wasn't sure what else but figured she'd be able to make do if he forgot anything.

Karl hefted the crate, began to walk, and then stopped dead in the kitchen. It was a complete disaster. The clinic had been spic and span, but her kitchen . . . He'd never seen such a mess. His first thought was to question if this was another underhanded threat, but then the truth dawned on him. The doctor couldn't cook. All of the tasty food she'd been bringing him came after she'd been on a house call. Other women had made everything she'd shared. It all made sense. *When would she have had time to bake the cookies or make a cake? She didn't have milk in her house. How could she have made pudding?* All this time, he'd been under the assumption she could cook—he'd even instructed her to burn food! Couldn't all women cook? Then again, weren't all doctors men?

Life with Taylor as his wife would be far from normal, but it would be interesting—if he didn't starve or die of indigestion. She, however, was more than worth the risks.

When he reached the forge, Piet came out. "What are you doing?"

"The doctor's been gone awhile. I thought perhaps she would need these things."

Piet nodded. "This is good."

Karl suddenly changed his mind. He shoved the crate at his brother. "Go take them to her."

Piet's eyes widened. "Me? You want me to take them to her?"

"Until now, I've done all of the driving because of my leg.

But now my leg is sound. You should do your share to fulfill the contract. I'll finish that order."

Karl picked up his hammer. He needed Piet to leave before he tried to look for clues about who'd been in the doctor's place. Had he told Piet anything, Piet would be underfoot . . . and very likely get himself stuck under a bed again. Pounding and striking sparks gave vent to his rage, yet brought no satisfaction. Until he hunted down whoever dared disturb Taylor's place, there'd be no peace.

◦◦◦◦◦

Shedding her pelisse and peeling off her gloves, Taylor quickly assessed the situation. Daisy Smith's baby was just getting the hang of sitting all by himself—meaning he was six or seven months old; yet the exhausted woman looked to be halfway through carrying yet another child. Though average-sized, the cabin seemed to have shrunk because of the harsh sounds of several children's coughs. Miserable, the children wandered about and whined.

"Mrs. Smith, I haven't learned the children's names yet. While I get them to sit in bed and do a quick check, please write their names and ages on a scrap of paper and pin it to their right sleeve."

"I'll do that, Daisy," an older woman with a toddler on her hip offered. "Children, girls on the red quilt bed, boys on the brown."

Harsh coughs shook several of the children, but only the youngest three weren't struggling to breathe. It didn't make sense. As a rule, the younger the child, the more fragile the health. "So the bigger boys and girls are having trouble. Has anyone at school been sick?" Quickly gathering information, Taylor washed her hands and made a hasty circuit around the beds, pausing at each child just long enough to assess the rate of breathing and lip color.

"Suzannah, go sit over by the fireplace and read to Jackson for a little while. Mandy, why don't you help your mama and grandma by stacking blocks for the babies?"

Now Taylor could concentrate on the other children. She opened her physician's bag and pulled out her stethoscope. She had work to do. After listening to Gilbert, she nudged him onward and pulled Nathan toward herself. She listened in silence for a moment and then gave her instructions to Grandma. "Keep Nathan over by the stove there and rub some of this vaporous salve onto his chest. Then have him dress in a flannel nightshirt and help him to stay warm."

The woman everyone in town called Grandma nodded. "I'll do that."

An expectorant Taylor had made of inula helenium and althea officinalis would loosen the secretions. She drew it from her bag. The first spoonful went to little Lila. "She's going to require a warming pack, if not a poultice."

"I'm clean out of flannel," Daisy said, her voice crackling with pain and worry.

"There's a length in my bag." Taylor didn't permit anyone to reach into her medical bag. They could get poked or cut, or they might jumble the order of things. "I'll get it for you." After seeing to that and giving all of the other children a dose of medicine, Taylor coaxed everyone to have some tea. "The warmth will help keep the chest loose. Each of the children needs to be drinking plenty."

One of the little boys let out a rumbling cough. Grandma smiled. "Looks to be workin' like a charm."

Taylor walked over to Mrs. Smith. "How are you doing with Lila?"

"Not so good." Deep lines of worry carved haggard furrows in Daisy's face.

Taylor's heart went out to the woman. "Well, let's take a listen to Lila." She lifted the earpieces to her stethoscope. "She's too weak and tired to bring up the secretions." Without delay, Taylor took the child over to the bed and laid her so her head and chest hung over the side. Immediately, she massaged Lila's back directly over the lungs. "Sitting upright has gravity pushing the secretions downward. This position will allow me to shake them from the lungs and have them flow out."

The method worked. Taylor didn't mind applying logic and new solutions to problems if it was in her patient's best interest. In this case, though, she didn't delude herself. Once the medication wore off, Lila would be in distress once again. "I can leave you medication and directions on how to care for the children, but they still require far more care than you've been trained to render—especially Lila. She's exceptionally delicate."

"Little Lila, she's my only early-born babe. Puny and weakly most of the time. Sorta like a runt kitty. The cutest one that stays small and soft and steals your heart."

Smoothing back Lila's stringy hair, Taylor smiled. "You are a beautiful young lady, Miss Lila." Knowing how long the expectorant would last before it wore off, Taylor determined she could stay through an entire cycle or more still—even if Mr. Smith didn't like having her there.

He'd come into the house a couple of times already, casting visual daggers in her direction. Now, hand on the door, he stated in a rough voice, "Goin' to get the boys now." The door slammed.

Daisy looked at him like a whipped puppy. She whispered tearfully, "I called you without my husband knowing."

"You realized your children needed help and reacted appropriately."

"But all this medicine and everything you've done—we don't have any money."

With a houseful of children and a meager-sized farm, that fact had nearly shouted at her as she rode up. From Mr. Smith's conduct, Daisy couldn't very well publicly endorse Taylor's care. Taylor thought about it. "We can make a deal."

Daisy looked more terror-stricken. "Don't think of the list," Taylor said quietly. "I wouldn't ask you to add your names to it." As a guilty flush filled Daisy's cheeks, Taylor spied a jar on the table. "I don't know how to put up preserves."

"You don't know how to put up preserves?"

Lord, thank you for putting the right words in my mouth. "No, Daisy. I don't."

"Won't matter much," Gilbert said. "Pa says you're not going to stay."

Taylor turned to Grandma. "I won't have any chance to preserve anything other than life. So . . ." She looked from Grandma to Daisy and back.

"Better food's not to be found. Daisy's snap peas are sweeter'n any you've ever tasted."

"I'd be willing to barter canning for medical care. Of course, I'd provide the jars."

"I'll tell Pa."

Suzannah knocked Gilbert in the arm. "You will not, tattletale." The children began fighting. All of a sudden the coughing increased again.

"You children cease that at once. If you don't, the sour balls in my medicine bag are going to have to stay in there."

The children stopped immediately. "Sour balls?"

"Yes, sour balls. At least I think that's what I have in there today. I always keep a special treat in my bag, and I give one to each child when I leave if they've been very good."

Immediately the Smith children behaved better—but the minor exertion had tipped them back into wheezing.

"Guess I'll brew up some hog's hoof tea." Shoulders slumped in defeat, Daisy rose.

Hiding her revulsion at that cure, Taylor asserted, "A mustard poultice would be far more effective now." Truth be told, she had little else to suggest. Having dosed all of the children once with one curative and a combination of others, Taylor's supply of medicaments had hit an all-time low.

Lila then crept across the bed and raised her arms to Taylor. Lifting the little girl, she felt a tenderness wash over her as Lila straddled her hip and wound her arms about Taylor's neck. Her clinical side, telling her to remain detached, flew right out the window.

The sound of a horse approaching the farmhouse caught everyone's attention. "Something better work quick. My man's back with our oldest sons. Since you haven't cured the others already . . ." Daisy's voice cracked.

Footsteps stopped out on the porch and Taylor braced herself. She couldn't cure Mr. Smith of his bad mood. All she could be was accountable to the Lord for taking care of these children as best she could.

Knocking sounded. A man didn't knock on the door of his own home, so Grandma got up and opened the door. "Piet Van der Vort!"

Piet shouldered his way in. "Dr. Bestman, my brother said you might be needing these things."

"Let's see what he sent." She peered inside the crate. *Oh, Lord Jesus, thank you!* Karl *had* been paying attention to what she'd been doing all of these days. Surprising attention.

"So," Piet said, "are you ready to go now?"

Mr. Smith came in. "Yeah, haul her outta here."

Grandma stood up. "Okay. She's ready to go, Piet. Pick up that crate for her and take it right on over to my house."

Mr. Smith jarred. "What's this?"

"I'm not going to speak disrespectfully—not in front of anyone, not your wife and not your children—but I want to make sure these children get the care they need; so I'm taking the children who need Dr. Bestman's care over to my place. Soon as Daisy's done making us that mustard poultice, it'd be right nice of you to bring it on over. It won't do for her to take a chill with her expecting."

Taylor stood still.

Mr. Smith's eyes narrowed as he stared at her holding Lila. "That's my child."

Daisy's voice shook. "And we want to see our Lila grow to be a mama herself one day. Let's keep the doctor just a little while longer."

Mr. Smith ground out, "Thirty minutes. She gets thirty minutes."

Taylor nodded. For the next half hour she worked and prayed.

Grandma took her hand and whispered, "If need be, I'll come to town with the children. I can drive a buckboard."

Taylor prayed it wouldn't come down to that. Thankfully, it didn't. The children's chests loosened; the wheezing lightened. She mixed some teas and powders and left very careful instructions for Daisy and Grandma. They each agreed to take a shift so one of them would be up at all times with the children.

"If at any time you need me, send for me." Taylor shot a look over at Mr. Smith. Would he come for her if one of the children had a crisis? She dispensed last-minute advice and the promised sour balls.

Taylor left the house and went out to the buggy. As Piet put the crate into the rig, Mr. Smith stepped closer and glared down at her. "Don't think me and my kin are goin' on your list, because we're not. You're not welcome here. Don't come back." He turned abruptly and strode away.

While she had worked on the children, Piet had rehitched so his horse was also on the buggy. He assisted her up, then got in and spread a scratchy wool blanket over Taylor's lap and drove to town.

Rain started falling by the bucketful just before they pulled into the livery. "You can warm up by the forge while I find an umbrella." Piet helped her down and escorted her to the smithy.

Hearing the clang of hammer on iron warmed her more than any fire ever could. Smith's words had chilled her to the depth of her soul. How could a father be willing to sacrifice a child's health— perhaps even her life—in order to prove an argument?

"Your life is more important than your limb." Some of the very first words she shared with Karl echoed back to her. Karl would have sacrificed his own life rather than to have lived without his leg, but she knew he'd have gladly sacrificed both of his legs if it meant a child would be well.

"Sis!" Enoch fell into step with them as they entered the smithy and frowned as her teeth chattered. "You're half frozen."

"What are you doing here?"

"Since there weren't any lights on at your office, we thought you might have gotten back and were just trying to warm up here. Sweet pea, I found her."

"What is Mercy doing out in this weather?" Taylor asked.

"Showing off the new coat your brother got me," Mercy said as she came toward the fire's warmth and gave her an embrace. "I'm so glad you're all right."

"Perfectly fine." It was a lie. She felt sick inside.

"She looks fine. You needn't worry about her." Karl nodded, turned away, and started hammering again.

That's all? No "Hello"? Not, "How are the children?" Just, "You needn't worry about her"?

Mercy fussed over her. "You need to warm up."

"I'll be okay. Your coat is lovely!"

"The doctor is chilled, and she needs to eat," Piet tattled. "Smith, he pushed. He said she could have thirty minutes more to treat the children and then she had to go."

Enoch's jaw went square and tight. Taylor shook her head. "It's not our decision. I go when called. I help as best I can."

"He's a fool," her brother said.

In her heart she agreed. "He's their father. Where's Heidi?"

"Spending the night with the Clarks." Mercy smiled. "She, Fiona, and Audrey are inseparable."

The rain let up, so they crossed the open area and got to her back door. Enoch pulled out his key and opened the door. Just as she stepped into the kitchen, Taylor suddenly remembered. "Oh, dear mercy."

"Yes?"

Taylor laughed but blocked the entrance. "I'm home and I'm fine. I'll just take the crate and you two can go home now."

"Sis, don't be silly. Let us in."

"No."

"Sis."

Taylor couldn't stand it. This was the humiliating end to a terrible day. She couldn't let them see. But Enoch gave her a little shove. Mercy, on the other hand, wrapped an arm around her and nudged.

"You poor thing you, you're so frozen you can hardly move."

Enoch pushed his way in, shut the door, and lit a kerosene lamp. The entire mess of the kitchen became wholly and completely apparent.

Taylor heaved a sigh. "I'm so ashamed."

Mercy took a look around the kitchen. With every second that passed, her eyes grew bigger and her jaw dropped just a little bit more. Taylor's heart sank further, and she felt worse and worse . . . if that were possible.

Mercy collapsed into a chair. "Oh, praise Jesus! I've been feeling like such a failure around you, Taylor."

"You, a failure?" Taylor swung her arms to gesture around the kitchen. "Look at this. No, wait a minute, don't look at this. I can't cook. I can't cook a blessed thing. There isn't a meal I don't spoil."

Bafflement contorted Enoch's features. "You mean you really haven't been cooking for yourself?"

"How could you even imagine I'd learn at this late date? Singed, charred, burned—"

"Cremated," Enoch tacked on as he recalled.

"Exactly." She turned back to Mercy. "So you cannot possibly tell me you feel completely—"

Mercy laughed until tears were streaming down her cheeks. "But what about that chicken?"

"What chicken?"

"The day I came over and you'd cut apart that chicken so beautifully. I've never seen anything like it. Every piece was matched perfection. You've read hundreds of books, speak three languages, practice medicine, and up until that day, I admired you tremendously—but when I saw that silly chicken laid out with flawless precision I knew there wasn't a thing you couldn't do. I felt so worthless in comparison."

"Oh, good heavens. And to think I've been looking at how you can bake and cook, and how you keep house, and all those other wonderful things you do. Other than seeing patients, I'm hopeless."

Enoch sat back and looked from his wife to Taylor, then back. A slow grin crossed his face. One side of it faded and the other side of his mouth kicked up in a bigger grin still. "So."

Taylor looked at him. "So?"

"Why are you looking at me like that?"

"It's not just that I burn things. You know I'm helpless in a kitchen. You've been keeping that from her?"

"I haven't been keeping that from her. Think about how competent you've become—killing and dressing and plucking your own chickens."

It was Taylor's turn to laugh. "Hope Stauffer comes to town twice a week with eggs, butter, and milk for the mercantile. We have a deal: I give her two clucking, scratching, noisy things, and she trades me for one very neat, plucked, dressed pullet."

"It makes sense, sweet pea." Enoch caressed Mercy's cheek. "The two women admire what the other can do. It's just like the body of Christ. Each part has a different function, but they all work together."

"Exactly." Taylor nodded. "It's how the Lord wanted it to be— His children helping one another."

"Good. Then we're all agreed." Mercy rose. "Taylor will be eating with us from now on."

With her secret out, Taylor would no longer struggle with meals. But two things hung heavy on her heart: the number of patients she still needed on her list, and the fact that Karl was acting like he wanted to be more than a friend.

If she were honest with herself, however, Taylor realized she wasn't all that bothered by his interest.

Seventeen

I've got a small job for you." Tim Creighton stood by the partition in the smithy, giving Skyler a good behind-the-ears scratch.

Karl set down his hammer. "What can I do for you?"

"Sydney, her uncle Fuller, and I discussed it. We determined we don't want our baby growing up on Forsaken."

Karl jolted. "You can't be leaving!"

"No. We're changing the ranch's name, and I need you to make an addition to the arch over the entry gate. Sydney sketched it out. Think you can do this?"

Karl looked at the paper. " 'Never.' That is very clever. So now it will be Never Forsaken."

Tim hitched a pant leg and sat on the edge of the smithy's worktable. "Other than the salvation message, it's the spiritual lesson I want our children to learn most. I lost years of my life and untold opportunities because I couldn't comprehend how God would stand beside me in the fiery furnace."

Karl hadn't lived in Gooding long enough to have been there when it happened. He'd overheard gossip he'd rather not have heard about any number of people, but he knew grief had left Tim sorely bitter after he'd lost his first wife and baby. How had Tim gotten over that when he and Piet couldn't break free from the shackles of resentment because God took their little brother? Yesterday had been the anniversary of Lars' death, and Piet was upstairs, drunk. It was the first time since Karl's accident that Piet had drunk, and he'd made up for the dry spell with a vengeance.

Tim stared at the anvil. "There's nothing worse than burying a child. They're supposed to outlast us. I assumed it was my right to have my son grow up and work alongside me."

"No one faults you." *Least of all, me. Lars wasn't my son, but I still imagined him growing up, the three of us brothers living and working together far into the future.*

Tim shook his head. "I fault myself. Being a Christian didn't guarantee me I'd have no heartache; it promised when heartaches came that I'd have a refuge and strength. Instead of keeping my eyes on the Lord, I suddenly looked only at myself—and in doing so, I cut myself off from accepting the solace of God's loving presence and the consolation of knowing my family and I would be reunited for eternity."

Tim's statement set an avalanche of thoughts into motion. Karl tried to quell his emotions—yet for the sadness that welled, shafts of hope started shining through. "The doctor—she says heaven wouldn't be heaven if there were no children or babies there. That notion carries much truth in my heart."

A smile split Tim's face. "That's a fine image. A comforting one." Drumming his fingers on the sketch, Tim thought for a moment or two. "By weeping over Lazarus, Jesus showed us that grief is normal. My problem started when I wallowed in my grief and cut myself off from God and the people I loved. One day I woke up to a startling realization: Clinging to my anger and sadness didn't make me feel any closer to those I'd lost."

"No, it doesn't," Karl agreed under his breath.

"I'd forsaken my past and forfeited my future—and it shamed me. Louisa and Timmy would have wanted me to be a better man than that. I'd been shaking my fist in God's face, yet I'd squandered every opportunity He'd given me."

"You?" Karl couldn't hide the surprise in his voice.

Tim grinned. "Yeah, me. Repenting and resting in God's promises isn't easy. But I do know that I've never regretted doing either."

Concerned that he might reveal too much about himself or show too much emotion, Karl changed the topic. "You might not regret repenting, but that is because you have never read your cousin's diary, like I did as a boy." As Tim started chuckling, Karl added, "If I had repented, I couldn't have told everyone she was in love with the storekeeper who had hair growing out of his ears."

Tim studied him. "Psalm nine, verses nine and ten is what gave us the idea for adding *Never* to the ranch's sign. 'The Lord also will be a refuge for the oppressed, a refuge in times of trouble. And they that know thy name will put their trust in thee: for thou, Lord, hast not forsaken them that seek thee.' You're talking about assessing whether the benefits of what you gain are worth what you'll relinquish. If you ask me, it's one of the best deals you'll ever get." A smile creased his face. "Better than telling all about your cousin's secret admiration for the hairy-eared shopkeeper."

Karl managed a chuckle. The conversation was too personal, too convicting. He tapped a pencil on the sketch. "After I finish this rack, I'll ride out and take measurements for the sign and get to work on it right away."

"Thanks."

After Tim left, Karl couldn't separate work from the message the sign carried. Forsaken. Never forsaken. All this time, he'd felt God had abandoned him. *God was to be my refuge in times of trouble. That verse—it pointed out how I was to seek Him and trust in Him. I did neither. Forsaken—I've forsaken Christ; never forsaken—He's never forsaken me.*

Squinting at Sydney's sketch more carefully, Karl tried to determine whether she'd intended for the word *Never* to be in italics or if it was simply the slight slant to her ornate penmanship. Under normal circumstances, he'd have paid more attention—but Tim had gotten him thinking. *Even so, heaven holds a million children. What would it have hurt for God to have let us keep Lars?*

Shame scalded Karl as he caught himself having that thought. *I felt I deserved to live a life without sorrow, or I shouldn't have to accept God's sovereignty.* Fingers tightening around the paper until *Never Forsaken* lifted off the worktable like a banner, Karl stared at that stark and beautiful truth. *Heavenly Father, I beg your forgiveness. I've been so foolish and stubborn.*

After he prayed, Karl felt a sense of serenity he'd lacked for years. Finally the chains of doubt and pain had fallen away— unlocked by the key of faith. As he pulled iron from the fire and started hammering, a hymn started going through his mind, the lyrics keeping the heartbeat-like cadence of strike and rebound strike of his hammer. *"Whe-en. Pea-eace. Like. A. Riv-er. A-ttend-eth. My. Way."* He set down the hammer and sang, " 'When sorrow like sea billows roll. Whatever my lot, thou hast taught me to say, It is well, it is well with my soul.' "

Piet trundled in from the outhouse. "Doc Enoch wants you to go see him at the barn."

"All right."

"I'm sure it's about his sister," Piet added. "He's concerned, and he doesn't want to worry her. Otherwise, he'd talk to you anywhere, anytime."

Eager to share the good news of having returned whole-heartedly to the Lord, Karl whipped off his apron. "There's no better time than now."

"Wait awhile." Piet hung his head and mumbled, "Till I feel better, so I can go, too."

Karl wondered how his brother would take the news that he'd gotten his heart right with God. Should he tell Piet first? Or tell him at the same time as Enoch? "When will you be better?"

Heaving a sigh, Piet buried his head in his hands. "Not for hours. Go. Tell me what he says."

"I will."

Piet gave him a bleary-eyed look. "You said nothing, so I will. I have no excuse. I got blind drunk, but it didn't take away the grief. Nothing brings back our Lars. God—He let me keep you, and I promised to stop drinking. I went back on my word. But I won't. Not again."

Karl wrapped his arm around his brother's shoulder and led him toward the stairs. "I pray you won't. But God is faithful to His promises even when men aren't. So go sleep the rest of this off. Instead of dwelling on the sadness left by losing Lars, why don't we begin to remember the joy he brought us while he was with us?"

"Hmm." Piet trudged upstairs.

Karl fought the impulse to go check on Taylor. Recalling seeing her open the back door to Widow O'Toole's a short while earlier, he knew for the moment she was fine. With Skyler trotting alongside him, he made a beeline for Enoch's barn.

The inhabitants of the barn were always a surprise. A soft touch, Enoch only had to be shown a sick or suffering animal and he'd render aid. Sensing that, children counted on Doc Enoch to help them rescue whatever animal earned their pity. At present a piglet was the celebrity. Emmy-Lou Stauffer had helped Enoch with splinting her piglet's broken foreleg, and children wandered in after school to see how Pinkie was faring.

Nearly a dozen hens fluttered and hopped about as Enoch opened the small door and came out into the yard. "Good morning, Karl!" he called.

"It's not a good morning; it's a great morning." When he'd started over to the barn, he'd savored the sense of rightness and peace within his spirit. Suddenly, another emotion joined it: elation. He'd always tended toward being optimistic, but this differed from that. He'd lived on the edge of darkness for years, and now Light flooded his soul. "You're the first to know what a fine day it is."

Enoch grinned. "Did you win another hammer toss against Piet?"

"Far better than that. I didn't walk over here alone. I'm walking with the Savior again."

"Praise God!" They went into the barn and Enoch gladly listened to his testimony, then they prayed together.

Afterward, Karl looked around. "What do you have going on here?"

"A horse with lampas. Some places, the blacksmith does the equine dentistry. Other places, the liveryman acts as the 'hoss doctor.' It's a nasty case. I thought to have you assist me."

"Ask Smith. He's the expert around here. Till you came, he

kept the animals patched together as best he could. For lampas, he favored stabbing the roof of the horse's mouth with a hot stick. The first time I saw him do it, I thought it was barbaric, but he didn't have anything else on hand to use. Second time, he could have used something different and just plain didn't bother. I didn't have the stomach to watch a third. Struck me as a cure being worse'n the problem."

"Ah. Now it all makes sense. He made it clear that he voted against my coming, and he's been hardhearted to Taylor. Our arrival equated with a loss of income for him, but Lloyd working for me helps make up for it."

"Whatever he earned was under false pretenses. He was the animal's equivalent to that quack Doc Wicky. Piet says you needed to tell me something." He patted his leg and ordered, "Skyler, stay put."

An odd expression crossed Enoch's face. He glanced down at Skyler. "Actually, I need to show you something. Come over here." They walked to the far corner of a stall, and Enoch squatted down.

Karl hunkered down, too, and nearly lost his balance when he caught sight of what was in the box. "Those pups are—"

"Nursing off a cat. Accepting mamas, cats are—I've seen one nurse skunk kits." Enoch studied his expression. "So that's not what you noticed. Blood shows—or doesn't, as the case may be. White was counting on selling off Queenie's pups. He's fit to be tied."

"Her litters bring top dollar. She's the best coon dog for miles around. Only this time . . ." Karl lifted a mewling little puppy and a rueful chuckle rumbled free. "This isn't a purebred. Nowhere near pure. Handsome rascal."

"You ought to think so." Enoch swiped the puppy. "Skyler's

the sire. First couple of weeks, it wasn't readily apparent, but it's glaring now, and White was set to drown them."

Outrage surged. "Not while I'm still breathing!"

"They won't suit his needs, so they're worthless to him." Mewling and grunting, the pup tried to nip Enoch's fingertip, so he stuck him back in the box. "One of the kids brought in the litter. They'll fare well enough since the cat has plenty of milk."

Widow O'Toole entered the barn, a covered birdcage in her arms. "Doc Enoch, could you please come take a peek at Goldie?" She pulled the cover off the cage, and the canary let out a poor excuse for a song. "She was fine just yesterday. I love her so. Millie and Daniel gave her to me, you know."

While Enoch went to examine the canary, Karl sat in the hay and stole the pups one at a time for a good look. White was an idiot. He didn't get exactly what he had expected, but how could he ever want to do away with these helpless little balls of fluff? They'd undoubtedly be as smart as could be and easy to train. Good with children. Delightful and loyal, too. Certainly a far sight better looking than anything Queenie ever had before.

Goldie let out a trill. "Oh, that's so much better! I can't believe I missed that thread. What a horrifying accident. It could have cost Goldie her life."

"She probably thought it was a worm." Enoch sounded quite soothing. "I'll carry her cage back for you. It must have grown heavy for you. Before we go, you might take a look over in that stall. Karl's got puppies."

"Puppies?" A moment later, Widow O'Toole was kneeling in the straw and hay beside him. "May I?" She didn't wait for an answer but scooped up a pair. "Aren't they beautiful? They favor Skyler."

"Ja, they do." Karl couldn't hide the pride in his voice.

Enoch crooked a brow. "White was ready to drown them because they favor Skyler."

"That dreadful man. Just yesterday he told that new family that's moving here to have Velma deliver their baby because no one could trust a woman doctor. Is there no end to the paltry hearts and narrow minds some of these men are showing?" Cradling the puppies close, she cooed, "At least you don't know they're being mean. Poor Dr. Bestman—she's getting the same treatment. Men look at the outward appearance and judge her as being less than what they want. According to them, she's not good enough for them to sign on as a patient—never mind the facts that she's far better educated and has proven her skill several times over by now."

"Beginning with my surgery," Karl tacked on.

"And Mr. Toomel's shoulder. After each time, more folks saw reason." Widow O'Toole made an aggravated sound. "Even so, at this rate, there won't be anywhere near a hundred names on the list by March."

"I've covered Goldie's cage." Enoch looked over the stall gate at them. "The barn's far too drafty for her. I'll carry her back to your place for you."

"Thank you." She popped to her feet quite spryly and followed Enoch outside.

Karl didn't move. Thoughts assailed him. Taylor was better educated, more competent and cultured, and more forgiving than anyone else in town . . . her brother included. If she'd been male, the mayor would have sprained his shoulder, patting himself on the back for his town attracting such a professional. If anyone had been tested by fire and proven their mettle, surely it was she.

Anguish twisted within him. *Some of that fire is my fault. Because she's different, I first didn't support her. Remaining silent is just as wrong as to do the wrong deed. It's impossible to remain neutral in the face of prejudice or cruelty, and that's truly what it boils down to. I'm just as wrong as those men who don't want a woman doctor and refuse to sign up on her list of patients. Even worse because I didn't think. I purposefully didn't see or hear anything. She knew I wasn't walking with Christ and still befriended me, yet I never once considered that I would be an unsuitable mate because I was a prodigal son. Lord, never let me forget that loving Taylor means embracing all she isn't, just as it means accepting her for all she is.*

"Well . . ." Enoch's voice broke into his thoughts. "What do you think?"

"I want Taylor to have the pick of the litter."

"In the long run, it wouldn't be a bad idea for her to have a dog. Until things simmer down, I want to hire you to guard my sister."

"No need. I'm going to marry her."

⚬~⚬~⚬

Christmas fell on a Sunday, and it was the most beautiful Christmas Enoch had ever seen. He set Heidi down on the church steps. "Wait inside for Mommy and me." He walked back over to the boardwalk in front of the boardinghouse and held out his arms. "Here we go."

Mercy looked over at him. "I feel ridiculous."

"Feel cherished." He swept her up. "There's no way I'm having any wife I love walk through the mud to church."

"And how many wives do you have?"

He laughed. "One is plenty enough, ma'am."

"Good. You just keep it that way."

"Feeling sassy today, are you?"

"Yes, I suppose so."

"How sassy are you feeling?"

"Well, it all depends."

"Sassy enough for a kiss out here in the middle of the street?"

She thought for a minute, and he paused. "No." She smiled. "But sassy enough for a kiss right before we hit the church steps."

He laughed. "Yes, I guess this is a good Christmas after all."

Once he got there, he claimed his kiss and went up the steps.

"Daddy, I saw you and Mama kiss."

"Yes, you've seen us do that a few times now, haven't you?"

"Aren't you 'posed to wait till you're at the front of the church to do that?"

"Oh, sweetheart, I love kissing your mommy anytime."

Heidi tilted her head to the side and studied him. "Should I give you a kiss now?"

"That's a great idea." He knelt down. She gave him a peck on the cheek, and he returned it. "Ah, that was a wonderful Christmas kiss. Thank you very much."

They walked down the aisle and sat in their pew. He knew his sister would be joining them soon.

Stomping sounded. Footsteps time and time again could be heard outside the church as people knocked the mud off their boots. Laughter filled the foyer. Folks kept coming in. Hearty shouts of "Merry Christmas" were exchanged over and over again.

In walked Piet. In walked Karl. *That clod forgot my sister! On Christmas Sunday of all days!* Hands fisting, Enoch leaned over and whispered, "I'm going to get my sister." He started to ease to the edge of the pew.

But just then, Karl reached back and tugged on something. "Are you going to talk all day, or are you going to sit in church? It's ready to start."

"I'm sorry, Karl," Taylor said. "I just wanted to see the baby."

Karl turned and looked at the newest Bolington baby. "Ah, it is a beautiful baby, Mrs. Bolington." Mrs. Bolington beamed. Enoch had told Mercy about Karl's courting plans the night before, so they'd allowed others to take seats on their pew. Taylor's eyes widened when she saw she'd been ousted.

"We have many visitors today." Karl gently tugged her. "Come, there's room here for the three of us." He made sure that Taylor sat between him and his brother, the two of them forming sentinels on either side of her, insulating her from the ill will of some of the group.

Enoch looked down. His hands were still fisted. Mercy reached over, smoothed her hand over his fist, and stroked it a couple of times. "God's will, will always have its way."

Enoch thought about those wise words. *God's will, will always have its way.* It was true. He had to have faith. Whatever God wanted would occur. No matter what differences Enoch tried to make, none of this fell within his control. In the end, it came down to one verse. *"The fervent prayer of a righteous man availeth much."* He needed to be praying—fervently and more that acceptance and peace would fill the congregation and Taylor's practice would flourish.

Parson Bradle read the Christmas story from Luke, and they sang carols. The music rose to the rafters and reverberated in the cold air. It was beautiful. Afterward, congregants wished each other a merry Christmas and walked on out to their horses, wagons, and buggies again.

Old Mrs. Whitsley leaned heavily on her cane and beamed at

him. "Got us a mighty nice Sunday. Times were, everyone came to church. It's not that way anymore, but today most everyone showed up."

"Yes, ma'am. It seems everyone in the township came to worship. There are a few I've met only once, if at all."

Mercy leaned on his other arm. "Several of these people only see one another on Christmas and Easter." Exuberant greetings and hearty laughs supported her assertion. Greetings were exchanged, embraces held. Laughter bubbled up all around them. Kids ran about, playing tag. It didn't matter that the ground was damp, that little boys jumped in puddles and little girls screamed because the mud landed on their pretty dresses. Everyone was just delighted that it was Christmas Sunday.

Heidi tugged on Mercy's hand. "Can I go play?"

"Go ahead and have a good time," Enoch told her.

They exchanged a few more comments with Mrs. Whitsley and then the old woman toddled off.

Suddenly a girl's high-pitched scream rent the air and a horse and wagon whizzed past.

Eighteen

Heidi!" Enoch and Mercy croaked her name in unison. "She's right here." Hope's reassurance freed him to help and not feel he was abandoning his wife in a time of need.

Enoch saw his sister start darting across the churchyard. "Move for the doctor!" Karl mowed a path for her at an impasse and lifted her directly over Mrs. Richardson's swooning form.

Enoch cut across the other direction and met her where Bethany Richardson lay in the mud. The little girl's leg was skewed at an awkward angle, but Taylor only gave that a passing glance. Immediately she put her hand on Bethany's chest to make sure she was still breathing. It rose and it fell three times before Taylor nodded.

"She's breathing well." Taylor then inspected the little girl's head. Swiftly, deftly, her hands moved. "She didn't get kicked in the head." She checked Bethany's eyes. "Pupils are equal and constrict to light."

"Her leg's busted. What're you doing looking at her head and in her eyes?" Mr. Smith said. "Dumb woman don't even know what end to look at."

Karl growled, "That's enough out of you."

Somebody else stepped forward. "He's got a right to speak his piece."

"Yeah, he does."

"Yeah," others chimed in.

Taylor ignored them all. She lightly assessed Bethany's little chest, checking her ribs, then ran her hands down both arms, hands, and fingers, taking swift, careful inventory.

Mrs. Richardson screamed, "My little girl. My little girl. My little girl." Enoch caught her right before she grabbed her daughter.

"What are you doin' stopping her? Let her go. That's her child."

Enoch didn't release her until Karl brought Mr. Richardson over from beside Bethany. Enoch handed Mrs. Richardson to her husband. "If your daughter's pelvis is injured and she's moved right now, it might cause her grave damage. She can't be shifted whatsoever until my sister makes sure everything else is all right."

Some of those who were disbelieving a few minutes before suddenly didn't seem quite so sure of themselves. Enoch went to kneel across from Taylor as her hands efficiently mapped out her patient's hip bones. "What do you need?"

"Stay right where you are," she murmured. Taylor opened up the leather purse hanging from the chatelaine at her waist. From it she pulled some gauze in which she hid a small vial with a dropper. She didn't want people to know that she had narcotics in her chatelaine. Such knowledge could be dangerous, because if someone were desperate for the drug, they might rob her. Taylor didn't so much worry for her own welfare, which terrified Enoch, but she fretted because she knew the contents of the vial were sufficient for several doses. If someone were to ingest all of it at once, it could cause cessation of breathing. Enoch said nothing.

"What's she doing?"

"What's that for?"

Enoch wedged open Bethany's mouth, and Taylor quickly administered just two little drops under the child's tongue. Karl saw what was happening, but Enoch trusted that he'd say nothing.

Quickly, Taylor put the vial back into her chatelaine. She stroked the little girl's throat to get her to swallow. "Mr. Richardson, I've given your daughter some medication. This will help her swallow it. She'll still awaken when we move her, but I want her to have something already working to alleviate the pain."

Some of the drug probably got absorbed beneath the tongue—a trick their father had taught them long ago. The remainder would be absorbed more slowly in the stomach, but that meant smoother, longer relief from the pain.

The little girl groaned.

Taylor finally looked up. "Please step back. None of us wants Bethany to be frightened."

"Yes," Mrs. Bradle agreed. "Let's all give her a little air."

The little girl groaned louder, then cried, "Mama—"

Mrs. Richardson knelt in the mud. "Oh, my little girl. My poor little girl."

Bethany's eyes opened. "Mama." Her arms came up to her mother.

"Her arms are working." Taylor touched Mrs. Richardson's shoulder. "Have her move her left leg, but not her right." Mrs. Richardson was too upset to give the command. Mr. Richardson tried to kneel down, but tears clouded his eyes. Taylor pulled one of the little girl's arms from around her mother's neck. "Bethany, I need you to listen to me. One of your legs hurts. It has an owie. This other one here, the one that I have my hand on, I'm rubbing it right now. I want you to take that knee and bring it up for me. Just lift it up just a tiny bit."

She sobbed, "I don't want to."

"Just a tiny bit, sweetheart."

"My leg hurts."

Enoch got down. "Just a little. Come on, just a little bit. Heidi would do it." When Bethany opened her eyes wider he repeated, "Heidi would do it."

Bethany lifted that leg a few inches.

"Excellent!" Relief rang in Taylor's voice. "Heidi couldn't have done it any better."

Two men carried Bethany over to the surgery, then stepped out to allow the women to go in and help undress and clean her up. Enoch knew Taylor wished she could keep a select few there to help, but no woman was willing to be left out.

Mercy went home and got one of Heidi's little nightdresses. "I thought she could use this," she said as she took it on in.

Heidi came over and held Enoch's hand. "Daddy, is Bethy gonna be okay?"

"We'll wait and see, sweetheart. Her leg got broken, but your auntie can make it better."

"Okay, Daddy." With all the assurance in the world that her auntie could make it better, Heidi skipped off.

A few short minutes later, the door opened again. Taylor stood in the aperture, and women lined up along the far wall of the surgery. The variety of expressions warned Enoch that the situation was still volatile. Taylor nodded toward Bethany's father. "Mr. Richardson, we need to discuss the treatment for your daughter."

"Yes."

"Pa, what she says—do it," Linette Richardson said. "I trust her. She knows what she's doing. Pa, we need to do it for Bethany."

"Linette, you pipe down. This isn't your decision."

"And it's not yours, either, Daisy Smith," Linette shot back.

Daisy sucked in a deep breath. "That's no way to talk to your elders."

"You have no right to speak, Daisy," Velma snapped. "You were giving your opinion a minute ago, but Bethany's not your daughter. At least Linette waited until her little sis fell asleep before she spoke her piece."

"What we're going to do," Taylor said in a carefully modulated tone, "is have everyone leave with the exception of the Richardson family."

"No cause for that." Cutter planted his feet. "This surgery belongs to the town. We all care about the girl and have—"

"—made wise provision in your deal, Mayor Cutter," Taylor broke in smoothly, yet forcefully. "You yourself said the fathers were to make the decisions regarding their children's care. It's been that way throughout history, and you judiciously set that same guideline for Gooding. This decision is the Richardsons', and theirs alone. The rest of you need to leave now."

People started to shuffle out. Mr. Richardson cleared his throat. "Mercy, I'd be obliged if you'd stay. Not that I don't value the doctor's judgment, but you've got yourself a little girl, and since my wife's a bit on the emotional side here, I'd like a mother's opinion. Doc Enoch, you've got some medical knowledge, too. I know this here's your sister, but I'm expecting you wouldn't side with her just because of that. So let's hear what's to be said."

Taylor nodded. She went over to the table and checked to see if Bethany was sleeping before she gestured. "What's happened is that both of your daughter's bones have been broken in two places—here and here. As you can see, these bones in the lower leg are very fragile and thin, especially in a small girl. If I try to put very much traction on them, they're not going to mend properly. The leg will break, because the traction will pull it sideways. Though it would eventually mend, it won't knit together correctly. The best way to set a fracture like this so it does align and mend straight is to have Bethany lie on the table here at the surgery for a couple weeks. I'll affix long, flat cloth strips going down her leg and have a rope dangling from the strips with an iron hanging from it."

"An iron?" Mr. Richardson sounded incredulous.

"Yes, an ordinary iron." Taylor's voice remained factual.

"An iron," he repeated.

Taylor went to the kitchen, picked up one of the smaller irons, and brought it back. She held it in both hands, then set it down. Next she picked up Bethany's healthy leg, closed her eyes and balanced it in her hands, as well. "They weigh about the same. Try for yourself."

"I'm not good at small weights," the farmer said. "Mama, you try."

Mrs. Richardson tried, as well. "They're close."

"I don't want to be wrong on this." He looked at Taylor. "We have a boy in town whose leg is twisted. It got broken and the last doctor did a bad job when he mended it. That boy's always gonna be lame, and I don't want that for my daughter. Why would this work instead of making her leg turn out?"

"Because if I apply a heavier weight, her leg's not strong enough to handle the burden. Let me have your arm." Taylor patiently demonstrated with a heavier weight on his arm, and then a more temperate weight, showing how his hand would either stay straight up or turn to the side.

Richardson's brows shot up. "It makes sense!" Then he shook his head. "No one else would think to use an iron, though."

"The shape of something often doesn't dictate whether it can serve the purpose."

"Papa, do it," Linette urged him. "I've seen what other things Dr. Bestman's done. You know I've helped with a few small things in the office now and again. If Bethany has to remain here for a couple weeks, we wouldn't want her to be alone. You and Mama have to be home with the others, but I could stay here with her."

The Richardsons looked back at Taylor. She nodded. "Of course we would want her to be with Bethany."

"Then go on ahead. Setting it's going to hurt." Mr. Richardson drew in a deep breath. "Linette, you take your mama on outside now."

"Pa, I'll stay and help Dr. Bestman. Mama's going to need to lean on you." Linette went to her sister's side. "I'm going to be taking care of Beth, so I ought to see how everything's rigged up from the start."

"That would be wise." Taylor motioned to her. "Loop your arms beneath Bethany's and clasp your hands together over her heart. We'll slide her up higher on the table. . . ."

They set the leg and put it in traction. As soon as they finished, Taylor ordered, "Go home to your wife and daughter, Enoch. It's Christmas."

"We'll bring Christmas supper over here."

"Don't." She tilted her head toward Linette and Bethany. "Just soup and maybe a few cookies. Thanks for all your help."

He shook his head. "You did this on your own." Enoch turned to the Richardsons. "Don't stay too long. Remember it's Christmas, and you still have your other girls."

Mr. Richardson smiled sadly. "It doesn't feel like a very merry Christmas."

Taylor looked at him. "It was the best Christmas of my life when I realized your daughter was breathing and could move everything."

◇~◇~◇

Finally. The Richardsons left, and Karl yanked on his coat. He didn't really need it, but if things went the way he hoped they would, he'd be glad to have it in a short while. That morning he'd wanted to start off Taylor's Christmas with the news of him reconciling with God. Piet had tagged along like a lost, starving puppy and wouldn't give them a minute alone. The words that needed to be said were private. Now he'd go say them. He thought to sit out back to ensure their privacy.

"Karl!" She tipped her head to the side. "Are you worried about little Bethany?"

"I thought to come check on her and share some coffee with you."

"I'll get the coffee." While he prayed over Bethany, Taylor took a pair of mugs out the front door. A smile kicked up the right corner of his mouth. Let others see him with her. They'd know soon enough that she was his woman. He accepted the coffee, but before taking a sip, Taylor looked at him. Fatigue painted her features, but she'd never looked more lovely to him. "I'm not sure whether Gooding is going to give me a chance to prove myself. The resistance shown to me as I rendered emergency care today was significant."

"You're here for a reason. God brought you here." *To become my bride.*

She set aside her coffee and turned toward him. "You're an extraordinary friend. I recently came to a startling realization. It's logical when I think of it, but—" Color filled her cheeks and she dipped her face.

On the pretext of warming her, he'd adjusted the collar of her pelisse in the recent past. Now he didn't bother with subtlety. Sliding a hand along her jaw, he marveled. His rough, callused hand against the silk of her skin drove home the vast differences between them—differences like education, refinement, and wealth she never seemed to notice or care about. Desperate to know what she thought, he rasped, "What?"

"Please don't take this the wrong way."

Dread swamped him. He drew his hand away.

"Enoch was always my best friend. Since we came here and he met Mercy, his attentions shifted—as well they should. I knew that day would come. He's still more dear to me than I can express. It makes sense, you know—that having a man for my best friend all those years, it would be natural for me to be comfortable with a man becoming my best friend and confidant again. Of everyone in Gooding, you know more about my daily life and what's really happening. I know I can trust you. It's not something I see men do—to speak of having a best friend—women do it as a matter of course. And even though I've built strong foundations for friendships with Millie, Sydney, and Hope, I still know the truth. You're my best friend, Karl Van der Vort. Today you stood in the breach. You helped me get to Bethany and stood like a guardian angel so

I could do my best for her. I want you to know how very much I appreciate not just all you've done, but how you've lent your kindness and strength and offered your friendship regardless of the opinions of others."

Taking a long, scalding gulp, he let her words sink in. At first, when she'd spoken of her brother, he'd felt sick that she only held a brotherly affection for him. Then, as she went on, hope sparked. She'd acknowledged her trust in him, that he meant more to her than anyone else. Yes, even if he followed her reasoning, he meant more to her than her own twin. The woman loved him back! He just had to get her to realize it.

He wanted to choose the right words, say the things a woman would want to hear. A man making a declaration need not get down on his knee. That was reserved for proposing. Then again, depending on how things went, he might wind up doing just that. . . . For now, he covered her hands with his. "I've never been more proud to be a best friend. You've earned my admiration, Taylor." He purposefully left out any other hint of his emotions. "Everything you do, you do with all your heart. You're that way in your professional life, in your friendships, in your love for your family, and in your walk with the Lord."

"No, Karl. I fail. Often, I fail. I've spent plenty of time repenting and apologizing. Probably not as much at either as I ought. It's because of the very intensity and zeal with which I do things that when I'm wrong, I'm terribly wrong."

As you were about going off on house calls at night all by yourself. He didn't remind her of that. He wanted to keep the discussion channeled in another direction. "Taylor, I want you to know something. Suddenly everything has come into focus for me. I can see how I've wasted years of my life, and I don't want to waste any of my future by having the wrong priorities. It's important for you to know I've reconciled with God."

A beatific smile lit her face, and her green eyes shimmered as they filled with tears. For a moment, she was speechless. "How wonderful! I've been praying for you to find the peace that passeth understanding. Our heavenly Father must be delighted to see his son return home." She disentangled her hand and opened her chatelaine purse to pull out a hanky. Wiping away tears of joy, she let out a blissful smile. "This has to have been the best day of my life."

"Is that so?" *Should I propose now, Lord?*

"The cliché is 'saving life and limb,' " she said. "We saved Bethany's limb together today, and something even more precious than life—your soul—has been restored. Yes, this was a perfect Christmas!"

How I love her! She finds the good in everything and makes me want to be a better man.

Cold reality washed over him. He couldn't ask her to be his wife until she no longer felt at risk. It wasn't fair to taint what was to be a woman's most special time with memories of fear. His Taylor trusted him. As a friend.

Lord, I've seen those advertisements about asking for something for Christmas. They disgust me. But here I am, and I'm going to give you a whole list. Please safeguard Taylor and help me catch whoever is causing her problems. Take off the blinders so she sees the love I have for her and let her return it.

"Karl, I can't tell you how happy I am. Every Christmas I'm going to remember the special joy of this time we've had and the wonderful news you shared."

Sliding his hand over hers, he nodded. "Ja. Memories—they are like a forge where bonds are joined. The goed feelings, the happy and sacred ones we share now—those are ones I would want joined together in our hearts and minds."

∼•◦•∼

The next morning Taylor came downstairs to the smell of something baking, but she couldn't be too excited, because Linette's cooking meant a little girl was hurting.

Linette might make a good nurse. *If she were interested, I could send her back to Chicago to attend a nursing program. If she chose to go away for a while on such an adventure, how wonderful would that be?* Her sisters were getting married and no one was interested in her. It might soften the rejection and equip her with a way to provide for herself in the future. But how would Taylor explain that to Mercy? She counted on Linette's help with the boardinghouse and baking. The smell of the breakfast sure sweetened the deal. With a full stomach, Taylor figured she could get along with just about anybody.

She walked over to Bethany and smoothed back her hair. The little girl moaned restlessly in her sleep. Adults could endure pain; children, on the other hand, were so very innocent and helpless. Pain bewildered and scared them. Taylor bent down and pressed a kiss on her forehead, readjusted the blankets, and went into the kitchen. "She's still sleeping."

"I know." Linette took muffins from the oven. Their aroma blasted through Taylor, making her mouth water. Oblivious to the effect her baking was having, Linette continued on, "The mud in her hair is dry now. Later this morning I'll brush out the dirt."

"It's a going to take a while. Her hair's a rare mess."

Shuddering, Linette nodded. "I'll get to it straight off.

Mama will have a conniption if she sees just how filthy Bethany's hair is."

"Why?" Taylor looked at her in absolute amazement. "Haven't you all been that dirty before?"

Linette reared back. "Of course not."

"What've you been doing with your time?" Taylor grabbed a muffin and tossed it back and forth between her hands because it was far too hot to hold. She noticed with delight that it had raisins in it. "If I'd been living out here, I would have been swimming in the creek and sledding down that hill back there in the mud. I would have gotten filthy twenty times over by now."

Linette tried to muffle her laughter. "You wouldn't have!"

Taylor cocked an eyebrow and said nothing.

"You really would have?"

"Linette, worrying about what people thought would have prevented me from becoming a doctor. Some things you do because they're the right things to do—and you always do them. But there are other things you do because your spirit needs to take flight or you feel called. Becoming a doctor was both of those things for me—it was in my heart and soul." She pointed her muffin toward the window. "You'll see Widow O'Toole go by in about three seconds, and I don't doubt for a second that her spirits soar when she rides her velocipede."

Linette's eyes got big. "Does everybody have something they want to do that's different?"

"Mmmm. This muffin is delicious. Yes, everyone has desires. Some fulfill them, while others deny themselves and never reach for their dreams. Instead of ridiculing someone for being different, I admire them for their courage." She took another bite. "Ohhh, this muffin is good. God bless the hands that prepared it!"

Laughing, Linette put two bowls of oatmeal on the table. After they both sat down and prayed, Taylor swirled her spoon in the bowl—brown sugar and a big chunk of butter, just the way she loved it. "So, Linette, what's the thing you've always wanted to do?"

"I'm not real sure. We get the newspapers and I see things that other women do, like the suffragettes. Or you. I didn't know women could be doctors! Other than being schoolteachers or working in the mercantile or sewing, women don't have jobs around here. Those are the only choices I have since—" She sucked in a quick breath and blurted out, "I'm not getting married because nobody wants me."

Bethany moaned and let out a sharp cry.

Immediately Taylor left the table, and Linette followed after a few seconds.

"I hurt," Bethany whined.

Linette petted her. "I know you do, sweetheart."

"Of course you do, Bethany. What little girl wouldn't?" Taylor made a face. "After all, you had a whole horse and . . . and . . ." She stuck her forefinger in the air and spun it around like a wheel, trying to get Bethany distracted.

"Buckboard?" Bethany said.

"Buckboard! Yes. Thank you. You had a horse and buckboard roll over you and break your leg. Accidents like that kill grown-ups, but Jesus and the angels were taking very good care of you. You'll stay here for maybe two weeks. After that, I can put a cast on your leg. Since you're on this special table bed here, during the daytime, I can tuck some pillows under you so you can look out the window. Sometimes we'll shut all the curtains and you can take a rest or we'll just have some fun all to ourselves. And other times when I need to work, we'll make sure you have wonderful books to read."

"Can I have my friends come see me?"

"Yes, your friends may come pay you visits. Linette, how many hundreds of friends does your sister have?"

Linette got into the spirit of things. "Let me see."

Bethany laughed. "You're silly."

Taylor got down next to her and held her hand. "Okay, Bethany, I'm done being silly. Now I'm going to tell you what to expect, because big girls deserve to know what's going to happen." She explained about traction and boredom and discomfort. "In the end, it'll be worth it because your leg will grow nice and straight and beautiful."

"So I can dance with a prince on my wedding day?"

Linette leaned forward and gave her sister a kiss on the cheek. "Yes, so you can dance with a wonderful man on your wedding day."

What must it have cost for her to say that to her little sister? Especially after what she just said in the kitchen.

"I'll lay on the hard table if I get to have a pretty leg, then." Suddenly Bethany's eyes got big. "We're not supposed to talk about legs with men around. So what do we say if somebody comes to see how I am?"

Linette pointed at the odd weight on the traction and started laughing. "I think we should tell them Bethany's ironing is doing just fine."

Feeding and medicating Bethany and combing the dried mud from her hair took a while. They'd just gotten back to the kitchen and Linette had pulled their bowls from the warmer when Taylor heard a commotion. She walked out onto the back porch and saw four men. One rushed up the steps. Blocking the door, she asked in a sharp tone, "Gentlemen, did you need something?"

"We come for the girl."

"I'll ask Linette to step out and speak with you."

"Not her. The little squirt."

"This conversation is over." Stepping back, Taylor started to shut the door. It flew open.

Nineteen

The men pressed past Taylor and into the house. She grabbed hold of one man's suspenders and pushed another man back. Linette shoved the table and managed to nail another against the wall, then yelled at the last, "Sam Jinks, don't you go in there and upset my sister."

From the next room, Bethany's high, sweet, slightly slurred voice reached them. "Hello, Mr. Jinks. Did you come to visit me? I'm getting all better. My ironing is going just fine."

Almost immediately, he backed out into the kitchen. One of the men who'd broken free from Taylor shoved him. "Hey, what are you doing, Jinks?"

Jinks pushed him. "We're not going in there and scarin' that little girl witless."

Karl burst through the door. "You're right, you're not." As he spoke, he moved to shield Taylor.

She spoke to his broad back. "These gentlemen are leaving now."

"My lady and her guests are to be left in complete peace." Karl's voice rumbled like the threat of distant thunder. "If you have a problem, you come to me. Even if you're sick or hurt, you come to me first. Got it?" The men grumbled and growled as they started to walk away. Blocking their exit by keeping a meaty hand on the doorframe, Karl asked in a quiet tone that vibrated with fury, "Want to explain what was going on here?"

One of them pointed a finger at Hank Parson. "His boy's got a gimpy leg. Never gonna be right because the last doc was a quack." He jabbed his finger toward her. "Now this one's using cloth strips, rope, and an iron. Last time we all gave Doc Wicky a bunch of chances. This time we tried to put a stop to it."

Jinks cranked his hand around and stabbed his finger into Karl's chest. "You got in the way. When that little girl is all gimpy just like Hank's boy, we're all gonna hold you to blame." The men started to push on out.

Karl didn't yield an inch. "You remember every time you see Bethany run and play on a perfectly sound leg that it was our skilled doctor who treated her." He then permitted the men to go.

Her quaking limbs still held her up, but Taylor couldn't be sure how much longer. Part of her wanted to thank Karl for coming, because things could have turned even uglier. She'd been scared. She'd been scared a lot recently. There'd been times when she knew someone was watching her. This was the first time, though, that anyone had caused a physical confrontation.

On the other hand, she couldn't always depend on somebody to bail her out—even if he had expressed great confidence in her skill. She looked at him. "Didn't I tell you once I didn't need you to rescue me? And I am not your lady!"

Karl stared right back. "I remember telling you somebody had to rescue you from yourself. You can't cook worth a plugged nickel, so as long as Linette's cooking and there's something good on that stove, I thought I'd invite myself over." With that, he walked in front of her, sat down, and finished eating her bowl of oatmeal.

Fighting with her stank. Matching wits and debating was fun; bristling and wanting to shout until she absorbed some common sense held no charm at all. He hated it. And he hated brown sugar and butter on oatmeal. But he ate the whole bowl. Loathed it so much, he ate another bowlful. The whole time, he smiled at her—a grin so big his molars almost cracked. He kept his fist wrapped around that spoon so tight, it was amazing the spoon didn't melt from the heat. If he dared to let go of it, he just might grab hold of her and rattle her until some sense got into her brain. He'd never touched a woman in anger. Never had, never would—but she had no idea how much danger she'd been in. Absolutely none at all. She didn't think she needed to be rescued. She'd been absolutely unaware of the gravity of the situation. And why would she? A lady from proper Chicago society couldn't be expected to grasp just how raw and undisciplined men could be.

Those same men didn't respect Linette. Even if she cried or complained or got hurt, she didn't much matter to them. But if those men would have picked up little Bethany and carried her out of there, they would have lamed her for life. And why? Because they thought they knew better? Because they wanted to show they didn't want a woman doctor? Stupid, stupid men. They didn't understand the treasure they were rejecting—both as a professional and as an individual lady. Anyone who frightened or manhandled a woman deserved to be leveled. Anyone who so much as put a finger on his woman better be all prayed up.

Karl kept smiling at Taylor. He was going to keep at it until she realized just how irritated he was. Funny thing was, she was smiling right back at him the same way. It took him a moment to realize she knew exactly what he was doing. Why had it taken him so long to figure that out? How long had she known what he was up to?

She was real good at these games; he'd met his match. The realization invigorated him. She could kick and fuss and deny it all she wanted, but he'd staked his claim and knew deep in his heart she was the only one for him. Linette asked, "Would you like some more oatmeal?"

Taylor poured a cup of coffee. "Do we have any more?"

"I think I could scrape probably another tablespoon out of the pot."

Karl laughed. "I'll eat it. Just give me the pot." She put it on the table. He stuck his spoon in and proceeded to give one big, long scrape. Holding the spoon aloft, he shook his head. "Nah. Not even one bite." Linette laughed; Taylor didn't.

The stubborn woman had a temper that wouldn't quit. He knew she was biding her time, waiting until the next time she came to the livery to give him an earful. Well, that could go both ways. How many other situations had she been in that she hadn't told him about?

Karl swiped her coffee mug and emptied it in one gulp. "You might have some customers coming in, Doc."

"How is that?"

"It seems that Widow O'Toole has taken it upon herself to get a shotgun."

Linette dropped the pot in the sink. It clanged loudly. She turned so fast that the water on her hands swung in a big diamond arc across the room.

"What is Widow O'Toole doing with a shotgun?" Taylor sounded remarkably serene. "More important, is she a very good shot?"

"She doesn't have to be a good shot; she loaded it with buckshot. Anyway, word has it she thinks somebody's been prowling around her place. Made me wonder if you've felt like anybody's been here when you haven't . . . if someone's been watching you."

"No."

Casually turning the mug round and round, Karl let a few seconds stretch out. Her answer came just a shade too quick. "That surprises me. The widow told me she'd been here a couple times when you hadn't been around. I would have thought you'd notice when things got used up or moved around."

"But she'd explained those to me, so I was aware of those things. Discounting those occasions, no. Nothing else."

He shrugged. "Okay."

The silence sat heavy between them. Taylor looked at him. "Orville."

"Orville's been here?" *I'll throttle that weasel. . . .*

"No, Orville hasn't been here. Orville Clark mail-ordered a bunch of snake oil cures. He's been going around the neighborhood and—"

"Yes, I know."

Taylor gave him a jaundiced look. "You knew?"

"The whole town knows about it."

"Yet you said nothing to me?"

Exasperation got the better of him. "Why would you expect me to tell you? Why not someone else?" There. He got her on that one.

"Why should anybody else tell me? After all, I spend significant time in your company because you insist on driving me around rather than letting me drive the buggy myself. They probably presume since you have a monopoly on my time, you'd tell me the news."

"Oh, for crying in a bucket. All right. Let me tell you something, Doc. Orville Clark got himself a box of snake oil cures, and he's wandering around the neighborhood selling them. There. Are you happy now?"

"No, I'm not happy to know it, and no, I'm not happy that you're telling me, because you resent it. But worst of all, I'm not happy that you didn't tell me long ago. It is imperative I know of anything that could potentially affect the well-being of my patients. A lot of those so-called cures have things in them that react chemically with my medications."

Vexatious woman. He gave her what she wanted and then she didn't like it. He rose and set down the mug. "Okay, Doc. It's like this. I just mentioned Orville's so-called cures because Widow O'Toole thinks alcohol is the demons' breath. If for some reason Orville lost the little tiny bit of sense he has and went knocking on her door to sell her any of that, she'd be liable to take out that shotgun of hers and plug him from here to Sunday."

A shiver ran straight up her ramrod spine, and her voice quavered a little. "Perhaps I ought to pay her a visit."

"Good, Doc. You do that."

Fire sparked in her eyes again. "You still should have told me sooner, Karl."

"Didn't need to, Doc. You already knew."

She quirked a brow. "You didn't know I knew."

He walked toward the door. He wanted to tell her, "You shouldn't always depend on me." But he wanted her to. She was making him daft. Savagely, he twisted the doorknob.

She tapped him on the shoulder. "Aren't you going to go see how Bethany is?"

He shut the door, turned around, and went to see her. After a quick visit and a peck on the girl's cheek, he straightened up. The little girl was very drowsy. He couldn't resist. He dusted her cheek with the very edge of her pigtail. "You be a good girl."

" 'Kay."

"I'll be back later to see you."

" 'Kay."

He headed toward the back door. "If you're leaving here," he instructed Taylor, "you make sure either Piet or I am with you, and we'll let the other know so we can keep an eye on the place."

She nodded. He shut the door and walked away. She'd tell him what was bothering her soon enough. He wanted to go back in and find out, but he'd bide his time. If he went in right now, she wouldn't tell him. She was just that stubborn. She was just that frustrating. That impossible, too. And he was in no mood to deal with her.

He went back over to the forge. Regardless of how cold it was, Karl pushed all of the doors wide open so he could see out the door to the back of her place. Suddenly it struck him. *Taylor didn't scrap with me. She didn't argue whatsoever about me going on all her visits or watching her place while she's out.*

Normally, she would have fought, or if she were frightened, she would have stopped and thought about the offer before accepting it.

The episode today was frightening, but there was more going on. *She's terrified. But of what? Or of whom?*

Twenty

The tang of terror filled Enoch's mouth. His wife looked up at him, her eyes huge with worry. Smiling to lend a reassurance he was far from feeling, he adjusted his coat he'd draped over her delicate shoulders. Mr. Richardson hadn't wanted to leave town with Bethany laid up, so Enoch had offered to check out for him a bull located several hours away. He'd taken Mercy along for the ride, and they'd made a vacation of the two-day trip. "Are you warm enough now, sweet pea?"

A full mile must have passed by the train's window before she responded. "Yes, thank you." Beneath his coat, her posture straightened, showing strength and gumption. A smile flitted across her features, as did a beguiling wash of pink. "Enoch." She cast a shy look at the open doorway. Though they were alone in their Pullman compartment, the door to the narrow hallway traversing the train car was open.

He lifted her left hand and kissed the back of her fingers,

paying special attention to her wedding band. Pitching his voice low, he professed, "I'm proud you're my wife." He heard the small tearful gasp and turned her hand over, pressing a kiss to her palm. "You've blessed my life with love, and—"

"Enoch." Anguish tainted her voice.

"Shhh." He looked up at her and manufactured a scamp's smile. "I'm trying to be romantic."

"You've been very romantic."

"Mmm. Good." He winked. "Now where was I? Let me see. Right about here . . ." Dipping his head, he brushed his lips on the inside of her wrist. The pulse there fluttered. "Sweet pea, sweet pea, sweet pea," he murmured in time with the thrum of his own heartbeat. He turned her hand over and kissed the back of it. "Sweet pea." Kissed her fingers and wedding band. "Sweet pea." And last, the tips of her fingers, looking deep into her eyes, willing her to see the love in his eyes, hear it in his voice, feel it in his touch.

"Oh my."

He tucked her close to his side once again. For a few moments, he'd helped her push away the fear and enjoy being a woman—his woman. "We've a ways to go. Rest your head here and take a nap." He didn't give her an opportunity to demure. Instead, he slid his hand along the far side of her face and drew her head down. He had no answers for her, no honest reassurance. He'd do anything he could, though, to make this easier on her. Easier? Immediately revising that to be truthful, he corrected himself. Less hard.

Overwhelmed, she snuggled up next to him.

Short as the trip was, every minute had seemed to last an hour. Enoch knew he'd bought only a few minutes at best. Those moments counted, though. *If you're only going to give us a short time together, Lord, help me make every second count. You know my heart, though.*

*I've waited for this woman, and if you'd grant me a long lifetime with
her, I'd count it a great blessing. Bowing to your will . . .*

Mercy's hand came up and rested over his heart. "Could we
do something?"

Anything. "What, darling?"

"Let's get off one stop early and sneak into Gooding."

"Sure." Until this matter was settled, no one else needed to
know anything. Even afterward, no one else needed to know. Never
before had he been more thankful for Taylor's unsurpassed medical
talent and her incredible tact and discretion.

"Especially with it being so late, we'd probably be able to ride
horses through the woods and sneak over to see—"

"Our sister," he inserted, trying to keep her from having to
say doctor.

Mercy tilted her head up and gave him a startled look.

"Just because Taylor's my twin doesn't mean she's not your
sister now."

Tears glossed Mercy's remarkable eyes. "Yes, that's right. I'd
like to see our sister, and I don't want to scare Heidi."

"Of course not."

He kissed her nose. "It could be nothing. Let's not borrow any
worries from tomorrow." His soul told him his assertion was true;
his medical mind jangled alarms.

◦~◦~◦

"I've performed several of these surgeries before." Taylor set
aside the tablet of paper with the quick sketches she'd drawn and
looked directly into her sister-in-law's fright-filled eyes. *She needs
my confidence and strength. So does Enoch.* Resisting the temptation
to downplay the gravity of the situation, Taylor curled her hand

around Mercy's and reached for Enoch's. "The most important thing is, we're going to go through this together, and God is with us. I trust Him to guide my hands during the operation and to bring you through recovery."

"If it's not just a cyst . . ." Mercy stared at her lap. "If you have to . . . well . . ."

"I'll do whatever is necessary to remove the threat to your life." As a rule, cysts were smooth and regular in shape; cancerous tumors grew in irregular shapes with uneven edges. Her examination revealed a walnut-sized lump in Mercy's breast—and the jagged outline presaged bad news. For that very reason, she wanted to discuss the worst possible surgical treatment. "As a new wife, this must be especially difficult."

Mercy's hand clenched tighter. "It's dreadful. I've ruined everything."

"You haven't ruined anything. I'm thankful we caught this when it was small and that Taylor is so experienced. Think, Mercy—how God had His hand on this with those provisions and that you live now instead of back when surgery was barbaric."

"They didn't have to do . . . that, though."

"Yes, they did mastectomies. That's what the surgery is called, and it's been done for a long time." Taylor kept her voice matter-of-fact. "John Adams' daughter had a mastectomy while fully awake, without anything to dull her pain. Her cancer had been noticeable for quite some time and she'd not gotten any treatment. By the time she sought surgery, the tumor had completely overtaken her breast—yet the mastectomy drew away enough malignancy that she lived another two years.

"Your examination reveals something quite small in comparison to Nabby Adams'. Since it is movable and away from the chest wall, those are excellent signs for a full recovery; but if this is a cancerous tumor, I must remove the entire breast so none of the glandular tissue is left." If she gave no realistic preparation with honest glimmers of hope or heaped-on pity, her sister-in-law was doomed. Taylor knew the importance of instilling the belief that she'd recover and lead a normal life—not just immediate recovery, but also for Mercy's ultimate outcome. "After healing, women with this surgery wear some padding at the bosom and no one is the wiser that they've had the surgery at all."

"You'd know," Mercy whispered to Enoch.

He lifted her face to his. "And I'd still love you every bit as much."

Taylor turned away. She didn't want either of them to see her tears. "Enoch, I'll prepare everything. Go fetch Velma. She can assist me."

"No!" Mercy and Enoch said in unison.

Mercy wrapped her arms around his waist. "Only Enoch. No one else. Please, Taylor. I trust him. He's helped you with other surgeries, and—"

"He's too emotionally involved."

Enoch glared at her. "I vowed before the Lord to protect and cherish my wife. You and I work as a team, and no one else has half my skill. You're not going to stop me, Taylor. I'm assisting you."

She looked from one to the other and got ready to argue. Mercy's eyes held desperate trust, and Enoch stared at Taylor's with a fierceness she'd never seen in him. Medically, Velma would be the wiser choice for an assistant; but they wanted—no, needed—this semblance of control. "The two of you are insane."

"I sure am. Crazy in love." He must have thought she was out of earshot when she went across the hall to prepare her surgery, because he said, "I'm madly in love with you, Mercy-mine."

Heavenly Father, please, can't you grant a miracle? Can you make this a mere cyst after all? They're so in love. Heidi's just a little girl, and she needs her mommy.... Prayers lurched from Taylor's heart as she set out her carefully sterilized instruments. Trying to sound calm and maybe even a little lighthearted as she reached for the chloroform, she called out, "Okay, Enoch. It's time for you to give your bride a good-night kiss."

A short while later, Taylor paused. In a second, the tumor would be visible. Some tumors spidered out in all directions, clear into muscles and the lymphatic tissue—even into the lungs in a few cases she'd seen. In such instances, the cancerous disease had gone so far into the woman's being that putting her through the hardships of recovering from the removal of all of the tissue was not only useless but cruel. She stopped praying just long enough to order, "Give Mercy a little more chloroform."

"She's had enough."

"I'm the doctor here." She didn't want her twin to see the tumor until she'd first had a glimpse of how involved it was; only he wasn't cooperating. "I knew I should have gotten Velma to assist me."

"She wouldn't administer more chloroform, either. It'd be too much, and you know it." Enoch's voice edged close to a shout. "Stop delaying. The truth isn't going to change."

"I love her, Enoch."

"I know."

"I love you, too." She drew a deep breath and pressed ahead.

❧

" 'Beautiful dreamer, wake unto me . . .' " Enoch crooned softly as he sat at the bedside and coiled one of Mercy's little wisps of hair around and around his finger. She was hideously pale, her lips pinched in pain, and her body dwarfed by the bed and the stack of pillows Taylor had used to keep the covers from rubbing against Mercy's chest.

Mercy's eyelids fluttered.

Holding her right hand in his, he brought it to his lips and pressed a kiss to it. " 'Beautiful dreamer, wake unto me. . . .' "

Slowly, one eye opened. "You need glasses."

Bolting up out of the chair so fast it slid back and crashed against the wall, Enoch chortled. "You need a kiss to sweeten your disposition." He gladly obliged, then fearing she'd ask the one question he didn't want to answer, he insisted, "You have to drink some of this. Taylor extracted a promise from me that I would make you down the whole cup when you woke up."

"What—"

"It's a mixture of juices and some medicine. I think you're fairly safe. Taylor can't cook, but no one can ruin juice."

Mercy rewarded that with a small smile.

"And voilà! I have a straw for Madame." He tucked the paper straw into the cup and aimed it between her lips. "I bought a whole box of them. Think Heidi's going to like sipping lemonade with them?"

"Mmm . . ."

"She's fine. I'll bring her by later on." He tapped the straw to urge Mercy to drink more. "You ought to see how much fun she's having, sticking her tongue out through the hole where her tooth was. I caught her trying to wiggle another tooth loose." Enoch twisted the straw. "Keep drinking. Taylor and Karl argued about her wanting to pay too much for coal today, and I'm not getting in the way of her temper. You've seen Taylor when she's got her back up. She hisses at everything."

Her lids drooped.

"You're tired, sweet pea. Go on and take a little nap." He drew away the empty cup and pressed his lips to her temple. "Praise God, you're doing fine."

He stepped out of the room and Taylor grabbed his sleeve. Hauling him over to the room that had been his bedchamber, she whispered hotly, "You can't do that, Enoch. You can't. She's not fine. It's wrong to tell her otherwise."

"I'm doing what's right for my wife and family. It's my decision." For the past three days, they'd been squabbling over this issue. He'd continued to argue, assuming that Taylor would eventually give in. First, he'd attributed it to the stress they'd both been under. Then, the sleepless nights. But now—now things were hitting a critical point.

Eyes afire, Taylor kept hold of his sleeve and shook it. "How dare you relegate Mercy into the same category as you would a naïve child. She's a grown woman who's cared for herself and her daughter and run two successful businesses. Suddenly, since you put a ring on her finger, you know so much more than she does about herself that you get to decide what she's told about her own condition? No. Absolutely not."

"Not everyone is as headstrong and autonomous as you. Certainly not other women. You can't judge what my wife needs based on what you'd want."

Taylor released his sleeve and stepped back. "I based what I said on what other patients have desired and on the character of the woman I know Mercy to be."

"My decision stands."

"It's not your decision to make, Enoch. Mercy is my patient. When she asks me—and she will—I'm not going to lie."

"So then you lied when you told me you love her . . ." He couldn't force himself to add *and me*. He knew better. Taylor and he shared a bond that was unmistakable, undeniable. But he couldn't reconcile how pitiless his twin planned to be toward his bride.

"Go home, Enoch. Spend time with your daughter. She's hardly seen you these last three days. Get some sleep." Taylor turned and started out the door.

"I'm not leaving my wife."

"Velma's coming in to sit with her. You can go on home." Taylor descended the stairs without looking back.

Enoch felt the distance between them grow wider with each step. The day of the surgery, the aftereffects of the chloroform had kept Mercy asleep most of the time. Taylor hadn't skimped on dosing her with laudanum the second day or yesterday, either. Drifting on the cloud of medication, Mercy hadn't been aware of much more than someone being nearby to give her something to sip or turn her when she woke. Today would be nothing short of hell. Used for even modestly long periods, laudanum could cause addiction, so the blessed relief it had brought these last few days now had to be taken away. Taylor had spoken with him about it a few times, preparing him—and he'd agreed, the medical part of him saying all the right words. Deep inside, he railed at the thought of his wife hurting. The only thing Taylor could offer was acetylsalicylic acid—nothing more than a chemical name for willow bark scrapings that was suitable for headache relief.

Velma was coming. Plainspoken Velma would state facts without considering the consequences if he wasn't there to stop her.

Sure of that, Enoch strode back to Mercy's side. He ought to do something—anything—to help her, yet he was powerless.

A tap sounded at the back door. "Yoo-hoo! Anybody home?"

Giggles twinkled up the staircase. "Yoo-hoo!" Heidi copied.

For the briefest instant, delight filled him. Next came the crashing realization that he had to protect Heidi from the harsh realities every bit as much as he needed to spare Mercy.

"Hope! Heidi!" Taylor sounded genuinely surprised and pleased.

"Auntie Taylor!"

"Shh, dear. Bethany is resting," Taylor said. They had moved Bethany temporarily into the kitchen so the surgery would be free for Mercy's operation. And apparently Bethany enjoyed being in the midst of the action.

"I brung a chicken, only I decided to do a swap. Heidi, you be a good helper and put this basket on the table there."

"Okay."

Enoch walked into the kitchen in time to see his little girl stand on tiptoe, seeing to the chore. The minute she spied him, she shrieked, "Daddy!" and sprang into his arms.

The way her little arms and legs wound around him and she clung to him like a little monkey never failed to delight him. He held her close and dipped his head to press a kiss on her rumpled hair. "Ahhh. Here's my girl."

"I heard tell your missus is under the weather, so's I went to the mercantile. Millie and me, we haggled."

"They fighted, Daddy. 'Bout wanting me."

"Because we both love you," Hope said. "The Clarks have had you for a few days, so now you're gonna have a fun time playin' with my Emmy-Lou. But to make 'em feel a little better, I gave them the chickens I usually get from Dr. Bestman. And y'all can enjoy the soup I made for the next few days. Since they was your chickens to begin with, the swap was fair all around." Hope beamed.

Heidi squirmed. "I wanna see Mama."

Enoch pressed his forehead to hers. "She's sleeping."

"I could give her sleepytime night-night kisses like you and Mommy give me," she whispered.

"Okay," Enoch agreed and swung her around and onto his back. "You have to stay quiet, though. Mama needs her rest so she can get better. Just a few quick kisses, and that's all."

In the end, it was ridiculously simple. Heidi gave her mama a dozen sloppy little kisses, and Mercy roused just enough to call her by name and say, "I love you." Reassured everything was fine, Heidi waved as she rode away with Hope.

Enoch waved until she was out of sight, then turned to his sister. "What did you tell Hope?"

"You know my ethics and oath. I don't discuss my patients."

"Good."

"Velma, however, is a professional associate. Though she doesn't have formal training, she's proven herself skilled and capable of giving care and rendering simple treatments."

Disbelief flooded him. Enoch knew most physicians stepped back and had someone else treat a family member—but not when the substitute was nothing more than a ranch cook! He gritted his teeth. "Velma—is—not—treating—my—wife."

"No, she's not. But she needs to be informed of the diagnosis and extent of the surgery since she will be sitting with her. If the pillows aren't positioned with exacting care, Mercy's arm will swell more. Pain inevitably results from such swelling, and we both want to spare her as much as possible."

A ruckus sounded out on the porch. "Doc! Herman got his-self shot."

Taylor whirled away. A second later, he heard her order, "Remove his shirt and have him sit on my examination table."

"Don't want you. Want Doc Enoch."

Another man tacked on, "He's not over at his barn."

Enoch went to the doorway. "Get it through your thick heads. If you don't have four feet or wings, I won't treat you." He pushed past three men and went up the stairs. His wife needed him.

But with three men smelling like a brewery down there, his sister could use his help, too. He didn't even glance over at Herman. Digging a bullet out of him wouldn't be easy. The man had to be as big around as he was tall.

A man's first allegiance belonged to his wife, though. He went into the room and decided the pain medication was now working well enough to reposition Mercy. Drawing back the covers, Enoch took care not to let them brush against her chest.

Lord, let me have her for a long time. You gave me this love for Mercy, and I'm selfish enough to beg for years of it. Don't take her from me. Please, God, don't take her from me.

Moaning lightly as he finished tucking the last pillow into place, Mercy curled her fingers around his wrist, as if searching for him. "That's right, sweet pea. I'm here." Then just as quickly, her grasp loosened and her hand slipped away.

Lord, no. Please don't let us be like that. Not just a momentary coming together and tearing apart.

"Wondered if you'd be up here." Velma's low voice took him by surprise. "That sis of yours has her hands full. A couple fools at the Nugget used each other for target practice."

"Go on down, Velma. You'll establish order in no time."

Velma looked at Mercy, and then at the arrangement of the pillows. For an unguarded moment, shock widened her eyes, then she steeled herself with a deep breath. Hands rough and reddened from washing thousands of dishes petted back his wife's hair, and Velma murmured softly, leaning down close to assess Mercy's breathing and check her pulse. Not bothering to straighten up, Velma lifted the bedclothes a few scant inches.

Enoch encircled her wrist and tilted his head toward the door.

Velma settled the bedclothes back in place with great tenderness. Once she made it out into the hall, she grabbed both of his hands. "Just the left one?"

He nodded.

"Did your sis get it all? Cut it out and get an inch or so of healthy tissue all around just to be sure?"

Again, he nodded.

Velma let out a huge gust of air. "Good, then. I'll be sure to let Mercy know that I'll keep her secret. A woman's got a right to her privacy. You get on down there now and knock a few heads together. If you don't, folks are gonna think you staying up here all the time means something bad's wrong." She turned loose of his hands and started pushing him toward the stairs. "Up till now, they've chalked it up to you bein' a doting groom."

Enoch didn't want to leave, but Velma's comment carried some validity. She'd shown herself to be more capable than he'd imagined. More knowledgeable, too. He went on downstairs.

"Now see here, young woman," the mayor blustered. "There are considerations."

"Indeed there are. Your wound can wait. Mr. Clark's cut is

more serious." Leaving Herman with his upper arm bandaged, she washed her hands.

"Orville Clark is white trash; I'm the mayor. That's as serious as matters get." Cutter yanked the towel from her and grabbed her wrist.

"Get your hand off her, Cutter," Enoch snarled from the doorway.

Twenty-One

It took every last shred of self-control Enoch possessed to keep from launching across the room and throttling the idiot. "Don't ever touch her again or you'll suffer the most serious injury she'll ever treat."

Once freed, Taylor swept right past the mayor and over to a chair in the corner. Along the way, she grabbed a stack of towels. "Let's see to you now," she said to Orville Clark.

"Girlie, go have a tea party. I need a real doctor."

"Mr. Clark, if you had bothered to read it, you would have seen that that's my name on the medical diploma. As for tea—you might consider switching to it yourself. A drunken brawl and a broken bottle fight have left you in bad shape." She took a pair of shears and whacked his sleeve.

"Hey! This is my last good shirt!"

"It can be mended." Staunching the blood with a compress, Taylor picked up tweezers with her other hand.

"Since she's busy, you'll have to tend to me." Mayor Cutter stuck out his hand toward Enoch, displaying a jagged cut. "I have more important things to do than sit here all day waiting while she digs bullets out of a man who cheats at poker and then wastes more of my time while she stitches up a swindler."

"You have nothing more than a jagged surface cut, Mayor." Taylor's tone remained wry. "I daresay the alcohol in the bottle you broke causing the injury has sterilized it quite efficiently."

Puffing up indignantly, the mayor hid his hand behind his back. "Who says that's how I got hurt?"

"Maybe you ain't so dumb after all, Doctor." Orville Clark started chuffing air. "Holy cow, woman! What did you do?!"

"Having removed the glass, I obliterated any germs so you'd not suffer blood poisoning." Taylor set down the steel flask of her special mixture of hydrogen peroxide and a few drops of iodine. The combination never failed to impress—it stung, bubbled, and left a rim of color that lingered for a few days as a reminder that care had been rendered.

"Least she's smarter'n you, Mayor. She didn't waste good whiskey on a wound."

Mayor Cutter leaned closer and cast a glance at Taylor, then looked Enoch in the eye. "Treat my hand." From the looks of Orville's arm, Taylor would be suturing it for a while. Enoch jutted his chin toward a bench in a silent order to sit down. For all of his dramatics, the mayor needed nothing more than for his hand to be cleansed and bandaged, but what he said left Enoch glad he'd finally agreed to step in and render care.

Forty-five minutes later, with all of the men gone, Enoch helped Taylor clean up. Her shoulders slumped with fatigue. He'd been sitting with Mercy, but Taylor was still at anyone's beck and call around the clock. Had she gotten any sleep at all?

Turning toward him, she stuffed a wad of bloody cloths in a basin. "I can't for the life of me imagine what happened at the saloon. I don't know who Herman is, but all the men seem to. No one said who shot him."

"Orville has a big mouth, and Gustav Cutter's temper is swift. I'd attribute a fight between them to that combination, but they weren't baiting each other or waging war here. Do you know what happened?"

"Yes." He took the basin from her and carried it to the kitchen sink. Cold water rinsed blood out best—especially if done right away.

"Well?"

After the mayor confided in him, Enoch hadn't had much opportunity to decide how best to share some of the information with his twin while leaving her ignorant of other portions of it. He put the words together quickly. "In addition to selling those patent medicines, Orville's been trying to earn some money using those crazy machines Dr. Wicky left behind."

"They're working—at making people crazy." Taylor shook her head. "I understand Orville's part in the whole matter. But the mayor? Gustav Cutter hardly seems the type to rely on such quackery."

Enoch pumped the water furiously, hoping he'd turned in time to hide his expression. Starting to rinse the cloths, he strove to sound nonchalant. "I believe that was the general cause of the disagreement."

"Ohhhh. I suppose then it probably had to do with Dr. Somebody-or-Other's magnetic girdle."

Water splashed all over him. "Girdle?"

"Yes. Sydney and Velma told me about it as well as some other items Orville carted out of here. Sydney's amusement over that one item's advertising made it stand out in my mind. 'For the treatment of social ills and baldness.'" Taylor barely paused to draw a breath. "If Orville was foolish enough to suggest the mayor might be in need of a treatment . . ."

"Someone might get hurt." Enoch didn't look at his twin—he couldn't. She'd stare at him with such intensity, she'd read his every thought. "So that settles it. I'll take care of the rest of this. Go on up and get some sleep."

"That does not settle it." Anger vibrated in her voice. "When it comes to the welfare of the citizens of Gooding, I'll do whatever I deem best. I don't need you to take care of this or to tell me to go take a nap as if I'm an irritable toddler. You're nothing like the brother I knew a month ago. That Enoch respected my professional ability and judgment and never once interfered with my patients."

"I did not interfere. If someone confides in me, I owe it to them to be worthy of their trust."

"But if I'd treated my patient, he wouldn't have confided in you."

Her accusation hit home. He'd made a determination, stepped in, and treated a human patient—her patient, in her surgery, without so much as having glanced her way for permission. The magnitude of what he'd done struck him. By interfering, Enoch had given the mayor an excuse to say he didn't need the doctor, when otherwise he'd have needed to either sign on to her list of patients or proclaim himself to be a hypocrite.

Still upset, Taylor kept right on talking. "The twin I had in

Chicago would have respected a woman's mind and sought her wishes."

"Of course I did."

"Not anymore, you don't."

Though tempted to argue the point, Enoch gritted his teeth. He'd earned her wrath, so he'd take it.

"The Enoch Bestman here in Texas is a complete stranger who acts as though neither his wife nor sister ought to be troubled by anything."

"Come on, Sis. What kind of man would stand back and allow a lady to endure something when he could take the brunt of it?" *I wouldn't want you hearing what the mayor said.*

"We're not talking about a threat where a man's physique would protect a woman's smaller frame. The issue at hand is one where you've determined that it's your place to be the gatekeeper of knowledge, weighing information and determining what is acceptable and what is deleterious or unacceptable."

"That's an oversimplification—"

"Ignorance is never admirable nor attractive, and if that has become your feminine ideal, you may as well go wear Orville's girdle."

~·o-O·o·~

Weak rays of sun slanted across her mattress, awakening Taylor from a short nap. Exhaustion and years of learning to sleep in short snatches helped . . . some. She had let her emotions loose in full force and felt none the better for it. As a matter of fact, she felt worse. Her twin was carrying an unbearable burden, yet she'd added to it. *What is wrong with me? I used to be able to tease him. We once laughed things off or compromised. How is it that we fight over things now? Is that the way it's going to be from here on out? A few months ago, I would have appreciated his bandaging a simple hand wound.*

As soon as she tidied her hair, she went to check on Mercy. Enoch sat beside her, and Taylor murmured, "I'm here. You can go sleep now."

Enoch shook his head.

They'd already argued enough. Taylor chose not to pick a fight, and certainly not while standing over Mercy's bed. She assessed Mercy's respirations and pulse and prepared to fold down the covers so she could inspect the dressing.

Enoch's hand stilled her movement. " 'Beautiful dreamer,' " he began singing.

Mercy moaned.

"Do you hurt, sweet pea?"

Her eyes opened, and she bit her lip. Taylor smoothed back a few stray wisps of her sister-in-law's hair and strove to ease the awkward moment. "Of course she hurts, Enoch. Your singing has to be one of the more painful things known to man."

"Mmm-hmm," Mercy agreed.

"You can give me voice lessons later." Enoch reached for a glass and eased the straw between his wife's pale lips. He seemed so casual and relaxed, but the tension in his shoulders and the infinitesimal shake of his fingers gave away his fear.

Is he afraid I'll tell her the truth, or is it just that he hates the truth himself and doesn't like her hurting? Whichever it is, I only made it worse today. I have reasonable matters to discuss with him, but I was unreasonable. Instead of being able to lean on me when he needs me the most, he's on his own.

After a few sips, Mercy cleared her throat. "How long have I slept?"

"Four days."

"Four days!" Mercy's right hand flew to her mouth. "It can't be. Heidi. The boardinghouse."

"Everything's being taken care of," Enoch assured her.

"And now you need to be taken care of, too." Taylor drew down the covers with great care, yet used a brisk move so it wouldn't look as though she was fussing. "I need to inspect your dressing."

Mercy fingered the button at the high neck of her flannel nightgown. "Yes. Of course." Faint color washed her cheeks as she cast a quick look to her right. Her lashes lowered, and her grip on the button tightened.

"Let me help you." Enoch reached for the button as he spoke.

"No!" Silence hovered over the three of them. Then Mercy whispered, "Please leave me alone with the doctor."

"No." Enoch said the word quietly, calmly, firmly. "I'm your husband, and my place is by your side."

Her brother needed her. Her patient needed her, too. How was she to decide whose decision to support? *Lord, please give me wisdom now and all of us help in the days ahead.* Her stethoscope hung on the bedpost, a poignant reminder that she wasn't there as Enoch's twin sister, but as Mercy's physician. Taylor steeled herself for the battle ahead when suddenly words threaded through her mind. *What God has joined together, let no man put asunder. . . .*

"She's my patient, and you're her husband, and you're making a pest of yourself. Being by her side puts you in my way. Go stand by the window, Enoch."

Enoch gave Mercy a peck on the cheek. "Hurry up and get well. Sis is far too bossy for us to stay here much longer."

"If you don't like that window," Taylor said, making a dismissive gesture, "go look out any of the others, and polish them while you're at it. After all, you still haven't hired a housekeeper, and that was part of our deal."

"Deal?" Mercy asked faintly as she watched Enoch walk toward the far side of the bedchamber.

"For me to agree to come to Texas. You're my sister now, so I expect you to stand beside me on this and make him hurry up. I think I've been remarkably patient." Taylor pushed her sleeves up. "You just lie still. Your gown is nice and full, so I can leave the covers here at your waist and lift the gown instead of having to unbutton you and bother with the sleeve. I'll inspect your dressing now. I do that a few times each day and change it once a day. Eager as Enoch is to escape from me, you can come have me change it as you continue to heal."

"I'll just do it for her at home."

"You, Taylor. I want you to."

"Hey!" Enoch protested from over at the window.

The stricken look on Mercy's face cut through Taylor. If this was how she felt without knowing her diagnosis, how much worse was it going to be when she learned it was cancer? Patting her sister-in-law on the shoulder, Taylor used her crispest voice. "Enoch, don't you dare say another word. You only treat animals."

Enoch made an impatient sound. "The two of you are going to stick together, aren't you?"

"Yes," they said in unison, then Mercy winced as the gown snagged for just a second on the dressing. Intentionally, Taylor left the gown bunched up so her patient couldn't see the bandaging.

If there was any complication whatsoever, Mercy could be told about that later—not now. Not when she'd likely be absorbing at least part of her condition as soon as Taylor drew the gown back down. Whether Enoch wanted her to know or not, Mercy was too intelligent not to figure things out. It wasn't fair to have her deduce the situation by herself; she deserved to have her doctor and family be honest with her.

"Excellent. The dressing is nice and dry."

A whimper escaped Mercy.

Taylor didn't look at her patient's chest; she looked at her face.

Eyes huge and lips tremulous, Mercy stared downward. She'd lifted her head slightly and could plainly see the dressing. Her right hand came over and she barely grazed her fingertips over the flat surface. Too weak to keep her head up, it lolled back.

Slipping her fingers beneath Mercy's, Taylor gave them a small squeeze. "Enoch—"

"I don't want him here. I don't want him to see me. Not like this. Oh, not like this."

"Shhh." Hastily, Taylor pulled the gown down and the bed-clothes up. "You're covered."

Enoch hadn't waited. Upon hearing his name and his wife's anguish, he'd come at once. "Enough of that."

Taylor wanted to kick him. His wife was distraught, and he was trying to be logical. Of all the male things to do, Enoch couldn't have made a more boneheaded choice.

Mercy dissolved into a fit of tears. Clutching Taylor's hand, she begged, "Make him go away."

He glowered at her. "Don't waste your breath."

A keening wail split the air.

She knows. She's figured it out. Taylor tightened her hold of Mercy's hand.

"It's gone. All of it. It wasn't just a cyst, was it?" Mercy's tear-filled eyes pleaded for reassurance.

Enoch said, "I'll answer that."

Twenty-Two

Everything within Taylor revolted. Enoch hadn't wanted Mercy to know, and he'd gone so far as to give instructions to avoid answering—but this? He was prepared to tell an outright lie and have her be his accomplice? "That's not right. I'm the physician here." *And Mercy is going to get the full truth.*

Ripping the covers off the bed, Enoch half roared, "For Pete's sake!" After shoving the covers into Taylor's arms, he lifted Mercy and sat on the bed with his back to the headboard and her cradled on his lap. "You women are trying my patience. I've waited for this moment for four days."

"Mercy, you asked me, and you deserve an answer." Taylor reached over and held both of her sister-in-law's hands—the small, slender right one and the left one that was painfully swollen from a common temporary circulatory reaction to the surgery. "It wasn't a cyst."

"It was a tumor, sweet pea. But Taylor got it all."

"Cancer." Horror and shock hushed Mercy's voice.

Enoch's head dipped. He brushed a soft kiss across her mouth. "Yes, but Taylor got it all. I've been waiting for four long days to give you the good news."

Taylor slowly, subtly released Mercy's hands and backed away from the bed. She couldn't believe it. Clear up to the very last second, Enoch had fought with her. For the first time in their lives, they'd been diametrically opposed and unable to find a compromise. He'd been impossible, selfish, overbearing, and . . . now, absolutely the most loving husband she'd ever seen.

"We didn't want you to hurt too much, so Taylor's been giving you laudanum." He nuzzled Mercy's temple. Such a display of affection wouldn't normally be acceptable with anyone else present—but this situation didn't conform to ordinary rules. "The only reason I could wait for all this time was because I knew it would let you sleep through some pain. But here you are in my arms, and I'm going to hold you for years and years to come."

Mercy's head dipped. Enoch cupped it to his shoulder and murmured, "Tired?"

"Heidi?"

Did Enoch notice how Mercy had avoided answering him by changing the subject? Taylor's eyes narrowed. The next minutes and days would form the ways this couple would deal with not only the challenge, but with one another during the recovery and beyond.

"Dan and Millie had her until today. Hope took her so she and Emmy-Lou could play together for a few days. And I'd guess you want to know about the boardinghouse now, too. Right?"

"Yes." Mercy's tone sounded flat.

"Linette's handling it all. After having helped you for so long, she knows your routines. Widow O'Toole's pitching in and keeping things going just fine."

Her brother was a complete dolt. Instead of reassuring Mercy, all he was going to do was make her feel unnecessary! Taylor immediately tacked on, "But no one can begin to truly fill in for you. All of those things are inconsequential compared to you and your health, anyway. Most women who hear the news you were just given have some questions. Is there anything you'd like me to explain?"

Mercy barely shook her head.

"Over the next days or weeks, things are bound to occur to you. You might feel a bit numb right now after having been given such a shock."

"Tell her how small it was," Enoch demanded.

"Here." In preparation for this moment, Taylor had formed a likeness of the tumor out of soap. "This is the size and shape. Not only did you detect it early, but when we did surgery, I was able to remove surrounding tissue that appeared healthy."

"Do you remember Taylor telling you how tumors put down roots or send out seeds, so she always makes sure she trims out extra to be sure?"

"But it's all gone."

"Yes, sweet pea, it's all gone."

Sensing they meant entirely different things, Taylor decided to help. "Mercy, we did the mastectomy just as we discussed so we'd rid you of the cancer. Your breast is gone now, but the most important thing is—"

"That Heidi and I will have you for a lifetime."

Understandably shaken and weepy, Mercy asked, "How long of a life?"

"Only the Lord knows that, but I fully expect it to be comparable to any other healthy young woman's." The strain had gone on long enough. Taylor motioned to Enoch to lie Mercy back down.

He ignored her. "I'm your husband, Mercy Bestman, and you're not getting away from me. You married me, and you're stuck with me."

"Are you sure?"

"*I* am!" Taylor exclaimed with a laugh. "I finally got rid of Enoch, and you're not giving him back."

Finally, Mercy slumped into Enoch's chest. A hiccuppy sob shook her. "I didn't want to give him back."

"Then see to it you don't. Oh, and by the way, over the next seven or eight years, I fully expect a couple of nephews and another niece or two. If there was justice in this world, the children would be hellions to pay their father back for all the times he's bedeviled me; but I love you too much to wish such a fate on you, Mercy. Instead, I'll pray for you to have children just like me."

"It's a good thing you married me, sweet pea. If you hadn't, I'd be stuck here with a madwoman."

❧❧❧

Karl helped Taylor into the buggy and then scraped the mud off his boots as he climbed in himself. "So Enoch took Mercy home?"

"Yes."

He wasn't quite sure how to phrase his concerns. "After two weeks. Is she better?"

"Recovery from surgery is never easy. You're a particularly hearty specimen, and you sprang back faster than any patient I've ever had. Even so, for the first week or two, you fatigued rapidly. As a small woman, Mercy's vital reserves are lower. I have every confidence she'll spring back as long as we don't cause her anxiety over her temporary weakness."

He pulled the buggy to the side of the road. Curling his fingers around the doctor's gloved hand, he searched for the right words. Until now, he'd not taken the liberty to make such familiar contact, but it came so naturally. "To do surgery on someone you love—it must be very hard."

She managed a tense shrug.

"We have spoken about whether it is good that you became a doctor, and I believe it was the right thing. If only for this, then it was worth it so you could help your sister."

"That would be very selfish."

He let out a disbelieving snort. She seemed to be regaining her mettle, and that was good, but he still wanted to praise her. "You're a scientist, but in many ways, you're also an artist. This case, I'm thinking, must have been your masterpiece."

Slowly, she pulled her hand from his. "Mercy is God's masterpiece. I'm thankful for all He's done for her."

"Why can't you accept any credit? You did the operation."

She let out a long, shaky breath. "Mostly with my eyes closed."

"If your eyes were closed, it was because you were praying. I've been praying, too. The difference God makes in the midst of difficulty . . . In my grief I railed against Him, and now I see how Enoch and Mercy turn toward Him and find strength. My aim is to walk so closely with the Lord that I lean on Him in every circumstance of life."

"It's a noble goal, and our heavenly Father must be pleased you're pursuing Him with all your heart."

"It is the way a marriage should be, as well."

"I agree." Hastily she tacked on, "But it's far easier for me to set lofty goals for marriage and child-rearing since I'll never marry and have children."

"Does it ever occur to you that just as I didn't turn to God in my grief, it could be that you're not listening to His will about your future? He could be demonstrating through Enoch and Mercy that you must have your priorities in order."

"Are you beating around the bush about the list? It's only up to fifty-six. But I won't stop practicing medicine. If Gooding doesn't honor the contract, I'll relocate to a town where my skills are welcome."

❧

Taylor entered her surgery, sterilized several instruments, and made a list of supplies and medications to reorder. She noted that some of her medical texts were missing and made a mental note to ask Enoch for them. She quickly finished her tasks, noting the quiet that surrounded her. Though she was grateful both little Bethany and Mercy were back home, she felt a bit lonely at times.

With a satisfied glance at the pristine room, Taylor grabbed her bag. She needed to make a couple of house calls, but first she'd like to stop off at Checkered Past and see the new mama and her newborn baby again.

Realizing she needed to remain close to home and be available to Sydney, Velma had started taking Taylor with her on prenatal visits and summoning Taylor whenever she was called for a birth. Having attended a few births together, Velma finally admitted she no longer worried about Taylor's competence and would be glad to share the maternity cases.

God couldn't have poured a sweeter balm of contentment on

Taylor to make up for the contention around her than to allow her to resume maternity care. Bulky winter clothing had kept the number of maternity cases a secret. Gustav Cutter had greatly underestimated Gooding's population growth when he had said he expected only two births. Word of mouth had quickly spread that Taylor wasn't merely competent; she was comforting, as well. Now that Sydney was past her due date, Velma refused to budge any farther than the ranch's clothesline. Fathers-to-be knew—whether they liked it or not—they had to come fetch the woman doctor to assist their wife. Invariably those proud papas showed their thanks by placing their family's names on Dr. Bestman's patient list.

If Karl accompanies me on this postpartum visit, he'll stand there and switch from one foot to the other and hem and haw about how we need to get going again. It wasn't that she planned more than a very brief visit, but she didn't want him dictating what she did with her time. He'd gotten pushy about her schedule, and she didn't want to admit that he had every reason to. The man spent more of his time than he could spare escorting her around.

Ever since he'd told her he thought she was beautiful—thereby essentially declaring himself, he'd become more assertive about her schedule. *Our schedule,* she amended honestly. He was a busy man, and he had a right to get antsy about being away from his business—but that was proof of her argument for why she'd never marry. Her profession required her attention whenever, wherever, however, and however long was required—regardless of anything and anyone else. No husband would stand for being treated in such a manner. Just about the time she'd been ready to tell him he'd gotten too bossy, he'd changed tactics. Instead of always accompanying her, he now asked Piet to take her on calls, too. Piet was far more placid. The difference in temperament only served to underscore the sparks that flew whenever she and Karl were together.

After the incident with the men breaking in to see Bethany, she didn't know if she wanted the Van der Vorts to carry the weapons or not. She and Piet had gone round and round about that. She and Karl had had a fight or two over it, too. What was she going to do? She looked around. Almost every man in Texas had a weapon on him. It really wasn't her place to dictate what grown men could or couldn't do. Karl and Piet did exactly what they pleased. They each wore a pair of guns whenever they weren't standing by the forge.

She donned her pelisse, took her bag, and carefully locked the door behind herself before going across the way to the smithy. "Hello, Piet. I'd like to go make some house calls."

He looked over his shoulder at her and set down his hammer. "Ja. I will hitch up the buggy."

Taylor went outside to escape the heat of the smithy while she waited, and Karl rode up in a cloud of dust, coming to a halt a few yards past her.

"Whoa!" he called, his gelding skidding to a halt. "Taylor! I was coming for you. You're needed at once!"

Twenty-Three

The world—it feels . . . new and fresh." Karl placed her bag in the Creightons' buggy and lifted her onto the seat. The buggy dipped ominously and swayed as he climbed in. He set it into motion, and Taylor lifted the lap robe so he could share it. The horses' breath left clouds of condensation in the frigid air. This ride was far more comfortable than the one they had taken to get there—when Karl had swept her off the ground and onto his lap, and rode straight back out of town. And less exciting by far. Amazingly colder, too—and that was saying quite a bit, because they'd ridden into a stiff wind that had barely let them get inside before it whipped everything with snowy-sleet needles.

Karl wondered, "Is it always thus after a birthing?"

"After a healthy one. Blessedly, there are more of those than not."

He turned. Piercing blue eyes studied her. "I never thought. Not of that."

"Don't. I shouldn't have said anything."

"It makes me appreciate more the miracle of holding Rose and sharing this day with Big Tim and Sydney."

Taylor cleared her throat. "Karl? My oath says I will not speak of anything that goes on in the sickroom. Since you were there only because you took me, it wouldn't be right for you to—"

"You can tell everyone about Rose. Sydney and Tim told you to."

"I wasn't referring . . . to . . . that." Keeping from smiling, let alone laughing, tested her sorely.

"Ahh. So what am I to answer about how she and that baby are?"

"They're beautiful."

Eyes sparkling impishly, he mused, "Then I'll say Tim is uglier than ever. Especially with those stitches you put alongside his forehead!"

"I don't believe in coincidences. God arranged that I'd be there when Tim sustained a freak injury. Not many men fall from that height and can later tell about it."

Karl threw back his head and belted out a laugh. "Is this how you'll say it? To protect his pride?"

"I don't plan to say a word. Nonetheless, it never hurts to be prepared."

"You're good with words. I'm not so diplomatic. I'd rather walk barefoot through coals than go to that Richardson wedding next week. There will be women crying. Tears of joy. Linette weeping in sadness. If you think of something good to say, let me know. Better still, if you think of a reasonable excuse so I don't have to go, give it to me."

⦿⧽⦿⧼⦿

"Wilt thou have this woman to thy wedded wife . . ."

Though Marcella and Katherine Richardson stood at the altar by their grooms, Enoch couldn't help himself. He slid his hand beneath Mercy's. Even though she'd healed, he always sat to her left. The action he'd started weeks ago to protect her still remained, and now it arranged for him to subtly encase her hand. To his delight, the swelling in her hand scarcely was an issue anymore.

Parson Bradle continued to read the matrimonial vows. "Wilt thou love her, comfort her, honor her, and keep her in sickness and in health; and, forsaking all others, keep thee only unto her, so long as ye both shall live?"

Meaningfully rubbing his forefinger over his beloved's wedding band, Enoch very quietly whispered, "I will."

Mercy dabbed at her eyes with a hanky. Women were like that—all sentimental at weddings. No doubt she was recalling their very own wedding.

Good. He wanted her to remember everything about their special day—about the romance, the love, and how the Lord had blessed their union. Even more, though, Enoch needed Mercy to hearken back to the beauty and closeness of their wedding night. The memory of that splendor swept over him again, leaving a keen sense of longing in its wake.

Respecting the wishes his bride had expressed after surgery, he'd said nothing about Mercy going to Taylor to have the dressings changed. Trying to be understanding of how she'd need to recover not just physical but emotional strength, he'd babied, coddled, and praised her. Since her surgery, Mercy had needed more rest, so she'd gone to bed earlier and gotten up later than he had. At night, he curled around her and held her tight. During the day he told Mercy how beautiful she was. But in the last week and a half, when he'd finally made any overtures, she'd shied away.

When Parson Bradle read through the woman's portion of the ceremony and paused for the brides to declare, "I will," Mercy's hand clutched his more tightly.

"Who giveth these women to be married to these men?" Pastor Bradle asked, altering the words slightly to fit the situation.

Mr. Richardson took a red bandanna out of his rear pocket, honked his nose loudly, and quavered, "Mama and me." He gave his daughters one last kiss.

Since the front of the church was already crowded, the brides and grooms were serving as each others' maids of honor and best men, and the girls' youngest sister was serving as the flower girl. Mrs. Richardson sat in the first row. Sitting beside her, Linette was supporting Bethany, who sat sideways to keep her now-casted leg elevated. The minute Mr. Richardson plopped down by his wife, she threw herself into his arms and let out a wail. "Now, Mama, we still have girls at home."

Linette recoiled as if she'd been slapped.

"Repeat after me," Parson Bradle said a little too loudly, bringing the focus back to the wedding. He turned to the couple on his right. "I, Leopold, take thee, Katherine, to my wedded wife, to have and to hold—"

"No. I cannot do this."

Some of the parishioners started to snicker.

"I do not want Katherine," the groom continued. "I want Marcella. Katherine is nice for a sister-in-law, but it is Marcella I love and want to have and hold."

With the proper names paired, the vows sped by. As soon as

the organist started playing the recessional, Mercy leaned closer. "Will you please mind Heidi?"

"Sure." But why? He'd planned on their enjoying the reception together.

Country wedding receptions made city ones seem colorless. Folks took care of their chores during the morning, ate a quick lunch, and came to town for the doings. Glad to be together, folks sought to have fun. Sure, the women all cooked and helped out—but accustomed to feeding a whole boardinghouse as Mercy was, merely taking a few covered dishes and helping serve would be like a vacation.

After everyone had been through the line, Enoch had to track her down, press a plate into her hands, and make her eat with him. He defined having fun as having her by his side.

"Isn't the phonograph music fascinating?" Mercy commented. She waved at Linette, who turned the crank on the phonograph and reset the needle. Static sounded, then "Old Folks at Home" came on.

"As much as we're both enjoying the music, perhaps we ought to get one. It would be nice to have in the parlor while you knit and I fall asleep over the newspaper. After all, we're the old folks now."

Looking stunned, Mercy nearly dropped her plate.

Enoch steadied the dish and whispered, "It's been six weeks since your surgery. I've thanked God for every one of those weeks."

She gasped and thrust her plate entirely into his keeping. Popping up, she babbled, "I forgot something!" and ran off.

Visually, he followed her until she exchanged a few words with Velma, then slipped behind a group of women and disappeared. It might be something minor—food left in the oven, a milk pitcher too close to the stove, maybe even a glass of water for Sydney. Only

Mercy didn't return. After a considerable lapse of time, Enoch ate all the food from both plates.

Hope Stauffer came over. "Let me take them plates from you. Sure does my heart good to see a man with a hearty appetite."

Much as it galled him, he asked, "Have you seen my wife?"

"No, but she ought to be done botherin' any time now."

"Botherin'?"

"Like the tradition." Clearly gathering from his expression that he didn't understand, Hope glanced about and lowered her tone. "You know. For weddings. 'Something old, something new, someone bothered with something blue.' Sydney bothered for me, then I bothered for Mercy."

"I see." Enoch shouldn't have been surprised that Hope had her own twist on the old expression.

"In Gooding, the last bride bothers for the next," Hope finished. As she beamed and dashed off with the plates, Enoch's mood lightened.

Taylor came over and sat with him. "When Mercy comes back, she can sit on your lap. I'm not budging."

"Fine." The notion appealed greatly to him.

"Skyler could learn some tricks from Mama Richardson about herding people. That woman has four plans and as many contingencies to make sure as many unmarried women as possible are present to catch the bridal bouquets."

"Stop sounding so disgruntled. It's to spare Linette's feelings of being the only one."

"Dance with me," Karl said from behind them, curling his beefy hand around the back of Taylor's chair. If ever there was a possessive move, surely that qualified. He'd just staked his claim. Again. Taylor kept trying to treat Karl like a pal, and he'd have none of it. Others wouldn't notice, but Enoch knew his twin felt flustered. He found the whole situation vastly amusing.

"Thank you, Karl, but no. It wouldn't be . . . right. I need to remain professional."

Karl's tongue slid inside his cheek. "Now normally, I think a man should take a woman's refusal gracefully." Assurance filled his tone as he looked to Enoch for support. "In this case, I think the lady just needs a little coaxing, don't you?" He came around, took her hand, and pulled her to her feet.

"Apparently coaxing works," Enoch mused.

"I'm sorry, Doc Enoch," Grandma said as she stopped in front of him. "Did you say something to me?"

"No. Just talking to myself." He grinned. "I've solved a problem."

"In this case, I think the lady just needs a little coaxing." Enoch echoed Karl's words, but with completely different intent as his hand curled around the cool brass bedroom doorknob. He wrenched it and pushed open the door.

Mercy let out a squeal and whirled to face the far wall. "Go away. I . . . I'm not dressed yet."

Enoch entered anyway and shut the door. "I've seen you undressed. Do you think Parson Bradle mixed up the names in the wedding to stop everyone from gawking at Linette?" As he spoke, he shed his coat and vest while heading toward the armoire off to the side.

Turning in response to his moves, she bowed her head and fumbled with the hooks on the corset's busk. "I don't know. Please, Enoch. Give me a few minutes."

Swiftly hanging up his clothes, he winced at the pain in her voice. "Sweet pea, I vowed a lifetime. Don't ask me for a few paltry minutes."

A man who took off his shoes intended to stay someplace, so he did just that, and whimpers spilled out of her. She gave up on the corset and tried to fight her way back into her shirtwaist while he unbuttoned his own shirt. He stopped behind her and kissed her nape.

Clutching fabric over the place where her left breast had once been, she ordered, "Leave me alone and give me some privacy. Please."

Spirit. Good. He could handle that far better than tears. She'd decided to fight? Fine. "Why should I?"

"Because—just because." Defiance straightened her spine and tinged her voice.

"If that's the best reason you have, I'm staying."

"I want my robe."

I don't want you to have it. Making concessions could be wise, though. With it on, she'd be comfortable enough to turn and talk face-to-face. *Coax her*, he reminded himself. Just one tiny step at a time until I can actually gain ground. "I'll get it for you. It won't fit over these, though." He tugged at the puffy sleeves on her shirtwaist. He held the robe out as a screen while she made the necessary changes in wardrobe.

Robe on, she sat in the rocking chair—the one place he couldn't get close enough to easily touch her since she had it going to and fro at a good clip. "You owe it to me to leave me alone." The rocker went faster. "I requested it, and that's reason enough."

Two could play at being implacable. He pulled down the covers. "I'd say your logic escapes me, but there is no logic involved."

"There is, too!" The rocking chair didn't go at much of an arc, but she had it swaying at breakneck speed. "It's a dying request."

Whoa. He jerked the rocker to a stop. "It sure is. That request just died, because you aren't. Do you hear me? Taylor is honest to a fault, and she gave you a prognosis that you'll have a normal life-span. I'm not going to spend the next fifty years married to a woman who expects to keel over dead any minute."

"She can't be sure."

"So you've decided to give up? The only things you can be certain of are that you are God's child, I love you with all my heart, and someday all of us will die."

"But you'll be left with Heidi. Our marriage has been nothing but a disaster for you from the start."

Anger surged through him. "You won't leave me with Heidi. Even if the Lord does take you before He takes me, I'll feel lucky to have our daughter. God blessed our marriage. Every day has been a miracle to me, and I won't have you desecrate it by saying I feel otherwise."

She tore her gaze away, then bowed her head. In a hushed voice, she choked out, "Ugly. Deformed—"

Immediately pressing fingers to her lips, he interrupted. "Beautiful. You'll always be beautiful to me. Nothing could ever change how I see you or feel about you." His fingers slid from her lips, down her neck, and carefully lower. She stiffened and tried to stop him, but he pressed his hand against the flat plane of the left side of her chest. "I enjoyed your breast, it's true. But now that it's gone, when I hold you, I'll be much closer to your heart."

Her chest heaved with the sound she suppressed.

"Matthew six, verse twenty-five, says, 'Therefore I say unto you, Take no thought for your life, what ye shall eat, or what ye shall drink; nor yet for your body, what ye shall put on. Is not the life more than meat, and the body than raiment?' You can fault me for the first part of that verse. With your good cooking, I think plenty about what I'm going to eat. The second part, though—now, I'm after you for that. In front of others, if you're self-conscious, then wear some padding. But other than that, no more concerns. Not about your health. Not about how you look to me. No more hiding from me or turning away."

She started weeping. "Don't ask that of me."

Lord, what am I to do? How can I reassure her? The closer of the two kerosene lamps went dim. Casting a quick glance over, Enoch noticed it had run out of fuel. Odd that Mercy had allowed that to happen. Such details were her bailiwick. He kissed her hair, then walked over and lifted the now extinguished lamp. "There's enough in the other lamp to split between—"

"No," she blurted out. "Don't."

Maybe in a dimmer room. Is that it, Lord? Enoch set down the lamp and walked most of the way back toward her before halting. "Do you love me?"

She nodded.

"Are you ashamed of me?"

Her head flew up. "No!"

"Repulsed by me or disgusted?"

"Enoch." She rose from the chair. Hands extended, she approached him and took his. Tears were still running down her face, and her shoulders were shuddering with sobs. Vehemently, she shook her head. "H-how could you s-say such t-terrible things? You're the most beautiful man I've ever known, inside and out."

"Exactly my point." Lifting her hands, he kissed them and looked into her swimming brown eyes. "You're the most beautiful woman I've ever seen, both inside and out. So how could you think such terrible things about me?"

"I don't."

"You do. When you think those things about yourself, you think them about me. About us. Because two became one."

"It's not like that." She tugged her hands free. In a purely defensive move, she bent her left arm and held her right shoulder so as to block any view of her missing bosom. "A man expects certain things—"

"I do." He stepped closer.

She retreated and continued as if he hadn't said anything. "A whole wife who can spark his desire and suckle his children. I—"

"Stop right there. If you believe you can't nourish our babies, you're wrong. Taylor specifically reassured you, you can. As for sparking my desire . . ." He reached up and pulled down her arm. An incoherent sound of protest curled in her throat as he unfastened the robe's uppermost button. By the time he reached the third, her fingers were desperately tangling with his.

"Do you have so little faith in my love for you that you think this could destroy how I feel for you?" He stared at her, willing her to see the answer in his eyes. Tears had to be blurring her vision, though. "Nothing could do that. Nothing. Ever."

"It's hideous. I ca-can't even bear t-to look."

"Then don't. Just look at the love in my eyes." Finally, when he saw the freshly healing incision, he ran his finger lightly beside it with his fingertip, then with his lips as he spoke. "Is this all? This, sweet pea? Just a red line?"

"That's just it." She jerked away and sought her robe. "Just a red line. Nothing more. Nothing that a woman should have."

Enoch yanked off his shirt and wrapped it around her. Fine

tremors shook her, like those of a high-strung mare about to bolt. *She's scared. So scared. She didn't want the lantern relit. I wonder . . .* "Sweet pea, do you want me to extinguish the other lamp?"

"Yes."

He took care of it—a silly matter as far as he was concerned, but if it lessened her concerns, he was glad to do so. He searched for the right words . . . the ones to express his heart and to let her know of his love and desire. *I should have paid more attention to Shakespeare. Or Burns or one of those other poets. Song of Solomon? The only verses that came to him wouldn't work. Lord, this is too important. I can't mess this up. Mercy needs to hear the right words.* As he reached her, the tumult inside stilled. The words filled his mind and heart.

"I, Enoch, take you, Mercy, to be my wedded wife." Gently, he lifted her into his arms. "To have and to hold from this day forward." He curled his arms and squeezed to emphasize both *have* and *hold* and began walking. "For better or for worse—and the worst was waiting for the surgery. For richer for poorer—and I've never been more impoverished than in these last days and nights when I was foolish enough to let you turn away from me instead of turn toward me to share your worries. I'll be the richest man on earth as long as you believe in our love."

Her breath caught loudly.

Enoch thought about skipping the next part of the vows, but he refused to. "In sickness and in health, fully counting on you to take plenty of time to recover after bearing each of our children so I can spoil you shamelessly." He nuzzled her temple and stopped at the bedside. "To love . . ." He kissed her deeply. "And to cherish. . . ."

❦

The day after the wedding, Karl was working in the smithy when he heard some horses race past. He ran outside in time to see three riders stopping in front of Taylor's place. Hoarse with terror, two women were screaming for the doctor. Big Tim Creighton and his huge mount—there was no mistaking them. And the little blanketed form in his arms? Karl's heart stopped.

Not Tim's baby girl. Not little Rose. Sydney will be— Suddenly Karl realized Sydney wasn't there. Tim dismounted and dashed inside. Flinging herself off a horse, Velma kept shouting for Doc. Clicky reached up to the other. "Here, Mrs. Smith. Let me help you down."

Karl knew Smith had come into town that day for fence posts and barbed wire. The second he overheard little Lila's name, he tore out toward the feed and lumber store. By the time he made it there, Smith had finished loading the barbed wire into the buckboard. "Smith! Get over to the surgery. They brought Lila in."

"We'll see about that." Smith peeled off his leather gloves and flung them into the wagon bed, then stomped across the street.

Karl knew he had no notion of the severity of the situation. He deserved to have some kind of warning. "Creighton and Velma brought her in. She's in a bad way."

"Daisy babies that girl because she was early-born. All of the kids have a cough. Lila just whines more with hers." Their boots clomped in a rapid-fire report on the boardwalk. Once they reached Taylor's, Smith flung the door open wide. "Daisy, we're going home."

Tim clapped his hands on Smith's shoulders. "It looks bad."

"Daisy's wont to worry," Smith said as he pushed past him.

He strode in a few more yards, then turned to the left and stared inside the surgery. "Enough. Let's go."

"Come on, sweetheart." Dr. Bestman lowered her mouth over Lila's and breathed into it. After a few breaths, she'd straighten just a little. "Come on, sweetheart." After a few more times, her words changed. "Please, Jesus . . ."

Smith demanded, "What're you doing?"

When Enoch arrived, Karl didn't know. But he interposed himself. "Trying to push air back into the lungs, as Elijah did to the boy who ceased breathing."

Everything inside him quaked. Karl saw the stunned look on Smith's face, the way his features twisted. *God have mercy on him. Spare him. You didn't spare me. At least spare him. . . .*

Taylor straightened up.

Karl's mouth went dry.

She whirled around and yanked open a drawer. Hands steady as could be, she unrolled the white napkins she wrapped her sterilized instruments in. "Daisy, there's a very small chance here. It would be a miracle. But if I open Lila's throat, air might get through."

Calm and precise as could be, Taylor did the procedure. Daisy's crying and Tim and Enoch's praying blurred in the background as Karl strained to hear any rasp of air going through the little girl. He listened in vain.

After gently covering the incision with a cloth, Taylor looked at the Smiths. Daisy leaned into her husband's side, weeping. "I'm so sorry. Lila was such a sweet little girl."

"Sorry? Sorry? She was right as rain this morning, and you messed up." Smith's volume rose with each word. "A simple poultice woulda cured her, but you cut her throat and she died."

Velma unashamedly wiped away tears. "Lila stopped breathing on the way to town."

"The doctor was making a last-chance effort, Smith," Tim tried to reason.

"Talk all you want. The proof's right there under that cloth. She ain't just a quack; she's a killer!"

⌖

Subdued after yesterday's tragedy, Taylor spent much of the morning in the Word. Big Tim and Velma both asked her to come see Sydney to assure the new mom that Rose was healthy. She wanted to do that for her friend, so Taylor went to the livery, where Piet was cleaning a horse's hoof. "Piet, I need to go to Never Forsaken."

"Ja. The buggy, it is already hitched. I'll meet you there."

Taylor walked over toward the corner where he normally hitched it. It wasn't there. She wandered through the side door of the smithy so she could go out the front.

Skyler barked a greeting, and Karl looked up. "What are you doing here?"

Patting Skyler on the head, she craned her neck to look out the wide-open door. "I'm looking for the buggy. Piet said he's hitched it, but it's not in the back corner."

Karl looked and didn't see it, either. "Perhaps he took it around the front." He strode around the building with her close behind, but it was nowhere to be found. The Van der Vort brothers always attended their animals, kept up their rigs, hitched things with precision, and were careful with their gates. "Hey, Piet!" Karl hollered.

Piet didn't have time to answer before a gunshot split the silence.

Twenty-Four

With more shots fired in the air and a couple of whoops, the rig came around the corner and down the street. Two riders preceded it and two followed. Waving from inside the buggy, Orville was putting on quite a show. A banner fluttered from the back of the buggy reading *Orville's Cures: Better Than the Doc's.* They'd taken rags—a red one, much the color of her blouses, and a burlap bag that they had dyed black, and stuffed an old hat above it so it looked like an effigy of her. They had tied it all together and affixed it up where Skyler usually sat atop the buggy.

The cavalcade went down the street, turned, and started back up toward them. Karl set her back while emitting a piercing whistle. No sooner did he turn around than he shouted, "Whoa!" to the horse that was pulling the buggy straight toward him in response to his whistle. In an awe-inspiring show of obedience and fine training, the horse came to a complete halt. Karl smoothed his hand down the beast's neck and gave it an affectionate smack, then took another two strides and wordlessly fisted his hand into Orville's shirt, yanked him right out of the buggy, and slammed him onto the earth.

Taylor marched over. She didn't know what she was going to do or say, but she refused to stand by silently and permit violence. Piet held her back the last few steps. "Don't."

"We were just having some fun," Orville whined.

Daniel Clark walked out into the street. He grabbed his cousin by the shirt, hauled him back up, and gave him a healthy shake. "What do you mean, fun? You were mocking a lady! What kind of man mocks a woman? That woman is a thousand times better than you'll ever be, Orville." He dropped his cousin back down.

Orville popped up to his feet and dusted off his backside. "No woman ever measures up half as good as a man, and that woman ain't healing folks any better than the cures I'm selling out of my kit. Folks can go pay her big doctor bill and she can fix them up something, or they can buy something from me for a heck of a lot cheaper."

"Hey, watch your mouth. We got women present," somebody shouted.

Skyler jumped up onto the buggy, grabbed the dummy in his teeth, and shook it until the pieces flew in all directions. He then jumped back down, stood back on stiff legs, and barked furiously at one of the parts.

"Let me get this straight." Clicky came over and held out the banner before him. "You admit you have cures and claim yours work better than the doctor's. Seems like you were advertising to me, so I'd like to know if you paid for the rig."

Taylor could have kissed Clicky. Bony and scrawny as he was, every once in a while he showed a stroke of genius.

Orville shuffled in the dirt. Skyler growled at him, and he scooted to the side. "I was just having fun."

Everybody started to square off, fighting back and forth about who was better: Taylor or Orville. Karl remained silent. The one time when she most wanted him to say or do something, he didn't stand up for her in the least. Skyler came and sat beside her. Even Karl's dog supported her, yet his master remained mute.

She'd been ridiculed. They'd taken her in effigy and run her up and down the street, yet he stood silent.

When Karl held up one hand, everybody else finally fell silent. He stared at Orville. "That is my rig. That is my horse. My brother left them carefully hitched within the gate on the property of our livery. You did not have leave or permission to come onto our property. You didn't ask to borrow or hire them. Instead, you took my rig and stole my horse."

"In Texas," Piet added, "we hang horse thieves."

Karl's voice began to vibrate with outrage. "And you did this at the expense of my woman—a woman who has done nothing more than devote her life to healing and helping others." He took a step forward, but Piet held his arm.

Taylor couldn't believe it. Karl had claimed her in front of the whole town, and no one seemed to hear it but her. More amazing, not a man in the crowd lined up behind Orville. Every single one of them turned on him. Orville barely escaped being mobbed when the sheriff took charge of the situation. He put handcuffs on the man and carted him off, promising the crowd that justice would be done.

Taylor carefully picked up her medical bag, walked over to her office, and set it down on her desk. She needed to think. Karl had called her his woman. Should she have said something to him right then? Let him know that was wrong? . . . *So why didn't I? Because the man stole the breath right out of me.* "*My woman,*" he'd said. The most frightening part of it all was how wonderful it would have been had she not made the choice she had and taken her oath.

But the spark his words put in her heart got thoroughly doused in the realization that he'd put his horse and rig ahead of her. Appalling as it was, the truth couldn't be denied. His first thought had been for his horse and his rig; he'd argued his case based on that value. Even with him tacking on a nice sentence about her, that's all it was: tacked on. She didn't want to have to face him again—at least not privately. The only way to avoid that was to purchase a mount of her own.

Clicky walked into her office. "Doctor, did you need anything?"

"Yes, Clicky, I do. I'm in need of a horse. Could you please help me purchase one?"

"You know, the livery has pl—"

"Clicky, I'm in need of a horse. Let me give you the funds, and if you'd be so kind as to purchase one for me, I'd be most appreciative. I don't want anyone to know who is purchasing the horse. Simply get a bill of sale and a horse."

"Well, ma'am, I don't know if I should."

"Clicky, you offered me assistance. Are you willing to give me that help or not?"

"Well, um . . . yes, ma'am. Miss. Doctor. Yes."

She gave him a large sum of money and he left. Twenty minutes later he returned. Of all of the horses he might have returned with, it was Dimples, the mare Karl most often hooked up to the buggy when he drove her to call on patients. She had Clicky take the horse over to meet her at the side of her home, where Karl and

Piet couldn't see her. "Ma'am, I'm not sure this is such a good idea," Clicky said, though he helped her mount anyway.

"Could you recommend a place to board my mount? I don't believe the livery will be an amicable arrangement."

He got a stricken look on his face.

"Think about it while I'm gone." She'd barely ridden three hundred yards from town, however, before thundering hooves sounded behind her.

Karl whistled, and Dimples halted at once. Karl let out another little whistle.

"Traitorous horse. You traitorous little . . ." Taylor jerked on the reins. Taylor kicked. She twisted. She pulled. She begged and sweet-talked. It didn't matter what she did, she couldn't get Dimples to stop. The horse turned and walked straight back toward Karl.

Smug as could be, Karl sat on his big old buckskin horse as Dimples' dainty little princess steps carried her ever closer to him. When finally the horses were nose-to-nose, he said, "Taylor?"

Absolutely at her wit's end, she shouted, "Don't you take that tone with me! Don't you dare, Karl Van der Vort! You and your friends were more worried about a horse than a person."

His expression didn't change one bit. His tone didn't, either. "A Texan has to have his priorities."

That did it. Taylor wasn't going to argue with him or waste another breath. She jerked on Dimples' reins and tried to wheel around. Karl nudged his mount forward, reached over, and took the reins right out of her hand. She glared at him. "I understand horse thieves are treated poorly in Texas."

"Yep."

"Then I suggest you let go of my horse."

"Now how do you figure that, darling?"

"Don't call me darling."

"Would you rather I called you Dimples?"

She put her hand on her waist. "Are you calling me a horse?"

"Well, now, do you really want me to answer that? Because I'm probably just going to be calling you a certain half of a horse if you really want me to tell you the truth."

Taylor looked at him and burst out laughing—partly out of humor, but also to hide her embarrassment. "Of all of the crude and awful things a man could say! I don't believe you actually said that to me."

"You deserved it." He yanked off his hat and raked his fingers through his hair in a single savage swipe. "Wait . . . no you didn't. You're impossible and maddening, but that was wrong of me."

It was hard to tell who was more embarrassed at the moment. She tried to grab the reins again. He wouldn't let her. "It's my horse," she reminded him.

"Can't be."

"And why not? I have a bill of sale."

"Possession is nine-tenths of the law."

"It's the other tenth that matters."

"Christians tithe the other tenth to God. You can't claim that tenth." Karl gave her a smug grin.

"God's my father. He wouldn't mind my borrowing His horse because I need to go out and pay a call."

"Okay." Karl got them turned around to both face the correct direction.

"You can give me the reins back."

"No, I'm not going to do that."

"Karl?"

"Ja?"

"Give me my reins." When he didn't, she reached up and grabbed his.

Releasing them, he gave her an amused grin. "What good is that going to do you?"

She stared pointedly at the reins he held. "I gave you credit for being smarter than this."

He shrugged off that insult. "Where else are you going to try to get a horse?"

"I don't need to find another place to get a horse. I have a horse. I'm sitting on her."

"Fine little mare."

"Dimples is huge, and you know it. She'll take me wherever I want to go."

"She wasn't taking you where you wanted to go just a couple minutes ago."

Irritating man. "We were doing fine until you whistled."

Karl gave her a maddening look. "She'll come whenever I call. Other women should learn to mind, as well."

"Well, when you find another woman who's willing to follow those dictates, go ahead and grab her up."

He smiled—that irritating smile men have when they think they know something a woman doesn't. "You still haven't answered where you think you're going to get a horse."

She turned to him. "Karl, I don't want to call you stubborn, even though you are. I don't want to call you dense, though you're acting that way. I don't want to insult you, though I'm tempted. I'm trying very hard to keep my patience, though it's in short supply. So let me put it succinctly: I bought this horse. I'm keeping this horse."

"Where are you keeping your horse? I'm concerned. There's

not a man in Texas who'd abide by seeing such a fine specimen of horseflesh mistreated."

"You Texans and your horses, and your rules about horses, and your guns, and your rules about guns." She shifted in the saddle. "Are there any other things you have rules about?"

"Could be."

"Am I going to have to sit all day before you deign to inform me, or are you going to stop making a production of it and just tell me?"

Karl rubbed his nose with the ball of his thumb. He appeared to be thinking hard to answer the question. "Well, ma'am, let's see. We have rules that you treat your mama nice. Always greet folks. Those are all I'm going to tell you for today."

"So you can make up some more tomorrow?"

Resting oh so easily in the saddle, he gave her a teasing look. "Are you going to tell me that people haven't said howdy and they haven't treated their mamas nice?"

"Well, yes, but . . ." Somehow he'd managed to turn the tables.

"So I'm not wrong."

"Back to your making me crazy. Why don't you just go away, Karl? I'm going to make my house calls." She grabbed back her reins, and he released them to her. "Just go and leave me alone."

"Can't do that, darlin'."

"Why not?"

"Orville had friends riding with him today."

"Well, obviously he did. There were two before and two behind."

"Only four that you saw. Anytime you've got men planning

something like that, it's a safe bet you've got at least twice as many if not more behind it all."

"I don't know that that's possible. There aren't that many more people in Gooding."

Karl stopped his horse again. "There are many who stand with you."

She looked at him, knowing he was speaking of the list. "Not enough."

"There's still time left."

"Three days. I haven't said anything, but after Lila died, two men struck their entire families' names off my roster. Until then, my practice was growing steadily and it looked like God was opening doors for me here in Gooding."

"He has."

"I don't know that, Karl. I came because I signed a contract to practice medicine. In the New Testament Paul writes about learning to be content wherever he is, and he wrote those very words from prison. And so, when I started out here and things were bad, I promised myself I'd learn to be content no matter what, and I've tried hard to do that."

She could see the look in his eyes. She could see that he wanted to deny all of it, yet she could see the truth just as clearly that he couldn't. "So, Karl, I've tried to be content, and most days I'm doing very well at it. My brother is happy, and I could never ask for something better than for Enoch to be content. He has a wonderful wife, and Heidi is a darling little girl. He's established his family and his practice. Even with their difficulties, God is drawing them closer together."

"You have me, Taylor." Karl hammered his way right in. "I'm the man who loves you and is waiting for you."

Taylor could feel her heart begin to accelerate and her cheeks flush at his words. "Yes, Karl, between our debates and all of those buggy picnics, we forged a unique friendship."

"Friendship? Ja. But there is far more to this. You know it, too, my Taylor."

She found she couldn't look him in the eye. "Friendship is all that's possible. And I treasure it. But I'm getting desperate to add ten more names to my the list or I'll no longer be Gooding's physician. In that case, I'll have to accept that God wants me to go elsewhere. That's why I'm married to my job. Because God can take me anywhere, at any time. I'm free to get up in the middle of supper or the middle of the night and go answer anyone's summons. I can stay with a laboring woman or a dying man without concerns for my hungry family or a baby needing tending back home. The contempt people aim at me—prompting harsh words and cruel deeds—would grow into hatred if I were a married woman who rejected her family obligations. You see, that's why I'm married to my job. I'm able to share Enoch's family, and my patients' needs are met." There. She'd explained it. Now he would finally understand.

"But you, Taylor. What about you? What about your needs? When are they met?"

"I made my choice when I chose medicine. Medicine is my love. There isn't room for anything more."

They spoke no more as they traveled out to the Bunce farm, then over to Checkered Past before coming back to town. As they rode the last mile into town, Karl directed his horse so close to her that their clothes brushed. It made everything inside her tingle. "That'd be a real shame if what you said about not having room for anything more in your life were true, darling. But you know things can change. They have changed. I'll give you time to figure it out."

He helped her dismount out in front of her surgery. "I'll board Dimples for you, but it's silly for you to have bought her. She was already at your disposal."

"No, Karl. Once I make up my mind, I don't change it." *Not about the horse, not about medicine, not about marriage.* Taylor thanked him, unlocked the door, and went into the empty—and yes, lonely—place that was both office and home. Her steps echoed in the silent void. Pressing her hands to the top of her kitchen table, she allowed her head to hang low. Karl's questions pounded at her like his hammer on his anvil. *"What about you? What about your needs? When are they met?"* Deep inside, a cold, awful ache spread, chilling her to the core and making her crave things she'd sacrificed because she'd been so sure medicine would be more than enough. For the first time, it fell short. Frighteningly, heart-wrenchingly short.

But I took my professional oath. I can't have everything.

⊰•◦•⊱

"One of your breakfasts is a wonderful way to start a day, Eunice. I was thinking last night about what would make me happy, and you came to mind."

Widow O'Toole gave a start. "Me?"

"Yes. I need someone to help me out. You already do it—as you did the day Enoch and Mercy married and that night when you stayed over. Often, you've come taken my laundry off the line when I've been out on a call or brought over food. I'd like to make it official and hire you."

Now if only I could ignore the feelings Karl stirs up. . . . Taylor opened her mail and found the usual "We don't want no wimmin docter" notes. A rueful smile twisted her lips. *It's a pity some of Karl's warm feelings can't be siphoned off and administered to some of these other people.*

Over the next few days, she wished she could fully depend on Karl's protection and safety—but that wasn't right. Bad enough, she had to mind her actions and reactions around Karl at every turn because he'd made his feelings clear and she couldn't be anything more than his friend. But added to that, strange things kept happening, and she'd gone through an entire tin of chamomile tea trying to keep herself calm. Odd sounds in the night, manure on the porch, dirt and worms in drawers, mean grease pencil messages on the windows, missing food—those had been sporadic since her arrival. All were things that sounded like imaginings of an overwrought woman. But over the last few days, she'd sensed she was being watched much of the time. Small items got moved or were missing—and she was sure Eunice had nothing to do with it. And this morning, there was the note on the inside of her top dresser drawer. She shuddered and lifted the stove burner.

A thump announced Karl's entry. "Goed morning. Mrs. Ochoa—she has need of you."

Hastily tossing in the note, she slapped the burner back in place. "Let me get my bag."

Karl's eyes narrowed. "What was that?"

Too embarrassed to tell him, she turned away. "You know better than to ask questions, Karl."

He tugged her back around. "I know you better than to be fooled. What was on that note?"

"I'm sure word's gotten around that I need ten more names and there's less than a week to go. If the men who don't want me here can't vote me out, one of them thought maybe he'd scare me out. Obviously he didn't know how stubborn I am."

Keeping hold of her wrist, Karl tugged her toward the stairs. "You're packing a valise and staying at Mercy's."

"I'm going to the Ochoas'."

"We're not done talking about this."

Good as his word, Karl harped on her the whole time they were making calls. Finally, when they returned to town after making a string of calls, he went into her place and assured himself all was safe. Since Eunice O'Toole came over, he left them alone. While Eunice went upstairs, Taylor headed for her surgery.

Once there, she heard a cabinet door creak. It wasn't a loud sound, but just enough to let Taylor know she wasn't imagining things. Everything within her cried that something was wrong. She never left cabinets or drawers open or even ajar. When Bethany and Mercy had been there as patients and she'd heard a sound, nothing odd or frightening had happened, and as the day progressed, she'd convinced herself she'd been the butt of a sick joke. Right now, the light creak of the cabinet door warned her the dangers she'd faced weren't all in the past.

Though it was just afternoon, heavy clouds darkened everything, promising another storm. She lit a kerosene lamp and stepped inside.

The skeleton hung undisturbed, the microscope curled precisely where the sun would slant first thing in the morning. Those things registered in a mere instant. Most people didn't know she kept the addictive medications such as opium, laudanum, and Brown's mixture in a locked drawer. To feed their insatiable cravings, people who were desperate for the substances were known to sometimes break into doctors' offices to obtain the drugs. Even though such medications weren't available to whoever had been there, that didn't mean they'd . . .

Oh, Lord, no. Please, Lord—no.

Twenty-Five

Mouth dry, Taylor knew for certain whoever had been in her surgery had also tampered with her pharmacopeia. Only this wasn't the pillaging search of someone desperate for a medication his body craved. The glass-fronted cabinet doors rested shut—except for one that barely hung ajar. Order mattered—but so did precision. As she scanned her shelves, the evidence was undeniable. The royal blue Latin script indicating the contents of each white porcelain container always faced directly forward, and she always kept the jars two inches apart, set back from the edge.

Only now, not all of them were in the correct alignment.

It wasn't Enoch. He knows my protocol. Mercy's too short to be able to reach the jars on that top shelf. Widow O'Toole was gone before I left, and I locked the doors. One realization after another hit, each striking harder.

I've been naïve to think the men who want to discredit me and run me out of town wouldn't try to tamper with my materials. They already did that stunt with the bugs and worms on my sterile instruments.

This was far worse, though. After the other stunt, she could notice the damage and correct it before treating anyone with the compromised instruments. This time, she couldn't be sure precisely what had and hadn't been moved. A deep breath filled her lungs, then whooshed out. *Lord, grant me wisdom.*

After lighting more lamps and carefully assessing everything, Taylor knew for certain seven jars had been moved. Or at least seven. Maybe more. Immediately, she took down all seven jars that were off-kilter on the shelves. Setting them apart from one another, she tried to determine what her foe had done.

It was worse than she could have imagined.

Whoever it was had taken it upon himself to dump the contents of a jar directly into another, stir it, and then return a portion back into the first jar. The slight difference between a granular and a powdery texture of the first pair tipped her off. For the second pair, the scent was wrong. Each medication had a specific aroma—whether sweet, acrid, oily—just like foods did. Immediately the mingling of scents gave an odd bouquet that qualified as suspicious—if not downright malicious.

Which left three last jars. Three. Meaning they'd put away another jar and she'd not detected which one. By opening up those three, she'd try to find out what the other jar was. Valeriana officinalis—valerian—and Tanacetum parthenium—feverfew—were the more important of the three. The third, Caccinium macrocarpon—cranberry—didn't matter as much. Carefully prying off the tops of the first two, she peered inside. Then it hit her. *He didn't care that she knew.* She'd been so taken in by the trappings of stealth that this was a slap in her face—he was showing her what a cat-and-mouse game he was playing. He'd toyed with her, letting her anguish over what had and hadn't been adulterated, then he'd mixed three different colors together.

Anger surged. No one was going to harm her patients. She secured the lids, pushed the jars to the back of the counter, then marched to the oak hall tree. Eunice came down the stairs. "Was there anything you needed while I'm here?"

"Goodness, no. Thank you for doing the laundry."

Gloves, hat, and pelisse on, Taylor stepped outside, as did Eunice. A savage twist of her key, and the lock clicked shut.

Experience had taught her the value of pausing to take a deep breath instead of rushing headlong into something. Invariably, the seconds used to gather her thoughts saved several minutes of trying to redeem lost time due to a poor decision. *I'm not going to give whoever it is the satisfaction of seeing me look rattled.* Plastering a smile on her face, she stepped out into the rain and waited for Eunice to go home before going down the boardwalk.

Daniel Clark subscribed to three different newspapers so the mercantile patrons could read the paper and enjoy coffee while playing chess or checkers. Papers had just arrived, declaring the stock market was plummeting and the railway system's financial underpinnings showed signs of grave instability. With everyone distracted, Taylor selected some cabinet locks and had Millie put them on her account.

As Taylor walked home, she looked out at the rainbow. *Lord, I have plenty to thank you for. You've ironed things out for Enoch and Mercy, and Tim and Sydney have a healthy baby. I'm in need of your wisdom and help. I don't want anyone to be hurt because someone is trying to discredit me, Father. Please, protect everyone.*

⌒·⌒·⌒·

"Botheration!"

Karl paused outside the doctor's house and didn't bother to muffle a chuckle. He tapped on the window, and Taylor yelped. "Open the door."

Scowling, she met him at the front door. "Did you need something?"

"I thought perhaps *you* did. You're making plenty of noise in there." He glanced down and squinted in the dim light. "What happened to your hand?"

She shoved it behind her back. "It's cold out there."

He shrugged. "Since it's too early yet to go to bed, I thought to go for a walk."

"Where's Skyler?"

"Drinking from a puddle. Still, he will not drink from the horse troughs."

"Skyler's an intelligent dog."

Hoping for an invitation to come in, since he'd just scorched his own pot of coffee, he angled, "Your coffee—does it taste any better than the trough water?"

Her chin came up. "Are you calling me a horse, Karl? Do you think I drink out of those troughs?"

He sidestepped the second question. "A while back, I paid you the compliment of calling you a Thoroughbred."

"You most certainly did not." She arched a brow. Her eyes were sparkling too much for him to think she'd taken any offense. "You likened certain admirable traits to a Thoroughbred. There is a vast difference." She bit her lip, but a smile broke through. "Logic dictates that you, on the other hand, have inadvertently made an admission that you've tasted the water from the horse troughs since you believe a comparison can be made."

Guilt hit as he saw her shiver. "You're cold."

"I'll get some coffee." They spent some time sitting on her front veranda, sharing an entire pot of coffee. Bundled in her pelisse and beneath a lap robe, she seemed . . . different.

"You're acting nervous."

"Too much coffee tends to make my hands tremor a little. For that very reason, I rarely indulge in more than a single cup." She set aside the mug. "It is, however, cold and late. If you'll excuse me . . ."

"Of course. I shouldn't have kept you up or outside."

Rising, she gave him an amused look. "We're friends. As long as we're outside, there's no reason we cannot appreciate a pleasant evening together. Good night, Karl."

"Good night." He opened her door. Skyler sniffed, started growling, and pushed past her.

"Skyler—"

His dog didn't listen to her. Then again, neither did he. Karl barreled on in. Skyler's hackles stood straight up as he ran about the surgery. Low growls continued to curl in his throat.

Once Karl was sure no one was there, he spied the lock she'd started to put on one of the glass-fronted cabinets that held her medicines. Fury billowed off him. She'd wasted time hiding this from him when he could have been tracking down who'd been there. "Why didn't you tell me someone's been here?"

"That's not what's important."

His hands itched to grab her arms and yank her out of there. Maybe shake some sense into her along the way. "Nothing is more important than your safety."

"You're wrong."

She was so scared, she wasn't making any sense.

"Other peoples' safety is more important." She drew in a breath. "Someone got into my medications and has tampered with them. In trying to discredit me, someone—or a group of people—is exercising horrendous judgment that could prove deadly."

Horrendous. It wasn't just the word she chose, but the way her voice shook when she said it that struck Karl. Suddenly it hit him. "Sharing the joys like Rose's birth the other day—that was good; but I am here for you in times of fear and sorrow, too. Come to me." He reached over and took her hands, pulling her closer. "Come to me, good or bad, right or wrong, day or night. Promise me."

Slowly, she withdrew her hands. "No, Karl. I made—"

"Don't tell me about your oath. Your oath was not meant to put you in danger or isolate you so you couldn't be effective. I'm putting those locks on. Now." He knew he was pushing her, but it was for her own good. The woman he loved was in danger, and she hadn't come to him. It tore at him. If she wouldn't come to him, he would at least make sure she'd get help elsewhere.

" 'Bear ye one another's burdens.' You think you're supposed to help everybody else handle their burdens, but you hide your problems and carry everything on your own shoulders. That verse isn't just about you doing it for others, Taylor MacLay Bestman. That verse is just as much about you letting others share your load. It's time you stopped trying to handle all of this by yourself. As soon as the locks are on, I'm going to haul you over to Enoch's and we're going to tell him just how far things have gone." Angry, he grabbed the screwdriver.

A moment later, he heard the front door click shut.

Karl put the locks on her cabinets, but he'd taken the shutters off her eyes. Shaken and humbled, Taylor walked over to the boardinghouse and asked Enoch and Mercy to come over. Mr. Michaelson promised to listen for Heidi in case she woke up before her parents returned. She then went to get Daniel and Millie Clark, who came at once, their butler and cook happy to mind the little ones. Last, she went to Piet.

When Taylor walked back in, Karl was standing off to the side. She went and tapped him on the shoulder. "Remember what I told you? When I'm wrong, I do a spectacular job of it." In the next hour, she proved her case.

No one had known everything that had been happening. After completely unburdening her heart and revealing everything, exhaustion pulled at her.

"Mercy, my sister needs to feel safe to sleep. I'm going to spend the night here."

"I'm staying." Karl didn't ask. He stated the fact.

Enoch gave Piet the keys to the barn so he could let Ozzie and Lloyd in to muck in the morning, and Daniel escorted Mercy and Millie home.

The next morning, when Taylor emerged from her bedchamber, Enoch met her in the hall. "If you're serious about wanting a puppy, Sis, you ought to come see what I have in the barn."

"That's the nicest way I've ever started a day!"

Karl opened the door to the patients' room and leaned against the doorframe. "Seeing you first thing is the nicest way I've ever started a day. Looking at puppies with you will be a nice second thing." Suddenly, in comparison to the compliment given in Karl's deep, husky morning rumble, Taylor wasn't so sure the offer of the puppy was the best start after all.

They'd just started walking down the boardwalk when the desperate shouts of men cut through the morning air, barely to be heard through the most tortured, panicked horses' sounds she'd ever heard. A rifle shot boomed through the air. "Doc Enoch! Hurry!"

"Watch her!" he shouted to Karl and took off at a dead run.

Karl grabbed her, wheeled to the side to shield her as much as possible from the street, and held her impossibly close. His huge body protected her from the maelstrom that passed by.

As soon as it went by, she stared up into his fathomless blue eyes. "You can watch me run to help," she told him, "or you can run with me."

He put her down and grasped her hand. In that moment, suddenly, her heart fell into place. Karl trusted her. He respected her. When it came to a matter of physical danger, he had shielded her; but now he was her partner.

They cut across the field. By the time they reached the barn, Piet had the door wide open. A buckboard jounced up with Mr. Toomel driving, and Todd Valmer sat in the back with not one but both foals. Their dam had apparently followed them all the way to town without so much as a halter on. She neighed in distress. Todd rasped only one word that said it all: "Wolves."

Hearing the ruckus, Dan and Clicky showed up. Clicky, Ozzie, and Lloyd hurriedly lit every lamp they could find while Piet and Dan slammed the barn door while keeping the dam outside. Toomel, Valmer, Enoch, and Karl gently removed the injured foals from the wagon. Piet came back in for a lasso. "I'll take their mama over to the livery."

"Don't," Enoch said. "She'll be anxious here, but if you take her away she'll panic and be liable to hurt herself and anything or anyone in her way." While he spoke, Enoch knelt on the ground and began to assess the foals.

Taylor opened the cases and pulled out the drawers with the most essential instruments. She handed three to Karl and took two for herself, and knelt just off to the side. Instead of getting into the thick of things, she started threading suturing needles and poking them into her bodice. "What do you have?"

"Month old. Fast runners." Enoch started out with age. When his patients' family or owners were around, it was always smart to begin with a couple of positive statements. Calling them fast runners when they'd both been downed warned her that what came next would be grave. "Both have flesh at their necks torn. One has flank damage. The other's hindquarter is laid bare."

Enoch finally looked up. "I can't make any promises, Valmer. They're both in a bad way. Saving even one will be a miracle. With that flank wound, the guts could be infected and any effort to save it would be for naught. Even with the best of repair work, that kind of hindquarter damage could render a horse a cripple."

"I'll take the one on the right," Taylor said, solving the dilemma.

Word got out, and farmers came to lend support to Valmer as he waited during the surgeries. A man ought not have to face such disaster alone. The dam made her presence known, racing around outside the barn and trumpeting her fear. Her babies, having been given occasional whiffs of chloroform, didn't answer—which made their mother all the more desperate. Valmer sat between the foals, able to touch each one's muzzle. He'd spoken to them a little, but as badly hurt as they were, that didn't make much difference. He looked up, saw his friends, and nodded.

Taylor lost track of time when she did surgery. In terse phrases, she and Enoch exchanged information as they each tried to save the foals. On both, the jugular had been laid bare, yet not punctured. Taking that as a heartening sign from heaven, they worked with feverish determination. When she'd finished entirely, she went and knelt beside her twin, assisting with the remainder of the repairs.

"I'll get these last few sutures," Enoch told her. "Go ahead and stand up." He didn't say more, but she was grateful. A well-made corset worn at a sensible tightness ought not be uncomfortable. One of her secret indulgences was in buying the very best. Even so, the garment wasn't designed to permit a woman to fold over double.

Hovering and assisting as he had, Karl scarcely waited for her to sit back on her heels. Helping her up, he murmured, "Millie's cook just put hot water and soap in Enoch's sleeping room. She brought you a change of clothing, too."

The men noisily started the task of moving the foals to stalls and making sure they wouldn't damage their incisions while Taylor made her way to the boardinghouse.

The warm water felt heavenly. Taylor relished the few moments washing up and moving to ease the aches her odd positions had caused. Using Enoch's comb, she stood by the mirror and disciplined her hair, twisting the sides first and gathering it all in the back for a sensible chignon. The black wool skirt fit well, but she paused for a moment when she saw the shirtwaist. Before medical school, she'd often worn that exact shade of deep green because it brought out her eyes. Would Karl notice?

I want him to. Taylor buttoned up the shirt, fluffed the sleeves, and emerged back into the main part of the barn.

Karl's eyes flared and smoldered. Then a teasing smile tugged at the side of his mouth. "You were both wrong and right, Taylor."

"I think you search for reasons to tell me the first part of your sentence."

He stalked toward her. "That day you came to have me take you on your first house calls, you asked, 'What difference does the outside make? Man looketh on the outward appearance, but God looketh on the heart.' The second part is from the Bible, so of course it was right. But the first part?" He gently tested the silk sleeve between his fingers. "The outside does make a difference. It is not just what flows in veins that deserves your concentration, but what beats in the heart and radiates from the soul." He took hold of her hand. "The color has come back to your life."

"A very colorful man brought it back."

"That does it, gentlemen." Enoch's voice held relief.

Taylor wished she and Karl had left and had this discussion elsewhere so it wouldn't have been interrupted.

Valmer walked up and stuck out his hand. "Thank you."

Enoch shook his hand. "They're not out of the woods by a long shot. We did our best for them, but it's still chancy."

"I didn't think even one'd be alive by the time the school bell rang," Toomel stated. "You and your sis did fine work."

"It's because of my sister that we got so much done."

"That's right." Mayor Cutter swaggered over from a knot of men. "Everyone wants to give credit where it's due. And it's the perfect solution to our little difficulty. Dr. Bestman can become your assistant—or partner," he quickly corrected himself when he saw Enoch's thunderous expression.

"No," Enoch and Taylor said in unison.

"The town will still appreciate Dr. Bestman's contract has been kept in spirit, and she could continue to treat some of the women and children if they want her to."

"She saved my life." Karl stared at the mayor. "I'm not a woman or a child."

"At least not most of the time," Piet said. A few people laughed. He walked out and jabbed his finger in the air. "You, Toomel. Just fine your shoulder works, ja?"

"Yep, and I'm neither a woman nor a child," Toomel agreed emphatically.

"Don't forget Tim Creighton," Karl said, standing behind Taylor and slightly to the side, cupping her shoulders. "On the very day his daughter was born, Dr. Bestman didn't just deliver the baby, she staunched the bleeding and stitched his head from that fall."

As he spoke, Karl scanned the barn and realized most of the men who liked and supported his beloved weren't present. Oh, she'd won over plenty, but in the middle of a working day, once they were convinced things were going well, many had gone back to work. White was there. Smith, too. The mayor and a few of his cronies—coincidentally, men who shared his low opinion of Taylor. *I was a fool. I should have been on guard for her.*

"Now that we've established that Dr. Bestman's practice is inclusive of all human beings, I'm ordering you all out of my barn."

"It ain't your barn," White drawled.

"Shut up, White," the mayor growled. "The town deeded him the land, and he paid for the lumber. It's his free and clear. But we're not leaving."

The men all sat on hay bales at once, proving Karl's suspicion. Like vultures, they'd gathered and swooped in to take advantage of this misfortune. Enoch obviously sensed it, too. Immediately he headed for his sister.

The mayor continued, "The complaint comes up that ladies are present whenever we talk frankly. It's just us here now."

"There. Is. A. Lady. Present," Karl bit out.

"She's always parading around in her red shirtwaists and dress," the mayor sneered. "Everyone knows exactly what that means."

"What it means is that I'm practical." Taylor's steady voice didn't show a hint of concern. "Blood doesn't show on my clothing."

Piet loomed over the mayor. "Which will come in handy when she treats your broken nose."

"No. No violence." Clasping her hands at her waist, she looked around at the men. "If we must have a difference of opinions, then please—let's be civil."

"You can all talk about how she fixed up a few folks. She didn't fix up Lila." Lloyd Smith's accusation cut through the undertow of conversation.

"You cannot fault her, boy," Piet said gently. He left the mayor and approached Lloyd. "Your father . . . I was there. With my own ears I heard him tell the doctor she could not return to your home."

"I'm not a boy. I'm a man. Dad didn't let her treat Lila because he couldn't put his trust in a hussy."

Karl shook his head vehemently. "Your father's judgment was wrong. Still, you can't blame Taylor."

"Taylor," Mr. Smith said in a mocking, bitter tone. "If that's not proof of how familiar she is with men, I don't know what is."

"The girl has no modesty. No shame." The mayor leaned forward and leered. "How many naked men have you seen?"

Karl bellowed, "Enough!"

Enoch had been moving toward his sister's side. He jerked toward the men and snarled at the same time.

Ignoring them entirely, Taylor looked directly at Smith and Cutter. "Counting the corpse I had to work on in dissection class, there's been one, Mr. Cutter. All other men have been either fully dressed or have been draped by an assistant, and that assistant remained present in the room at all times."

Reaching the mayor, Enoch stood close and said something.

Cutter shot him a vicious grin. "Confidentiality." He was so self-assured that he didn't bother to drop his volume much, and he'd said it with the same obnoxious way he had the night he'd destroyed the ugly swan sconce his wife treasured.

Enoch said something more, and the mayor's grin melted and he went pale.

Unaware of the quick exchange that had occurred while she'd paused to allow the men to absorb the arrangements she'd used for decency, Taylor continued, "Mayor Cutter, in interviewing a male physician, would you ask how many naked women he'd seen?"

"Or any man for any important public position, for that matter?" Enoch inserted.

Thrusting back his shoulders, Cutter blustered, "Of course not. That's . . . that's different."

"I'd hope not!" Taylor gave him a shocked look. "You've been entrusting your wives and daughters and mothers to male physicians, allowing them to render the most intimate of care. Ascertaining that those men haven't conducted themselves in an untoward manner or shown a licentious nature would have been wise."

"You don't know what you're talking about." Lloyd stood. "Doc Wicky wasn't like that. You can't deny it." Shaking his finger at Taylor, he half shouted, "You in those red shirts. You know what they mean, and they're all you wear. It's your fault no one trusts you."

Taylor inhaled sharply. Karl braced her and murmured, "Ignore him. He's being a dumb kid."

She looked up at him with suspiciously moist eyes. "I'm afraid," she said softly. "I'm afraid it's far more than that."

"Sit down, kid." Toomel sounded bored, but he looked livid.

Taylor said, "Lloyd, I'd like to have a private word with you, please."

"You ain't corrupting my son, woman!"

"Mr. Smith, I'd welcome you to be part of the conversation."

"Nope." He folded his arms across his chest. "Anything you gotta say, you say in front of everybody."

Suddenly pale, Taylor sighed. "If you insist. I want to ask Lloyd one simple question. Will you all agree to remain quiet?"

"Just that one question?"

When they agreed, Taylor's shoulders rose and fell as she steeled herself with a deep breath. "Lloyd, what color shirt am I wearing?"

"Red."

Her hand covered her mouth and her head dipped as a pained sound curled in her chest. Sheltering her against himself, Karl bit out, "Green. Her shirtwaist is as green as her beautiful eyes. Don't take my word for it. Ask any of these others. They can tell you."

"What's all this nonsense about color for?" Smith asked, standing by his son.

Enoch put all the pieces together. "The inability to distinguish between red and green is a medical problem for a very select number of males. It's called color blindness and is inherited."

"Can't be. None of my kin nor Daisy's—"

Lloyd turned on Smith. "I'm not your son. Grandma dragged me out here, but you're no kin of mine."

Grief over losing Lila had already carved lines in Smith's face. Betrayal now twisted it into a mask of pain.

"Karl, he couldn't have done this alone." Taylor looked into Karl's eyes and could see that he, too, was putting all the pieces together.

"I know. I also know you wish me to walk you over there so you can be in the midst of this discussion."

"Because you know I'm going no matter what, and we belong together," she told him.

He groaned, "Of all times, you pick now to tell me we belong together, when I cannot be joyful?"

She squeezed his hand. " 'Come to me. Come to me, good or bad, right or wrong, day or night.' She repeated exactly what he'd said to her last night. "We have the good and right. Let's face the bad and wrong."

Lloyd was getting an earful from White about how ungrateful he was for all Smith had done. When he and Taylor walked up, Karl saw no trace of worry on the boy's face. "The doctor has something even more important to say," Karl told them.

"Nothing's more important!" came at him like a chorus from all the men.

Taylor ignored them. "Lloyd, didn't you realize when you mixed the medications that it could be deadly?"

"No, it couldn't."

"How could you be sure?"

"Hold on here a minute." Smith grabbed Lloyd by the collar. "What's this about mixing medicines?"

Karl wasn't about to let Lloyd get a chance to wiggle out of any responsibility. "He mixed the medications in the doctor's jars. Only he couldn't tell the difference between the red and the green—and that is how he just gave himself away."

"But what made you certain the mixtures weren't dangerous?" Taylor persisted. "They were. Depending on the disease and dosage, it could have been deadly."

"You don't know what you're talking about. He told me—"

"*Who* told you?" Smith gave the kid a good shake. "You mixed up drugs? Someone tells you to do something so stupid and you just do it?"

"You're making me quit school! That's stupid! All you care about is having me help with the farm."

Taylor reached out. "Lloyd, just as you were blind to color, you were blind to how someone was using you—"

"He's not using me. He's teaching me! I'm going to be a doctor just like my dad was."

Karl said, "Doc Wicky."

"Doc Wicky?" Smith dumped the boy. "That quack?"

"You've cast your lot with a charlatan we ran out of town?"

Folding his arms across his chest, Lloyd sassed, "You really didn't run him out of town after all, did you? We made a plan. Soon as you figured out the new doctor wasn't any good, you'd ask Doc Wicky back. Then I could be his apprentice."

"Wicky's an idiot." White spat. "We wouldn't take him back no matter what."

"He's smarter than all of you. We almost made her leave on her own. You shoulda just stayed outta it. Doc and me, we were doing you all a big favor. See? Toldja he's smart!"

"Sure he's smart," Karl agreed in a carefully leashed voice. "He had a thirteen-year-old do all of his dirty work. What did it cost him?" Karl noted how the boy's coloring changed slightly. "He paid you nothing but empty promises. He would teach you to be a fine physician as your father was. How could Wicky do such a thing when he is a failure when it comes to medicine? Now you're the one in trouble. You did the wrongs—and he did nothing."

"Yes he did!" Lloyd broke out in a cold sweat. "Orville traded him—all those machines for a key to the mercantile."

"Orville sold the mercantile to Dan," Piet said loud enough for both Taylor and Enoch to hear.

"Things have gone missing," Dan said.

"Yeah. And he has a key. To her house." The kid pointed at Taylor.

Everything within Karl revolted at that revelation, yet he acted completely controlled. His woman needed him to be calm for her.

"Those books—the big medical books—he stole them. And I only put dirt and worms in a drawer once—he did it the first time. It wasn't nothing a woman couldn't wash up. That's what she is, anyhow. Nothin' but a woman with biggety ideas." Lloyd twisted around and craned his neck up toward Smith. "Ain't that right, Dad? That's what you're always saying. Fit for washin' and scrubbin'."

"So now he is your father again?" White mocked.

"Keep your nose outta this. It ain't your business." Smith looked around. "Go on. All of you."

"I'm staying with my foals." Valmer headed toward the stall. "Piet, they're going to be tied up. I'd be obliged if you'd come keep an eye on them with me for a while."

Karl nodded curtly to his brother. Whether Piet needed to remain for the sake of the animals didn't matter. He'd still be there as backup. Karl didn't have his gun; Smith did.

"The boy did wrong. Smith'll handle it on his own." Cutter bent his arms akimbo. "That still doesn't change the facts. A woman doctor isn't right. She's almost out of time, and she still needs to get twenty-one names on her list."

"Twenty-one!" Taylor shook her head. "Ten."

One of Cutter's cronies gave him a baffled look. "Pastor Bradle told me yesterday there were ninety on it."

"Ah," the mayor stretched out the syllable with relish. "But that was when Gooding only had a hundred twenty-five citizens, so one hundred was eighty percent. Now with those new families moving here and the babies being born, we have a hundred thirty-nine. Eighty percent is a hundred eleven."

"You said a hundred." Karl clenched his fists and fought to keep them at his sides. "Nothing about any percents. A hundred stands."

"No one asked you," White snapped.

"Honor," Smith said heavily, "is built over a life and can be lost in a moment. Lloyd is learning that lesson today. He and Doc Wicky did wrong. More than enough wrongs have been done. I'm not going to be party of changing rules and playing dirty. The doctor was told a hundred, and it should stay at a hundred."

Resting his hands on Taylor's shoulders, Karl looked at all the men. "Lloyd needs us all to be Christian examples. Narrow is the path, but we can light the way. We must be men of integrity and fairness."

Heads nodded and mumbled agreement echoed in the barn.

Lloyd looked at Taylor and mumbled, "Sorry."

"Sorry means you also try to make it right." Karl waited. When the boy said nothing, he prodded, "To make this right, you must also tell us how to find Wicky."

"Before he does, I have to make a confession." Mr. Smith swallowed hard. "Pride cost me my Lila. It's nearly cost me my . . . boy." He rested his hand on Lloyd's shoulder. "I judged Dr. Bestman and resented her. Those two actions were sins. But me disparaging her—it sowed seeds of discord. Like a fool, I watered and tended them until I reaped a crop of death and destruction in my family. Doctor, you need ten names on your list? Daisy and me and Grandma are three, and I got me . . ." He stumbled on what number to give. "I got me a passel of kids." He clenched Lloyd's shoulder in a possessive move. "You put us on that roster."

"Me and my missus, too," someone else said.

Three more men also pledged their families.

Karl let out a victorious whoop and spun Taylor around. "Abundantly above all that we ask or think."

"Yes," she agreed breathlessly. It's even over Mr. Cutter's new figure."

"It is, and for that I'm grateful." Karl looked at her and his voice dropped. "But you, my Taylor. You are abundantly above all I could ask or think."

❧❦❧

"Come with me," Karl said later that evening after the men had returned from what they euphemistically referred to as a "successful trapping trip," where they caught "one prime hide." She slid her hand into his large palm and appreciated the way he enveloped it with a heart-stopping blend of gentleness and possessiveness. He led her into the smithy.

"It's pitch black in here!"

"Depend on me. I know the way. Sometimes to see the light, you have to be patient."

Taylor laughed. "I'm not the patient type. I'm the doctor type."

He led her on, and she trusted him to get her through the opening toward the forge, since they were headed in that direction. He stopped and searched for something. "Ja. So this was you. And this was me." He put two hard objects in her hands.

"They're cold . . . hard . . . one's almost smooth and the other's jagged."

He took them back. "You are the smooth one. I'm as rough as they come."

"Not rough. Rugged. There's a vast difference."

He made a pleased sound. "And so there was you and there was me. We bumped into each other. We jostled in the buggy. But then, something changed. I put myself back into the Master's hands. Then . . ." He struck the objects, and sparks flew.

"Flint and iron!"

"With God all things are possible. He provided Mrs. O'Toole as a housekeeper before you ever came here. He gave us Enoch and Mercy to be baby-sitters whenever the need arises. Most of all, He gave us one another." In the dark, Karl moved yet again. "That is the tinder. Do you like that? Tender. For you and me. That is how I feel for you. Now one more strike." A spark hit some tinder and a wisp of smoke rose. They both bent to blow on it together. "That was the one. That certain spark—only in us, it will be a spark that will stay bright for years to come."

Resting her cheek against his, Taylor whispered, "You're a poet at heart. Don't ever call yourself rough again."

As the flame started, they rose and fed it. "I love you, Dr. Taylor MacLay Bestman. Come with me through the years. Whatever

God has in store, I want you by my side." He took her left hand in his and started to move.

"No, Karl."

"Taylor—" Anguish the likes of which she'd never heard echoed in his voice.

"Karl! Oh, no!" She threw her arms around him. "You were going to kneel, weren't you?"

"Ja, that is the proper—"

"This is what I think about proper." She slid her arms upward, daring to have her hands meet behind his neck, went up on her toes, and grazed a kiss on his jaw.

Karl gave her a wry look. "Since when did you do things halfway?"

"I have to! There's something I have to say first." Her heart nearly beat out of her chest as she looked up at him. "I love you, Karl. Why would I want you kneeling down in the dirt when there's no place I'd rather be than by your side or in your arms?"

A sound of exaltation rumbled out of him as he wrapped his arms about her in a never-let-you-go embrace, and then he kissed her with the promise of a fiery future.

CATHY MARIE HAKE is a nurse who specializes in teaching Lamaze, breastfeeding, and baby care. She loves reading, scrapbooking, and writing, and is the author or coauthor of more than twenty-five books. Cathy makes her home in Anaheim, California, with her husband, daughter, and son.

Cathy Marie Hake Serves Up More Humor and Romance!

When a whirlwind decision intertwines their lives, it's merely a matter of convenience. Or is it?

Whirlwind by Cathy Marie Hake

There's no one else quite like her…but holding on to Hope is harder than he thinks.

Forevermore by Cathy Marie Hake

What happens when you need an escape plan *from* your escape plan?

Fancy Pants by Cathy Marie Hake

A secret love…a shotgun wedding…and a sudden death. Sometimes the journey to love is truly bittersweet.

Bittersweet by Cathy Marie Hake

If Ruth's clumsiness doesn't land her in trouble, her mouth will. But her arrival at the Broken P Ranch stirs up more mayhem than even she is used to.

Letter Perfect by Cathy Marie Hake